VENENUM

Taylor Slade

VENENUM
TAYLOR SLADE

Venenum

Venenumous Books LLC, Independent Publisher.

For Business Inquires, please contact us at: VenenumousBooks@gmail.com.

Book Cover by GetCovers.

Identifiers: ISBN 979-8-9888701-0-4(Hardback), ISBN 979-8-9888701-1-1(Paperback), ISBN 979-8-9888701-2-8(Ebook)

Subject: Mythology—Fiction, Fantasy—Fiction, Romance—Fiction

Printed in the United States of America. First edition 2023

 **For Philip Slade,**

No matter what I chose to do, you always said, "I'm proud of you."

February 7th, 1956-May 10th, 2022

·ONE·

They say a first kiss should be like fireworks. Shooting thin lines of bright colors into the night sky and blossoming into star-like petals. Carrying sweetness and joy to everyone who experiences it. Dancing around in pure bliss.

But what if a first kiss is like the smoke that falls after? Dark, asphyxiating, hazy, and dangerous. Leftover embers cast down with a slight burn.

As the stereotypical good girl, I always expected the former. But I was **wrong**.

He called me. Blowing smoke into my mind with his devilish grin, I knew he would swallow my heart whole. My legs move on their own to meet him. Good girls don't get eaten alive, but in his presence, I'm enthralled. A deer caught in headlights, and now this dangerous person's prey.

Strong hands gently graze my face while his striking green eyes glow in the dim light. The corners of my eyes grow peppery, black spots creeping up to the center of my vision. Shivering at his touch as it tempts me and calls me closer to him. Only a centimeter apart, it's easy to see his eyes are the size of saucers, with deep emerald flecks. Is he a man or a beast? Whatever the answer, it doesn't matter because I already fell for his trap.

He leans in too close to stop what happens next. Our fate is sealed.

With our bodies pressed together, my heart starts pounding, and my armpits begin to sweat profusely. Why am I doing this? As if I'm a puppet in my own body, I look back at the boy. Lifting my hand to my face, placing it on top of his, everything's shrouded in a dark mist. Everything except him. The world stops, and the music fades away. A jolt of electricity dances on my lips, traveling through my body. Head to toe. What is this burning sensation that hurts but feels so good simultaneously? My first kiss is bittersweet, burning my core like coal, making my legs buckle from under me. His arms wrap around me, maybe to keep me ensnared or to give me leverage. I'm not sure. Bodies melt into one as I let the dizzy feeling pass through me. Those few seconds are timeless. Addicting.

The world spins as I rest my heavy-laden head on my palm. A strange rattling off in the distance ricochets in my ears, slowly dissipating as the mysterious boy walks away from me. Leaning onto a wobbly table for support, my eyes drift to someone's abandoned drink. The suspicious amber drink carries the image of my eyes. I blink once more and try to clear my fuzzy head. What just happened?

Green eyes survey me from a distance. As our stares get entangled again, his eyes disappear in a flash of neon lights without a trace.

I push ahead in a blurry search for that guy. Where did he go? Bodies bump into me left and right as I hear a familiar voice.

"Raine," I hear my friends call, but I don't turn around. My eyes stay locked onto the spot where he disappeared. Something about him makes my spine shiver, but I need to know more.

"Raine?" The fog around my eyes starts to clear as I turn around to see all my worried friends. Cutting through the massive dancehall's opening, the shadows leave their faces as they walk into the more lit bar area. I look down and scratch at the big 'X' drawn on my hand and remember I originally came to get a soda. Turning to my side, I squeeze through the standing patrons enjoying their drinks. Wicks of sweat smear across my shoulders and arms as I meet my friends. We all stop in the middle under a bright blinding light that swings to the song's beat.

"Where'd you go? We lost sight of you after those three bimbos pushed you into the crowd," Sofia asks, grabbing my arm like a child.

"I'm sorry. I should've stayed still so you guys could find me."

"Yeah, gurl, we're right next to West End. We still can get shot," Sofia nags. I nod in silence, thinking of the boy's cold, forest-green eyes.

"Are you okay?" another friend, Kasha, says.

"I just have a headache but took an aspirin," white lies pour out. I could never tell her what I just did seconds ago. Good girls don't kiss guys they just met.

"Oh, feel better. We still got lots of dancing to do!" Sofia pats my back. "Raine, I know I said you were crazy for wanting to go to a teen club, but this place is awesome," she confesses.

The ice-cold water, a gift from Jay, soothes my feverish skin. It certainly has had some unexpected events.

"Yeah, this is fun. Can't believe we are almost seniors! Playing *Fantasy XII* is fun, but this is a nice change. Thanks for forcing us out of the box, Rae," Jay agrees. I meekly smile with the spiraling haziness of my mind finally clearing. My phone vibrates. I get a notification on my phone. Oh God, please don't be my mom! I pull it out, relieved to find no new messages—instead, the latest chapter of my favorite visual romance novel updates. I have to check it out later.

"Well, come on, a live band's gonna play," Kasha whines. *What band?*

A low rattle sets off in my head once more, sending a searing pain into my head. I flinch, sucking in air sharper than usual. "Yeah, let's go," I say despite my sudden migraine. I rub my forehead one more time. Ragdolling, I let the girls pull me away to enjoy the rest of the night.

Burn Alice's Snake sounds like an edgy rock band, and these boys gave us the works. They all have messy, post-sex hair and dark, grungy clothing. Tattoos run down the lead singer and drummer's arms. Scanning through each bandmate and rating their looks with Sofia, Kasha, and Cassie, we annoy our poor guy friends. "What would you give the guy in the gray shirt?" Cassie's lips curl up like a cat as she points to the guy on the end. My eyes follow her guidance expecting to drool over the next cute guy, but my jaw drops in horror. Oh no. This wave of embarrassment could only be described as a person hearing the word 'moist.' Unwarranted and uncomfortable. I gasp at the familiar face on stage.

A familiar face and the most stunning boy I'd ever seen towers over the crowd. Nothing can be helped but to stare into his unnaturally bright green eyes. My eyes trace him, following the lines on his sharp jaw. Parts of his long, messy black hair cover his pale neck—what a beautiful disaster. But what's set on his face seems to be his most famous feature: his scowl. Plastered on his face, I can't tell if he was kidnapped and forced to play here or if he hates everyone around him. It's hard to tell, but it sparks something in me.

His face drifts me into a faint memory.

"I'm sorry!" I broke out of my trance and felt like a moron. "I bumped into you."

"Not your fault. Ah-rin pushed you into me." He smiles. There was something off about it, though. His wide mouth showed off his sharp canines.

Tripping over my words, I continue my apology. "S-s-still, I'm sorry! M-my name's Raine! Fun fact, it has a silent 'E' at the end. My name means noble presence. My mom thought I would be a queen because I was sensitive and could feel every spring in my crib. You know the princess and the pea story," word vomit flies out, sharing my whole life story. We lock eyes for a moment. I awkwardly laugh, causing more tension. Why would he care about my name and how to spell it? I was too eager that a guy was even talking to me. After all, I am a dull girl with boring dreams in a boring house with a boring life. There is no way a guy like him is interested in me.

"I'm Nathair. Fun fact, it rhymes with fair," he says, trying to play along with my foolishness.

"That's an—"

"Interesting name, I know."

Rustling me out of my daydream with a sharp shove, a high-class girl says, "Move it!" She plows another victim out of the way too. She looks like a supermodel with long dark hair, a long face, and structured cheekbones, and is wearing a long-sleeved crop top with a low-rise plaid mini-skirt and platform shoes. She is giving serious ABG vibes. So sharp. So aggressive. As quickly as she pushes me, she turns to her friend, smiling. "Aethelfield, this is a good spot to see Nathair perform!" she says sweetly to her friend. I scrunch my face. *Aethelfield?* What kind of name is that? Aethel. Aethel would be better.

With curly, golden diva hair, caramel skin, and a perfect smile, Aethel is stunning in her own right. Though it's a shame that her face is caked with makeup so thick—you could scrape it off. She looks at me in disgust. I gulp. They are too pretty and intimidating to tell off, which is mega-annoying, but I'll let it go.

My friends steady me, avoiding their eyes and shrinking away from the girls. No need to cause unnecessary confrontation. Rule number one in a nerd's survival book.

Nathair still holds the same grimace from earlier as he starts to strum his guitar. He looks up for just a second to set his eyes on me but then immediately averts his gaze. My heart flutters. Is this rejection or longing? To be honest, I can't tell. Sweet phantom kisses linger on my lips with a slight sting. Eyes graze my back. I touch my lips and look in the direction of the daggers. I look over at Aethel; she clenches her jaw.

"Watch it, Cleopatra, an asp bites." Aethel's sharp eyes snap toward me and glint under the bright stage lights. Green light casts on her skin. After a few uncomfortable seconds, she turns away and gives Nathair a cute wave. Plopping down on his stool, he tinkers with his guitar before diving into the performance, not paying Aethel or me any mind.

Lights undulate to the beat of the fast-paced song. It's hard to follow along, and my dancing feels like flailing. *Try to have fun, be adventurous, and embody your inner goddess,* I remind myself for the hundredth time as I struggle to stay present in the moment. This affirmation may have been motivational earlier, but not anymore. The humidity and steam in the air from the many hot-breathed teenagers crowd around me as I try to stay close to my friends in the club. I am out of my element, which is apparent as I fight the urge to cross my arms over my midriff. I take a deep breath of the thick, dirty air, trying to shift my mind to one positive thing, the music, my friends, anything but myself, and the gross, steamy air. *Ugh, it is impossible to focus on anything in this heat!*

The goal is to be pretty, confident, and outgoing. But maybe I am trying too hard. Despite wearing my new black boyfriend jeans and gray crop top, I can't feel the transformation I craved. It certainly contributes little protection from the gush of hot air pulsating through the room with each joyous scream or cheer from the crowd. I eye Nathair, who ignores the girls who hold their hands out to him to touch. He steps over the ladies' advances and keeps going with his riffs. He looks up again, meeting my eyes. We hold our looks for a moment as he exhales and looks back at his guitar. *Are you okay?* Rings in my head, followed by more rattling. There must be something wrong with my ears. Probably from all the loud music. Nervousness and heat rush to my head.

This is too much. I'm going to pass out at this rate! I desperately scan the room when I see the sparsely decorated streamers wave. Searching through the sea of people, I find the perfect spot. It doesn't take me long to figure out why. I squint my eyes and peer over the streamers at my favorite invention: air conditioning!

Moving to the beat, I hurry and grip my friends' sweaty palms, dancing as we go. Much better. The low buzz of the air conditioner charges my social battery. My friends and I jump around on the solid concrete floor and try not to bump into the exposed industrial piping. There are lots of good songs playing. We dance in the corner, having our little private party for antisocial kids. Awkwardly footed, we jump around with our poor excuse of dance moves, but the bright smile of my friends keeps the mood high. We dance the night away in a giant, hazy, neon-colored warehouse.

A huge round of applause erupts through the club during the band's final song. The band mates high five and fist bump each other with puffed-up chests. The main singer goes to fist bump Nathair, but the dark boy continues to keep his hands glued on the guitar and leaves him hanging. In one quick move, the drummer comes to save the day and finishes the fist bump. *Yikes, he's a real character.* Despite their dodgy teamwork, I still hum their last song to myself as the party winds down.

I try to catch up with Nathair as his band packs up. I have two choices: tell him how they did a great show, or I can run for the hills. What would the main character in a fiction book do? That is obvious. There would be no story if the main character didn't take risks. Looking at his long face reminds me of the word encounter we had. Is it okay to talk to him?

He rips his face from mine. Forcing me back to reality, the music booms, and the loud buzzing of people talking hurts my ears. The smell of coffee and food overwhelms me. I press my fingers in my ears, trying to adjust to my setting. Focused again, I look back at Nathair. His expression twisted in frustration instead of bliss. "Crap!" he exclaims, turning his back to me.

"Did I do something wrong?" I ask, feeling down from the sudden switch.

"Um, no." He pauses, turning back to me. "I shouldn't have done that, sorry. Are you okay?" Puzzled by the strange question, I nod my head. He furrows his brows, making his eyes smaller and sharper. He checks his phone. "Got to go. Nice meeting you." He walks off before I can say anything.

I sigh and get back into the present. Such a frustrating thing to always be stuck in the past. But why would he ask that? I shake my head and get into this complicated social puzzle. Let's do this before my shyness gets the better of me. "Hey, Nathair, great show." He doesn't look at me, nor does he reply. "I just wanted to say bye before I went home." I blab, feeling nervous. His aura freezes everything around him, standing still like a cornered animal ready to strike. Before I can say anything else, he walks off. Ouch, such a harsh rejection, but it is to be expected. I am pretty ghost-able. Still, it's a hard pill to swallow, so I shudder and walk faster to catch up with my friends.

Sofia looks back at me and the mysterious boy in pure shock. Her face crinkles up in anger, glaring hard at the door he exited from.

"What was THAT about? Who's that jerk?" Sofia asks. Even while mad, her smooth, tanned skin shines as the light hits it from different angles. Her kinky blowout is still perfect after hours of dancing.

"How do you know that guy?" Kasha asks. Everything she says sounds like she's speaking in slow motion. Which many people can mistake for her sounding calm. As I watch her eyebrows furrow and her hands land on her hips, I know she is pissed off, too. My guy friends, stiff-jawed, roll up their sleeves. Uh oh. Looks like I need to do damage control.

"Earth to Raine! Spill it, girl," Sofia snaps. My friends close in on me, and it makes my lips quiver. Twiddling my fingers, I mull over what to say. Do I tell the truth or lie? My friends would understand, right? Not having all the details myself on why I kissed him seconds after meeting him is hard enough, but to fear their judgment would also be hard to endure.

I blink away the droplets forming in my eyes, feeling overwhelmed and disappointed. "I ran into a boy earlier after I got separated from you guys, and we kissed!" I confess, covering my eyes, and internally screaming at all the dumb decisions I made tonight.

My friends all stand silent, mouths agape. "WHAT?!" they shout in unison.

· TWO ·

The car tires quietly hum in the background of the Uber. Gently rocking me into a somber state, the existential dread builds inside me. This is the latest I have ever stayed out before. The night is beautiful, only seeing street lights here and there. The crystal-clear sky and crisp fresh air are filtered by all the deep green trees lining the street. Many cars are still taking the backroads, so my face glows a gentle yellow as we pass by the other vehicles. My eyelids are sandbags making me nod off every few minutes or so. Gravity jerking my bobbing head is the only thing keeping me awake.

Can I tell Jasmine what I did? I touch my lips, now chapped from the unexpected makeout session, and smile. My horrid brain, foggy and self-destructive, reminds me of the awkward ending. Ugh, he's interesting all right, but he can never take that sweet memory away from me. My first kiss was unusual but perfect to me, just like how I read in books—adrenaline-inducing and solemn, wrapped in one. But he's not my type. My mom and stepfather would hate him. I play with my fingers, glittering from the chipped silver polish Sofia gave me, and melt at the thought of his eyes. Glimmering crystals, inhuman and hypnotic.

Oh, Raine, stop thinking about him! I think. *You'll never see him again if you keep playing the "good girl" role.*

My mom always says, *'We are all entitled to a slip-up now and then, but if we continue to do the wrong things, they will become a habit.'* My life flashes before my eyes as I slip into a dangerous routine that could follow me into adulthood. I sit up straight, trying to feel confident but bash my head against the headrest instead. Luckily for me, the driver isn't paying attention. He's too busy gripping the steering wheel, speeding through the empty roads, and ignoring as many traffic signals as possible. Regardless of his rush to get home, I can't help but return to my worrisome thoughts. It is a must to look prim and proper at all times. Though ill-gotten, the agreement is still valid. I represent my mother and can't embarrass or upset her, even in a late-night Uber. Perfection is a requirement for my last remaining parent because nothing else went right in her life.

The car slows down, and the driver slams down on the brakes, causing us to jolt forward. I launch my hands forward, hitting the headrest in front of me. Good thing I have my seat belt on, or else I would be catapulted out of the windshield by now!

The driver turns around. His voice is groggy—a light stench of alcohol leaking from his mouth. "My bad," he says. I wave it off and unclick my seat, stumbling out of the car in a hurried frenzy. My shoes click against the concrete as I run to safety.

He's not getting a tip. At least I'm home and alone.

Shuffles nearby give me hints that I am sorely mistaken. I jump at my older sister's sudden appearance. "Oh!" I exclaim as I cover my fast heartbeat, thumping like a rabbit, with my hand. "You scared me." Jasmine doesn't respond. Her mouth is so heavy with alcohol. She trips over her bag. I shake my head, mildly annoyed, and pick up her things. She leans on me and giggles in my ear. At least she had fun. "Shut up, or they'll hear us!" I whisper, fumbling with my drunken sister and my house keys.

"Hurry up. I need to puke!" She gags, making me rush. The sound of my keys breaks through the silence like a gunshot. We both freeze, hoping no one but us hears it.

Finally, the door creaks open. It cuts through even more of the deafening silence. The obnoxious bright yellow door with chipped red paint underneath not only needs a new paint job but oil for the hinges too. We pause again, praying we get in without causing too much noise.

Did we get away with it? As my anxiety relaxes, I see a dark figure in the hallway. "Are you drunk, too?" My stepfather's voice is a cannonball blasting through our eardrums. My sister and I both instinctively straighten up with a flinch. My mom rushes out, flipping on the lights. The living room lights burn into my retinas, and all I can see is that God-awful vintage puke-green couch Mom thrifted last summer. We've gotten many lectures on that couch, and it looks like we'll get one more.

"No, sir, just a long drive," I respond. Being the alert one of the two, I must take care of everything.

"I can't believe you two," my mother starts. She ties up her robe, covering her fancy black nightgown, and agitates her silk bonnet that slumps in her face. "Jasmine is getting drunk, and Raine, you're past your curfew. Did you forget you're seventeen?" In typical mom fashion, she crosses her arms and glares at us. Brandishing her slipper, she is ready to throw it at one of us any moment should the conversation go awry.

"Mom, I didn't do anything wrong. The place I went to closes an hour before curfew. It was just a little far." All I did was kiss a hot guy whose name I barely knew, but Mom doesn't need to know that tiny bit of information. It's a game in which sister gets punished first. We even keep a tally. Normally Jasmine gets the slipper, but it would definitely be me if I confessed tonight.

"Besides, coming home at one in the morning. You're not even supposed to be out this late!" Richard storms behind us and slams the door. The four small windows in the center vibrate under his force. He locks it, securing the house but trapping us.

"And what are you wearing? I can see your stomach!" My mom nags, whipping me around to see me from all angles. "And what is going on with your hair? Why do you have these two crazy buns?" My hair isn't exactly the most pleasant thing to look at. The shoulder-length kinky curls only behave on the occasional good hair day. But I like my space buns.

"Mom, it looks prettier like this," I say, looking down at the floor. Why am I the only one being interrogated? Jasmine is sitting on the couch drunk, for goodness sake!

"You are a beautiful black queen, and this is how you chose to present yourself?" She throws her hands up. "It looks so messy. Did someone touch you?" My mom gasps. I avert my eyes and smooth any flyaways, hiding that she is correct. "Was it that Jay boy? I knew I couldn't trust him! His mom seemed like such bad news at the church bake sale!" She interrogates, getting into my face. Her bonnet slides in front of her eyebrows again, so it's hard to take her seriously without the threat of picking a belt for her to hit us with. We're not eight anymore. Shoes and belts don't scare us. But that doesn't stop her from trying to keep us in line.

"Oh, God! No, Mom, we're just friends!" I say, flustered. My guy friends are good-looking, but there is no way I'd do anything with them. Sorry to disappoint the masses, but I believe in the friend zone. "I was just dancing too hard," I explain, but it's pointless to argue with the unreasonable, as it only makes my social battery go down to the negatives.

"Dancing? Did you go clubbing?" Richard scrutinizes, stepping up behind me. The hair on the back of my neck stands up, and my stomach is in the pits. He's too close for comfort, so I step away from him and get closer to my mom. They say pick the devil you know, after all.

"Richard, shut up." I stare in horror at Jasmine's slurred words. "Take out that wedgie you have up your butt," Jasmine continues, a cheeky smile creeping on her face as she plops down into a more comfortable position on the couch. "If you don't leave my baby sister alone, I'll chuck all over this place," she threatens, trying to sound intimidating and failing. On the bright side, if she did throw up on our sofa, no one could tell. Her foot kicks the gaudy, ornate Persian rug that Richard bought last year.

"Jasmine, I haven't even started on you yet!" Richard fusses. Jasmine gives me a subtle "ok" sign on the side of her head closest to me, playing up her drunkenness to our parents. Her feet rock the broken cherry wood coffee table as she hauls them on top (Richard's pet peeve). I get the memo. It is my time to bounce.

"Well, I'm going to bed now!" I announce before Richard can jump down my throat any longer.

As I walk away, he complains to my mom, "Monica, what are we going to do with them? We can't have another Jasmine. Coming home this late?" I clutch the door harder than I usually would. My nails dig into the parts of my hand that are not wrapped around the handle. Is it possible to hate a man your mother loves so dearly? I screw up one time, and now I'm condemned?

I storm into my room and close the door to prepare for bed. I collapse once I put my face on the pillow. Void of comfort, my mattress and blankets cover me. I toss and turn. My room, no, *Richard's* room, is upsetting. This isn't my bed, my desk, or my curtains. Nothing is mine. It is all Richard's. This is no longer 'our house.' Even though we've had this house long before he showed up, he came in and claimed it. It just hasn't been the same ever since *he* left us. I shut my eyes in determination and fall asleep.

A girl stares at the stormy sky. With her blacked-out face, it's hard to make out the details, but she looks about seven years old. A man is standing right next to her—his face is also obscured. He grips his daughter's hand, gentle and protective. Cradling her small hand in his giant one, almost swallowing it. Lightning flashes through the black clouds next to them, setting off spikes of debris around them. The destruction follows but never reaches them. Ash-like snow falls behind them. Eerie and beautiful.

The little girl doesn't scream or run. Her father looks around, dodging the lightning strikes, and shields her ears from the ferocious thunder, but the little girl doesn't cry nor react at all. This is normal to her. This is her life. All she does is turn to her father, who quivers under a tree with her. Scared for her or of her. Words choking him, all lumped together in his throat, he asks, "Did you eat the apple?"

She opens her mouth, but lightning strikes between them, covering her voice with the following thunder—

I shoot up in my bed. Panting and sweaty, I peel my body off my sheets and head to open the window. How could I forget to close it? The rain pours in, soaking everything on my desk. Annoyed, I get some paper towels from my drawer and wipe the water off. I am lucky that only rain bothered me in my one-story home. The possible danger is only a screen away. As I go to close the window, the boy from earlier crosses my mind. It was probably a dare from one of his bandmates. I overanalyze again, a bad habit of mine.

I stare at his reflection in the rain, those eyes lure me in once again, but this time I'll fight him. The boy's phantom is gone forever once the window is slammed shut. Walking back to my bed, I silently challenge myself to not think about anything for the rest of the night. *Just give me darkness. Just a bit of sleep, please.* Visions of him plague my mind. I turn on my side and hit my pillow. So much for being left alone.

I get up and head to my desk. The old squeaking chair shifts under my weight. I open my notebook and press the pen to the paper. The ink flows, but the words don't follow. They're clunky and emotionless. My nails dig into my palm. How can I have so much to say but no idea how to say it? It's a frustrating challenge that I don't have the patience for. It's late, and I have school. With my mind in a tizzy, I scribble down my obsessive thoughts, hoping to trap them inside forever.

> Mr. Right, filling me up with fright.
> Mr. Right, are you a beast or a shinning knight?
> Cause I know I shouldn't get close to you,
> but in my mind you always running through.

These are the worst song lyrics in history. Groaning, I grab a loose sheet of paper and pen more manic notes. Another failure. I crumple up the paper, cringing, and toss the paper in the trash, making a successful shot. I huff, continuing to write things that could never actually leave my lips. Sleep is for the weak, anyway.

As per usual, I got the 'Monday Blues.' It is just any other day, but far from anything exciting. Where I live doesn't help either—stationed at the epicenter of boredom and restrictions, Hoss County. With its confusion about how it presents itself to people, Hoss County has nice parts, and others are not. I often refer to it as "falsely owned" because it looks like a lovely, quiet suburb. It is full of kids desperately wanting to gain clout in the most ridiculous ways possible. The adults here are also pretty bad, ignoring and neglecting their kids, who want nothing more than love and guidance. It is going on eight years of being trapped here. I am ready to get out of here, maybe settle in a nicer part of Atlanta for college, then leave Georgia to start my career.

My local juvenile corrections facility, also known as Darlson High School, controls every move you make. If you even sneeze in their perfect air, you'll get suspended. Unfortunately, despite the extreme tyranny of our administrators, the students of DHS are wild. ISS, or In School Suspension, is a class only allowed for the most boisterous of kids, the class clowns. Of course, since DHS is so strict, they also falsely accuse innocent kids. No one is safe in Darlson. It is an excellent school, but as a public school, they can't pick the kids who decide to attend. Other schools often frown on us, though we do decent in state competitions.

Then, of course, there is my class. With any person you can't put a basic description of them unless you know them, but I can say that most people in my class are uniquely prejudiced. Sure, they don't discriminate on your ethnicity or gender identity, but they judge you on everything else. If you don't like their music, dress in name brands, or take school as a joke, congratulations, it's weird! So, enjoy a high school career of constantly being bullied. Being nothing to them besides wasted air and enduring four years of being pushed out of the way in the hallways, just like me. I've always been a background character. Keeping my mouth shut with a smile kept me out of the spotlight. Suitable for survival, but I can't help but crave more at times.

One thing I hate the most is presentation day. My sweaty palms dampen the paper, and I grip my essay for dear life. My topic is controversial, but I didn't even pick it. Guess who did? The King of Evil Stepdads, Richard, of course. I was forced to follow his views on the legalization of marijuana in Georgia. It's nerve-racking talking about this to a room full of people who do it recreationally. I read out loud monotone and dry, in hopes that everyone in the class will zone out. "The CDC has stated that frequent use of marijuana can increase your chances of having disorientation, unpleasant thoughts, anxiety, paranoia, depression, and even suicide. Studies have shown that temporary psychosis and schizophrenia are more likely to be developed by those who use marijuana regularly. Since many strains are laced with other drugs, it can lead to other substance abuse, such as opiates and methamphetamines," I read verbatim. I know it is ridiculous and closed-minded, but I have to make my step-monster happy.

As expected, my classmates are not too happy with me, whispering to each other and laughing. Jerrod raises his hand, holding a mischievous grin. "I got a question," he interrupts my reading. Great, not this again.

"Yes?" I look up from my paper, feeling tense.

"Look, Miss Mouse. You seem like you mean well, but what about those who need it for anxiety and depression? Also, why is alcohol okay to legalize but not weed? Alcohol is linked to kidney disease and high blood pressure. Yet, you seem to be worried about a little grass?" he asks with a damn good rebuttal.

"These studies are done with individuals who do it excessively," I say, fanning myself like I'm trying to put out the fire that is my social anxiety. There is no good answer to give him.

"What about those who use it for fun? When people use it a little bit at a time?" he counters with no mercy. His jaw twitches in delight and he's leaning closer and closer to me. Or it feels like it. He is trapped at his desk, but if set free, he'd roast me like a suckling pig.

"I'm not sure of the long-term damage it can cause with recreational use," I answer. The all-too-familiar choking feeling pools into my chest and throat. *Don't get upset. Don't get upset. Stay strong, or else he is gonna pounce like a hungry lion.*

"You don't know?" He slowly claps, making everyone giggle at my expense. Too late. "All those big words, and you don't know? Hmm, maybe talk about something you know, like how to be a virgin for the rest of your life. Or about cults."

"Mr. Banks, that's enough of the inappropriate comments!" the teacher says, horrified. I shrink in embarrassment. This fish bait is floating in a sea of sharks.

"Hold on, Teach, one more thing!" He raises his hands, appearing to surrender. "The only reason it is not legal right now is that the government doesn't know how to tax it. There are many successful cases of turning it into a moneymaker."

He pauses, staring into my eyes with a smirk. He throws his final strike. "Lucrative, for Miss Big Words over here." The class laughs again on cue. "Before you mindlessly follow what people say, think about stuff, use your critical thinking skills. I'm sure you got some." Putting his hands peacefully on his desk, he finishes his thoughts. My heart is pounding, and tears are welling up in my eyes. I have nothing else to say.

"Thank you," I mumble and look down. My lead-filled legs do the walk of shame to my desk. Locked in the same position for the rest of the class, I can't look at any more presentations.

"I'll show you how it's done." Jerrod taps my shoulder, trying to be friendly now. I shrug him off, feeling the condescending undertone. Soaking in my shame, I can only think about the word *green.*

Green.

Green.

Green.

It is the only thought that keeps me sane at this moment. Or is it the thought that makes me crazy? A wave of desire crashes over me. I have to see the boy with green eyes again. The bell rings, freeing me from that God-awful class. I bolt out the door, knocking my shoulder into it, but the stinging in my shoulder numbs the longer the storm brews in my mind.

I used to like school when I was a kid, but now, I rescind that statement.

Walking through the long sterile white hallways of Darlson, my brain is fried. Without much thought, I walk to the cafeteria. Hopefully, my friends might walk by and join me. My chest still hurts from the humiliation I suffered moments before.

Swiping away a few tears and shaking, I pull out a book. Within a few seconds, I hear a *plop* right next to me. Looking up, I see a random guy going through his backpack. How disappointing.

"Nathrech." The sound of the strange name startles me, not realizing who said it. Aethel stands before the mysterious green-eyed boy I'd been dreaming about for the past two days. Am I the only freak who obsesses over a guy who kisses you once? Probably.

"Don't call me that, Aethel. What do you want?" Nathair asks, crossing his arms and tilting away from her. She tries to touch his shoulder, but he shrugs her off.

"I just want to know what you need help with," she says, doing a piss-poor job whispering in his ear. I can hear everything. Too close to his neck, she tries to graze it with her lips, sending Nathair's body into shivers.

He backs away. "No."

Those sweet-looking eyes Aethel set for him turn sharp. I snort quietly at his curt reply.

She then turns her sharp, deadly hazel eyes toward me. Uh oh, she must be thinking I am eavesdropping. I am, but I'm not going to admit it. But just when I think she will come over and rip out my jugular vein, she turns back to Nathair. "I saw your *minor* indiscretion Saturday night, and I have forgiven you. We can't have obstacles in our way. Let's come together about this." She smiles with a saccharine voice. I want to vomit just from hearing her. Considering his face is set in a permanent scowl, I can't imagine how he feels.

"I don't have to do anything I don't want to," he interrupts. Are these two going out or something?

"Yes, of course, I understand you need a break. I'm just here to help remind you of the right choice when it's time—"

"To let me go," Nathair finishes. "Find another pawn, please," he replies just as coldly, simply walking away from her.

I jump, pretending to read my book. "And you, come on." He nabs my wrist, pulling me up too fast to get everything.

"Where are you taking me?" I ask, trying my best to shove everything I have into my backpack.

"Why were you listening to my conversation?" Nathair counters.

"E-excuse me?" I stutter.

"Is this a girl thing? Look, can't you take a hint? Leave me alone. I don't have time for this," he says, sounding exasperated.

"Wow, no need to be misogynistic. I did leave you alone if you don't recall. You kidnapped me!" Inspired by the stupid books with witty character dialogue, I spit out some lovely word vomit.

"Please, I saved you. Aethel would've eaten you alive. Just trust me on this. She is not the kind of girl to mess with," he scoffs.

"You think I haven't been surviving at this school? I'm used to girls like her. She is not special!" I say, still wondering why I'm talking to him like we're friends. And why am I seeing him? Has he always gone to this school? Is he new?

"No, she will literally eat you alive. Look, I'm sorry about what happened at the club, but if you ever see my face again, or Aethel's, run," he pleads.

"But I've only met you twice, and both times you came to me! Also, a bit dramatic? It's not life or death!" My mind tells me to shut up, but my mouth keeps running.

"Look, will it make you feel better to think I was on someth—" Nathair stops mid-sentence. His green eyes grew murky and harsh. He leans closer, throwing me off mentally because he was yelling at me seconds ago. He pauses, shaking his head. Hearing a rattle in the distance, I look around, confused.

A small pop goes off in my head. "Um, you need to use your words if you want me to understand you," I comment. Right afterward, I cover my mouth. I have never been this direct with people before! Where is this coming from? Why does it feel *good?* I shake my head. "I'm sorry, I'm being rude."

"It's happening again," he hisses under his breath—no, literally hisses, like a snake. Maybe he really is on something. "I need to leave," he turns away, covering his mouth.

"Why?"

"Look, you seem like a nice girl and everything, but stay in your clique and date one of those nice boys who love anime," he says.

"Excuse you?" I scoff, mirroring my mother when she's upset. Hands glued to my hips with my eyes ready to turn him to stone. *What's wrong with anime? He doesn't know a thing about me!* With his own Medusa Eyes, he turns away and walks down the hallway without another word. *What is wrong with this boy?* I throw my hands in the air and kick the locker in front of me. A red string tied to my finger catches my attention. It slithers down the hall on its own. Rubbing my eyes, I try to figure out how that got on me. More and more string pulls away from me. I step on the thread, only to be greeted with the smooth, blank tile. The string vanished.

Maybe it is my imagination or maybe my lack of sleep is catching up to me, regardless, it's time to head to class. My thoughts are a maze, thinking of that weird dream I had last night.

Did you eat the apple?

· THREE ·

You can say I am being a good girl and not talking to him, but he never said anything about waving or smiling. So that's what I did. He seems nice about it, returning a smile or a raised hand in my direction. It is innocent. Just innocent. I can look but not engage. Don't engage. Did I mean disengage? Whatever, I'll look it up. Casually pulling my phone out of my bag, my pen falls out and rolls across the tacky cafeteria floor smeared with smashed peas and dried milk. I huff, mildly irritated. But before I can get up, he stands in front of me. With a meek smile, he holds out my pen to me. "Thank you," I say, retrieving it from him, creaking my seat as I lean back on the long table. He nods in my direction, turning away to head to his class. I smile, hugging the pen to my chest. Just innocent.

THUMP! I flinch, looking around for the culprit of the loud noise. Sofia stands in front of me with her hands on her hips, attitude activated. With a repulsed look on her face, she spits out, "We're not done talking about this, by the way." She shakes her head in disbelief.

Sofia is my longest friendship of eight years. We met in fourth grade during an awkward conversation about Barbies (which she had no particular interest in, but I still shamelessly owned) that ended in me hitting her and walking off. Somehow, we became best friends ever since. Though we grew older, our relationship hasn't changed. With her flawless caramel skin, long, thick natural hair, and dominant personality, people find themselves in love with Sofia in seconds. But at times, she can be—well, *Sofia*.

"What?" I say cluelessly.

"Are you kidding me? The fact that you made out with the most stereotypical bad boy that you could find. You're practically drooling over him." She throws her bag down with an aggressive thump and plops down in her seat. Crossing her legs, she continues to give me the side-eye of the century.

"Keep your voice down!" I hush her, looking over my shoulder to see if anyone heard. Thankfully no one heard her. The endless rows of filthy long tables hold hundreds of distracted teens. I turn back to Sofia. "I am not drooling over Nathair." I lower my voice, covering half of my face.

"So, you know his name?" she probes, picking off the dead skin on her cuticles.

"Yes, we have had a few conversations."

"He was so rude to you at the club, and after, he shamelessly took advantage of you nonetheless!" Sofia put a chip in her mouth. Sofia could argue all day, so winning her countless debates is impossible.

"He apologized, Sofia. Besides, I'm just being friendly to the new guy. Is that so wrong?" I ask while batting my eyes at her.

"It is when you treat my best friend like that. You are too nice. You always try to find the good in people," she nags. The loud chatter in the background engulfs her voice, but I can hear her snark loud and clear.

I put my hand on the table but instantly regretted it. My fingers peel off the dirty table. Wiping the strange substance on my jeans, I look back up to reply. "He probably was just having a bad night."

"No excuses. One bad night will turn into many, so don't think about it!" The bell rings after she gives her unwanted advice, which means the argument is over. Sofia: 51 and Raine: 0.

"Happy Friday to you, too!" I yell off to her in the distance watching her thick frame disappear with each pillar she passes. Sofia waves me off as she struts down the sterile white hall. I gather my things but get stuck. I look down, confused. My bag brushed against the wall. The bag clings onto the texture-painted brick, and I have to give it a little tug to free myself.

Each frilly lamp lights up in my room. The Fifty Shades of Beige room has terrible lighting. I have to plant my face so close to the mirror to be able to see anything. I comb through my curls with my fingers at my vanity, spraying it with leave-in conditioner. My mouth is as dry as fall leaves. Separating each coil in a daze, I accidentally brush up against my princess bed. The canopy blows in the light breeze, filing into the room. Maybe the cool air will keep me from passing out.

Nathair stays living in my head rent-free. I'm not sure what about him draws me in, but something needs to happen. Staying stale like this makes my soul waste away. What was his big secret anyway? What if Nathair is a dragon keeper? Or what if Nathair is a vampire? No, calm down. This isn't a teen romance novel. Plus, he doesn't sparkle in the daytime. It is pretty sunny in Georgia. But what would the main character do in this situation?

"Try to have fun, be adventurous, and embody your inner goddess." My affirmation falls flat, as usual. I fetch my pen and rapidly tap it against the vanity. Ripping off the cap, I write my goal for the week in my journal.

> Chance, I need to seize it.
> Because chance can turn into a reward.
> Or it can explode in my face, I'm not sure.
> Have confidence. Have courage.

Feeling more confident, I underline it twice and close my book. I hope everything goes to plan. I know it's crazy. I know it's stupid, but I am sometimes a bit self-destructive. It is the first time in a while that I feel alive. Like the main character I want to be.

This may or may not be a great idea on my part, but I am here now, and it's time to enact my plan. The club is just as packed as last time, so it's very possible they might do another live show. My white pom-pom earrings smack my face as I swing my head to look for Nathair. Do I look desperate? Probably. Gross, my makeup is creasing in my dimples and smile lines. *Stay positive, Raine.* Would he like my makeup? Should I even care? I know I shouldn't, but I do.

He is there but not performing. Disgruntled faces seem to be his staple—RBF is a serious condition after all. Pushing past dancing teens, he lifts his hand and calls for someone. The music is too loud to hear anything other than the pounding bass, but he tries again. Who is he looking for? A sinking feeling of disappointment settles in. A girl, maybe?

"Nathair!" I call, hoping he'll hear me over the blaring music. I wave at him, trying to get his attention, but to no avail. Getting shoved around at every angle by party-goers, I try my best to weave through the dance floor. Guys dance past me, gently putting their hands on my back to scoot by. My eyes follow Nathair. His eyes furrow once again, looking frustrated as he turns in every direction that isn't mine. I cough at the thick smoke that fills the air. It doesn't smell like a regular vape or even cigarettes. (Ugh, I never want to smell weed again after that disastrous presentation earlier this week.) The beat of the music thumps under my feet. I wave in Nathair's direction, but he continues searching for whatever or whomever it is. I huff, now annoyed, too. He pulls out his phone to text someone. Perfect, this is my chance. I push through the crowd at a more frantic speed. How hard is it to get a boy to notice you? Girls in movies make it look so easy. Finally getting close enough to call him, I start to open my mouth—

But Nathair vanishes in the crowd! Where did he go? The back door? I contemplate what I should do for a few seconds. It should be okay to go see him outside, and he would be able to hear me out easier.

The back door is heavy. I grunt, putting all my weight to open it. The loud creak allows me to peek outside. There is nothing in sight, only a dark alley with one single light surrounded by flying bugs. The crickets and cicadas chirp in the distance. I shudder, getting ready to go back inside.

"*Mhmmmhmmmm,*" I turn around, searching for the source of that noise. It's not a bug. Nope. Nope. I should go, don't go investigating that. I'm not that dumb! The noise gets closer and closer to me. They would surely hear if I went back through the door. I hide behind the trashcan nearby.

"Crap, it's scratched. I need to get home quickly." I can see a lanky man with tan skin dusting off a necklace. Relief runs through me. It is just another teenager. His head is small, but he has a massive head of curly 3C hair. I'm jealous. His hair is bra strap length. Good for him since he doesn't even have a bra. But either way, it's a false alarm. I exhale, stand up, and make my way to the door.

A gust of wind starts to swirl around. An overwhelming pressure follows, causing me to duck down. The ground shakes under me.

I jerk my head back in the same direction as the man, but he's vanished. A giant being stands in his place. It stares me down. Fire and smoke come out of its nostrils. The air grows heavy, and the dark sky looks surreal. Sulfur burns my nose and my eyes blur with tears and soot. Its long snout draws closer to my face, giving me a better view of his huge sharp teeth. Each one bigger than my arms. Its goldish-brown scales are sharp and rough. Sulfuric, volcanic air blows on me. The heat is unbearable. I start sweating, unsure if it is from the heat or just out of fear. Its big, golden, diamond-shaped eyes leer.

What is this thing? My eyes focus on the gargantuan creature. Enormous scaly wings, breaths fire, huge sharp teeth, and claws. Is it a dragon? Am I face-to-face with a REAL DRAGON? Screaming and backing away from the monster, I trip and fall to the ground. A sharp pain emerges on the back of my calf. I scoot away from the beast.

The beast's long tail snakes over my legs, dragging me closer to it! Holding me up to its eyes, the monster inspects me. I continue to scream, shut my eyes, and thrash around—expecting myself to get eaten at any moment.

This is it. This is how I die, at seventeen years old. The short life of a loser who's never even smoked behind her parents' back, or snuck liquor. I haven't even thrown a huge party and vomited in one of my mom's flower vases!

But then nothing comes.

I pop open one eye. The dragon sniffs me and places me back on the ground upright. In place of a tail, a hand appears. What is going on here? I gape at the man from earlier. "It's okay! You don't have to be scared. Are you a friend of Nathair?" he asks, dusting me off. "Did you need our help? What kind of creature are you?"

Still petrified, my mouth remains open. "What are you?" I mutter, shivering in fear.

He pauses, looking concerned about my reaction. "Oh, my God. You're a human," he says, matching my nervous energy. He knocks on his head, swiping his hair out of his face.

"What's going on?" Nathair's booming voice pierces through the quiet air.

"I wasn't careful, man," the man-beast replies.

"What does that mean, Alister?" His voice is flat with anger, ripping me away from him.

"My amulet is broken, so—shesawmeinmydragonform!" he blurts. Nathair grows red from fury. Grabbing my arm roughly, he pulls me closer to him.

"How could you be so irresponsible?" he hisses, keeping a tight grip on me.

"Take it easy, man. All you have to do is just erase her memory!" Alister tries to pull me away, but Nathair pulls me closer to him, our bodies now touching. His smell is so comforting like fresh rain falling on the cool concrete. But I shouldn't be thinking about that right now by the look in his eyes.

"You know, I haven't mastered it. What's gonna happen if she remembers?!"

"Little Bear, you can keep a secret, right?" Alister pleads. I nod, a little confused. "See? She's fine!" Nathair shakes his head, his eyes turning a haunting green. Is he one too? Trying to run away is futile because his steel grip keeps me locked in place.

"Hold still, and I won't make this painful!" he says in a husky voice. I struggle, but less fear builds up in my chest with every throw. His fangs are long and thin, resembling more of a snake than a vampire. His green eyes flicker. Like a moth, I am drawn into his deadly flame. I'm not scared. A strange but familiar tickling feeling in my stomach develops. A giggle comes out, soon turning into laughter. My whole body shakes, involuntarily chuckling. Instead of fear, my body goes into shock from all the laughing. The fact that I have no control over my body is scarier than the thin needles coming close to my throat. "I told you to leave me alone!" he warns. I still cackle, feeling jovial and tears run down my eyes.

"STOP IT!" Alister tackles Nathair, taking me down with them.

He hisses, sounding like a snake. The familiar rattling sound rings into the air.

"This isn't fair. You used your seduction power on her in the first place! Plus, she probably was sick afterward. If anything, it's your fault!" Alister growls back, his eyes getting darker and growing into diamonds.

"You know I can't control my powers fully! And if I knew she was going to be a problem later, I would've used more of my venom on her." My laughing stops instantly as he argues the morality of killing me. I drop onto the floor, curling up in a ball. This is just a bad dream, right? Something I can write in my journal later!

"So, you're going to kill her because you screwed up?" Back in my confused, scared state—whatever Nathair just did to me is off for now.

"Then what am I supposed to do with her, please? I'd love suggestions!" His sarcasm spills into his anger.

"Just let her go, man. You don't have it in you to hurt her."

"Why do you care? She's just a human! There are billions of girls like her walking around!" Nathair's voice cracks.

Is he trying to convince Alister or himself?

"She has a line, look! I thought she was a Fabulous Creature at first. She's different," Alister says.

Nathair's eyes dart back and forth between the two of us. He inhales, releasing me from his death grip. My eyes widen, and the hammering in my chest slows down. Nathair looks down at me, huffing. The snake-like slits in his eyes dissolve, turning back to regular pupils. "She does," Nathair mumbles.

"I won't say anything. Just let me go!" I croak, wondering how this "line" thing was essential to my survival.

Nathair pauses for a moment. "Ugh, okay, it's your lucky day." He sits on the ground, exasperated, looking up at the dark violet sky.

"What's this line you're talking about? What are you guys?" All the fear surges through my body like a waterfall.

"It's okay. We're not gonna hurt you. I think it is fate that we met today," Alister says gently. Alister gets up, Nathair following, making me the last one on the ground. Nathair holds out his hand to help me up. I shouldn't trust him. He just tried to kill me.

"I couldn't kill you even if I wanted to. We're stuck together now," he says monotone as if he has read my mind.

"What do you guys mean?" I ask, still not taking his hand.

"We can see a thin line connects two beings together. Only certain creatures can see it, and Alister thinks you and I are connected. Follow us. We can't tell you here," he says, still expecting me to take his hand.

"My mother said never to follow any teenage boys to a secluded area. And I think that includes magical creatures—or whatever you guys are," the words slip out of my mouth.

"Actually, we prefer to be called Fabulous Creatures." Alister hits Nathair on the back. "And, Little Bear, we're not going to hurt you." *Little Bear?* They almost kill me, and now they want to give me weird pet names? What kind of sick game are these creatures playing?

"I was leaning more toward the thought of you eating me." My voice grows steady but still raspy.

Alister laughs even harder. "Dragons don't like humans, too many bones, and Nathair eats cows."

"Really? My bruised body says otherwise."

"That's what you get for following me," Nathair replies.

"Well, you seduced me! Wait, what do you mean by seducing anyway?" I finally take his hand.

"It's how I get food. I convince creatures to do or feel what I want. Sometimes when I do it to humans, it can get out of hand." His loose curls frame his prominent cheekbones. *Focus, Raine. Focus.*

"That's not helping your 'I'm not gonna eat you' case. You literally use it to catch prey," I reply warily, the rough gravel scratches my feet as I try to scoot away from him.

"Well, right now, you don't have a choice not to believe us. So, come on." Nathair leads me to the white Mustang in the parking lot next door. "You took an Uber here, right?"

"Yeah, how'd you know that?"

"Good guess, you coming or not? Not like you have a choice, but it'll be nice to think you have one," he says.

"I'm driving!" Alister calls, running to the car.

"No, I said we're not gonna hurt her." Nathair smirks, commandeering my hand. I look into his eyes. I can't help it—I feel safe, even though minutes earlier I was going to die. Is it his powers or my naivety?

"Stick to what you know, flying."

"Alister is an A-lister in driving. The ladies always give me five-star reviews," he boasts.

"With these puns, you're not getting any girls," he adds, smirking when Alister gives up and flicks him off. "Get in, loser. We're going to the house."

The car ride is smooth until we go up a long windy hill. Shrouded in trees, the path is lined with tiny mushrooms, small, cute rocks, and patches of wildflowers. The stars twinkle, peeking through the forest. We're heading to their house—Alister's home, to be exact.

We finally reach the top of the long hill, a light fog lifts to show a two-story old Southern Gothic house. It's a beautiful dark blue that subtly matches the night sky. The car slows down as Nathair pulls into their driveway. My jaw drops. Its chimney, crooked but friendly, stands tall on the black shingles, and the roof sits on top of the house like a hat—patched up with mismatched tiles in certain parts. The front porch is massive with two rocking chairs perched under outdoor ceiling fans. On a warm spring night, it's strange to think of a dragon enjoying sweet tea out on his veranda. The car door slams behind me, scaring me. Nathair holds up a guilty hand, uncaring of my jumpiness—like I didn't have a right to be.

Alister gently grabs my arm. "Come inside! You're our first guest. I'll make us some drinks." His eyes are bright and wide. Innocent and sweet. The exact opposite of his grumpy roommate who trails behind me like a ghost. Despite my better judgment, I let the dragon lead me in. It's not like I can outrun them.

The inside is only better. There are warm paintings all over the house and a huge fireplace in the living room. In beautiful, cohesive colors of burgundy, blue, and brown, the living room makes you want to fall asleep on the floor—which is covered by a ginormous faux black fur rug. Alister hangs his jacket on a coat rack made of dark wood. "We have seven bedrooms. The two on the first level are Nathair's and mine." On cue, Nathair tosses his keys on the foyer table near the door.

Venturing into the magical house, covered with hanging plants that threaten to tickle the top of my head. A wind chime sounds as we enter the living room. "Where's your family?" I sit on the beautiful couch. It is like sitting on a cloud, warm and cozy. The house makes a sigh of relief, and the decorative pillows fall onto my lap.

"Oh, it's just us," Alister says, throwing a sad smile. "Plus, they wouldn't approve of the company I keep anyway."

"Why?" I settle into the deep plush of the couch, getting comfortable. Alister tosses a blanket next to me, which I happily use.

"You know the story of Adam and Eve, right?" Nathair says.

"Of course, Adam and Eve lived in the Garden of Eden until a—" I pause, realizing what he was getting at, "serpent tricked them into eating from the Tree of Knowledge."

"Well, I am a serpent. We are descendants of the snake that got Adam and Eve banished. The legend states that we were created to tempt more humans into sin. That is why we can temporarily control people's minds and trick them," he explains. Hence, why I kissed a guy I didn't know that fateful night. A sinking feeling of disappointment runs through me. So it wasn't my choice to be bold and take something for myself. It was just me being influenced. I allow the serpent guy to continue, "Serpents are horrible, evil creatures with venom that can make you sick or kill you. Unfortunate for you to have met one because we're very dangerous." Nathair's shoulders slump and his eyes drift to the floor. Then he sits next to me.

"We had a rocky start, but you don't seem *too* bad," I assure the two boys, hoping it will cheer them up. Nathair starts fidgeting. I haven't seen him nervous before. Though, I should be the scared one. I am in a house with two strangers, two non-human ones.

"Serpents are repulsive creatures. That's why I'm here. I'm trying to change." Nathair shakes his head, still looking down.

"Change what?" I have no clue what he is talking about.

"Myself, period. I want to be human, like you." He gives me a once-over and grimaces. "Maybe not like you, exactly."

I scratch my nose at him with my middle finger and purse my lips.

"Out of all the wonderful things you could be, you want to be human?" I ask.

"You wouldn't understand because you can't stand your so-called 'boring' life. That's what I want. I don't want to live like an awful, manipulative creature anymore. I hate being like this. I hate my people. You see, my best friend is *a dragon*," he says with emphasis.

"So, you hate your race?" Nathair presses two fingers into his temple and inhales so deeply into his bottomless lungs. He is probably contemplating his life choices at the moment. I should keep being obnoxious. "You know, they have talk shows for people with your problem," I add.

"Yeah, I could tell a talk show how I'm a giant snake who hates other giant snakes. It would make the perfect TV," he says, his voice thick with sarcasm. "Now, let's discuss your method of payment." He swings his arms down, resting them on his knees.

"Payment?" I don't recall owing him anything.

"For not killing you, I figured you have to be useful to my cause." He smiles, similar to the first night we met. Mischievous.

"Sorry, Little Bear, he's right. You are a human holding a damaging secret. We have to make arrangements so that you won't run and tell the media. I don't feel like being experimented on," Alister agrees, shivering in fear. His dragon snout shoots out, and he shrugs and pushes it back in. His human nose comes back with a short puff of smoke.

I look at him in horror. "Why do you keep calling me that? Is this some weird roleplay that you Fabulous Creatures do before you kill me?" I dig my fingers into the soft, velvety couch. The cushion in the couch makes a slight creak under my touch. This is not a dream.

"You remind me of someone." Alister beams.

"What?" I say, throwing my hands up to my sides. Alister just keeps grinning, not elaborating. I glare at the two boys—creatures—whatever they are! "When did I sign up for this?" I plant my hands on the couch and catapult myself out of my seat. I tower over the boys, only winning the height contest for a moment. How dare they try to force me into this! It's not my fault Alister decided to be a dragon when I walked outside.

"The moment you went to the club tonight. It was obvious you were looking for me since you came by yourself. Besides, it's not common for a serpent and a human to be paired. I'm curious to see why fate was stupid enough to bring you to me. Maybe you're supposed to help me." Nathair muses.

"Like what? What possible use could I have for you?" I demand.

"I've seen you in class. We were reading *I Am the Cheese.* Whenever the teacher asked critical thinking questions, you would answer them perfectly and state your evidence verbatim. I saw your profile for English class. You have impeccable scores on Reading Comprehension." He gets up, gripping my arms passionately. He gives a light shake for effect, steadying me right after. My temporary insanity of how attractive he is flashes in my mind for a second. Fortunately, I get back into my right mind.

"What? We're not in the same English class, and how did you get my profile?" Profiles were self-evaluation booklets showing you scores on tests and projects. Only the student and the teacher are supposed to see them! "And how do my test scores have anything to do with why you want me to help you?"

"I had to watch you and make sure you wouldn't tell anyone about me, and it's called 'stealing.' I thought you humans are well-acquainted with that word." He smirks at me, so smug and irritating. "And I need your perfect reading skills to help me find legends!" I look deep into his excited eyes. I think he's demented for wanting to become human, but it's his body.

"Legends?" I repeat, sounding slow.

"We found hundreds of books from all over the world, and we can't just read them with only the two of us," Alister answers, even though I didn't ask much of a question.

"Well, sorry, I'm not fluent in languages from all over the world. How am I supposed to read them?" I challenge. They can't be serious, right? Will they eventually let me go?

"You think we know all those languages too? I have to make potions that translate the words in our heads. It's like the opposite of dyslexia," Alister says in a silly tone.

"Okay, so it's settled. You're our researcher!" Nathair concludes, clapping his hands in excitement.

"What! I didn't get to say yes!" I protest.

"Your life is a yes."

"What makes you think I can read all those books, too?" This is unfair. I can't be some book slave for a snake and an overgrown lizard! My body drops back onto the couch.

"We'll help, but one more set of eyes won't hurt," Alister admits. I glare at the two. *How could this be happening anyway? This is real life. Serpents and dragons don't try to make you an indentured servant in real life!*

"What if I'm not up to your expectations?"

"Then you die, simple as that. Look, it's your choice. Die or help us. I'd choose the latter, but maybe that's just common sense," Nathair says, void of emotion.

"Why can't you just let me go?"

"Humans can't be trusted with secrets."

"So you give me more secrets to hold? What about my friends? I can't lie to them. I can't pretend everything's okay when you just gave me a horrible ultimatum!"

"Don't be like that, Little Bear. You'll still be just a normal teenage girl. Your friends will be fine. Besides, you don't want them to be brought into this, do you?" I shake my head. It's my mistake, not theirs. Nathair hands me a tissue, and I snatch it away to have control over something. Still overwhelmed, Nathair comes over to sit by me again, making me slightly happy that I can scoot away from him.

Though I've made it obvious I'm angry with the situation, Nathair still takes it upon himself to put his arm around me. "All you have to do is read, and last time I checked, you liked reading."

I shoo him away and check my phone for the time. It is getting late. Alister and Nathir talk amongst themselves to work out the kinks. I can hear them, but I can't understand. Zoning out, my eyelids are iron oars, and I fall under its wrath. Nathair looks over at me, expressionless. Is this my own body calling me to sleep?

My eyelids shut on me before I can ask.

·FOUR·

The moon shines directly into my eyes, stirring me from my slumber. A pillow glides against my face, and my body sinks into the cloud-like mattress. *Ah, this feels so nice. Wait!*

"Ah!" A small shriek leaves my throat as I shoot upright. The sudden movement leaves my brain rattling for a second. Scanning the room, there's no canopy bed or my vanity, and the walls are *blue*. This is not my room.

While comfortable and calming, the unfamiliar room still sets me in a panic. My phone, which was lovingly plugged into a charger on the bedside table, falls out of my trembling hands.

Is it three forty-five? "They are going to KILL ME!" Going home this late is never an option. This is my chance to run away and join a commune.

Practically falling out of bed, I scramble to call Nathair and Alister. "What? Why are you screaming?" Nathair yawns, scratching his messy black hair. He leans in on the doorframe, relaxed and with one arm resting on it.

He's mighty casual for a kidnapper. I stand up and stomp over to him, pushing him off the doorframe. "It's almost four in the morning! My mom is probably worried sick about me!"

"Calm down. I sent her a text saying you were staying at a friend's house," he says, holding me off with one hand.

My chest puffs up, ready to strike him when his defense is down. "Snake Boy, I'm not done with you! That can't be true. My mother would've asked whose house I was staying at!" I argue.

"I used your phone to find the first name to pop up on your speed dial. I think it was Sophie, Serena, something close to that." Rubbing his eyes, Nathair tries to walk off.

Yanking his arm back. I continue to give him my two cents. "It's *Sofia!*" I correct him, holding up my phone as proof.

"Go back to bed!" he says as he snatches his arm away and walks off.

"No! I shouldn't even be here!" I look down at the beautiful white nightgown I had never seen before. "Where are my clothes? You pervert!"

"Alister! I told you she wouldn't like it," Nathair, still tired and agitated, shouts, banging on Alister's door.

"You've got to be kidding me! You guys had the nerve to strip me!" My nails dig into his shoulder, whipping him around to meet my eyes.

"It was his idea! He put you in some old things we found when we moved in. Don't worry. He used magic. Besides, he doesn't need to see mosquito bites." He chortles mockingly. "Why are you complaining anyway? Bed thief." Yawning, he pulls his droopy sweatpants back on his waist. For a second, I can't help but look at his six-pack. This is so unfair. Why does he have to be so hot?

I shake my head, bringing myself back into the present moment. I have to fight this violation of privacy. "I would've preferred for you not to change my clothes! And what do you mean I took your bed?" I tilt my head and cross my arms.

"The other rooms don't have furniture, so I generously donated my bed to you," he says with a fake shining knight accent. I finally look at the room. It has simple white furniture, giving it a gender-neutral feel. The laundry basket, full of male clothes, is the only giveaway the room belonged to him. "Anything else?" Who knows what these guys did to me? My eyes are rabid and wild with anger. I stare up at my kidnapper. Nathair rolls his eyes. "How many times do I have to tell you? We didn't do anything to you." Alister finally opens the door after Nathair's assurance.

"Could you guys get any louder? It's four a.m.!" a very groggy Alister complains. He rubs his eyes and ruffles the curls out of his face.

"Hello! You took off my clothes and put this on, and you're complaining about sleep!" I pinch Snake Boy.

"Raine, we've seen curvier girls. Don't worry," Nathair says, attempting to reason. My anger only gets bigger.

"My body is none of your business!" *He is so aggravating!*

"Guys, you need to calm down. Little Bear, I swear changing your clothes was completely innocent. I used magic, so we didn't see a thing. Nathair, stop being a prick. Women's bodies are not here for you to objectify. I am too tired to be an ally right now. So please, let's all hug and go back to bed," Alister says as if a single decibel higher will set us off—which it did.

"May I remind you that—" Nathair starts, but I shove my pointer finger in his face.

I interrupt him, "Do not blame this all on me!"

"Well, I told you to leave me alone!"

"GUYS!" Alister snaps at us, finally causing us to shut up. "We are a team now! Nathair, I don't care if you have a kink for bookworms. Raine, I also don't care that you have been staring at his abs this entire exchange. Just because you guys can't be together doesn't mean you have to jump down each other's throats—"

"Oh, shut up, Alister! This isn't TV!" Nathair snaps back.

"And I'm not staring! Who would stare at him? He's awful!" Looking once was a minor mistake, one that I will no longer repeat.

"I'm going back to sleep." He rushes back into the living room. Our adrenaline coasts down and calms me down enough not to follow him.

"I can't deal with you two. All this tension will drive me crazy," Alister mumbles and marches back into his room. All alone in the hallway, I look in the direction Nathair went and walk into the snake pit.

"We need to talk," I say rather loudly. It is not in a voice I should use this late at night.

"Nothing to talk about," he dismisses me, but there's no backing down now. It must be him. Something about him makes me feel stronger, with some ability to control emotions.

"I need to know about your conditions before I do any work with you," I keep going.

"It just lasts a couple of months, don't worry about it," he replies, sleepy, almost pleading.

"No, I do need to worry about it. We were just arguing. How am I supposed to work well if I am concerned for my safety?"

"Six months."

"What?" I ask, looking confused.

"Work for me for six months."

"Why six months?"

"Generally, you decide if that person is trustworthy in six months." He is testing my ability to keep secrets. I continue my sharp glare. "You don't trust me to keep my word?" His demeanor grows darker.

"Why should I?" I say, shaking my head and pushing him off.

He holds out his hand, looking at me with an unamused face. "Give me your phone." I stare at him uneasily. But I hand him the phone anyway. He turns around, hiding his face from me. In the distance, the rattling sound comes back, his figure slightly glowing in the moonlight. Scales form around his neck, and his skin becomes a striking blue. My heartbeat is loud in my ear, a Tell-Tale of my own. Snap! My camera's shutter goes off. Just as quickly as he changes, his snake features revert. He faces me again. Typing away at something on my phone.

"Why did you do that?" I ask.

"Now you have dirt on me, but be warned, if you leak this, the other Fabulous Creatures will come for you. When our magic is exposed, it is a big deal, and they will try to clean it up. So this picture gives you power but will hurt you simultaneously. Now you can hurt me just as much as I can hurt you. We're even." He hands my phone to me, staring deep into my core.

"I still don't understand. If you are trying to enslave me, why risk exposure?" I am bewildered.

"I'm not. We're partners. Look, I'll even let you go home tomorrow. You can come and go from the place as much as you like. Deal?" He holds his hand out for a handshake. His hand is blue now from the light reflecting in the room. I nod, take his hand and give it a firm squeeze. An idea pops into my head.

Maybe we can help each other.

"On the condition that you show me everything about your world. I want to experience wonders that no other seventeen-year-old girl can see." We shake on the promise. Our fate is sealed.

"I can do that," he says, eyes flickering again.

"And don't use your powers on me anymore!" I nag, smacking his arm.

"Ow, I can't control it sometimes. I'm still developing, too, like any teenage boy," he confesses.

I cross my arms at him. "Then try harder!" He looks a little pathetic, still very tired and groggy. "You know, snakes are cool," I say, looking away from him. "I bit a kid in second grade because he broke my toy snake."

He quirks his head and raises an eyebrow, looking moderately impressed. "Hm, you might be crazier than I thought."

A smile creeps up on my lips, and I clear my throat and hit my chest. What is this feeling? Am I really happy, or is it his seduction powers again?

"Let's go back to sleep," I say, turning toward his room. He yawns as he heads back to his makeshift bed. I leave the living room afterward.

As I shut the door to Nathair's room, I see a student I.D. card lying on the small desk in the corner of the blue room. I look around to see if anyone will break into the room to reprimand me, but the halls are silent. I tiptoe to the desk and slide my finger over the picture on the card. His picture. As per usual, Nathair's face is set in a grimace. Smiling must be torture for him. I furrow my brows at the sight of his full name. *Nathair Vanos*. It is a strange name, but it must be difficult to come up with any name that follows *Nathair*. I place the card back where I found it and crawl back into Nathair's heavenly king-sized bed. The couch has nothing on his bed, not to mention the earthy, fresh scent radiating from the sheets. It isn't hard to get back to sleep after inhaling the wonderful aroma, carrying me back into a peaceful dream.

My eyes flutter open, feeling fully rested and happy, something I haven't felt since last summer. Whatever Nathair sleeps on every night, I want it. Though it is late March, a chill passes over me as I climb out of the big bed. Stretching and yawning a little bit, a delicious smell creeps into the room. I open the door, hearing a shower running in the process. Despite its unconventional residents, this house has the "white picket fence" feeling.

The beautiful kitchen is straight out of a home and gardening magazine. Vines drape the top shelves and windows, and the counters are gleaming marble. The tiles consist of some strange circular pattern that resembles glass. The salty aroma of bacon sizzles in the pan with a plate piled high with bright yellow sunny-side eggs. Pieces of eggs hang off the edge—a trickle of oil drips onto the table. A huge fruit salad glistens in a wooden bowl next to a freshly squeezed orange juice jar.

"Nathair is in the shower. Too cold for him to focus on doing anything, so don't expect any hot water," Alister warns, handing me a plate. The clink of the ceramic against the kitchen table brings me joy. This would be heaven if I didn't know the harsh truth about these boys or their house. "Nathair told me about keeping you hostage for six months," he says. I look down at my plate of food, hoping that this is a dream I'd wake up from. "It's not that simple, you know."

"I figured." My usual morning misery settles in. The world is in balance again.

"You have six months of endless research, lying to friends, and dealing with Nathair's crappy attitude—"

"Wait, I have to lie to people? I am horrible at lying!" My hand bumps into my plate. I settle it with my hand before glancing at Dragon Boy.

"Well, it's not like you can tell anyone that you are working for a giant snake and a dragon. They'll have you committed or probe us," he explains. What have I gotten myself into? Why couldn't I have followed the example of a realistic fiction book, not a fantasy book?

"Oh." That's all I can say. I am flabbergasted. What can you say to a commitment like that? My life is on the line, so this isn't something I could back down from.

"Can you handle it?" Alister's hazel eyes shine, flashing some concern. I nod, not able to speak. "Are you sure?" I nod again, starting my breakfast. Alister's jaw unhinges and swallows a huge pile of eggs in one fell swoop. He winces, hitting his chest. A burp slips out of the dragon's mouth, followed by a small flame. He balls up a fist and hits his chest. Sulfuric smoke leaks out of his nose and ears. "Sorry." He clears his throat.

"Eat slowly!" I giggle, handing him a glass of orange juice. He takes a sip.

Nathair walks in about five minutes later, wearing a thick leather jacket and dark clothes. Although it has warmed up a little since earlier, he is bundled up. He hasn't said anything to me, nor is he eating. All Nathair does is drop a book in my lap and hand me a vial of purple liquid. "Can she finish breakfast before you harass her about her duties?" Alister throws the kitchen rag at him.

"Nope," Snake Boy says, sitting right next to me. Does he hate me at random times? I scoot a centimeter away from him. The chair lightly scratches the floor, squeaking under the shift.

Pretending like his harshness doesn't faze me will surely upset him, right? He seems like a guy who likes big reactions. "Thanks, buddy!" I smile.

"We're not buddies," he says with a blank face, slowly blinking at me. He averts his eyes and leans against the chair with his jaw locked.

"Sure, we are. First, we hate each other's guts. Then we become friends." My chipper voice makes him shuffle in his seat, leaning farther away from me. His face turns into a frown. At least I get to see him squirm, too. Maybe I have my own seduction powers. I trace a finger along his arm, and he springs out of his seat.

"Just help me find the information I need, and we'll be acquaintances." Nathair brushes my cooties off his jacket, storming off.

I stick my tongue out in his direction, causing Alister to bust out laughing. "Really, Little Bear?"

I cave, trying to hold in most of my laugh with my hand, but it squeezes out from the sides of my mouth. Alister high-fives me.

"I saw that!" Nathair exclaims from the living room. Alister and I pause and lock eyes, then laugh harder.

I swipe a small tear from my eye. I am different today. From now on, everything is different. The monotonous life I was used to is gone. Is it supposed to be scary or exciting?

Before, my only talent was escaping my misery. Not with drugs or alcohol—as most would think—but with books.

Books are the reason I got into trouble. They are like my silent gurus for life. They advise what adults can't: the impossible is possible. But now everything I fantasized about and imagined is coming to life.

Now the main character in my story, I look back at the two creatures. I turn to the sunrise shining into the kitchen, smiling at the new day.

My phone vibrates on the table. It's a message from Jasmine. My blood freezes as I read: *get home now, devil-dad wants us.*

· FIVE ·

Jasmine gives me the once-over, ready to pounce with her interrogation. "Where were you last night?" She cocks her eyebrow and uncrosses her arms, doing a quality TSA pat-down. Like the wonderful sister she is, she decides to smack my butt. The loud sound echoes through the living room. I give my sister a soft shove.

The car pulls away without a sound. Alister offered me a ride after I took a shower. I adjust the baggy shirt—one of Dragon Boy's. My hair is haphazardly brushed back in a bun, and my daisy skirt from last night pokes under. To be honest, anyone would think it's sketchy. "And don't say Sofia's, I called Serena, and she told me you were not there." Having a best friend whose sister is also best friends with your sister is a total drag.

"I guess you caught me," I say with fake remorse. Dramatically throwing my hand on my forehead, feigning a distraught look.

"I can't believe you went over to a boy's house! I thought you would be a nun for the rest of your life! I'm so proud of you!" Jasmine squeals, throwing me into a bear hug. "My little sister's growing up!" I hug her back, barely having enough arm strength to pat her back.

"Is this what you consider growing up?" Technically, it isn't a lie. I did stay over at a boy's house.

"What type is he? Bad boy? Church Enthusiast? Nerd?" Jasmine rapidly fires. Aren't big sisters supposed to discourage these things? But then again, I forgot who I'm talking to.

"No, I just stayed over there, and he's emo, kind of indie." I stroll into the house.

"Ugh, you're still the same. What'd you do, study?" Her face sinks into a frown, spelling out her disappointment in getting a 'not fun' sister like me. We don't look much alike, but we have the same annoying pout. Her bottom lip pokes out. I pinch it, forcing her to fix her face.

"That's exactly what we did," I agree, laughing at her wiping my germs off her mouth.

She goes back to normal and closes the door behind me. "Isn't he new? I think I've seen him around. That emo kid doesn't seem like the studying type of guy." She catches me, knowing I always trip on this stupid gnome in the entryway. Richard has an obsession with them. They randomly pop up in our house like magic.

"Oh, you'd be surprised about the kind of guy Nathair is," I say, steadying myself with her arm. Jasmine's face drops, confused. She isn't the best at reading my thoughts. Too absorbed with her own life, she doesn't pay too much attention to me. This is the most she has acknowledged me in a while.

"I always knew you'd fall for a guy who wears eyeliner," she says, shaking her head. Nathair wouldn't be too happy to hear her say that. This morning, he yelled at Alister for his eyeliner joke, saying his eyes just "naturally" look like that. Sure, they do, Snake Boy, sure they do.

"Yeah, what can I say? We bonded last night." I smile at the irony. Jasmine would never guess it, though she was taught about it every year in English. She still doesn't know what it is, let alone how to spot it.

"Hello, Raine, how was Sofia's?" Richard saunters into the room, his back to us, preparing a snack. Silent for a second. I am hoping he doesn't expect an honest response. "Raine?" I slap my face, dragging it down. I always have the worst luck.

"Sofia's was fun. We played video games and watched videos on YouTube," I lie, sneaking to my room before he notices Alister's shirt.

"That's good. Sofia is a nice girl. I'm glad you two had fun!" He hums, doing a little dance while fixing his fresh-cut fruit. Richard must be in a good mood today. For once, he isn't complaining about every little aspect of our lives. Still waiting on a baby sibling. That way, he can focus on them and not on us. But sadly, we've not been blessed with a cute little scapegoat. "Can you get ready? I want to take my precious girls out today." Both Jasmine and I become wide-eyed. Whenever Richard wants to take us out as a "family," that means a whole day of torture.

"Where are we going?" Jasmine asks, anxiety rising at the thought of a whole day with Richard.

"The mall, we want to get you some nice outfits, and afterward, go to a nice restaurant downtown. Doesn't that sound fun?" *Richard, don't you realize if Jasmine and I had the chance to punch you, we'd take it?*

"Sure, it does," Jasmine says, mouthing *'or not'* to me. She isn't afraid to be outwardly rude to him. Even when my mom first married him, Jasmine always made it essential to let Richard know he would never be welcomed into the family. Though it was mean of her to do, I fully agreed. If Richard didn't try to pretend to be our dad, maybe things would've been different. My mom could quickly slide in a replacement, but it was hard for us to follow her lead.

My father was a kind and loving man. He didn't show many emotions, trying to look strong in front of us, but you could see that twinkle in his eyes. We were his world. He was a stern, intimidating figure, but when we needed something, he melted, holding us in his arms for hours.

But good things always come to an end.

I hate you.

I wince at the intrusive thought. We all carry the guilt of what was said in his final moments. So now, buried away in an attic, is my father's history.

And now we have Richard.

I focus back on my step-headache. "Good, I only had you in mind when I planned this," Richard says. I walk into my room, thankful he didn't notice Alister's shirt. All right, time to overthink all of my clothes to find what's 'appropriate.' I toss on a loose shirt, baggy jeans, and some sneakers. The items are easy to change out of but decent enough to go out in public. Not like I'm planning to have anyone look at me. Richard would drive them away faster than the speed of light.

I look down at my wrist. Nathair gave me a bracelet before I left for home. He said it was an old leather-bound charm that people from his village used to know the location of loved ones and friends. I twist it around. Why does it bother me so much? Not every person in the world will like me. Maybe it is because of the kiss, how much electricity we got whenever it happened. Whatever the reason, we are supposed to be something other than what we are now: master and servant.

It takes me about twenty minutes to salvage what is left of my unmanageable hair. I know better. As a black woman or any person with kinky, curly hair, it is essential to wrap your hair with a scarf unless you're comfortable with frizzy hair the next day. No one cares as much as my mother. I look fine, but I want to appease her by living up to her standards.

I sit at the table, eating a frozen Trix yogurt. It changes from a block of tasteless ice to too-thick bitter yogurt. I make a face, regretting picking up one of my sister's favorite snacks. "Jasmine, these are disgusting!" A little yogurt dribbles onto the big kitchen table. I quickly wipe it up, knowing I'll hear something about the price later if I don't.

"If you can't handle this, you are lame." She shrugs, sticking her tongue out and licking some yogurt out of the top. I cringe at her. She gives me a mischievous smile. I never thought of my sister's reputation at school until now. Kids at school say that all Jasmine does is hang out with boys. Being her sister, I know the truth: she hasn't gone past kissing a guy. She just likes the attention people give her. Jasmine is a Renaissance woman, great at everything—drinking, partying, and throwing out dirty jokes. There are plenty of things I can list, but then I'd spend the whole day coming up with reasons why she needs to attend an all-girl college.

"What if I want to innocently enjoy all the calories and high fructose corn syrup of a popsicle?" I put the rest of the snack in the trash. The metal lid makes a loud thump. Jasmine side-eyes me. "Put the claws away, sis," I say. She has to know this ain't good.

"You have a boyfriend now. You should start being more mindful," she says through her teeth.

Richard is still in the kitchen, finished with his fruit, and is now playing on his phone. He puts his phone down at the word 'boyfriend.' I freeze in fear, hoping he doesn't hear. "You girls ready to go?" he asks, sounding like he suspects what we are talking about.

"Yes," we say in unison. My mom floats into the room, smiling. Her floral perfume wafts in the air. She leans in and kisses the step-headache. I may hate Richard's guts, but when he isn't instigating our 'bad behavior,' he makes my mother happy. After Dad died, her smiling was an impossible feat.

"Hey girls, it's family date night!" My mom does a little jig.

"Yay," We both say in unison, the fake enthusiasm dying in a millisecond.

"This is a good time for our perfect little family to get out and have some fun." She hip-bumps me.

There's that word again, *perfect.*

Monica Court (maiden name Kane) is your typical forty-one-year-old woman with a perpetual sadness that she hides as best as possible. She is a giving and loving mother by herself, but she is the type to be easily influenced by men.

With the prematurely aged face of a beautiful *Brown University* graduate, she often shows her broken dreams without speaking. Eyes are the windows to your soul, and Monica is an open book when it comes to her dull, tired eyes. It doesn't matter that she wears nice clothes and expensive makeup and has the best of the best wigs. Mom is a sad woman.

It is a mystery what the actual dream she never lived out was, but she is the type of woman to replace what was missing in her life with something else. She wanted her master's in business when she didn't have enough money to return to college. She decided to fill the void with a husband. She wanted to be the best married couple on the street, comparing herself to the robot wives in her neighborhood who were a part of all the community functions. When she couldn't get that, she stuffed it in by having kids.

Then when her father died, a man we were all close to, dear ol' Mom took up volunteering. She hates being in the presence of homeless people, but I guess the satisfaction of helping them gives her some purpose. When David Thomas, her husband, and our father passed away, my mother filled the ultimate void with a dog training business owner: Richard Court. She figured we all needed to fill the void of a male figure to be happy.

My life's goal is to never be like her. I have bigger and better ideas. Unlike her, I want to finish college. Unlike her, I don't want my whole personality to be a 'housewife.' Unlike her, I want to make my own fate.

"Ma, when are we getting our *girls'* day?" Jasmine asks, eyeing Richard. She holds eye contact and takes a sip of her drink.

"Another time, baby. Right now, we're gonna all go together. Let's go to Piedmont Park another day." Mom fixes my hair, smoothing as many flyaways as she can. "Raine, you need hair gel sweetie."

Richard clears his throat and straightens his collar. "All right, let's go, girls! Today will be a perfect day," Richard says. I frown to myself, walking to the car. Of course, *perfect*.

I can tell the 'rents tried to be calm and normal, but as the day went on, so did their patience.

Dresses, skirts, shirts, pants, none of it is safe from Richard's cruel comments. He doesn't want us to wear anything form-fitting or showing skin. However, even under Richard's tyranny of inappropriate clothing, I still manage to sneak a faux leather skirt—tucked under the pile of basic tops my mom agreed to buy. Reckless, she sends me to the register alone. Holding back a satisfying smile, a victory song plays in my mind as the cashier bags up my things. "Thank you, have a nice day," I say, sticking my little secret into my purse.

My phone rings. I frown slightly, forgetting about the gravity of my new situation. This may be the last time I can have a normal conversation. "Hello?"

"Raine Alyce Thomas, why didn't you answer my calls yesterday?" Sofia's voice is hoarse, words coming out so fast that they jumble together. Her face is most likely red, puffed up in anger behind the phone's screen. She never uses my full name.

"I was asleep," I lie. What do you say to the person who's supposed to be your alibi? My mind is drawing a blank.

"Bull, Jasmine called Serena. I swear if you tell me you were with that psycho g—"

"Fine, I was downtown. I met an old friend and went to visit her. She just started college. I knew you'd be mad that I went by myself," I lie once again. If she knew I stayed the night with two boys, my story would turn into a murder-mystery novel.

"Yeah, right. You know someone in college? Okay." She pauses. "Give me her number so I can text her. I'd love to make a new friend." Uh oh, busted.

"Um, sure, hold on." I hang up, turning my phone off afterward. It is very suspicious, but I can always tell her the half-truth and say I was in the mall with lousy service. "Where am I going to get a new friend from?" I whine, putting the cellular device to my head.

Once again, air flows past me. Not in an open window way, but an unmistakably Fabulous Creature way. Why am I noticing so many lately? The smell of flowers wafts around me. It is too natural to be a perfume. And I hear a slight jingle in the distance. Should I call Nathair? What if I run into something sinister?

"I'll be your new friend." A girl laughs behind me. I whip around to see the cutest little redhead I've ever seen. Her small pale face has freckles sprinkled all over. Her button nose wrinkles as she smiles at me and waves. "Hi, my name is Maebh." Her eyes shy away from me. Her hazel eyes turn sienna when a tuft of hair falls from behind her ear. She fixes it, looking back at me with a grin. "I'm new to this town. I just thought it was convenient since I need a friendly face, and you need a cell phone number." Maebh waves her cute phone in my direction. I look at her quizzically. "Oh! Right, I overheard the conversation," she explains, almost like she read the question in my thoughts.

"Okay," I say. It's unusual for people to want to do me a favor. Sometimes, I drown in my thoughts and think about the power dynamics of my relationships. I was the one who does favors but never receives them. My mother always taught me to do kind things and never expect things in return. There's no kindness in your heart if you want someone to reciprocate. So over the years, I grew accustomed to helping others but only relying on myself. Anything more than that makes me uncomfortable. If I accept, will the person offering request an even *greater* favor from me later?

Nobody can be that nice in Georgia, even with Southern hospitality. That free tea or cold water on a hot summer day will cost you something.

"Well, turn your phone on and text her!" She laughs again. It isn't some annoying, unattractive laugh. It's cute. I eye Maebh carefully, trying to find a patch of green skin or abnormally pointy ears. If Fabulous Creatures exist, maybe aliens do too. Instead, I find a tiny pixie frame with long red hair with light waves.

My phone screen turns back on. Sofia called five times in four minutes. Her ringtone starts. Already hearing the cuss words in my head, I click accept. After hearing an earful, I send her Maebh's number. "How do I spell your name?" I ask, texting Sofia her details.

"It's a little hard. My name is pronounced like M-a-e-v-e, but it is spelled M-a-e-b-h," she explains. I nod, hearing a ding from Maebh's phone. "Okay, so how did we meet?" she asks. Her natural reactions are so cheery. It can brighten anyone's day.

"We went to the same daycare. We used to play together during break time. You found me on Facebook after randomly remembering my name." I say, making up everything off the top of my head. Even though I never get on my Facebook, it is realistic to lie and say I checked it and saw her message.

"This is fun! What daycare did we go to? And what is your name? I must have thought of it because it's really pretty." There's a glint of mischief in her eyes.

"In Loving Arms Daycare and Pre-K, and I'm so sorry. My name is Raine." We shake on the formal introduction. Hopefully, she can remember all this.

Maebh smiles wider. "I was right, it's a very pretty name."

I can feel eyes on me. I groan, seeing Richard's ugly face up ahead. "What now?"

Maebh tilts her head like a puppy. "What's the matter?"

"My evil stepfather is coming, and I haven't found an outfit for this dinner I'm supposed to go to," I reply, wanting to hide from Richard. He is so negative when it comes to anything I like. Then again, he isn't that great to Jasmine, either.

"I can help you pick out an outfit," Maebh offers, sounding so earnest. Maybe there are just kind people in the world.

"Okay, sure, but I don't know what to wear. My unwanted stepfather criticizes everything I look at or do," I warn.

"He can't be that bad," Maebh insists, amused.

"I told Jasmine I wanted a Lady Gaga t-shirt for my birthday, and Richard spent the whole day saying I was brainwashed." That fight was so bad that I had to stay at Sofia's for three days.

Her perfect face finally breaks, looking very confused. "I love Lady Gaga. She's like fae. Magical and alluring," Maebh says while dragging me into a store I'd never seen before.

The clothes in the store are weird, like a trend two months into the future. All the dresses are beautiful, with bright colors or dark lace creations, depending on the designer.

A beautiful snake necklace is the only item that stops my eye from roaming. Silver adorns its body, shaped like it's winding down the chain, and has one green crystal. It reminds me of Nathair. "What about this? Green is the color of royalty." Maebh snaps me back into reality, showing me an emerald velvet two-piece skirt set. It has long billowing sleeves and a structured sweetheart bodice with a matching pencil skirt. I love it, but I know who won't.

"Richard will hate it, so my mom will hate it, but I don't care because I love it." I shrug, still thinking about the snake necklace. I happily take it from her. Shortly after, she hands me a white button-down with a dramatic collar to go underneath. She nailed the fairycore aesthetic. "Shoes?" I ask. She seems to know this store better than I do. Grinning, she pulls out these black leather Mary Jane shoes and knee-high socks. "Those are beautiful," I approve. Very pleased with her trendy picks, Maebh skips over to the accessory wall, plucking the snake necklace.

"I saw you looking at it." She bats her eyes at me.

"I couldn't." I hesitate, thinking of my captor, Snake Boy. I swear, I'm not going to obsess over him anymore. I promise. I can't allow myself to be a doormat just because of his little secret.

"Yes, you could, it's fifteen dollars, and it's real silver. You must have it!" She chucks it in with the rest of the outfit.

"I'm sure all of this is expensive enough."

"Then what are fifteen more dollars?"

"I guess you're right." It doesn't have to be worn all the time, and I would've bought it before I found out about Nathair. Could the tiny snake's eyes at least be a different color? Shuffling through the other necklaces, none are as pretty as the one I fell for.

With one last look, I stare in the mirror at myself. It is very different from my regular style, but I love it. Turning to look at myself from every angle, maybe the fairycore aesthetic is for me. Thanking Maebh, I purchase my outfit. "Nice meeting you. Let's hang out sometime!" She gives a sweet wave, looking like a ray of sunshine.

"Absolutely! Give me your Insta and your number!" I say. I feel guilty for judging Maebh earlier. She is just lovely.

Moments pass, and I return back to my misery. Just as I expected, Richard hates the outfit Maebh picked out. "Raine, why is the skirt so tight? You do realize this is a family dinner?" he questions after I walk out of my room, fully dressed. "Even Jasmine found an outfit appropriate." Jasmine groans, texting away on her phone. Adjusting her clothes in just the few minutes she's been in them. It seems like she's disgusted with her outfit. I know what Jasmine likes to wear, and this is not her style. Jasmine is into the Insta-baddie aesthetic. She dreams about a metallic gold jacket—something loud and creative. I often love bold things too but never dare to wear stuff like that. This outfit is the first risky thing I own.

"I bought a jacket," I say. Richard, who doesn't look any less unhappy, just nods.

"Well, let's see." The gorgeous velvet cape rests on my shoulders, covering a bit of the back part of my outfit. Feeling Richard's eyes burn into my skin. My apathy sets in because I know what is coming next. "Raine, as lovely as you look, that is not an appropriate outfit for dinner, and you need to change. You look like you are wearing a costume." He shakes his head in disapproval.

"But—"

"Raine, you know how to dress, and this is not a good outfit to go out to dinner in," Mom backs him up. She always sides with him.

This is when I threaten to run off into the arms of a handsome troublemaker. However, I don't have a handsome troublemaker, nor do I have the guts. So I take the easy way out and change into a bland tank top, black blazer, skinny blue jeans, and black heels. Frowning, I let my mother tell me how beautiful I look now that I am not giving guys the "wrong" impression of me. "Perfect! Keep acting good, and maybe I'll let you get that blue-black low-lights you've been blabbing about for months now." She kisses my head, not making me feel any better. Her interpretation of "good" matches Richard's. And there it is again, *perfect*. If I have to hear that word again, I swear I'll pull a Van Gogh.

"Okay, girls, get in." Miserable, we walk to the car. Jasmine pulls out her phone, scrolling through TikTok, hiding her headphones with her long hair.

One of Richard's rules is not to listen to music in the car. He thinks the sound of him complaining about us is good enough. Following her example, I turn mine on too. Pink's "Split Personality" starts playing. One of the few songs I have that doesn't have a lot of screaming or is sung in a different language. "Raine!" I snap my head up to a furious Richard. "You know better. Take that out of your ears!" Eyes wide and confused, I comply. Jasmine is still on her phone, making me green with envy. I look out the car window, just staring at it. I have nothing better to do besides stare out into space. A lightning strike flashes, but the skies show no signs of a storm.

Forty minutes pass before we get to our destination. It's a restaurant that charges twenty dollars for water. Overrated and overpriced. We all know at least one. But Richard is wasting his money, not me.

Despite its fifty-dollar price, our food is disgusting. I have caramel chicken with pralines. Jasmine has filet mignon with bacon wrapped around it. Though very pretty, the caramel on the chicken is too sweet, almost sickening, and the rubbery chicken has no taste. Jasmine's filet mignon is the exact oppo-site of my chicken. Black people like well-seasoned food, but her food is too salty! The salt burns my tongue when I try a piece. She isn't exaggerating. I gulp down the rest of my water, forgetting about the straw. "Raine, mind your manners!" My mom slaps my hand.

"This is salty!" Jasmine guzzles her water.

"Jasmine Aurora Thomas! Don't embarrass us!"

Jasmine continues chugging the water, not caring what they have to say.

"All I was trying to do was give you girls a nice day together, but if you're going to act like you're at a rave party, I don't think I can take you anywhere!" Richard nags for the two-hundredth time today.

"Geez, just send us to a boarding school already!" Jasmine scoffs.

I am out of it through the rest of dinner. Everything seems pointless. No matter what we do, it is wrong. *Raine, you know how to act better!' 'Jasmine, you need to watch your language!' 'You girls represent us, and we do not look good right now!'* These phrases ring throughout the dinner table, making me give up and sit there. It is a miracle once Richard pays the bill.

We march back to the car, still hungry and a little nauseous. Richard shakes his head, takes a deep breath, and unlocks the vehicle. He seems disappointed in how the night went. His eyes show pure exhaustion. We are a lot to handle at times. I feel terrible for seeming ungrateful, but I am tired and upset too. I think about the outfit that I wanted to wear. I think about how he hyper-analyzed our schoolwork and how our home looked. He brought this upon himself. Sucking my teeth, I get in the car.

The ride home is docile once I sneak in my headphones. The harsh beats of the rock music calm me down. I try not to be obvious, holding back my desire to bop my head to the beat or hum the song.

The world falls off my shoulders once I crawl into bed. Tossing and turning, leaving me with my thoughts.

Thoughts of him play over in my mind. An escape is needed, and the new novel I had just bought is calling my name. Getting comfortable at my desk, I open to the first page. The world starts to blend around me but then stops. *What's Nathair doing right now? Ugh, who cares?* I huff, putting it down.

Ugh, why am I thinking of him? Since it's so boring here, why don't we get started on this mission early? He said I could come and go, right? The forbidden name glows on my phone. Typing things that should stay in my mind and biting my lip, I hit send.

To say I've died and gone to heaven is an overstatement, but the library in the manor is beyond words. The vast room is filled with shelves that stretch to the ceiling. Built into the walls and covered with various reading nooks, the library resembles a hobbit cave. Crystal chimes dance with light from the sunset floating around like fairies during a festival. Rainbow beams decorate Nathair's black hair, stone-faced, as he opens the door wider to me. "This is your new dungeon," he throws a half-hearted wave to show the place.

Even with such an unpleasant person next to me, I still have love in my eyes. "Woah! When you said you collected books. I didn't think you meant this many!" I touch one of the books, filled with the intoxicating smell of old paper and leather binding. Strange symbols are engraved on the books of the world. Well, not my world. The world of the Fabulous Creatures has a long history like my own.

"Yeah," Snake Boy grunts, plopping down on a recliner.

I pick up several books and memorize their bodies with my eyes. I sniff one of the books, earning a disgusted look from Nathair.

His nostrils flair. "What kind of freak did I let in my house?"

"Each book has different paper quality, ink, and bindings." I analyze each new book around me. Some were thinner and made of papyrus. Others were heavy with metal accents. Each one is lovingly arranged by class and genre. Or I think because it's in a different language. "What language is this? It's used as a label."

Nathair ignores me and starts his reading. I frown at him and place the books back on the shelves.

"It's Theban. That's our common language." Alister steps in, holding three cups of hot chocolate and a bag of chips. His eyes are bright and shiny. He places the cups down and picks up a pen. "But you're with us now! So I should write it in English too."

Alister's willingness to help and translate the many labels warms my soul. I look over at Nathair furiously flipping through his book, potion bottle still in his mouth.

I raise my hand in dismissal and go back to Alister. "How did you get all of these?"

"It's inheritance," Nathair mumbles through his bottle before Alister can answer.

"It's also our personal collection that we got from doing various favors for different Fabulous rulers." Alister sounds humble, but if he were to name-drop, it wouldn't make sense to me.

"Careful, Alister, each word you give her can be used as a weapon later." Snake Boy says, finally putting down his bottle.

"Careful, Nathair, each time you deny how cute she is, I can use it as a weapon later, too." Alister chides, writing *Gwisin legends* on one of the labels. His movements are calm and relaxed, but his face is impish.

Nathair glares at him, downing a cup of hot chocolate in one gulp. "Try being more creative next time, *old pal*," Nathair emphasizes. With a dynamic like this, they must be best friends. "Also, I'd rather puke than call her cute."

"Likewise!" I shoot back, though he *is* cute to me. But to let it get in his head would be a sin. This crush is an affliction, and I'll get over it soon enough.

We all do a Western stare-down, waiting for the following smart-ass comment to fire. When the dust settles, I take a book off the shelf and relax in my new prison. I drink a potion. As the foreign words shift and arrange themselves into English, a welcoming feeling warms my heart.

Fabulous Creature Findings:

Fabulous Creature:

Dragon

Report to Nathair:

N/A

Realm: Nomadic Species

Human Country it is Associated with:

There are records of dragon sightings all over the world. These creatures are nomadic and travel, and there are hundreds of variations.

Notes:

A giant reptile with enormous wings that can breathe fire. Most are revered creatures but either keep to themselves or serve as guardians. They live very long lives and, with magical assistance, can shapeshift into humans. Alister relies on an amulet.

Fabulous Creature Findings:

Fabulous Creature:	Report to Nathair:
Serpent	N/A

Realm: Thebes

Human Country it is Associated with:

There are many types of Serpents rumored to be all over the world, however, most are said to be of European origin. There is also a South American relative called the Yacumama.

Notes:

A large dark creature with three forms: human, in between, and a full serpent. Most are wicked and base their strength on how much venom a being has. After researching, I found that Nathair's name comes from a mythical large mountain snake.

Fabulous Creature Findings:

Fabulous Creature:	Report to Nathair:
Gwisin	N/A

Realm: Woori Nara

Human Country it is Associated with:

South Korea

Notes:

Dark Vengeful spirits that didn't move to the afterlife. They often target specific people that wronged them before their death. There are many urban legends of children seeing gwisin as they are more sensitive to magical influence. Gwisin can transform but do not have the ability to transform others.

· SIX ·

The next day's drive to school differs from my usual bus blues. For one, we're riding in the car together. Then add that Nathair is interrogating me on what I've read. "What did those three volumes I gave you say?"

Why do I need a pop quiz? I finished one of the books last night, even taking notes, but none pleased him. "It mostly talked about different types of ghosts. I read mostly about the Gwisin, and there was nothing regarding their abilities to transform others. It's all in my notes."

My back and neck ache from the stress of last night, but I hold out the papers for him anyway. The car wobbles as he steadies the wheel on his leg. Our bodies sway as he drives, and my stomach lurches. He snatches the paper from me so fast that it starts to whistle in the wind, and he begins to read it.

"Um, do you mind watching the road? The papers aren't disappearing just because you don't look at them right this second!" It's unnecessary to risk our lives for three pieces of paper with useless information! I also kept some personal notes for myself at his house, but he probably wouldn't appreciate me giving him stuff he already knows.

"Do you wanna drive?"

"Yes, if you want to look at those papers." I reach for the driver's wheel, and Nathair gives me the evil eye.

"Well, too bad. I'm not pulling over to let you drive. Can you even legally drive? You look like a fourteen-year-old." He returns his eyes to the road finally. Can a giant snake drive a car? I have questions, but he probably would have some dumb magical or criminal reason behind his driving license. He is only good at those two things.

"I'm waiting on my mom to get me a car." I cross my arms and lean on the car door.

"I need to see a license because I don't believe you." Frustrated, I snatch up my bag and rustle around in it—throwing my license in his lap. "How do I know you didn't make a fake one?" His voice is condescending and rough, angering me to no end.

"You aren't even a legal citizen yet. You're one to talk."

"Nathair, leave Little Bear alone." Alister taps away at his phone on the passenger's side. Like a fly on the wall, he blends in at times. Usually, when Snake Boy's mouth runs rampant. Then like a knight in shining armor, Alister comes in to save me. Alister relaxes more in the car, letting his horns grow out of his forehead, and his claws sharpen.

"It's fun messing with her, so sue me." He laughs. I try to look mean and intimidating. I try to the best of my abilities to look mean, but this early in the morning—or as I call it, *mournings*—my glare runs flat. Nathair ignores me and continues with his friend. "And do you mind? People can see you when we drive past."

"I don't know how you do it. Sometimes my dragon parts feel like it is being cramped in this tiny body. I need to stretch something in this puny car, or I'll go crazy." Alister reclines peacefully as his feet extend into claws.

"You're the reason she's in this puny car. Keep showing your dragon form, and we'll have to buy a bus!" Nathair hisses.

"Lay off of her and me." Alister yawns, and a tiny flame comes out. I fan the smoke away from my nose.

"Hmm, I wonder what the average size of a snake's brain is. Let's Google," I say nonchalantly, typing the inquiry into the search engine on my phone.

"Serpents."

"As far as I'm concerned, you're just an overgrown snake."

He stops the car, rotating his whole top half in my direction. "I'll be nice and pretend I didn't just hear that," he says ominously, turning back to see the road. His gaze pierces through the rearview mirror. I am quiet the rest of the way to school.

For once in my life, I walk the halls of Darlson High School and exist in my peers' eyes. Usually, I go through the day being ignored, which I don't mind. When I'm visible to my lovely classmates, they just say rude things. I'm not hated, just not worth their air. Their eyes burn me at all angles, observing my company. Nathair and Alister don't seem to care about the imaginary circus we created just by walking together. Some whisper and gawk as if we are animals at a zoo, but all of them follow the three of us with their eyes. Heads seamlessly pivot to trace every step. I gulp, needing to think of an explanation to tell my friends at lunch. "Where are we going anyway?" I whisper as if it is a sin to speak.

"I found an abandoned classroom. We'll meet there to discuss what we've learned."

I cock an eyebrow at Nathair. "An empty classroom? In this school? It's so crowded that we have to rezone." The tension in everyone's eyes melts off me. It must've been Nathair's ability to make people feel comfortable around him because I was a nervous wreck a second ago.

"Oh wow, what an astute observation from the class 'Know-it-all.' It's almost as if I'm magic," he replies, rolling his eyes for the thousandth time. I can ditch these two for Sofia if I want to hear sarcasm all day.

"Fine, what room, Snake Boy?"

"Three-two-six."

"That's not empty! I have class there during 4th period," I shriek. Does he think he can just steal someone's classroom?

"Well, it's abandoned now." He snickers, stopping at the empty room of Coach Ramsey. He pokes his head in and wolf-whistles into the dark room.

"What did you do to my science teacher!" The fairly empty room only has a few desks in it now. At least he was humble enough to pick the school's smallest room. I could see why he was attracted to it. This room is the only one with built-in bookshelves and no windows. It's also at the end of the three hundred hall with no room across from it, so it's full of privacy.

"Let's just say he believes in ghosts now." He strolls in and switches on the fluorescent lights, beaming at me. The pale-yellow hurts to look at, but my eyes adjust soon after.

"You're so—" I take out my notebook and brandish it at him.

"So *what*? Look, it's just a classroom. He got a nice one in the two hundred hall."

"—Inconsiderate!" I finish, hitting his chest with the book.

Without even a slight flinch, he grabs my notebook and holds it over my head. I stare at him and cross my arms. He lowers it, trying to bait me.

"Oh well, why should I care again?" He taunts, threatening to put it on the giant cabinets by the door.

I try to make a pass for it—too quick, Nathair lifts it back up again. I stop, tired of his games. "If you're going to be human, you've got to understand you can't get your way all the time! You won't be able to turn into some scary mythical creature and convince people to do what you want once you're human!" I make one giant leap and snatch my book in one fell swoop. Landing on my feet makes my confidence increase. He makes a tiny clap, looking impressed.

"I'll learn that when I'm human, but I know I will not be a pushover like you." He laughs, getting closer and staring at me with his gorgeous green eyes. "You know, I can't wait to corrupt you." I suck my teeth at him. Is he a beast who can be tamed with some training?

"Really? How so?" I stare back, trying to look intimidating.

"It's already happening. Pretty soon, you'll bite back snide comments that your peers throw at you, fight, and talk back to your parents. Remember, originally. Serpents were made to tempt humans, so even just being around me will make you want to say your true feelings." He plots, making me uneasy, but I'll never tell him that.

With a guy who can control emotions, how will I know when it's truly my feelings? I remember the picture on my phone. I don't want to use it if I don't have to.

But despite my reservations, I wrinkle my nose and fan the air. "I thought Alister was the dragon, but your breath says otherwise."

He sinisterly smiles, backing away from me. "Yeah, it starts with me, but it'll spread."

"Get over yourself, Nathair. The world doesn't revolve around what you say. You don't know me." I change the center of my chest, now and lead with my chin. According to my studies, centers are body languages that affect a person's appearance and personality. Leading with my chin makes me look more self-confident, helping me to finish my sharp remark with a fake confident stride to one of the desks.

"Sure, it doesn't, babe."

"I feel left out of this conversation," Alister says with a pitiful voice.

"Why do you want to be in the conversation? She's just insulting me." Nathair looks at Alister, squinting his eyes and furrowing his brows.

"Because I'm supposed to point out you guys want to smash faces with all the arguing you are doing." Like a child, Alister starts making kissing noises and wraps his arms around his body, mimicking making out with air. The hair on the back of my neck stands up in disgust.

"Look, the only thing I use the girl for is brains. It is the only thing I like about the girl, so get that dumb look off your face." Nathair gags, pointing at his uvula. Alister grapples him, still making kissing sounds.

To be honest, this infuriates me. "Wow, good to know that time you kissed me meant nothing!" I am still like a statue, heat radiating from my ears. The creases in my eyebrows intensify, and I try to hold back my pout.

"Only because I'm a boy. I would've done it with another girl if not you."

"You—" I'm speechless.

"Lost your confidence, I see. I thought you were witty."

I attempt to glare at him, but that only makes him laugh harder. Once again, I would go find Sofia if I wanted to be ridiculed by anyone.

"Whatever. Can you explain why I'm missing quality time with my ACTUAL friends in the morning when we're not doing anything?" I ask, trying to change the subject. Nathair notices but decides to go along with it.

"So you can get used to coming here in the mornings."

"But we're not doing anything. I could be talking to my friends so they don't think I'm ditching them." I remember the lecture Sofia gave me. That was before I realized Nathair was more than a smoldering, tortured musician—he was also a classic sociopath.

"It's all that passionate tension clouding Nathair's mind. He wants to keep you all to himself." Alister puckers his lips at Nathair, causing Snake Boy to hit him. "What, it's true!"

"Or not." Nathair shoves Alister one more time.

"Okay, since I'm not needed. I'll just take my last ten minutes before we have to go to class and explain to my friends about our project," I announce cheerily, trying to tiptoe out of the room.

"You can't tell them!"

"Duh, smart one, that's why I'm going to lie and say we're doing a cultural research project together in our sociology class at Clayton State University." I smile, thinking it is a good enough lie. They know about taking college courses early for extra credits and would assume my mother had signed me up.

"Who said you could leave?" Nathair dusts my good lie off, being stubborn.

"I did," I reply, leaving right after that. He doesn't even attempt to follow me.

It doesn't take long to spot the "O.C. kids." Short for Outcast Kids, we decide to take back the power of that word. Our table is in the back of the cafeteria, the second to last table. My friends squabble in the distance, and our friend—and local womanizer—Jacob is chasing Cassie around, trying to tickle her. She screams and runs around the table. Sofia, eyes bright and alert today, is laughing at them. Jay sits next to her, eyes resting on her smile. I search the table for Kasha. She isn't far, sitting three rows down, writing emo poetry. Even though she is laughing, I know she is writing about the meaninglessness of life or something else equally existential. Even when she is happy, she writes poetry like that.

"RAINE-CHAN! HELP ME!" Cassie whines, causing everyone to look in my direction. I would've laughed and hit Jacob, which usually ends with him chasing me too, but I stop dead in my tracks.

My friend's stares don't look like their usual carefree glances. Sofia must've said something about my "lovesickness." Jay doesn't notice my nervousness, but Sofia does. She eyes me meticulously.

"Why'd you get here so late? Jacob didn't see you on the bus, and you didn't ride with your sister," she asks, not sounding suspicious, but her eyes tell a different story.

"I had to talk with Nathair, my mom forced me into this lame sociology class, and we have to work on a project together. He takes the class too. It's for college credit," I say, mentally kicking myself for stating the obvious.

"What about Maebh? I thought you were catching up with her."

"Maebh isn't in that class—she studies fashion!" I nervously laugh, making it clear lying is not my forte.

"Right." Sofia sounds completely unconvinced. The bell rings afterward, dismissing me from explaining anymore. Since I never had time to put my stuff down, it's easy to go to my first-period class.

I arrive early for once. For the past seven months since school started, I've made a bad habit of hanging out with my friends until we have one minute before being late to class. But now I'm so early that the teacher wouldn't even be in the room. It's eight twenty-three, seven minutes of freedom. I pull out a book about serpents that I swiped from Nathair's library and get comfortable. I sigh, leafing through the stories of people who have come across one. They never seem to end well. So what he doesn't know won't hurt him because I need to know what kind of creature I'm dealing with. He's a conundrum that I can't solve. How do his powers even work? Can I even beat it? So many questions that I can't ask him. So here I am, letting the world around me vanish as I delve for answers.

Beware the terrifying Nathair, for it will whisper sweet nothings in a lonely heart's ear and consume you.

Beautiful creature, tempt me, drag me down to hell, and swallow me whole. Calling me from afar like a siren song, I follow your tune.

Oh, mighty beast or unholy animal, your rattle makes me dance to your every whim, every beck and call. I trek up your winding path, through the stony maze, and past the thick canopies just to get to you, my love.

Why do I run to my demise? Others before me have met an untimely fate, all poisoned, the color drained from their eyes. Unlucky fellows. Now it is my turn to meet the same death. With no control of my feet or mind and my bloody cracked steps leave a trail behind, all to get to you, my dear.

The vast cave, your home, greets me with a blanket of darkness. My heart cries and rejoices at the familiar hiss rattling in my mad brain. I finally got to you, my joy.

But as fast as you strike the others, the dread fills my lungs, and the terror sobers me. Today is my last day. I have been fooled by a beast who suckled Lilith's teat. I walked right into its deadly lair. My mind is clear once I meet this demon. She plays with me, revealing her human form. Her smooth, silky skin, hair white like the moon, and gemstone eyes sinisterly smiling at her next meal.

If I strike her, I can run away, but she has me frozen in fear. Feet planted into the ground like roots, and helpless to her attack. She grows into a massive snake, baring her fangs at me.

It's time.

Never go into the mountains or the desert, for she is not the only one to live. These dark, Fabulous Creatures will be waiting for you. If you are so unlucky to meet one, then to avoid its call, all you need to do is—

Aethel swipes the book from my hands, throwing it on the ground. With an accomplished smile, she digs her heel into my book. "Won't be needing that, freak." She grins, lifting her foot from my book centimeter by centimeter. She kicks it toward me. The murdered book hits the metal of my desk with a horrible *thunk*. I stop, looking at my fallen friend. I touch its wound, so deep and fatal. Pages fall out like wilted petals.

"What is your problem? Why did you do that?" The now ruined way to stop a serpent's power lies lifelessly on the ground. I pick up the precious book like a dead loved one. Her heel was so sharp it ripped eighty of its pages! "Do you realize what you just did?" I ask, horrified at its current state, but I don't expect her to understand the deadly gravity of her bullying.

Aethel just shakes her head, her shiny curls wriggling like baby snakes. "Just a healthy dose of payback. Consider this your final warning. Stay away from *Nathrech*," she says, using a name I don't recognize.

"I don't even know who that is." Frustration boils up in me. I clench my chair.

"Uh, stupid human, I guess you only know the human pronunciation." Aethel suppresses a laugh. "Nathair."

"Look, I don't know your relationship with him, but I don't owe you anything!" Who does she think she is? You can't go around destroying property and expect people to let it go! I am about to yell more until her eyes turn into slits, like a snake's, and yellow.

CRUNCH! I cry out in pain, dropping to the floor. My heart wants to jump out of my ribcage, and black fuzzies form in the corner of my eyes as I examine my limp wrist. I look at her with eyes the size of dinner saucers. No one else is in the room to protect me. Trapped and all alone with Aethel and her two lackeys, my body erupts into shivers. What else could she do to me? She isn't a regular mean girl.

"Look, you stupid little rat," she hisses in a low, dangerous voice, "stay away from my Nathair. I don't care if he threatens to kill you. If I see you with him again, I'll do the job for him!" she whispers the last part in my ear.

A classmate waltzes in, but before he can register what's going on, Aethel hisses. Her eyes glow a daunting yellow, and it rattles in the background once more. His eyes grow blank and he stands up straight. His pupils are so small you can barely see anything, the boy goes to leave, and blocks entry from the others.

"You're a serpent, too," I say in a daze, blinking away the black fuzz, trying to regain consciousness. My wrist hurts so much.

"Congratulations, you just sealed your fate when you decided to piss me off. Yes, I am, and Nathair needs to stay one. You understand?" I nod. My head is a bowling ball, straining my eyes and neck even more. "Good, now stay out of my way, and we won't have a situation like this again." She grits her teeth, releasing me from her death grip. Then the three stroll to their desks, giving me dirty looks. Aethel releases the poor guy. He requests to go to the nurse, complaining about a migraine.

I excuse myself as well and skip class to go to the only person who could help me.

Life is only a surreal moment for me until I go to room three twenty-six. Alister strokes my hair, treating my wrist.

Snakes are pretty strong creatures, so I'm sure Aethel was truly just giving me a warning. Nathair doesn't make any smart-ass comments. Once I tell him what had happened, he brings me lunch.

"Aos sí dust cures stuff like this." Nathair dumps his bag on the floor. His things rattle around, spilling to other parts of the room.

"I think I left it at home." Alister wraps my wrist in bandages, confessing to Nathair.

"Why would we not need to be healed outside the house!" Nathair kicks the bag. I look pathetically in his direction, my head turning like a sloth. What is their relationship? I thought she just has a crush, but there is more to the story.

"Because I didn't think one of us would injure a human at a school," Alister says in a concerned voice without looking back at Nathair.

"She's not one of us! It just pisses me off that she would do this in public." He bends his head backward and puts his hands on his face, covering the red flush creeping up from his neck. His arms tremble.

"Don't be a prick just because Aethel knows how to push your buttons. Raine is the victim here." He gently pats my shoulder and gets up. "Calm down. I'll go get it. And be nice to her!" Alister demands, leaving the room. "Little Bear, I'll be back in ten minutes. You can go to your friends after I heal you."

Nathair, weary, looks over at me. "Did Aethel try to bite you too?"

"No." This is the first time I spoke since the incident. "What's her problem?"

"You should eat," he replies firmly. Too traumatized to rebel, I bite my soggy and cold chicken nuggets. We sit there in silence for a few minutes.

Slowly, I chew, focusing only on the task in front of me. It was me who broke the awkward silence first. "Ever thought of locating a witch," he looks at me, curious what nonsense I was spitting out, "to change you into a human?"

"Witches don't exist."

"But serpents, dragons, and nymphs do?"

"Well, I didn't create the world." He takes a nugget from my plate and takes a bite. Nathair makes a face, which is justified. The cardboard stale chicken slumped over into the mushy fries.

The soggy fry flops in my hand as I eat it reluctantly. "I just thought that was a little strange, is all."

"There are humans practicing white and black magic, shamans, psychics, but none fly on a broom," he teases, smiling a bit.

"Well, let me rephrase the question, have you ever thought of consulting anyone who practices white or black magic?" I earn a light laugh from him. It is times like this that make me want to be friends with him. He can be nice when he wants to be.

"We'd have to research more, see their locations. It could be possible, but I don't want to add anybody to this."

"But if we found someone who could do it, would you?" I press, leaning closer to him, and scoot my plate closer to him with my hand.

"Well, if you found somebody that could give you anything you wanted, would you?" He gives a small wave and declines my offer. Fair enough, cafeteria food is universally gross, but they always have to add the atrocious peas too. One rolls off the plate and onto the dusty floor.

"Yeah," I reply without a doubt.

"Well, that's pretty stupid."

"How so? Isn't that what you're doing?"

"Tsk, You humans are way too curious and don't think about risks. To be a Fabulous Creature is much more than that crap they put in fairy tales." He says.

"How so?" I ask.

He steals a chicken nugget from me, eating a few bites. He continues with his explanation. I can't expect peace from a dude who can't make up his mind on nuggets.

"Not all of us are violent and homicidal. But we always think about how we can progress and improve ourselves. Our evil comes from our ways of manipulation to get what we want. Light creatures do the opposite. I'm a dark creature, but I don't like hurting others, even if it makes my life easier. My people only focus on what they can do to strengthen themselves. We're selfish. We're heartless. We're all these things that I don't want to be," he admits.

"Still can't believe you want to be a puny human! Aethel is terrifying, and she snapped my wrist like a twig!" I say, a little too excited. He stares at me like I'm a complete freak. With a comment like that, I guess I am.

"You're so weird, but I don't care about strength. I want—" He cuts himself off. "Would you change yourself if you could? Into a Fabulous Creature?"

"Nah, I wouldn't mind staying human after you two traumatized me! But it's cool hearing about magic." We both laugh now, looking at each other with eyes that don't contain animosity.

"Nice to know you two can be civil with each other despite Daddy leaving you two kids alone." We both jump in unison after hearing Alister's voice. We couldn't have been talking for that long!

"I thought you'd be back in ten minutes." Nathair hurries away from my desk. "And never call yourself *Daddy* ever again unless you want me to vomit all over you."

"Ten minutes have passed! What, you two want me to leave you alone so you can make out? I get the hint," he jokes, sprinkling this queer, colorful dust on my injury. Instantly, the pain dissolves.

Testing it out, I roll my wrist in a circular motion and move my fingers. Nothing. "Now I have to explain so much to my friends," I say, lifting my body from the seat.

"Lie," Nathair commands, not meeting my gaze. Great, all's right with the world. He is his typical self again.

"No, I'm just gonna tell my friends a serpent and a dragon enslaved me. And how they are looking for a way to turn him human and that another serpent is out to get me," I say. Gosh, is this my new typical day? I had a lot happen this past weekend.

"Just reminding you, in case you have a horrible memory problem." He bends down and lifts my bag for me. Handing it to me without meeting my eyes.

"Get a room," Alister coughs.

"SHUT UP!" Nathair and I say in unison. I leave the boys to their matters. It's funny how I escaped Nathair's snake pit, but I'm about to throw myself into the lion's den.

<u>Fabulous Creature Findings:</u>

<u>Fabulous Creature:</u>	<u>Report to Nathair:</u>
Spellcasters	Transformation
Realm: N/A	spells available

<u>Human Country it is Associated with:</u>

Every continent has legends of spellcasters.

<u>Notes:</u>

Though witches are not specifically named in the books I read, many types of spellcasters exist. Most are dark creatures who have given up their souls to an evil force or to their grimoire to gain power, revenge, or by accident. Some of these spellcasters include: Shaman, Aos sí, Daikini, Iele, and Aswang.

·SEVEN·

Sofia and Jay are the only ones at the table when I arrive at my destination. Talking animatedly about some game they played, they both pause to look at me. "Hey, where is everybody?" I start twiddling my fingers, standing awkwardly in front of the table. Sofia's eyes focus on my hands. She squints and goes back to looking at Jay.

"Lunch line and microwave. Nice of you to join us." Ouch, I need water from her dry voice. Then again, Sofia always has a natural sarcastic tone in her voice. She can't help it sometimes. She motions to an empty seat. "Well, why are you standing?"

"Just feel like it." I've never really had to lie that much in my lifetime, so being dishonest is hard. The task is even more demanding when talking to your best friend, the person you share your deepest thoughts and feelings with. Best friends know you inside and out. Yet, I am hiding this deep, dark secret. My knees pop from how long it took me to sit down. I tap my foot, placing my bag on my lap. Sofia and Jay revert to their conversation. They forget I'm there in minutes, but I don't care. The less attention those two give me, the less chance I get interrogated. Undetected, I sneak my headphones into my ears and play hardcore emo music. The booming beat and guttural singing cure my slight depression. My chest feels lighter. Songs like this heal my soul.

Hands are trying to tickle me. I elbow Jacob as he greets me fondly, "Raine, we missed you!"

"Leave her alone!" Cassie squeaks, pulling Jacob away from me. He efficiently fights her off, pushing her to a chair. With big fluid movements, she settles into a pout. Making a noise similar to a baby.

Oh, Cassie, such a weeb.

"I miss you too, Cassie!" Jacob whispers, tickling Cassie now, causing her to squeal and run away as usual.

"SOFIE-CHAN!" Cassie lets out a high-pitched scream—similar to that anime girl trope where she falls on top of her crush. She hides behind Sofia, ducking Jacob's grapple.

"I don't know where your hands have been! Ya nasty!" She laughs, pushing Cassie into the jungle again. "Hey Jacob, she's right here!" She gives a hearty laugh and points at her.

"FML, I have a test next period and didn't study," Kasha complains without a stitch of emotion and is unbothered by the chaos surrounding us. She sits beside me with her warmed-up TV dinner, ignoring Cassie and Jacob's charades. She must be in one of her moods. I can sympathize with her on the FML moment, but not over a test. Sofia's knowing glance burns into the side of my head. She can smell my lies like a blind dog. I quirk the corner of my lips, trying to look like my usual self, but my thoughts are draining me.

"Well, you don't have an A.P. psychology test next. It's supposed to be one-hundred questions." Jay turns his head to look at Kasha, arm-wrestling Sofia. She puts up a good fight, but Jay smacks her hand on the table for the fifth time. He turns back to her to rub her hand, but Sofia takes it away quickly. She flicks him off, laughing at her defeat.

"FML, FML," Kasha chants, digging into her food. I put one of my headphones in her ear, letting her listen to one of our favorite songs by Flyleaf.

"So, Raine, how's that project going?" Jay turns his attention to me, his brown eyes wide like a puppy's. In stark contrast, Sofia's eyes snap in my direction like a vulture. I squirm at the sudden attention.

"Fine, we haven't done much yet, just researched. We looked up countries we wanted to examine closely in the first ten minutes of class." I glance over at Cassie's untouched lunch plate, and still peckish, I take a carrot.

"Sociology? Right?" Sofia leans in to lock her eyes with mine. The dry carrot gets stuck in my throat, and I cough up a bit. This is what I get for stealing food. With a straight face, Cassie hands her milk to me. I waterfall it, careful not to touch the carton with my lips.

"It is." I clear my throat, now lubricated with cow juice. I wipe away a single tear and continue on with my facade. My lies are coming out more smoothly. Is that a thing to be ashamed of or to celebrate?

"Oh well, that's cool. I should look that class up and go to the next session. I got nothing better to do." Sofia whips out her phone to type in the name of the class. I smack her phone on the table in one fair swoop. Sofia's eyes go wild.

"Uh, you should—it's three hundred forty-five dollars a week." I smile back, knowing Sofia wouldn't attempt to ensure it was legit at that high cost.

"I'll talk to my mom about it." She snatches her phone back, putting it in her pocket.

"Raine!" That all too familiar voice calls to me. I turn around to face Snake Boy, wondering what he wants now. Once he realizes he has my attention, he picks up his pace in a light jog. "I forgot to give you this." He hands me a small book. I trace my hands over the book, my fingers drifting over some bumps. The book cover says *The Wonders of Our World*, but underneath reveals a different story. Leather embossed with old yellow pages that crackle under my fingers, I briefly flip through and avoid my friends' curious glances to read what it is.

"Thanks." We stare into each other's eyes for a second. A pink flush develops on his cheeks, and my face follows, feeling hot. Nathair looks away, being the first to break the gaze.

He clears his throat. "I should get to class." He backs away, pointing to the two-hundreds hallway.

"Yeah, I don't want to miss anything over a personal project." I look down at the book, flipping through some of the pages. It is about black magic.

"Um, see you later then. Page twenty-three is beneficial." He waves, walking away.

"Bye," I reply, looking down at the book. Flipping to page twenty-three, I see a note scribbled on a small piece of papyrus. *Tonight. Seven p.m.*

"You like him," Cassie teases, snapping back into my reality.

"Do not," I disagree. I like the nice Nathair, but not so much the other side of him.

"Do too!" Cassie sticks out her tongue. Ugh, she and Alister would get along.

Sofia scoffs, lightly smacking Cassie's arm. "She better not like him." Sofia steps closer to me, crossing her arms. "He's bad news, probably a narcissist."

I shut the book with one hand and lean in, eyeing my best friend. "We can't go around misdiagnosing people, Sofia," I scold her. "And I don't like him." Sofia rolls her eyes so hard that it feels like they would disappear into the back of her head.

"Wow, Raine, I didn't think you'd try to date a bad boy." Cassie jabs at my stomach, making kissing noises at me. I need new friends.

"I do like bad boys, just not that one. One thing Sofia is right about is him being a total jerk. He's selfish and only looks out for his best interests!" I insist, getting a little carried away.

"Then why are you two partners?" Jay interrogates as he puts a stolen carrot in his mouth now. At this rate, Cassie isn't getting her lunch.

I shrug, "I didn't pick him. The teacher did."

"So, when is this project due?" Sofia warms back up to me, scooting closer to me.

"In six months." I wonder if that was the right thing to say.

"That's a long time." Jay whistles.

"That's a huge project!" Sofia exclaims.

"Well, what can you do? I've got to take this course to help boost my chances of getting into my dream school!" I point to the keychain on my backpack that I got from the school tour last year. The bright yellow bee mascot dangles on cue, distracting my friends enough from all the questions.

"Harsh, and I thought my 'rents were bad." Jay laughs, playing with my little bee.

"Well, Richard isn't helping at all. He's probably trying to convince my mom to send me away as we speak!" I drop my bag on the ground, and the heavy books land with a loud thud on the tiled floor.

"Ugh, are you ever going to be free from that control freak?" Sofia says, making a grossed-out face.

"He's going to take my mom out for the weekend. He doesn't like *intimacy* when we're in the house, so one weekend out of the month, he'll take her on this romantic getaway to get some." I laugh. Jay starts making inappropriate gestures. After a round of disgusting noises and laughter, I smack his shoulder. Sofia asks me where Jasmine will be this weekend. "She has a date. I overheard her on the phone with Serena talking about the perfect dress." I am most likely having a quiet night of studying whatever Nathair will give me for that night.

"Why don't we get together? I can spend the night afterward," she suggests.

"Yeah, I got nothing better to do with my life besides sit in the dark on a Saturday night!" I blurt out without thinking and mentally smack myself in the face. Can't forget about Nathair. It's only been a day of me working for him, and he is already sucking the fun out of me.

"Hey, can you invite Maebh? I've been texting her, and she is a huge Fantasy fan! I want to play *Fantasy XII* with her!" she adds. I nod, having my new 'reality' set in. Sofia points at our friends. "Great! Hey, O.C. geeks," Sofia says, "bring your own food or you starve. Thank you!" She says the last part in a high, fake-preppy voice.

I smile nervously at all of them. Here are my best friends in the whole wide world. I love them, but something tells me that this get-together is a bad idea. Let's see how well magic mixes with mortals.

Later that week, I head to Alister and Nathair's house. Perched on a vast hill, the manor sparkles under the setting sun's golden rays. The winding road to the house moves like a slithering snake in spring. The mysterious place is just as magical as its residents, but if you venture behind the house, you can find new treasures. Behind the house hides a colossal valley. Green pastures hold fruits that are so bright and plump.

"This is how we get the money to pay for the house and food." Alister puts his hands on his hips like a proud father. "We pick the fruit when it's ripe and sell it to markets or local grocery stores in the morning on weekends. I want to try to make blackberry jam in the summer," he says dreamily. The cool air blows past me, sending an intoxicating fresh smell. The rows follow the massive curves and turns of the hillside. At times they wind together, looking like they have collapsed into each other.

There are rows of grape vines, watermelon patches, apple, and orange trees. "What else is here?" My jaw drops at the beauty.

He chuckles. "We grow peaches, blackberries, tomatoes, and pumpkins along with what you see here." The trees are neatly arranged by their fruit type, showing all the care and love Alister puts into them.

"Aren't most of these fruits not in season yet? How do you take care of bills and other stuff when you can't sell the fruit yet?" The cool spring air isn't suitable for all the fruits they have. Most of these fruits are in season during the summer.

"A few wood nymphs owed me a favor, so they helped me build all this." He laughs, patting me on my head. Of course, it's something magic-related. That is a stupid question to ask a person who can fly and breathe fire.

"Dumb question, I'm sorry." I pick one of the apples, and it makes a crisp snap, the branch bouncing up and down from the sudden weight loss. The hose is curled up—looking like it is sleeping peacefully in the shade. Feeling a little remorseful, I unwrap the bundled thing. The cold, glistening water spurts out, running clean all over my snack. "Why is it so wonderful here? I don't want to leave!" I bite into the forbidden fruit. A beautiful deep ruby color, the appearance is just as sweet as its taste. My teeth dig into the apple with a satisfying crunch, leaving a bit of juice on my lip. A dribble of liquid runs down my chin. I wipe it away with my sleeve and continue to eat.

"I think this is my pride and joy. My greatest accomplishment." He closes his eyes, inhales the fresh air, and smiles. "As soon as we saw this place, it felt like home. It's been a year, and we are just now getting settled. This is almost everything I dreamed of." Alister's face drops, looking at an apple blossom still hanging on one of his trees. He exhales, turning back to me with his famous goofy smile. "This house will be a haven for anyone in need. Then I will consider it perfect." He crosses his arms and looks at his estate.

Alister has a young face, but his soul is bursting with experiences he might not feel comfortable sharing. I've been focused on what Nathair wanted all this time, but what does his best friend want? What does he even like? I realize how little I know about him. He's just there in the background, ready to help. "What did you guys do before moving in?" I stare into his eyes more. Flecks of yellow shine through his eyes, with slight dark circles underneath.

"When we left Thebes, it was hard for a while. But I made arrangements with the Elders of the High Court. And they set us up with this house."

"The what and the high what?" I say, words tripping over my tongue.

Dragon Boy puts his finger to his chin. "They are like the world leaders, but Fabulous Creatures. In rare cases, they will approve us to integrate with the humans if they think it will be beneficial. Nathair is a refugee. So it was easy as his guardian to get permission granted." Alister presses his arms closer to his body, lost in his thoughts.

"Huh? You're his guardian?" I pat his arm, and my eyes are so wide that they might pop out of my head. "How old are you? I thought we were all the same age!"

"Yes." He chuckles, like an older man laughing at his young child. "I knew his father, and I promised to watch over him. You'll have to ask Nathrech—" He pauses, looking at my confused gaze. "*Nathair,*" he corrects himself. "Anyway, I'm young for dragon years, but you probably will think I am ancient for humans." He pauses to calculate how old he is, counting on his fingers. "Maybe I am around two hundred years old?"

My mind explodes with thousands of questions, piling up so high in my mouth that it clogs. I stutter for a second, collecting myself. "Wait, if you are some old, powerful dragon, why are you in the body of a high school boy? This is the best you can do?"

Alister bursts out laughing, clutching his stomach. "No, I hate being in high school. It's so boring! But a certain someone loves it." He points off in the distance at the windy road. "You think it's bad to be normal in high school, but to others, it feels like a dream. A chance to be human is freedom for him."

"Wait, so if you're old, is he—?"

"Serpents age like you guys. So he is actually seventeen, don't worry."

"That's good. Nathair won't lose much when he turns into a human." I feel relieved for him. It would suck to give up aging slower. And he can live a good life after he turns human. One where he can get married and have kids and never wonder if he outlives them. My face gets hot, and butterflies churn in my stomach at the thought of him having kids. I shake the idea out of my head.

Speak of the devil. The subtle sound of gravel getting run over and the slight hum of a car engine. The white Mustang pulls up to the driveway. Nathair heaves as he lifts four metal cans of paint. He kicks the car door close. "You guys trying to re-decorate?" I ask Alister.

"You could say that!" Alister's eyes dart between grumpy Snake Boy and me. He steps in front of me, blocking my view of Nathair. "Hey, did you ask about the party yet?" Alister leans in way too close to my face, changing the subject. I back away, trying to look over his shoulder. Alister moves his head, blocking me again with his huge curly hair.

"Not yet. Chickened out yesterday." The get-together is tomorrow, and I have been procrastinating all week in fear he'd say no and make me stay over that night or something evil. This week, Nathair has been pretty decent. He kept snide comments to a minimum, but he could snap any second!

"You guys got anything better to do other than talking about me!" Nathair yells across the field. Of course, he'd assume that we were talking about him. It would only make his ego bigger if he realizes he is right.

"So sorry, my liege! No one should speak ill of the mighty King Nathair!" I say sarcastically in a very fake English accent.

"Your King shall forgive your grievances just this once! However, should you fail again, off with your head!" he returns the favor, copying my English accent.

"I'm lost. When did we get a hit online streaming show? And where is our period-appropriate clothing?" Alister looks clueless as his head whips between the two of us.

Nathair puts his face in his hands. "Alister! Get with the program, dude. You're ruining the joke." We all laugh, the sun smiling down on us with its golden warmth. It is so lovely of a day that even Nathair couldn't be a sour puss.

"Oh, by the way, boss man, can I have Saturday off?" I yell back over the distance. Nathair unloads more things into the house. It looks like a big renovation job. But he stops in his tracks, the question processing in his brain. Confused, he puts the house materials down and runs over to us. His feet hit the pavement. The echo gets closer and closer.

"It's pretty early to ask for vacation time, slacker." He snorts, a few feet away now.

"Slacker? I've read two thick books a day for you and taken notes in my notebook, and I'm the slacker?" I retort, holding up my Fabulous Creatures notebook. "I even took the time to decorate it! See? I used a cute snake stencil!"

"Ten books isn't impressive, and don't you think that is a little too on the nose?" He looks at my journal. Wrinkled brown paper and ripped pieces of the dictionary are scrapbooked onto the book. Sticky notes hanging on for dear life grace the cover. A piece of paper slides out. I tense up once I realize I forgot to throw the letter away. I peel it away before he can read it and ball it up.

"You must not have a realistic view of humans. In this realm, it's amazing to read even one thick book in five days!" I continue as if nothing happened, drawing attention away from my *personal* notes.

"Name which realm I'm from, and I'll just drop off a book for you to get to on Sunday." He crosses his arm, skeptical.

"Thebes, but not to be confused with the *human* ancient city in Egypt. They share a name, but the geography and cultures are different."

"What kind of creatures live in Thebes?" Nathair unfairly adds. He takes a step closer, now in my face. I lean back, trying to get him out of my personal bubble.

"Serpents and other immigrant Fabulous Creatures moved there due to war and famine." I am confident I got the answer right.

"What happens if you—"

Alister smacks Nathair's arm. "Oh, come on, give the girl the night off! She's been doing great."

"Fine, I'll deliver a book and let you call me on Sunday." It has to be killing him inside to let me have fun.

"Thank you!" I clap, excited.

"Don't hug me."

"I wasn't going to," I say, slightly confused.

"We all know about your crush on me, so let's keep this professional. No physical contact," he insists.

"Yeah, don't make me hate you again. You just did a good deed for once. Also, you are the one with the crush. You're obsessed with everything I do." I twirl one of my tight coils at him. Then with a mischievous smirk, I dismiss him with a curt wave before he could spew more nonsense.

"That's not true!" he says, trying to keep control. "I don't bother you when you are in the study." Unaffected, I grin at him and take off into the giant maze of grape vines. "Hey! Are you a kid?" He sprints after me. Alister, feeling left out, joins us. Laughing breathlessly, the three of us run into the pinkish-maroon sky.

My neck strains as I crack it from its frozen fixture again. I decided to study a few books before the party. "My brain is going to explode if I have to look at one more book," I mutter, stretching and extending my arms wide enough to knock over a snake trinket in Nathair's library. I steady it and look over nervously at him to see if he notices.

Nathair sits frozen in his chair. Face full of peace, but eyelids low and small. He yawns, covering up his mouth. His canine teeth still peek through, or fangs, I suppose. Nathair's eyes drift to me. "Fine. I need a break too."

Oh, is the master giving his servant a break? How unlike him. I perk up, looking at him, half expecting him to make a snide comment. But he only places his book to the side. "What do serpents do for fun?" I ask.

He shrugs. "Kill."

"Really?" I ask, full of surprise at his bluntness.

"No, that's a stereotype. But to be honest, I can't answer you. We're too busy working on getting food or fighting over things we need. So it's hard to do things that have no real benefit." Nathair flips through another book, looking for more information on spellcasters, but it's tossed on the ground seconds later.

"Okay. Is there anything you like to do?" He has to have some sort of personality other than mean and brooding.

He groans, placing his hands on his head, and leans back into his soft, lonely loveseat. "Thomas, stop with all the questions."

I continue on as if he had responded to my question. "I like to read and play video games. You should try one. My friends and I play this MMORPG called—"

He interrupts, "I don't care. Stop being such an annoying brat." He smooths his hair out of his face, huffing.

I smirk at him. Breaking him is kinda fun. "You can customize your character, choose their class, and develop teams with your friends online."

He lays his head on his lap, crossing his arms in front of me. His version of a white flag. "What do I have to do to get you to shut up?" He says, still huddled over.

My eyes widen at the humble but sudden power. "Let's play a round!" I jump up, slapping my hands on my thighs as I stand up too quickly to balance myself.

"I'm not playing this stupid game with you."

"Come on, get your laptop! Twenty minutes and if you hate it, I'll never talk about it again." I plead, eyes as wide as a baby bird.

Nathair collects himself, crossing his arms, with eyes half-closed as if he's internally saying *I give up.*

He reluctantly retrieves his laptop. Using my login to download a copy of the game, the keys of his keyboard click-clack away in hurried and clumsy thumps. "I think you're a thief class!" I beam.

"That's insensitive to serpents."

I swerve into a new class without thought. "Hero class is cool too. You can use a sword but still be agile."

Nathair leers at the hero character. "I want to use magic."

"Dark Magic?" I suggest. "I love using elemental magic, and you learn death magic later."

Nathair's face grows pink, and his cheeks heat up like a stove. "I want the healer." He points to an angelic blond boy with white robes and a long wooden staff. Standing four feet tall, if it was real, the character resembles a cherub.

I smugly pick the healer and let him decorate it. Nathair grows unnaturally quiet as he customizes his healer and gives them black hair and green eyes just like his. Not very creative, but I am proud he even changed anything on it. I follow after him, picking the hero. We would make a decent pair. I can hack and slash, and he'll heal me.

We played in silence for twenty minutes. I brace myself for him to declare the stupidity of the game, but to my surprise, he keeps playing.

"This is fun," he says plainly. No epic reaction, not even a smile, but I'll take his word for it because I am having fun too.

Fabulous Creature Findings:

<u>Fabulous Creature:</u>   <u>Report to Nathair:</u>

Elders of the High Court   N/A

<u>Realm:</u> Caeli

<u>Human Idea it is Associated with:</u>

Heaven

<u>Notes:</u>

Each Elder is the oldest and most wise of their species. They hold keys that can access all the portals to every realm to pass to the ruler of each kingdom. Only caring about keeping everything fair and balanced, they will do anything to keep it that way—including rewriting history or eviscerating those who break the rules. Only human-passing or shapeshifting creatures are allowed to live in the human realm.

· EIGHT ·

*D*ing-Dong. So much for bringing your own food. The door creaks open as I hold the crumpled, stained money my friends and I put together. The delivery man hands me the pizza, waving off the crumpled mess of money in my hand. It's no wonder why he doesn't want them. They need to be straightened up. Who the heck balls up their money like this? It was probably Cassie. As I go to fix the bills, the delivery man waves me off again and elaborates. "Don't worry about it. The redhead paid already." And just after that, Maebh steps out of the darkness.

"Maebh! You didn't have to pay." I say with a hand on my chest, feeling a little startled.

"It's okay, for the gift you've given me, it's well worth it." She beams. Cute as always, she's wearing a lilac dress with fluffy, layered tulle underneath and flower embroidery. She looks like a fairy character from a children's show—but in the best way. However, with her sweet smile, something is hiding behind it.

"I haven't given you anything," I say, ushering her in.

She looks at my neck, touching her own choker as an example. "Raine! Why aren't you wearing that snake necklace?"

Though lovely, keeping it hidden from prying eyes is a necessity. Especially from Nathair because he'll definitely get the wrong impression.

"Oh, that? I never had the chance to wear the outfit you picked out. Richard has been closely monitoring me since the mall thing." My laugh is nervous, with a hint of guilt mixed in. She worked hard to find me nice clothes, which never left my closet. Hopefully, she doesn't think I didn't like them.

"Well, he's not here, so let's at least get that necklace on!" She pulls me into the house and places the winding snake on my neck, its green eye twinkles in the artificial light.

The other hungry house guests attack the pizza once I put it on the stove. The poor pizza doesn't stand a chance against the pack of wild teenagers. No one even notices Maebh until after all of them have at least two slices. After the savage group stuffs their faces, they welcome Maebh with open arms and, in hours, fall in love with her.

"Maebh! It's nice to meet you. We are playing games in the next room. Wanna join?" Sofia puts her arms around Maebh's. She adores her, but it's hard not to. She is cute, sweet, and kind.

"I'd love to! I want to make a bunny girl! They are my favorite."

"From *Fantasy X*? Good taste!" Sofia winks at me, guiding her to the next room.

Halfway forgotten about by my friends, I follow them into the next room. We start to make our characters—I opted for the monkey person from *IX*. K-pop blasts in the background, and the air is coated with sticky, sickly sweets from all the candy and soda. Laughter, screams, and even curse words fill the house. We may have rage-quit a few times, but the mood is jovial.

We all gather around in a circle, telling ghost stories. It is Maebh's turn. Around midnight, the door rings. I get up, assuring my friends that Jasmine must be grabbing something. It was a simple lie because there was no way they'd be okay with the real person at my door.

Nathair and Alister, his right-hand man, stand in the doorway. "Wow, I'm not even human, and I've been to better parties." He shoves a book into my arms—no greeting, no questions, nothing.

"Nathair, it's so nice of you to ruin a pleasant evening with your sordid attitude and huge ego." I hug the book to my chest, concealing the cover.

Based on the small glimpse of the cover, this book seems to be about alchemy, which is more of a science, but perhaps certain creatures can replicate these spells. My morbid curiosity perks up, but it will have to wait. Plus, I can't look interested while Nathair is here. He'll never let me have a life!

"Aww, I miss those witty comebacks and scholarly vocabulary words! I miss it so much that I could just take it with me and stuff it with more knowledge," he threatens, tapping my nose. I move my head back in disgust and wrinkle my nose, sullied by his touch.

"Thanks, Snake Boy," I whisper, trying to shut the door on him.

"What, you're not going to invite me in?" He holds the door and saunters into the house anyway. Petty as usual, classic

Nathair. A piece of yellow paint chips off the old door and falls to the ground. Even my house doesn't want him here.

"Why can't you be a vampire? That way, I could have you just sit out in the cold." I bump against the door to shut it.

Alister gives me a side hug, probably pitying me. "You know he does miss you. That's why he's a grouch." He settles onto the hideous couch, immediately standing back up as a spring stabs into his back.

Even though I pity poor Alister, the longer he stays, the longer I will have to deal with Snake Boy. I carry on with the conversation. "Really? You know the whole 'boys are mean 'cause they like you' cliche is old and sexist." I glare at Nathair.

Nathair stops, turning his head in curiosity. Putting his face so close to mine, I back away, uncomfortable. The weirdo. He looks at my neck. Oh, right, the necklace! I try to hide the little charm, but it is too late.

"Well, that's ugly," he points out.

"Thank you for the opinion that I didn't ask for," I snap back, not offering him any food or drinks. I want him out.

Nathair inspects the necklace. A low hissing sound vibrates the air around us, growing thick and heavy the closer Nathair comes to me. Looking into his eyes, I notice they start to flicker. Is he using his powers?

"What are you doing? You said you wouldn't use your powers on me," I remind him. My neck starts tingling, and soon after, my necklace quivers under his touch.

"What are you talking about? I'm not—" The eye of my accessory glows sinister green light. Suddenly, the green lightning bolt shoots up his arm! We lock eyes in horror as his arm turns gray. Crumbling away like a decaying statue. Nathair kneels in pain, biting through the small shriek building up in him. His chest hardens, turning into stone! Cracks form on his neck. The necklace vibrates more erratically, stabbing his chest and twisting inside of him with that poisonous green light.

"Oh god, what's going on!" I ask, kneeling to his injured body. Big mistake. The light oozes over other parts of his body like rancid oil. Flecks of dust and stone spill over my living room floor.

"Raine, it's the necklace. Back up!" Alister yanks my arm, sending me to the couch to watch in horror. Alister's eyes glow a haunting yellow, and he rips the silver snake off my neck. Cracking into a thousand pieces of delicate crystal, Alister crushes the necklace with a heavy stomp. He freezes, eyes wide and mad. His chest rises up and down. Nathair is still alive but lying limp on my floor, moaning in pain.

I hop off my couch and slide down to him. "I'm sorry! I didn't know that there was anything wrong with it!"

Nathair struggles to breathe, whistling with each attempt. He looks up at my ceiling, closing his eyes in agony. His lips move, but no sound escapes.

"Little Bear, turn around. His body's going to regenerate." Alister helps me up and shields my eyes. Horrifying sounds of bones cracking and skin tearing fill the air. Grunting in pain, Nathair keeps his screams quiet. My fellow party-goers don't need to enter the living room and see the horror movie playing out by the front door.

After what feels like hours, Nathair gets up, dusting himself. He doesn't look angry at me, but he is pretty pissed. "Where.

The. Hell. Did. You. Get. That. Thing?" He points at me with his freshly grown pink arm. It resembles a sunburn, but only on the body parts he lost.

"A friend and I found it at this store in the mall." After this traumatic event, it's not right to withhold any information from him. I did almost kill him.

"Raine, you're missing everyone's stories," Maebh prances in, stretching. Alister's face drops and the air grows cold. Maebh looks displeased, turning her smile to a slight frown. Her whole demeanor shifts in an instant. Leaning against the wall, Maebh locks eyes with Nathair and Alister. She raises her hand. And to my surprise, crystals start to form over the doorway, creeping up like shimmering ice. Blocking the entrance.

"I'm assuming it was *this* friend," Nathair hisses, his black pupils shifting into small slits.

"Why aren't you dead?" Maebh, sounding so sweet and innocent, asks. In shock, I sit down, knees buckling. *Maebh did this?* I don't know her very well, but she has always been sweet and calm. "You were loud, by the way. I had to put up sound-proofing magic."

"You used Raine to kill me, didn't you?" Nathair demands, his fangs jetting out of his mouth, just like they did the night I discovered his secrets.

"Guys, what's going on?" I plead, holding onto Nathair's arm. He shrugs me off, lunging at her.

She stares deep into his eyes, void of any fear. She holds up her hand, and a sharp crystal stabs the air, stopping Nathair's attack. "Don't lose your head, snake. I know what can kill you." She gloats, now looking at me from the side of her eyes.

"I'm an Aos sí from the realm of Thebes, along with Alister and that *thing*," Maebh explains, smiling at Nathair and revealing her sweet face once again. "I came to look for Alister, but when I saw all three of you together, I had to do something about it. I'm so sorry to get you involved, Raine. I didn't want you to know about us, but the brash and brainless Nathrech decided to be curious about jewelry the day I was here."

"Why did you try to kill Nathair? He's my friend," I ask, still trying to hold onto Nathair's stiff arm.

"That thing? He ruined my life, Raine. Don't let him fool you. He's evil. He only thinks of himself and will step over people to get what he wants. He'll do it to you, too, I promise." She carefully approaches me, touching my arm. I jerk back from her. He hates being like this. She sighs, shrugging my rejection off. "Well, since he's used his seduction powers on you, you probably won't believe me right now. Alister, can you explain?"

"She's my ex-girlfriend. The Elder Court forbade us from seeing each other after they discovered our relationship. They threatened to kill us," he mumbles, standing on the other side of Nathair.

Maebh switches back to her sinister glare. "And who reported us?" she says, nodding her head in the direction of her least favorite person in the room.

Nathair gulps, fangs still ready to kill. "Look, the Royal Guards were already onto us running away. I did what I had to. They never play by the rules, who knew they'd report it to the Elders?"

She ignores him and her haunting eyes lock onto mine. "You know, he probably gave you the same speech he gave me. 'Oh, Maebh, I don't want to be like the other serpents! I want to be a good human and live an honest life. Can you help me?' I fell for it, too, and it got me almost killed," she says vehemently, snapping her head in Nathair's direction. She turns back to face me, her eyes full of sorrow. "We can't be together unless he's gone. I promise you, I meant you no harm."

Nathair's fangs retract. He twists his face in frustration. "Are you sure? Cause you sure made a big mess with your little stunt."

"This is rich coming from a literal hellspawn." Maebh raises her voice but ensures it is low enough not to be heard by the peons in the living room.

"You say I am manipulative, but it's okay for you to take advantage of Raine?" Nathair fusses. "You tricked her into buying a cursed necklace! What if she didn't know anything about us? You recklessly tried to get back at me!"

Her face finally breaks, looking hurt more than evil. "Because you left your friend for dead and took my love with you!" She casts away the giant crystal in between them and jabs him with an accusing finger.

"I'm supposed to be the evil one, but have you ever thought of taking some responsibility? You and Alister were breaking the law and drawing attention to us. I'm sorry if I had to make an executive decision," Nathair shot back.

Maebh explodes with fury, red enveloping her face. "So it's better to shirk all the blame onto me? They would've rather had him keep an Aos sí as company rather than a lowly, disgusting, vile serpent!" Nathair's eyes lower. Maebh continues, "I bring good luck and cast spells that help others. You only bring misfortune and death."

"That's enough!" Alister booms, stepping between them. His eyes glow, and smoke dances around him. Alister's voice grows deep and authoritative. "May I remind both of you that there are humans here? Innocent people who have no clue what's going on!" Alister's face is disappointed and distraught. This is the second time I've seen him serious. I was used to the cheery and goofy Dragon Boy, but I shudder in his presence right now.

Maebh's face relaxes and tears well up in her eyes. "Alister, how could you say you love me but then toss me away like I was nothing?"

He growls, stifling his anger. He looks down at her hands. "I had a plan, but you weren't patient." He dives in and holds her hands, releasing her floodgates. "I took you to the fairy kingdom, didn't I? Of course, I care!"

"You chose him over me," she whimpers.

"No, I chose you both, but I had to wait for you." Alister embraces her, holding her as if his life depends on it. Maebh's small body shakes in his arms, heaving.

"How much do you love him?" I mumble. All eyes shift to me—a nightmare I always try to avoid.

Maebh wipes her face, trying to regain her composure. "More than life itself."

Nathair runs his hand through his hair, huffing in angst. "We have a murderer in the house, and you pity her?"

"We're not pitying her, but she thinks she wants you hurt. She'd regret it just like you would've if you killed me," I try to explain without victim-shaming him, and though he doesn't say it out loud, I can tell he agrees.

"How can you be so naïve?" Defeated, he puts his arms down.

"Nathair, I had to give up a lot to help you. I have only one request," Alister starts, still holding Maebh tightly, "I want her to live with us. She can help us," he insists, making Maebh's eyes light up. "I love her. This is all I want. My dream is for us to be happy in that house together," he says wholeheartedly. Remembering our conversation by the farm, everything hits me. I look at the couple, smiling.

"I hate her," Nathair says with a straight face.

I jump in, ready to diffuse the bomb before it explodes. "Look, Snake Boy, here's a human lesson: Alister is your best friend who will do anything for you. Even things he doesn't like. Sometimes, we have to return the favor." I rub his arm, hoping it eases the burn.

"You really believe in this eye-for-an-eye B.S.?" Nathair says, frustrated.

I stand by him, staying calm. "I believe in second chances. I'll be on your side if she screws up a second time." While massaging Nathair's arm, I wonder if it is still sore. His eyes soften, conceding. I turn my attention to the other offender. "Maebh, please don't do anything to hurt my friends, or I won't be so nice next time," I warn. She nods, her head hanging low.

"And if you screw up, I will rip that pretty little head off," Nathair snarls, reverting to his complete human form.

"I could say the same thing to you, Nathair." Maebh turns to me. "Raine, be careful. Just know what you're dealing with. I don't want any misfortune to fall on you." I frown at her, worried as to if she learned her lesson. She springs up with a huge grin. "But you are lucky to have a super awesome fairy friend like me! I'll be here to help you." She pulls me in for a hug. I melt into her hug, letting her nuzzle me like a cat. Dang it, why is she so cute?

"It's a good thing I have one." I hug back.

"Raine and Maebh," Sofia calls in the distance. "You've been gone for thirty minutes! Is everything okay?" Maebh brings down the crystal wall.

"Be there in a second, I promise!" I call back. I look at Nathair, hoping he'll get the hint.

He huffs, fixing his disheveled clothes. "I guess I'll see you tomorrow then," he mumbles, scratching his head. He makes small steps toward my door.

"Thank you," I say, hugging him from behind. He lifts his arms awkwardly in the air, unsure of how he should react. He settles his arms and pats my hand reluctantly.

Alister throws his arm around Maebh. "We're going on a walk." They both have a twinkle in their eyes, excited to catch up on everything. I can see the chemistry spark in seconds, almost as if they didn't spend any time apart. The giddy couple glue themselves together and look at each other with small smiles.

Nathair yawns. "Whatever, I'm exhausted from almost dying." Sarcastic as always, I poke his side in hopes that it'll make him behave. Snakes can be charmed, but I'm losing hope for him.

"Join the club, Snake Boy," I say, sending him off to his car. Nathair starts the car, letting the engine rumble a few moments before he drives off into the night. I wave at him as he pulls out of my small driveway. His bright lights slowly grow smaller as he goes down the small dark street.

I turn my attention to the couple, wishing them well. They return the favor and walk away. Feeling good and stretching, I waltz back into my house, preparing to return to the party and act like nothing weird had happened. I eye the new hole left in the atrocious Persian rug in the center of the living room.

How am I going to explain this to my parents?

<u>Fabulous Creature Findings:</u>

<u>Fabulous Creature:</u>   <u>Report to Nathair:</u>

Aos sí   N/A

<u>Realm</u>: Ifeya

<u>Human Country it is Associated with:</u>

Ireland and Scotland

<u>Notes:</u>

Mischievous creatures with enormous,
beautiful butterfly-like wings. Their dust
cures many ailments and can reverse some
dark curses. Most are light creatures, but
some divert from their paths and find
darkness. They are very impulsive and
hot-blooded. They have the ability to put
a glamor on others but no permanent
transformations.

· NINE ·

I look at the purple room with wonder. "You're kidding me. This is mine?" I ask, surprised they made all this stuff look *good*. Alister and Nathair picked one of the rooms with the most abstract architecture. It has beveled walls on each corner—almost a diamond shape. The ceiling is cut out in the middle of the room, revealing a window pointing at the blue sky. Blue curtains line each window in case I want it to be dimmer. But who would want to turn this paradise into a dungeon? I tiptoe onto the faux fur pink rug and let out an elated gasp at the giant mirror in the shape of a swirl. It is a manic pixie's 70s-inspired dream house. It is so beautiful!

"That's what the stylized letters drawn on the wall say," Nathair says, trying to stay monotone, but I hear the relief in his voice poking through. I look over at the wall art that spells my name. Hand-painted, it is sharp but graceful at the same time. It makes me feel special.

"Nathair, how did you guys do this? Why did you guys do this?" I hug him, squealing. Bashful, Nathair pats my shoulders. The bright sun peeks through the many windows making the room light and airy. There is a custom desk and matching bookshelf, which looks hand-painted, featuring a rainbow swirl design.

"You've been staying over a lot for a couple of weeks now, and I got tired of you taking my room. I just guessed you would like this stuff." He shrugs, making it sound selfish and not a big deal. My eyes settle on a corner in the room. Blueprints, sketches, and a mood board lean against the wall and droop over, close to tumbling onto the ground. This cool-toned wonder beat my muted room! That room never felt like it was *my* room.

"This is the nicest thing someone has ever done for me," I say. Nathair's eyes light up, covering his mouth with his hand. I poke his reddening ear. "This looks better than my room in my house!" Erupting into delighted hops, I hold his hand. A small grin flashes, and then he clears his throat. He gives me a serious look.

"Cool, Alister got you some clothes this morning, too." Nathair holds a composed expression, but his now red skin betrays him.

"There's more?" Typically, I would've been worried about boys picking out my clothes for me, but I'm assuming Maebh helped. I walk over to the big closet, where clothes jump out at me, and even some shoes. The whole wardrobe is full!

There are dresses with different patterns and styles, lace shirts, tailored jackets, jeans in every shade, and cute graphic tees. The shoes are heels, Converse, and various boots, looking straight out of a catalog!

"Alister has already adopted you."

"I can't believe he got all this stuff!" The closet door is hard to close with all the fabric poking out, ready to break the shelves it sits on. I struggle for a second before his arms settle next to mine, and his body draws close to my backside. Nathair shuts the closet door with a soft thud. "Where is he? I need to thank him!"

"He and that *pixie* are getting groceries." He grimaces at the thought of Maebh.

I focus him back on my wonder and amazement. "Why would he do all this?"

"You look like his sister. Maybe that's why?" he muses.

I make a slight turn to face him. "His sister?"

"Yeah, he had a younger sister named Azra. We know dragons can live for centuries, but she was a young dragon. To humans, she'd look about twelve years old."

"What happened to her?" Nathair drops his arms and gives me more space to turn around.

His Adam's apple bounces and his lips grow straight and tight. "The Serpentine King killed her." He settles on my bed. "Her favorite animals were baby bears. I think that's why he gave you that nickname."

"Why would he hurt an innocent girl?" I ask, tearing up at the thought.

"There's an urban legend saying if you corrupt a dragon, they can turn into a demon, like a cursed serpentine dragon. The king is a sick, sadistic creature who experiments on the villagers."

"That's horrible! So he was just doing it to play with Alister?"

"There is more to the story, but it is hard to explain. There is some stuff he won't even share with me." Even his best friend found him a mystery. It gives me some serious mystery thriller vibes—but now is not the time to think of books!

"What do you know?"

"Well, Alister is being considered for an Elder position. The Dragon Elder passed away recently." He grimly continues, "An Elder is a Fabulous Creature full of wisdom, and as the name suggests they're one of the oldest in our world. They want creatures who think of the bigger picture and the greater good."

"Alister mentioned the Court, but I am still confused." I shake my head, feeling a headache forming.

Nathair continues, "It's this big organization that sits on their asses and determines right and wrong. They control everything, even the king, and he's a pretty powerful dude. My king rules over Thebes, but the Court rules over all the realms, even this one. Conspiracies, things you thought were tragedies, even natural disasters, are controlled by the Court."

"So Alister is a threat to the king?" I ask.

"Yes, but so am I." His eyes turn into slits, and with one blink, they return to normal—or should I say, human? Cause those eyes are probably more natural to him. My mind wanders, wondering what his complete form looks like. I still have his halfway form on my phone, but it wasn't right to look at it. He hid away from me for a reason. We still have this invisible barrier, and I don't want to push him.

"I don't know what to say to that. I'm sorry you guys had a hard time in your hometown." I plop next to him with a dramatic flair. We sit there in silence for minutes. The radio's alarm sounds off, scaring the life out of us. Both of us flinch, feeling the shock in the pits of our stomachs. I exhale, putting a hand on my chest. Nathair offers a comforting neck rub, chuckling at me now. "What's so funny about the song?"

"It just came out of nowhere!" He flops his back on my bed. His body bounces softly on my new king-sized bed. Covered with an Instagram-able marbled comforter—like melted crystals spread over the bed. His jump knocks over the cutesy radio they added for decoration. Nathair steadies it, accidentally pressing the button to turn it on with his thumb.

Feeling silly, I start to sing the song on the radio. "Find Your Love" by Drake bounces off the walls of my newly renovated room. Losing myself in the music, I shimmy to the beat. A deep and raspy voice mixes in with mine. In unison, we sing in different tones, accompanying the song with horrible choreography. Once the music ends, I'm happy to see he is playing with me. "I want to make a rock version of it now. Come on." He takes my hand and drags me to another unknown room. This one is full of instruments, and an amateur recording studio is in the corner. The bright red walls and simple black chairs make it comfortable. Nathair whips out his guitar.

"You know how to play songs by ear?" I ask, sitting next to him.

"Sing," he commands, starting to play the song.

"Excuse me?"

"Sing," he repeats, his eyes full of encouragement, not force.

"Um, okay." I am bashful about many things, especially when it comes to performing. My teeth chatter and my palms grow sweaty and clammy. This is probably the second time I've been this shy around him. "I-I suck at singing, though."

"Just sing." He strums a few notes. I comply, singing the song at a low volume. "It's rock. You gotta do it louder!" He laughs, still playing it but getting rougher and less structured, giving a sharper feeling. I sing louder for him, feeling more confident with each word. After a couple of tries, we have our version of that song.

"Okay, I've never done that before." I feel alive, exhilarated even!

"You were good—great!" He corrects himself, still strumming on his guitar.

"Please, I'm horrible! Singing is on my list of things I can't do." My high crashes down into a pit of flames. Stuff like this doesn't work well for me. How can I forget all of my past failures? I used to experiment to find my passion—something that would bring me to life. I've tried everything I dreamed about for years but can't recall doing something right. Even now, I struggle with my drama class, trying to get a role other than a tree. I like singing and dancing, but I suppose my stage presence is left to be desired. All I can ever do right is sit down and read a book. As soon as I was born, I was set up for disappointment.

"Not all of us have to sound like a pop diva. If you like singing, who cares?" Nathair is in his element, strumming his guitar. "I say we start a band," he says, determination underlining his voice.

"You're kidding, and what about *Burn Alice's Snake*?" I haven't heard anything about them since I saw him at the club for the first time.

"I'm not with them anymore. I was too focused on changing myself, so I left." He shrugs.

"Then why would you start a new band to distract yourself?" I challenge him—Snake Boy is going crazy.

"If I use Fabulous Creatures and a human who knows my secret, it would be easier to do both." He pats his guitar, cradling it in his arms. "I still want to be human before I do any serious stuff," he warns.

"I'm not a lead singer. I can't even think of singing in front of people." I jump up and start pacing around the bed. Throwing my hands to the sides of my head, blocking out his nonsense.

"You wrote a song once. I was bored and made a tune to it." Without another word, he starts to play an unknown tune. It is mesmerizing and pretty. I lower my hands. "It's your song. Sing to it."

"You looked in my writing journal?" I ask. Oh no, he found *that* notebook. It holds every embarrassing thing I've ever thought, felt, dreamed, or even wished for, and if given to the wrong hands could be catastrophic. I consider Nathair 'the wrong hands,' but at least all he did is like a song I wrote. *Did he read the letters to Dad? God, I hope not.*

"You leave your notebook with all our Fabulous Creature notes lying around the house all the time. I thought you had useful information, so I looked through it, but you only write stuff that is new to you. Sing." He continues his song, making me give up. Of course, he had to invade my privacy while also encouraging me to sing! I clear my throat, pulling power from my core. The lyrics, sentimental but sad, burn into my core—never letting go. Nathair starts strumming a mellow acoustic song, putting me into the zone.

"Feathers, feathers falling through the sky
Feathers, feathers, like tears in the night
Heavens, heavens, wipe your teary eyes
Heavens, heavens, I will make it right
We control the elements, we are strong
This is not a fantasy, they will know they were wrong."

Tears run down my eyes. I never thought I'd have the courage to sing it out loud. I feel accomplished, for once.

I look over at Nathair, who is beaming. "It's things like this that make me love music. That was beautiful, Raine. The lyrics are a little strange, though. What is it about?"

I chew on the inside of my cheek. I don't want to tell him, but he is the type to pry. So I confess. "It's a song I wrote about an old story my dad used to read to me. It was about a city in the clouds with dark-skinned angels. The story ends with them leaving their home. It doesn't say why they left, but the story is really sad, so I don't think it was by choice."

Nathair places his finger on his chin. Recollection flashes in his eyes. "Actually, we have a similar story, too. That's weird that it made it to the human realm. It tells of our former king's legacy when he tried to acquire new land for us, but he was killed by a traitor. I don't remember much of it, but it mentions those creatures. They are not angels. They went extinct, so I can't remember what they are called."

"My dad drew them once. They have dark skin because they live closer to the sun. And he told me they collected magical friends, like small magical birds that control the elements. A few different types lived there, like a storm bird. The more they collected, the more tattoos they got on their bodies. He said they are beautiful and kind. I wish I could meet one." I snap my head toward him in shock. "Wait! It is a real place? So I could at least see their home?" My voice starts off low but gets more excitable at the thought.

Nathair's eyes lower. "Well, not anymore. Not many creatures know where it is," he says warily. His voice is soft, juxtaposing his normally harsh tone.

"I need to go there." I walk up to him, linking our hands.

He looks up bewildered. "Why?" He cocks an eyebrow.

"Every night, my dad would tell me that story, and it makes me feel closer to him even though he's gone. I have to see it in person, Nathair. Please, I will do anything you say. I will follow you to the ends of the Earth. Just please take me there!" I hold his hands tightly in mine. Shaking them lightly, I eventually pull him close to me. Our chests touch, feeling each other's quickened heartbeats.

Nathair shakes his head. "I can't take you away from your family," he reasons.

"It will only be for a little while. Besides, I haven't been getting along with my mom and Richard. I need space from them, I feel suffocated. Just promise me, please?" I beg.

He gets up and looks me in the eyes, caressing my face. His face crinkles, biting his lip. He pauses and finally breaks down. "Okay, deal. You're helping me, so I can help you. And it's for your dad. I can try to find a map and see if I can locate it," he mutters, a centimeter from my face. My heart thumps out of my chest a mile a minute. The heat from his lips radiates next to mine. He presses his forehead against mine.

"Hey, guys, we're back from grocery shopping!" Alister calls, causing us to part abruptly. Walking out of the room, we hope silently that Alister won't see the guilty faces we have on. I tap each side of my cheeks, trying to get together before entering the kitchen. A smile is plastered on my face.

"Hey." I jump in to help Maebh pull the groceries out of the bag. Alister doesn't say anything, nor does he look in my direction. He purses his lips while arranging the food in the pantry like a jigsaw puzzle. His big, bulky wings and tail drag on the tiled floor. Making a light scraping noise.

"We already saw you two making out in the window, so don't think you're off the hook for ridicule," Alister says casually.

I sigh, pouting in defeat. After all, he is supposed to be my enemy! "We did not!" Quick! Do I have an excuse to cover up our heinous action?

"Oh right, we stopped them before they could." Maebh elbows Alister. Winking at him. Alister starts making kissing noises again.

"I have an excuse." Nathair storms into the room. "She came onto me first."

"Try again. We don't like liars in this house." I elbow him.

"So, how long is this civil communication going to last?" Alister asks.

"Oh, it'll end tomorrow. I hate her with the passion of a thousand burning suns, just slightly less now that Maebh is here. On second thought—I greatly dislike her with the passion of a hundred suns because I really hate Maebh," Nathair jokes back, though I'm sure he means the Maebh part. He glares daggers at her across the kitchen.

"He only hates me because it frustrates him that there's a girl who can match his wits and sarcasm. Especially since she's a cute, smart girl who won't take his crap," I taunt him.

"Really? How so?" He puffs up his chest and crosses his arms at me.

"Please, most of my friends are Scorpios! My whole life is dedicated to knocking you dry, sarcastic jerks down a peg. I dull sharp comments every day," I scoff.

"Get a room," Alister mumbles, earning a punch from Nathair.

"You forget I have fangs too, so I'm much sharper than your friends," he says, flexing his fangs. Is it wrong that they look good on him?

"I'm not scared of you." I lean on the table, staring him down. "You don't have it in you. You've gotten soft, Snake Boy."

"This is one hundred percent me. I am intimidating, smart ass." He leans across from me, staring at me with the same intensity.

I suck my teeth. "Ha, prove it." We have a stare-off before I hit the table and cause him to blink. I cackle evilly at him before settling down in a chair and relishing in my victory.

He closes his eyes in defeat, sighing. "Cheap shot," he grumbles. "But fine, Raine, will you go to that fair with me tomorrow night?" he blurts out, face red as a tomato. "Of course, you're a goody two shoes and wouldn't dare stay out past dark with a boy on a school night. Mommy wouldn't like that," he sneers, goading me in return.

"I am my own person. I don't need her permission!" I cross my arms and legs and look away from him. I give him an evil glance from my peripheral.

"Fine, see you in the evening!" He pushes himself up.

"Fine!" I yell, standing up with a hefty stomp. We stand and glare at each other for a moment before storming off in separate directions.

In the distance, a confused Maebh says, "That was the weirdest way to ask someone on a date I've ever seen."

· TEN ·

Out of all the billions of people and Fabulous Creatures in the world, I chose him. This is the ultimate betrayal to myself—the enemies-to-lovers trope IN REAL LIFE. The saddest part of all is that I am so excited.

I know it's *so* hard to believe, but I don't have that many date stories, and they all involve chaperones. Sofia would come along, or Jasmine would be forced to babysit us. So an actual date by myself is nerve-racking. It is *Nathair*, after all. The biblical baddie was created to bring everyone to ruin and sin. Even other Fabulous Creatures look down on them. But with all the knowledge I've learned about him in such a short time, I still find myself giddy.

The girl staring back at me in the mirror gives me a judgmental glance, ashamed of my choices. I am too dressed up for a boy who admitted his hate for me yesterday! My hands shake as I apply a thick layer of gloss. I only wear the wretched substance for special occasions since gloss is the messiest but prettiest thing to wear. I have previously destroyed a couple of my dates' white hoodies. However, I am safe this time, as

Nathair owns nothing white besides his car. He is always a black-and-gray type of guy.

"Stop looking at your reflection. It's pointless," I say, fidgeting with my hair. The front of my hair is pulled up in a top bun while the other half is down in a curly fro—two little tendrils hanging on my forehead. I've always had a bad habit of overdressing. Perfection is a must in my household, after all. Should I chicken out and wear jeans? Nathair wouldn't know the difference.

"Hey, Raine, Mom, and Richard left for another date night. You want pizza—" Jasmine pauses, looking at me. "Where are you going?"

"I was dared to go to the fair," I say, uncertain of my excuse. I can feel my eye glitter blinding Jasmine.

"You got a date on a Monday night?"

"Jasmine, it's not like that—"

"Just use protection. I don't want to be an aunt while I'm still in high school." She yawns, walking out casually as if I had just told her I was going to the store instead. Before I can judge my sister, the doorbell rings. No going back now. I can't dawdle any longer. Imaginary people gawk at me, judging me, mocking me. I need to get out of my head.

He leans against the doorframe. The contrast of headphones traces an outline that disappears into his pocket. His onyx hair looks sharper under the porch light. He squints with a hint of mischief. Imagine how smug he'd be if he knew I was checking him out! My eyes flutter, hiding how impressive he looks in his light blue button-up shirt. Snake Boy has decided to brighten his sexy, dark, gloomy look today. My eyes settle on his chest, and the top is slightly open. He is the first one to speak. "You look less like a dork today."

"And look at you, I see we have color today. Now you don't look so dead," I counter.

"Get in the car, Thomas," he commands.

"Yes, Your Majesty. Oh wait, you don't rule anything. Crazy." I saunter to the car, flipping him off as I slide into the passenger's seat.

"I want to see you in thirty years and see the dumb guy who marries you."

"Really? I was thinking the same thing about you. So when do I get to meet him?"

"Wow, the stick in the mud has jokes today," he says, lightly pushing me. "Well, let's get this over with so I don't get too nauseated by looking at you." A sensitive girl could never last with him.

"Ha, that was pretty funny." I fake laugh, going in for a high five. "Not!" I finish, moving my hand before he can smack it. Nathair does his signature eye roll and keeps quiet. He finally starts the car, moving the gearshift a little more aggressively than usual.

The familiar, friendly lights are clear signs of a simple night full of rides and funnel cake. I smile without worrying about Nathair ruining my mood for the first time tonight. I appreciate the seasonal fair. They only happen twice a year in this area, one in spring and the other in summer. The fair is always parked right by Wendy's and the Goodwill parking lot, lasting only a week. It's designed for little kids, but somehow teenagers flock here and ride whatever rides they can fit in. The air is filled with the aroma of sweet fried fair food, cars, and the bitter burning rubber from rides. These death machines are probably older than me, but nonetheless, it smells nostalgic, to say the least.

As promised, Nathair buys the tickets. I give my thanks to him and run into a line. He cocks an eyebrow at me and peers over my average height to see what they are making. Oily bubbles pop and shake as the stand owner squeezes sweet batter. The enticing air of fried dough wafts past us, and Nathair takes in a delighted sniff.

"You know, I've never had funnel cake before," he confesses. I mock gasp, throwing my hands over my mouth.

"What? You're lying!" I laugh, taking a small step in line. The other fair patrons zone out on their phones, unbothered by my disturbance.

"I'm serious," he says. His eyes widen like a puppy begging for food.

My mouth drops, still holding my smug smile. "You've been in Georgia for a year and never tried it?" There is no excuse for his neglect to eat local foods. "I can't believe you're a funnel cake virgin!" I accuse, playfully pushing him.

"Yep, my first time." He shrugs, pushing his growing black locks out of his face.

"Lucky for you, you're in good hands," I say with full bravado, patting my chest. "Imma Georgia Peach, I'll set ya straight.

If it ain't deep fried, it ain't alright." I toss in a phony Southern accent for effect. My parents were both from the north—New York and Illinois—so I never picked up a true accent, which only subjected me to more bullying when I was younger. But I knew the best food to eat, at least.

"In good hands? Woah, Thomas, a little inappropriate." Nathair jokingly backs up, but I tangle up our hands before he can escape me.

"Can't help it this time," I tease. I bat my lashes at him, a big mistake since I thought it would be great to wear falsies for once. Blinking feels like an exercise in these.

"Perv," he replies, ordering a funnel cake for us to share afterward. In minutes our delicious, messy pastry emerged. The sweet smell of powdered sugar and fried dough fills our noses. Nathair holds the plate closer to me, handing me a fork. He doesn't move, waiting on me to take the first bite. "Well, it's yours. Get the first bite." He gestures to the steaming dessert. A pink blush unfurls on his cheeks. What is his deal now?

"What, are you scared?" My voice comes out huskier than I'd like, but I still swipe at him with my imaginary monster claws. Honestly, I have no problem "showing" him it's safe, so I take a bite. The sweet, crunchy, oily substance sends fireworks to my tongue. So good. "Mmmmm!" I hum, doing a little dance. I nod in approval, giving a thumbs up.

"Dang, girl, save some for me!" He gingerly takes a bite of it, making me giggle.

"Good?" I ask.

"Delicious," he agrees, enjoying it to the point where a weird accent slips.

"What are you, Irish?" I joke. Mostly, he and Aethel have American accents.

"Well," his mouth pops as he touches his tongue to his molars. A feeling I know all too well since the powdered sugar and dough tend to get stuck in the back teeth. His eyes roll to the side, thinking hard. "I'm not sure." Nathair ponders as he walks back to the stand for a napkin. He points to my purse, miming out something that clicks. I hand it to him, completely lost. He digs through for a second until he finds a pen and scribbles a map like a madman. "Our universe parallels yours, but not entirely. We also had a Pangaea long ago, but our continents split up differently than yours. Also, Thebes is an immigrant land. So, my ancestors aren't originally from there, and multiple creatures exist. It's possible that my people are from Ireland or a nearby country."

I remembered that reading I did on the 'Nathair,' which is a mountain serpent, but neither my Nathair nor Alister ever mentioned Thebes having mountains. They briefly told me about the two terrains: a desert-like biome and a savanna-esque biome. Thebes was quite large, but a lot of land is unusable. I wonder why his original ancestors left the coastal mountains. Of course, like many snakes, there are different types spread out in different locations, so maybe that is also true for serpents.

"Wow, that's cool. I could never understand the maps in the books, so our worlds are connected but not parallel." I get close to his red face, swiping my pen back from him. He steps back a little, smirking at me.

"Yes, it's not perfect, but we are close enough that you humans have legends about us and even share some traditions with us. So while I know my serpent race, I can't get an exact pinpoint on my human race. It isn't hard for every Fabulous Creature. Some are so intertwined with the human realm that there is no question when they visit." He sits down, placing the funnel cake on a table.

"So if you are possibly Irish, why do you have an American accent then?" I ask, sitting next to him on a bench.

He shrugs. "Just to fit in since you guys can be rude to immigrants sometimes." Nathair bumps his shoulder against mine.

"That makes sense. If it makes you feel better, all I've ever dealt with are rude humans, especially teenagers! They never seem to care about anything except the 'somebodies' at our school. If you're not one of them, you're trash." I laugh, facing him. "Pretty cynical, huh?"

"You're talking to the master of cynicism. Besides, it's pretty cute, Thomas."

"Whatever, Vanos," I dismiss. His eyes flash a twinge of confusion from hearing his last name. I learned from my studies that many Fabulous Creatures don't have last names. Their home realm takes the place of their family name. "By the way, why did you pick Vanos?" It must be special because unlike a given name, which your parents select for you, his last name was his choice. His right to how others address him. Huh, it must be nice. My last name is so plain.

He scratches his eye and rests his chin on his now tucked thumb, pondering. "The mother realm of serpents is supposedly called Vanostro. Like your cloud city, it's lost. We only hear stories about it. My father had already named me after the serpents there. So I stayed with that theme. Nothing deep." He stabs at the funnel cake, clumsily dropping small pieces back onto the place. Clumps of powdered sugar gather on his shirt and hands.

Of course, he plays everything off, acting cool. I roll my eyes at him. *Maybe only Southerners can cleanly eat a funnel cake.* I pick up my fork and shovel it onto his since he struggles to eat it. "Hurry up and eat so we can get on the rides!"

We spend a couple of hours running around like children. Half of the time is spent with his uncertainty about an unknown ride and me ushering him on, only for him to find that he likes the rush that the rollercoaster gives. Or the innocent calm that the merry-go-round supplies. Even the slight squeeze he gives me on the tilt-a-whirl as I spin the middle plate with reckless abandon, throwing small yelps in protest. All of this shows me the other side of him. Today, he let the inner child run free, taking down a huge ball of cotton candy. He stops once he gets halfway through, pulls out a piece, and holds it out to me. I take the soft, warm cloud and pop it in my mouth.

Maybe he isn't as bad as I thought.

The final ride stands before us, the Ferris wheel. My stomach has little gymnasts doing cartwheels as the cart rocks under my feet. Nathair places a hand on my back, guiding me to my seat.

In a quick motion, he slides in after me. The cart wobbles as he sits down with all his weight. Anxiety grips my chest momentarily, but his presence immediately releases it. The cart lifts us into the air. The lights glitter and sparkle in the night sky. This area isn't the prettiest. The old broken pavement is full of potholes, and the nearby fast food packaging litters the parking lot. The old, dingy stores—half abandoned—surround it. It is dirty and run-down most days, but at this moment, it is the most beautiful thing I've ever seen. The neon lights of the other rides paint my face. I turn to Nathair, who isn't looking out of the cart.

"Whatchu lookin' at?" I ask.

"You," he says, entirely unbothered by his admission. No shyness, no sass. The word sends shivers down my spine. How can he be so bold?

A wave of embarrassment flows through me since I expected him to say something snarky. "Stop. I'm gonna think you like me or something!" I hide my face in my hands.

He chuckles, tapping my hand. "It's fun to tease you. You always get so worked up," Nathair confesses. I look back up at him, pouting. He looks down, furrowing his brows. "Can I ask you a personal question?"

"You asking permission for something? Yeah, go ahead," I say.

"You always talk about your mom and Richard, but what about your real dad?" His voice is gentle and cautious.

"He was a man," I say, a little bitter, shutting him down.

"That's a no." He takes the rejection rather gracefully. "Here, I'll tell you something about mine," he volunteers, leaning to face me. I perk up and look at him. Last time I checked, his dad was a sore subject too.

"What was he like?" I whisper.

"He was the greatest serpent in history, the only one I could say I cared about. He was kind and pure-hearted, helping many people in our community. To the other Fabulous Creatures, he was a hero. Saving them from starving and building houses for them, he would choose what was right when the laws were gray. He showed me that we could go against our nature. We don't have to be evil. We choose to be. However, those backstabbing snakes could never understand him. They would always say, 'The brother of King Vasska has gone crazy.' Even my mother joined them." He clears his throat, resting his thumbs in the corner of his eyes, swiping up in frustration to his temples. He sits back up and continues. "My father was next in line, but his brother sent him to live in the Cursed Lands, where serpents are trapped in their human forms with little power. He grew sick and died when I was young, the curse eventually eating away at him."

Speechless, I awkwardly babble out, "I'm so sorry." The guilt of not thinking of anything else to say boils over, but what can you say about something like that?

"He is after me too. I'm the only rightful heir," he confides, putting a hand on my knee. He lowers his head down, avoiding my worried gaze.

My jaw drops, "Wait—wait—wait! You're a prince?" I lift his head. His eyes are now red.

He turns away from me again, looking out the window now. He sits in silence. "Unfortunately, the Serpentine King sired no offspring. So, technically, yes. Thebes is my kingdom."

"Wait, so what about Aethel?" Please tell me I don't have Thebe's princess as my enemy.

He scoffs, waving off the mere thought of her, "Don't worry about her. She is from the Cursed Lands. She doesn't have much power. She is trying to gain favor with the king, maybe. So, she is trying to convince me to return and take my throne."

"Ugh, of course, she just wants to get ahead!" I toss my hands up in defeat. Nothing about this surprises me in the slightest. Though they're the same creature, they're total opposites. I look at Nathair, letting the guilt overtake me. There's no way I can top his story. "My dad was a kind man, but he always seemed off. He just always had his head in the clouds. His body was there, but his mind wasn't. He kept disappearing for weeks and sometimes months before he died. I used to think it was my fault he didn't want to be around. I wasn't the nicest to him when he was there. I never even got a proper goodbye," I stop, feeling my chest grow heavy.

"It's not your fault. Nobody knows when it's a loved one's last day."

"I know now, but when I was low, it just would play in my head over and over. Our fleeting time was spent arguing when all I ever wanted was to hug him and hold his hand." I shake myself back to the present. "Anyway, thank you for feeling comfortable enough to share all that with me. I know how hard it is." I hold his hand, tracing his blue veins with my thumb. I bite my lip, clueless about how to navigate this pained silence.

He shifts his hand to grab mine instead and reaches for the other with his free hand. He faces me again, pulling me to the seat next to him.

"I tried fighting it, but lately, I can't get you out of my head. You're a good person, Raine. Compassionate, forgiving, and positive, you've brought so much light to our home. It's weird, you are a human, but you fit perfectly in place," Nathair says. The moonlight shines on him, showing every part of his face. Dew drops dance on his eyelashes, showing his sincerity to me.

"You are a good person too. I see all your efforts. I want to be closer to you sometimes, but you put up a barrier. So, I had no idea that you felt that way," I say, my eyes softening at his vulnerability. His hands shiver in our grasp. My heart swells up, soaking in all his fears, pain, and warmth.

"It's complicated. I can't be close to you. Never forget this is not the real me. I am not a human. My kind is designed to only bring misfortune to humans, and if I told you everything about me, you'd be scared of me. You should be scared of me." The conviction in his voice stuns me. "If you had any form of self-preservation."

I look away, finally free from his hypnotic eyes. "The real reason you want to be human is to find a connection. You're lonely," I say. He gives a sigh of defeat. "Stop it. Do not put up any more barriers because I don't care what you are. Man or serpent, I'm here for you." I get up in his face, and each time he looks away, my face follows his. We have this dance until he gives up.

"Okay, I'll try." He pierces my soul with a whisper deep like tobacco. Sweet fingers trace the side of my arm, igniting a flame in me. Our fingers intertwine, locking in a promise—an understanding that there is no going back now.

· ELEVEN ·

We don't always study and sit in silence. Occasionally, Nathair will remember that he is supposed to be a teenage boy. So he settles any tension or frustration with the video game I shamelessly introduced. Furiously clicking away, we hack and slash our way through *Fantasy XII*. The boys and I sit in a circle, mashing our keyboards, trying to heal each other in this intense lair. Dragon Boy huffs, swiping his huge curls out of his face. "This isn't even accurate! Elves don't heal that way. They need a conduit!" His horns shoot out of his forehead in frustration.

"Alister, it's made by humans! Stop overanalyzing it and use your dark magic! The trolls are weak to fire!" My mouse clicks away, palms sweating and eyes wide.

"Someone heal me!" Nathair begs. His clicks and taps on the keyboard are foreign to him. He slowly sends out a special attack with his new weapon. It's his first time as an archer, and he hates the low defense and health that the class gives. He's been whining all night. As I am winding up my mana, a troll deals a damaging blow to Nathair. "This isn't fun anymore!" Nathair jerks his hand off the mouse, pouting.

"Hold on. I'll revive you!" I prepare my potions.

"Alister!" Maebh screams. Of course, her lover jumps up immediately, running toward the cry.

"Okay, never mind," I say, slightly disappointed. I get up, following the dragon and the snake. Maebh screams again. The sound echoes through the night sky, coming from outside. Is she not in the house? The front door swings open, hitting the cream walls. The glass on the door rattles, and Alister is already near the small house next door. She is in the farmer's hut. I stub my toe on the foyer table. Ow! I hold my toe and stumble. I balance myself and start to follow the boys again, my foot in searing pain. The wind blows my hair back as I hop after the boys. I turn to close the door, scared to let bugs in. Alister uses the hut when he is harvesting and doesn't want to mess up any nicer parts of the house. This is the only filthy thing about the place. Maybe Maebh is angry that Alister just left it so gross? Sprinting into the hut, we peer inside.

Tucked away in the small bathroom inside the mini house, a Yokai greets us! This one isn't those cute foxes you see in anime, either. It is ugly and smelly. The spirit has the body of a human, two big slit eyes, fangs, and a long slimy tongue. His head looks like a cross between a lizard and a human. The ugly brute grins wickedly, lapping away at the dirt and grime of the floor. He slowly drags his tongue across as if it is the most delicious ice cream cone. With his back to Maebh, he does not care about our presence.

"What is that thing?" Disgusted by its presence, I take a step back.

"It's an Akaname. It eats dirt and grime from untidy bathrooms," Nathair answers, walking behind me.

"Hello, barefoot here. I can't step on the floor!" Brandishing her mop like a sword, Maebh shakes in fear.

Nathair leaves the hut without a word. I look at him in confusion, but he waves me off. A few moments later, he returns with a magical-looking box. The sapphire box has beautiful ornate runes carved into it. Its gold accents shine under the fluorescent light in the bathroom.

"Akanames leave a poison behind on whatever they lick," Nathair explains, approaching the ugly spirit.

"I'm confused. Why isn't it in Japan?" Scrunching my face at it, I can't wait for it to leave.

"Yokai travel just like humans. Hold on. I have a spirit box." He snickers, opening the box. I don't know what is with magical things making weird sounds, but the box makes a small but charming chime. Similar to the jingle you hear at Buddhist temples. Within seconds, a giant gush of wind twists and whips around our hair and clothes. Making a small cyclone, the box sucks the Akaname inside. A foul stench blows around the room. Gagging, I pinch my nose and cover my mouth.

"Come here, Mae." Alister saves our precious Aos sí from the toilet. The Akaname leaves a weird gooey substance on only a section of the farmer's bathroom, so Alister tiptoes around the slimy puddle. Inching closer to his girl, he picks her up in one fell swoop. Wide-stepping over the slime, he sets her down next to me. Alister blows fire onto the slime. The goo combusts into a larger green flame. He gestures to Maebh. His fairy girlfriend pinches her nose but manages to summon small crystals. They circle and dance around the flames, lights refracting. I squint and watch in awe as the crystals sweep up the fire and bottle it into one fused crystal.

I look at Maebh, perplexed about why she needs to save it. Nathair rattles behind me. "She's confused," he announces for me as if it wasn't obvious.

"It's for potions," Maebh says, shaking the flame and turning it into a moss-green liquid. "It's a wonderful antivenom for poisonous Fabulous Creatures."

"Like Nathair?" I ask, a little too excited.

"No, he's a special case," Maebh says, suspiciously looking at me and then at Sanke Boy, "but if Aethel or someone comparable were to bite you, we could save you with this." She gags, holding up the crystal vile once more. "Too bad we had to meet a disgusting creature like him though."

"Well, fairy, this is a lesson here: don't mess with the farmer's bathroom." Nathair points finger guns at Maebh, snapping his fingers as he exits the room without a care. Maebh flicks him off, and for once, neither Alister nor I calm her down. I mean, she was in danger just seconds before, and he couldn't bother to mutter a simple, 'Are you okay?'

"How are you two friends again?" Maebh asks Alister, making crystals in the shape of Nathair's head, and then crushes them.

Alister shakes his head, resting his hand on his fro. "He has a good side," he says sheepishly, kicking her crystal dust into a pile on the floor. His eyes wander to me, widening. "Speaking of Nathair, Raine. The house has been quiet all week."

A nervous smile spreads across my lips. "He's been less of a jerk?" I start, making it sound too much like a question. To be honest, I don't know what is up with Nathair and me lately. Sure, he still says rude things, but they get on my nerves less, and morning meetings have been more pleasant.

"Or the tension has been released in the form of affection. K-I-S-S-I-N-G." Alister's infamous kissing noises come back. Maebh and I smack his arms on each side at the same time. "Ow!" He pathetically rubs his arms.

"Hey, Raine," Nathair calls.

"Yeah?" I answer, ignoring Alister's dragon mouth, which has a toothy grin poking out. Fangs and all. Maebh pushes his snout back in, making the human half of his face return.

"Stay the night. Tell your parents you're at Maebh's. Please," he says as he returns his attention to one of the ancient books we were reading. Transfigurations. I studied it last week but forgot to make notes on it, so I let him glance over it. He walks back out again, motioning me to follow.

"Okay," I reply, walking back to the manor with him.

As soon as the nice warm air hits my face in the doorway, I decide to move my homework into my room. This is turning into a usual thing for my double life. I went to the mall with my human friends, and at night I went to the manor and studied Fabulous Creatures, realms, and how they tie into transformations. It is fascinating how all these creatures humans thought were made up are real. Like people, they have homes and customs and looked very different! I love learning about the adorable Brownies in Scotland and the strange Ainu of the Pacific Ocean! It is like reading stories full of elements that tie into the culture of my world! The Japanese are very superstitious for a reason. With so many Yokai and spirits wandering around from their realm, it became an inspiration for anime and manga!

"And I'm getting you during lunch on Monday," he adds while settling on the couch.

"Why?" I ask. Usually, he tells me to show up at our headquarters, room three twenty-six, but leaving early on Monday would mean more questions from my friends.

"We're going on a magical field trip. Alister knows of an Elder that lives near Lake Allatoona. He can help us find clues."

"An Elder? So he can change you? I thought you said—"

"They have limitations too. One of them is not being able to transform others unless it is in the cosmic design. He wouldn't be authorized to do that, but he can help us to find who can."

"Well, who is this guy?" I question, not believing this guy is worth my precious lunchtime—this is the first year with all my friends eating in the same period!

"Andronicus the Wise. Also, I feel how tense you are. I am an empath, too. So chill out. Trust me, I would've done it by now if it was that easy to change." Wait, on top of controlling people's emotions, he can feel them too? My anxiety spikes at all the things he knew about me and couldn't be bothered to point out.

"Stop freaking out. It's not all the time," he says monotone, still reading his book.

"It's kind of important information that you left out." I pinch myself, hoping it hurts him, but he doesn't react.

"Emotional pain, not physical, Raine." He huffs. "Besides, I mostly use mine when I manipulate emotions. But that's not important, I don't use my powers on you. So focus, please, because the faster I turn human, the faster I can set you free," he reminds me.

"You're using them on me right now," I whine.

He shuts his book. "No, I'm not. Even the biggest idiot can tell you are an anxious mess."

"I need to do my math homework!" I turn toward my room, done with this conversation. "I'll be ready to see this scamming Elder on Monday," I say begrudgingly.

"It's Saturday night. You're just going to do homework?" He yawns.

"Well, what do you suggest then? In case you haven't noticed, I'm a bookworm, so I tend to be boring on Saturday nights."

"Go out with me. Let's do something together. I have nothing better to do either." He hops up, clapping his hands together.

"What about studying the book?" I insist.

Looking as if he is ready to drag me to Wonderland, he leans closer to me. "Trying to make up excuses, Thomas?"

"Yes, this sounds like trouble to me." I hide my arms behind him, swinging my body from side to side. My ears heat up again. Phantom kisses touch my lips, startle me, and make me look down at the ground in shame. No, he can feel that. I need to stop!

Honestly, I don't want to be alone with him after Monday's craziness. I feel different, but he stayed the same. Flashbacks of that night on the Ferris wheel run through my mind like a hamster wheel. He was having a hard time. So vulnerable, so trusting. But now, we are back to master and servant. Why are boys so confusing?

"You're right about the trouble part, but you're so innocent they'll let you get out of jail in fifteen minutes." He leans in and tips his head to get in my face. My stomach flutters and my chest feels like a fog is clearing. It is frustrating how I don't mind those fifteen minutes if it means I could be with him. Warmth spreads through my body as I stare into his aventurine eyes.

I blow out the air I was holding, straightening up. *Play it cool, Raine.* "Come on, let's go for a drive." I shrug, getting my jacket. He fist bumps the air in victory, trotting behind me.

The low rumble of the car relaxes me. Nathair can be a good driver, but most times, he is too impatient to follow traffic laws or drive the speed limit. Tonight, he is calmer, playing the radio. "I want a snack," I say, looking into the darkness. We are on the back road, the lights only showing me quick flashes of the trees creeping into the black lane.

"Me too." Nathair gets ready to turn back onto the main road. We drive in comfortable silence toward the closest CVS. Still looking out my window, I think about how regular of an evening this is. Suddenly, I feel a soft hand on my leg. It is awkward because it is on my thigh, but I allow him to stay there. "Wanna watch a movie after we get snacks?"

"I wanted to kick ass in the game, but I guess a horror movie would be fun," I joke, enjoying the slight friction of his thumb grazing my leg.

"Hey, Alister ruined it, not me!" He grins. His free hand moves from my leg to my hair, tucking a loose curl behind my ear. "I'll buy snacks as an apology." He winks, eyes settling on me. I giggle, pointing at the road. He obliges and looks ahead.

"Hmmm, deal!" The lights of the CVS brighten up the pitch-black road. I squint at a strange figure in the parking lot. Recognition instantly clicks in my mind. "Dad?" I say aloud. The wispy silhouette has his build, but something about him is off. He waddles to the car as we pull up. I can't see his face, but I am sure it is him.

"Raine? What are you looking at?" Nathair asks.

"You don't see him?" I question, trying to get out of the car. The car door locks snap shut, locking me in. I turn to him, confused, testing the door anyway. It doesn't budge.

"Stay in for a second," he requests while his pupils become slits.

"No, I need to talk to him."

"Raine, he's gone. You told me he's not alive," he explains calmly. "I think whatever this thing is might be using seduction on you."

"No, it's him. He's right there." I stare at the shadow. Its smokey body and inky eyes stare back at me, placing an inky-black hand on the car. It leaves a handprint of condensation on my side. Nathair's eyes flicker. He puts an arm in between me and the passenger's side window. The faceless man presses his cold face against the glass. My back starts radiating pain. The man backs off, mirroring me by rubbing his back. Groaning in pain.

"Raine... help me..." the figure whispers. I try to unlock the door, but Nathair stops me. Holding my hands. Getting frustrated with him, I yank my hands from his.

The black figure whispers 'help' over and over again. Nathair, looking worried, grabs me and holds me to his chest. I thrash in his arms, but he is too strong, his supernatural strength kicking in. "Let go! He needs my help!" I yell. Stabbing pain in my head shoots through.

"Come find me..." the figure requests, his voice fading. I rip myself away long enough from Nathair to see it is gone. What is that phantom?

"Are you okay?" he asks. I look at him cluelessly and nod.

"It's gone," I say sadly. Pangs of sadness ring through my body. What if it is him? He's hurt. He's scared.

"If you see him again, tell me, please. I don't think it's your dad," he instructs. I nod again, head slightly feeling fuzzy. A small lightning bolt flashes, guarding the door handle from me. Is Nathair doing that?

Worried, Nathair offers to pay for the snacks. I just let him, too scared to leave the car now. Nathair runs in as fast as he can, buying the snacks in minutes.

"Can we watch a comedy instead?" I ask meekly once he's back in the car with me. I've had enough horror for the night.

"Whatever you want." He rubs my arm. I grab his hand, desperate to feel normal again. My heart is still echoing in my ears, but it softens. "Don't worry, we'll figure it out," he assures. He couldn't see what I saw, but I must believe him now.

The car's engine roars awake in the quiet night, joining the crickets' night song. As he pulls out of the parking lot, I freeze in horror. Jay's car makes a sharp turn into the parking lot. The car slows down. I duck in my seat, hoping this won't cause me trouble on Monday.

I am indeed in trouble on Monday. Why can't a girl be nice to a guy without being accused of liking him? And if I do like him, so what? It is none of their business. However, Sofia isn't seeing it that way. She practically glares at me when I sit down. "People are talking about you and that boy."

"Really, what are they saying?" I say nonchalantly. I know Sofia wants what's best for me, but she can't help me with this situation. Dating or not, I still have to work for him for six months, and I'm not even halfway through my indentured servitude.

"You guys went out on Saturday. Is it true?" I didn't lie to my friends when I left the mall. I just didn't tell them any different plans. So, honestly, I have no reason to lie about it.

"Yeah, we did go out on Saturday."

"Are you two dating or something? I see y'all walk to class every day," Jay adds to the intervention.

"No, they're not together." Aethel walks up to our table. She's wearing her hair straight and long, pulled back by a headband. Her ultra-expensive black jeans make her look sweet and innocent with her Hollister long-sleeved, yellow ruched shirt.

Ah-rin and Alina, her two attack dogs, wear muted versions of Aethel's outfit. I stand up, ready for them this time. I anticipate whatever evil comes from Aethel's mouth. "I talked to Nathair, and he's not returning your big crush on him," she says, pouting a little.

I stand up and push her back, separating us from my friends. She's dangerous, I would never forgive myself if she hurt someone because of me. "Last time I checked, Nathair can't even be in the same room as you, let alone talk to you," I snap back in hushed tones, even though it is dumb to provoke her. After all, she broke my wrist the last time I talked to her. She could do it again or worse.

"The King will kill you too, and remember that next time before I send you on your knees again," she spits back in my ear so my friends wouldn't hear.

I laugh and puff up my chest. "It's funny how you are so insecure about your abilities to seduce guys that you have to threaten me," I whisper back.

"You don't know anything, rat!" Alina defends.

Ah-rin looks around before whispering, "Remember, Aethel has venom too!"

The trio walks up behind Aethel. "Oh really? Well, remember that the dark always comes to light." Maebh taps the evil snake on her shoulder. Nathair and Alister stand like bodyguards behind her.

"Want to try to bite our heads off, too?" Nathair threatens, his dark side out again.

Glaring, Aethel looks directly at Sofia before walking off. "Don't trust her. She's full of it." My friends all look confused.

"What just happened?" Jay asks.

"Aethel's a wicked little b—" Alister elbows Maebh. "What? You know it's true!"

"Aethel's just jealous of Raine. I wouldn't worry about her," Alister dismisses, but Sofia doesn't see anyone but me.

Her eyes water up as she stares into my soul. "Raine, what does she mean?"

"She said she lost her ring and was blaming me. She claims I took it." I try to play it cool, knowing Sofia is unsettled by Aethel's warning. It is a miracle I did the impossible by covering up all the unearthly things Aethel recklessly spat, such a slow girl.

"Is she seriously bullying you?" Her concern makes me feel a little sick. I don't like lying to people, especially since I do it so easily now.

"Yeah, but I'm taking care of it, don't worry." I fake a smile. I do it not to seem so cold to my peers or adults. My fake smile is always awkward because it is so hard to look grateful. The phony smile is frequently used on my parents and teachers but never on my friends.

Sofia's eyes flutter, but she doesn't say anything. "Raine, we got to work on that project today, remember?" Nathair reminds me. In the middle of all the drama, I forgot about the trip to Lake Allatoona.

"Yeah, I'll be there in a second. Wait for me in the library." More questions would arise if I said the parking lot. Nodding, Nathair and the others leave me alone with my friends.

"I want chips," Sofia announces. Before I can reply, she jumps up and storms off.

"Okay. Bye," I mumble, knowing she couldn't hear me. I look over at all my other friends, smiling at them. "Well, I'll see you guys later." I gulp. I am unsure if I was more nervous to finally start making headway on Nathair's transformation or worried about how distant my friends and I are.

<u>Fabulous Creature Findings:</u>

<u>Fabulous Creature:</u>

Yokai

<u>Report to Nathair:</u>

No transformation spells available

<u>Realm:</u> Spiritual Plane

<u>Human Country it is Associated with:</u>

While there are many types of spirits, Yokai originate from Japan.

<u>Notes:</u>

It is said that if people or animals do not receive proper burial services, people's souls can linger on Earth. They can eventually turn into Yokai and gain access between the human and spiritual realms. There are many legends of them transforming themselves, but none have the ability to transform others.

·TWELVE·

We drive in the Mustang for a distance. The icy rain drops on the car by the gallons. Nathair's fingertips, twinged with a sickly blue, tremble on the steering wheel. The windshield wipers slosh off streams of water that squeak against the glass. Alister sits on the passenger's side, phone navigation in hand. He initially offers to fly us there but decides not to because of the rain. Though it is springtime, Georgia refuses to let go of its killer winter rain. Alister's eyes dodge back and forth between Nathair and his phone. As he peers out of his window, the cool air seeps in.

It makes me feel alive, he says to me from time to time. As a dragon, immense heat is stored away in his chest, so the cold wind is the only thing that balances his core. He loosely told me once that his old home was a cold mountain, but that was before he lost his sister. Maybe on a cold day like this, he thinks of her.

Nathair adjusts his jacket, shivering more. Alister takes the icy air deep into his lungs one more time and then turns up the car's heater. He eyes me in the rearview mirror as I try my best to hide my discomfort, tucking away my shaking hands.

He smiles at me and rolls up the window. The warm air covers us like a blanket, and the rest of the inhabitants in the car relax. Warm and welcoming now, I cuddle up in the back with Maebh.

Maebh doesn't mind the cold. She said her Aos sí realm isn't the coldest place, but there is snow at least once a year. At eight, she experienced a tragedy that not even she would share with her worst enemy: the death of her mother. Her realm had many issues, *too many to share*, she tells me every time the details start to pour from her mouth. But in her refusal to relive the horror of her own country, she relays that Thebes was the only option young orphan fairies had at the time. Thebes had an orphanage that took care of homeless fairies. She said her ideals and views were Theban, but she never lost touch with her own culture. Her eyes still sparkle as she tells me old stories of how Aos sí came to be. It turns out they were originally fallen angels, eventually finding their own world. Their feathered wings turned butterfly-like because they couldn't fly to paradise anymore. Feathered wings gave you access to Heaven. There are many different types of Aos sí. The fairy-like creatures are like humans and choose their own destinies. Essentially picking their moral side—light or dark. Light fairies serve Queen Atena-Safiya. While dark fairies serve under their Aos sí King Zancan, who holds himself up in his castle and doesn't pay the rest of the realm much mind.

Hearing all these memories and history is like hearing an endless adventure. Aos sí has a bible like us, filled with different stories of encountering God, though they have another name for him, Dhia. Forty minutes into the drive, a glorious hymn pours from her lips like honey. Maebh's voice is sweet and delicate like a songbird, but the woe and sorrow hide underneath.

"Will you stop driveling on about your people? Some of us are getting bored," Nathair interrupts as he rests his head on his headrest, yawning.

"Well, I love hearing about it! Fae-folk are so mystifying." I stick my tongue out at him. Keeping his eyes on the road and steadying the steering wheel with his dominant hand. Nathair reaches into the back seat, half-heartedly trying to grab my tongue. I yank my head back, making a raspberry at him. I point at the road. He gives a curt laugh and grabs the wheel with both hands again.

Maebh scrunches her face at him. "This negativity is coming from a lawless, godless snake. Don't worry, Raine. No offense is taken."

"Lawless, godless *serpent*, thank you," he emphasizes. "You're right, I could care less about religion," Nathair interjects, causing Maebh to scoff.

She leans closer to Snake Boy. Her voice is deep and raspy, slightly menacing. "That's because you're a dark creature. You never have a set religion. Serpents especially are confused. They only worship their king." Maebh's words sting, but her delivery is smooth like velvet.

Nathair pulls away from her as far as he can in a small seat. "Alister, get your pixie." Alister turns his head to face his girl, sneaking in a kiss on her cheek. Her anger melts away, and a glimmer in her eye takes its place. Nathair gags.

"What about you, Alister? Are you religious?" I ask, wondering what his God is like.

"I'm agnostic. I can't put a name on who created all of us." He pinches the apples of Maebh's cheeks, enamored with her.

A thought pops into my head. "Nathair, wouldn't the mage be religious?"

"*Elder*," he corrects, "and I can talk to an Elder. I believe in things I can see and touch." His eyes look forward at the road, but a dumb smirk is plastered on his face—occasionally glancing at me through the rearview.

"But I don't get how you can't believe in anything." He shrugs. "But you believe in fate." I am not very religious, but now that I know about Fabulous Creatures, there has to be someone out there who created all of this.

"Lines can be proven." He holds his head high, stubborn as always, but the glint in his eyes says something else. Maybe his beliefs are only based on the horrors he has experienced in his past. "I told you I don't make the rules about the world. I just live in them."

Alister's eyes widen. A thick heavy slap lands on his best friend's chest. "Nathair, stop right now," Alister says in a cold, hostile tone.

"Ow!" Nathair rubs his raw chest. Alister is stronger than he looks. "Why?"

"I see a Five Guys, and if I don't get a bacon cheeseburger and a large fry, I will kill you," Alister says with a straight face, but I think he is deathly serious. With a man who can set us on fire at any moment, it isn't a good idea to take him lightly. I slap my knee and chuckle at the two boys. This had to be expected at some point from Alister—killing for burgers.

Snake Boy presses down on the gas, giving the car a low *vroom.* "You're going to make this trip longer! It's bad enough you couldn't fly us there because of the rain!" Nathair, determined, keeps driving.

In a tag-team combo, Maebh leans over to help her lover. "Drama queen, we're in Acworth. Lake Allatoona is only twenty minutes away, just stop for some food and stop starving us!" She whines, lifting off the corner of her mouth in disgust at Nathair.

"How about, no!" Nathair insists.

Being the peacekeeper at times is exhausting, but even I'm growing peckish. My stomach grumbles under all the arguing and fussing. I rub my stomach, getting hungrier by the minute.

Alister looks back at me, a man on a mission, his eyes settling into his golden slits. "Okay," Alister replies calmly, opening the door. A gust of wind and water rushes in. The chill air pierces our bodies, freezing us to the bone. Alister looks at Nathair, deadpan.

"Whoa! What are you doing?" Nathair keeps the steering wheel steady with one arm and stretches his body over the irate Alister to close the door but to no avail. Alister opens the door wider. I laugh at Alister and his determination for a good burger.

"Jumping out, I'll get the girls something." The dragon's hair whips around, reflecting his chaotic energy, but at that moment, he looks like a hero.

"Fine, I'll stop! Close the door!" Nathair slows down to get off at the next exit. The signal clicks reluctantly as he gets over.

Snake Boy gives the longest and deepest sigh imaginable once he parks at the restaurant. A friendly hand pats his shoulder, silently telling him it's okay to take a break. He looks at me in the back seat, trying to stop the corners of his mouth from pulling into a thin smile. "Thank you for stopping. I missed lunch." I grin at him.

His eyes soften, and he finally breaks into a small smile, his sharp canine teeth poking from underneath. "Raine, I got an umbrella. I'll walk over to get you." He unbuckles his seatbelt and rustles around in the backseat, eventually finding it.

"Forgetting someone?" Maebh clears her throat.

"Nope," Nathair says with a wicked smile, popping the car door open and hopping out in the cold rain. Maebh sucks her teeth.

Dragon Boy is back to his sweet self, beaming with his famous goofy smile. Even Alister can get hangry. "I got you, Mae," Alister assures as he pulls out his own umbrella.

"At least someone is a gentleman," Maebh says, letting her man come around to escort her in the rain. I look at my side, feeling the cold air rush in. Nathair smiles at me. The umbrella scrapes the roof as it shields me from the pouring rain. He holds out his hand. My body is frozen, but the warm fuzzies in my chest flutter about and give me the strength to take his hand and step out of the car.

We walk into the burger joint. It looks like a typical Five Guys restaurant. Boxes of peanuts cover every counter, reviews of the restaurant's success are strewn all over the walls, and the ample counter separates the workers from the customers. It's customary for Five Guys places to be messy. As expected, peanut shells are all over the floor. I remove the hood of Nathair's stolen jacket, still shivering a little. The warmth feels nice, but Nathair is even worse off than me. Though he doesn't show it, he is freezing to the point where he can't move. Was it wrong to assume that two of his jackets would suffice? He sits by their large indoor heater, trying to soak in as much heat as possible. I shiver in empathy, imagining the burning cold slowing down his fingers first and then slowly working up to his arms and limbs. When your limbs are frozen, they feel jammed, stuck in the position you left them in. Even in human form, serpents clearly can't function properly in the cold.

"You okay?" I ask, draping the jacket I borrowed over him. That is jacket number three.

"I just need a minute," he says with his eyes closed. I warm his cold, clammy hands.

Maebh slaps the back of his chair, scoffing, "Trying to rush us, and you can't even talk to this guy until it stops raining!" Nathair, still feeling ill, looks unaffected by her assault.

I push her into the line. "Lay off, Mae, and wait until he feels better." She frowns at me with full betrayal in her eyes, but I still hold her in place and wait to order.

A couple of minutes pass, and it is my turn to pay. I pull out my wallet, but a pale hand covers mine and stops me. "I got her," says Nathair, who recovers enough to move and drops a twenty on the counter. Ticked off at having to catch the falling twenty-dollar bill, the cashier hands him his change and tells me my order number.

Heading to the soda machine, the carbonated drink sizzles as it fills up my cup. "You didn't have to do that." I look at him and pop a lid on my drink.

"I wanted to." His voice is soft.

"Why?"

"I thought we agreed I'm not an evil being that is out to eat your heart." He leans in, making a small roar.

I giggle. "You're not evil. I never thought you were. A jerk, maybe, but you can never be evil." If Sofia was here, she would say something snarky. *Seems pretty evil to me. This is a setup to eat you,* she absently says in my mind.

"So, you don't hate me?"

"Nathair, I could never hate you," I say, soothing him. He stretches out his hand to touch my face. His fingers are cold at first but then melt into warmth. An earthy aroma wafts in the air. I close my eyes, taking this all in. Flickers of electricity lick my legs and arms. My body feels weak next to his, but I get pulled in.

"Hey, you two, stop messing around by the soda fountain!" Alister calls. My eyes snap open, back to reality. Nathair's other hand flicks Alister off. My fingers shoot up to my mouth to hold in my laugh.

Maebh makes gagging noises. Gripping her cup with one hand, she hugs the greasy bag to her chest. "I was going to get some iced tea, but I'll just eat my food without a drink!"

I snatch her cup from her and fill it up with ice and sweet tea. "You give Alister googly eyes all the time. I know you're not making fun of us!" The cup gets raised in the air, preparing to be slammed, but instead, I slow down at the last minute and gently place it down. The tea sloshes around but doesn't spill over.

Alister throws an arm around Maebh, kissing her cheek. "People can't get their drinks in peace without getting sick from looking at you guys being so lovey-dovey."

"I know." I smile, taking a sip of my drink. A split second later, my number is called. Nathair hops up, grabbing the brown bag dotted with oil, giving the rest of us a chance to sit at the table. The bag is a vessel for wonderfully artery-clogging fries. Crispy on the outside and fluffy on the inside, the steam warms our spirits. I push my prize to the middle of the table. Each magical friend takes one. Always filled to the brim in a large cup and with handmade beauties, we gobble up the bag like we hadn't eaten in days. Finally taking a bite of my burger, I can't help but look over at Snake Boy, who hadn't ordered a thing. Maybe it was due to him not feeling well, or him not wanting to waste more time. I take my knife, cut off a third of my burger, and hand it to him. His eyes look surprised, but he accepts it humbly.

Maebh's eyes reflect her empathy for Nathair. "So, are you going to be hard-headed and have us trek through mud just to find the old man? You'll be useless since it'll be cold."

"Georgia will not get the best of me like it always does in the winter." Nathair reaches for a fry, shrugging off his struggles just to get in the building earlier.

I chuckle, bumping shoulders with him, snatching a fry. "Georgia kicks everyone's ass in the winter."

Nathair leans in, squinting at me. "You're lucky you're cute. Never play with a snake and its food." I bat my eyelashes at him. He gives up and takes another piece.

Alister coughs up a small fire. We whip our heads around to check on the employees, but they are too busy talking in the back to see anything. Meeting the eyes of each other, we all laugh. Alister stretches. "And summers feel like death, too!" We all nod in agreement.

"So, what's the plan?" Maebh asks again.

"We're going, and I'll try not to lock up if it doesn't get warmer." He shrugs.

Alister grazes Nathair's hand, batting his impressively straight lashes at him. "I'll help keep you warm, love," he says sensually, but his geeky smile is in full force. Nathair shoves him off, letting off a displeased hiss.

We pause again to check the workers once more. Minding their business, they could care less if we hissed, meowed, or mooed. "We'll think of something," I say. Optimism has to keep us going with what we are about to deal with.

A few hours pass, and the rain pounds down on us out of spite. Georgia is ridiculous! Only minutes earlier, it was sunny and decent enough for all of us to trudge through the mud. My legs still itch from the massive battle with the bugs. Red dots cover my ankles. I lost the fight. Unfortunately, we have more than bugs to deal with.

A twig launches at me, hitting me in the forehead. "Ow!" I rub my forehead. The creature is relentless, tossing five rocks and three twigs in ten minutes! The downpour is cold, wet, and painful, and topping this off with sticks only infuriates me more. The animals don't bother us since they are hiding from the rain, but a Fabulous Creature is on the prowl. With the combination of Nathair and Maebh's constant bickering and bad weather, I can't deal with some creature chucking things at me too. "That's it! Where's a rock?" I yell in frustration, snatching the closet rock in my vicinity. Still soggy and covered in a bit of moss, it makes my skin crawl. But it is a fine weapon for revenge.

"Raine, what are you going to do with that rock?" Maebh asks, trying to block me. "Now, throwing something back at it is not the answer!" I'm a woman on a mission. Another slippery twig lands in my already ruined hair. Pinpointing the location, I chuck my weapon in its direction.

"Raine!" Nathair catches my arm, but he's too late to stop me from striking the annoying creature! The thick, shiny leaves rustle in the hightops, and the monkey-like creature falls out of the tree. What the heck is that thing? I inspect it, picking up his limp hand and dropping it. Its bulging eyes are closed, and its excessively long arms with human hands twitch. Is he cute? It's hard to decide since its appearance is shocking. Nathair shakes his head at me. "Great, look at you. The thing is knocked out."

My fabulous friends all look at me in horror. Half-crazed, I pant and look down at my victim, ready for another brawl. "Raine, he was so little!" Maebh wails dramatically.

His sad, sleeping face fills me with guilt. His pale skin and rough patchy fur prickle up at my presence. I do feel bad. "He's still alive!" I say, my anger turning into panic. I didn't mean to hurt the little thing—just teach him a lesson!

Alister grabs it by the shoulders, drags it through the thick leaves and mud, and props it up on a tree trunk. He kneels down and examines it, making a blanket for him with a pile of fallen leaves. "The poor argopelter didn't need your anger problems, Little Bear."

"I'm sorry, it's just so cold and wet, and the rocks hurt," I blab, feeling even worse. "I didn't mean to hurt you, monkey thing!" I rub his little head.

"Wow, I was expecting that from Nathair." Maebh heals the creature's head, sprinkling dust on his bump.

"Even I'm not that cruel!" Nathair steps away from the crime scene.

I settle into a pout. "I'm sorry, okay!" The argopelter comes to, jumping up. We back away from him, just in case he wants payback. I flinch, expecting a bite or something, but instead, he holds his hand to me, motioning me to put something in it. He points at my soaked purse. Nothing in there is worth much to a monkey except my candy bar. Confused, I hand him my Snickers, and he runs off. "Did I just get jacked?"

"Serves you right, Argo-beater." Nathair still has room for jokes, even in his state of vulnerability. He puts an arm on my shoulder.

I shrug him off. "We're all entitled to a violent moment. None of you can judge me."

Alister raises his hand. "Not me, I am a pacifist. I can never hurt a fly."

"I didn't ask you," I say, turning my back to them.

Finding the whole ordeal hilarious, Alister turns to Maebh, fake whispering to her. "Little Bear isn't as innocent as I thought she was." Nathair grunts in pain seconds later, causing us to turn in his direction. "You okay, man?"

Nathair clutches a tree branch, hunched over. "Yeah, my body is just locking up. We got to keep moving before I can't move at all."

"Why can't we just take cover for a while and warm you up?" I ask. His pride will keep torturing him if he continues to be sensitive about showing his weaknesses.

"I can handle a little rain and wind for my future," he says, grimacing. Though this whole thing is pointless to do in the rain, his resolve is admirable.

"A little." I gasp in disbelief. "I gave up on wearing a hood. That's how freaking hard this rain is!" I show my soaked hood for emphasis. "Not all of us have perfect hair. Unlike you Fabulous Creatures, there's nothing fabulous about me right now!"

"You look like the rest of us, wet, and we all can handle it," Nathair insists.

"You sure, man? There is nothing wrong with taking a break. We have no clue where he is in this place, and I don't want the girls to get sick," Alister states.

"I can still move. Why are we worried about me?" I say, pouting at the thought of being babied just because I am the only human here. All I am required to do is have a set of eyes ready to catch this Elder. "I can pull my own weight."

"We all can tolerate the rain more than mortals can, plus we have a healer in our presence." Alister gestures to Maebh. She poses regally, letting the glory get to her head for a second. Gently resting the back of her hand on her cheek, the fairy crosses her other arm to make a graceful open palm. She seems to belong in the pretty forest only for a second, but I know she is just a show-off.

"Just the dust, not me." Maebh waves, brushing it off as if she is being modest. I cross my arms and shift my weight to one side, skeptical of her little performance.

"Yeah, no one cares, pixie," Nathair says, trying to shut her down. He lays his back on the trunk of a tree and slowly slides down it to sit on the wet ground.

"First of all, I am an Aos sí. We are way bigger than pixies, so say my people's names with respect. Secondly, that's why you're almost paralyzed on the ground. Karma is a bitch, right?" Maebh always looks like a sweet angel, but the things that come out of her mouth are not.

"Language, please," Alister corrects, earning a listless nod from his girlfriend.

"Almost doesn't count," he insists, getting back up and walking in this harsh weather. Even in borderline hail weather, his determination shines through.

My ringtone goes off. The horror-themed riffs of "Scared" by Three Days Grace echo in the forest. Ugh, what do they want now? I rustle through my pockets until I find my phone. Step-douche's name flashes, with a demon mask as his profile picture—compliments of Jasmine. I whine, gathering myself and answering.

"Hello?" I shiver in the cold rain. covering up my phone the best I can.

"Raine! Why does your GPS say you're all the way in Lake Allatoona? It's school hours right now. Are you skipping school?" Richard screams through the phone.

I hold the phone away from my ear, saving myself from future ringing later. "My phone's GPS must be off. I'll try to reboot it later. I need to go to class."

"Oh really? How about I come to pay you a visit then? Or should I call the cops instead?" Behind my screen, I can envision his tomato-red face, spit hitting the screen. I hear him wipe his phone on his shirt. The quick rustling confirms my suspicion.

I keep my voice calm and stable. More anger will result in more anger. "Please, there's no need to do that. This is just a misunderstanding—"

Nathair takes the phone from me, his eyes doing that weird flickering thing again. "She's on a field trip and safe," he says firmly, rattling and shaking sounds off in the distance. My jaw drops as he hands the phone back to me.

"Next time, let me know you're on a field trip, Raine," Richard says, sounding a bit dazed. Without a word, he hangs up the phone.

I lower the phone in disbelief. "Thank you, but also, please keep the seduction thing to a minimum!"

Nathair looks down and swallows the lump in his throat. "I'll try."

After all these years of living in this hellhole they call Georgia, I am convinced that it has a mind of its own and hates us, or just me, who knows. It takes only thirty minutes of torture before the winter rain becomes blistering heat. That is the beauty of Georgia—trying to kill its residents. My hair's a hot mess, frizzy coils poking from every direction. And I am not even going to mention the shrinkage. It is unsavable. I pull it into a bun, trying to avoid looking like a troll doll in front of my attractive company. Buns are always my way of waving the white flag. I huff, looking at the beautiful waves of Maebh's red hair. She twists it into a French braid. "Maebh, it's not fair how I look like a beast, and you look straight out of a photoshoot," I whine.

Maebh flips her hair, flattered. "Not many girls can pull off the rained-on look."

"That includes me."

Maebh throws an arm around me. "It's all about self-confidence. I look sexy because I feel that way, so feel like a sexy rained-on vixen."

With a straight face, I stop and point to my unamused face. "Do you not know whom you are talking to?" I circle my face with my pointer finger. "I have middle school ugly-girl baggage."

"Well, screw them. You're beautiful."

"You're only saying that to make me feel better." I shake my head, walking ahead of her.

"Raine, you're fine, so stop worrying about what you look like and help us out here," Nathair buts in, sounding like he couldn't care less about my first-world problems. Now that I think about it, I'm positive he doesn't.

"Rude much? I'm trying to console this oppressed teenager, and you're doing the opposite!" Maebh snaps.

"And you can mend her fragile emotions when we are at the manor, but right now, just tell her she's beautiful and move on with it," he replies.

"I don't know if I should be happy that he called me beautiful or be sad that my self-esteem isn't important," I say.

He stops to look me in the eye, something I hate. His eyes, like swords, are always ready to pierce through me. "You are beautiful, and when we get back, I'll punch whoever says otherwise, but right now, we need to find that old man."

"You're getting soft." Alister holds his hands together and presses them against his face, and looks at Nathair lovingly. "It's so romantic." He sounds infatuated, but we all knew that Alister meant it mockingly.

"Shut up," Nathair says, deciding to ignore his jab. His walk is lighter and more agile.

"Ugh, where is this old man? My legs are killing me," Maebh complains for the thousandth time. She bends down to rub her legs, giving them a quick massage.

"I didn't know you all were looking for me," a smooth, mature voice cuts through the ambient sounds of the forest. We all jump, turning around to be greeted by an old black man.

He doesn't look like anything special. No fancy robes or a long beard. He wears khaki pants and a polo shirt instead.

"Andronicus?" I ask, stepping closer.

"In the flesh, doll," he says with a heavy Southern accent.

"No offense, sir, but," I drift off, clueless on how to verbalize it. "You're a little more casual than I expected." I was expecting someone who looked like he was a part of the *Lord of the Rings* series or something mage-like. He looks like a random retiree getting ready to get the early bird special at IHOP.

He laughs lightly. "I take the form of whatever society molds me to be. I enjoy Georgia, and I'm old, so I take the form of someone's grandfather. I want anyone who talks to me to feel comfortable." He does favor my late granddaddy, so I understand his reasoning. "And call me Andre. Andronicus is too formal!"

"That's the thing, sir. We're on formal business. I have questions." Nathair steps up, standing by my side. I want to joke about him being polite for once, but it's not the right time.

"I know why you are here, and I'm sorry you came all this way. I can't tell you everything you want to know." Andronicus'—Andre's—dark brown eyes are filled in deep thought, possibly pondering what he can share. He huffs, and raspy air passes through his thick lips. His gray mustache wiggles as he fixes his mouth to say something but then stops.

I place a hand on my chest, looking at him earnestly. "Any information is helpful, sir." I look at Nathair. Sweat or rainwater drips from his temple.

"All I can say is you must go to the highest form of darkness to remove the darkness in you, Nathair. You will have to go to the underworld." Andre's voice is sturdy like a tree, digging his words into us like roots. As the roots spread, horror settles in our bodies. The underworld? What could he possibly mean by that?

"Is there anything else that you can give us? I have no idea where to start. No one knows how to go to the underworld and get out alive." Nathair looks at his hands, and for a moment, scales form on them. Balling them up into a fist, the scales disappear as if nothing had happened.

"You need the phoenix. He will help you. A contract long ago was broken, but he will renew it in good faith. He is the key to your journey and has done this twice before. He will be a great adviser to you all." I want to ask more, but I'm afraid of sounding like a dumb human.

"What is its name?" Nathair asks, steadying his voice and keeping his respectful tone.

Andre's hand meets his chin, scratching the gray stubble underneath. He opens his mouth to say a name and then shakes his head. "No, his name in this life cycle is Bennu." He self-corrects. As the name suggests, maybe *Elders* jumble their thoughts like any old person.

"Is he reliable?" Nathair raises an eyebrow.

"He works for his own benefit, but he is knowledgeable and cautious. Sometimes he is a bit mischievous." The Elder chuckles to himself.

"How can we find him?" Alister asks, stepping forward.

"Oh, he is not a creature you need to summon. Chaos attracts him like a moth to a flame," Andre warns.

"He doesn't sound like he'll be interested in my cause. I have nothing to give him that will keep him loyal to me. Andronicus, please forgive me, but is there a way to get by without his help?" Nathair requests.

"You need his knowledge of portals. Only he will know if you are going down the right path. Others will point you in the wrong direction. Now, my time here is up. I wish you all good luck."

"No, wait—" Andre disappears with the gust of wind. "Great, now we have to find that thing." Nathair kicks a poor mushroom. White powder shoots in the air, covering his foot. Scowling, he plops down on the ground. Hunching over, he tosses his arms on his knees and hides his face.

"I'm missing something. What is wrong with phoenixes?" I ask.

"Phoenixes are dark creatures, so basically, they are evil. They do things that only benefit themselves. For example, if Nathair found a spell to change him into a human, the phoenix might steal it from him and use it to get stronger," Alister explains.

"They are at the same level of evil as serpents and demons!" Nathair's voice is muffled in between his knees.

"They are pretty bad," Maebh agrees, which is a miracle. "Andronicus wants him to oversee our research and aid us. Something phoenixes are incapable of doing."

Alister looks serious. "One thing you'll find out about phoenixes is that you can't even sleep in the same house as them. They are the type to kill you when you're asleep—"

"How can an evil creature help us? It's ludicrous!" Nathair throws his head up and looks up at the sky.

"Well, you keep saying how horrible serpents are, but you're pretty morally sound. Maybe Bennu is like you, good despite his race." My theory isn't exactly popular since everyone stares at me. Are phoenixes *that* bad? I always thought they were humongous flaming birds flying through the skies, looking fabulous and getting worshiped.

Snake Boy's eyes meet mine. "No phoenix is good. Serpents make mistakes like me, once in a while, but never a phoenix."

"Guys, you're not being fair. We don't even know him! Whatever happened to the benefit of the doubt? We're all prejudged, and doing it to him is unfair." I look at their not-so-sorry faces. "I'm a freak, Alister is an Elder-reject, Nathair is evil, and Maebh is a fairy criminal," I spit out harshly. They all shift angry looks my way, but I continue with my point. "It hurts to be prejudged, and that's what people would say about us, so let's not be like them. If he screws with us, we can insult him all we want, but we don't even know what he looks like right now," I reason, making everyone waver.

Alister pushes his mane out of his face, blowing a curl out of his eye. "You're right, Little Bear. It doesn't feel good to be a magical misfit. I'll try to give him a chance, though it will be very hard."

"Fine, I'll be nice too," says Maebh, who only volunteers because of her boyfriend. It makes me feel nice to be a voice of reason.

"Well, I'm not. I don't trust this at all," Nathair says, getting up from his fetal position. He starts to walk off.

"Hey, where are you going?" I ask.

"Home, I want to find another way. I don't need a journey," he announces. Half of his face looks back at me, but he still keeps walking.

"Whoa, you said we're connected, meaning something good is going to happen to us. Maybe this journey is a good thing," I touch Nathair's arm, "for all of us."

Face red with fury. He glares at me. "Do you even know what the underworld is?"

"Is it like what we learn in mythology class or something?" I scratch my head, feeling lost.

"Yes, the underworld, as you learned in school, isn't all evil. It sorts the souls of people. But if we go to the underworld, we can get in serious eternal danger if we run into the underworld's queen. *She* resides there and eats a portion of the souls there. Those who are eaten turn into Lemuri, evil souls." He holds direct eye contact. "I don't want you to think about going to the underworld, purgatory, or Heaven. It's just something no one should experience alive."

"Who is *she?* And Andre seems to think otherwise." I stand my ground.

"Raine, if any of us get caught by a Lemuri, we die and stay there for all eternity. We become Lemuri ourselves, or worse, we become *Lilithu.*" He whispers the last sentence. There is something about that word that frightens me.

"What's that?" I feel terrible for my ignorance, considering I am trying to convince him we must take this journey together.

"Lilithu are terrifying demons. Lilithu are the children of Lilith, the creator of all dark creatures. She gave birth to all of us, serpents, demons, phoenixes, leyaks. You name it. But the lilithu are her most terrifying and vicious creation. All our evil and darkness come from her resentment. You know Adam and Eve?" he says low in my ear. "Adam had a wife before Eve. Her name is Lilith. Legends have it that she was exiled from the Garden of Eden because she wasn't subservient to Adam. She wanted to be equal to Adam, but no one saw it that way. So, they got rid of her. Being exiled angered her and twisted her into what we know her as now, the Queen of Evil." I fall silent, which I'm sure he is happy with.

Please... help... me... I hear a familiar voice whisper. I look around, concerned. A gust of wind blows on my face. I shake my head in disbelief.

He wants me to stay out of it, but I know I can't. I'm tied into this reality somehow. This is my story, no, *our* story. And I'm not sure how, but I have to make it to the city in the clouds. Maybe this journey will lead me there.

"This is just a puzzle for us to figure out. Don't worry." More wind blows past me in agreement.

Nathair stares deep into my eyes. "I'm not worried about me." Everything stops. The trees, the wind, the leaves blowing over the forest floor. A sinister chill runs down my spine. Who is he worried for?

<u>Fabulous Creature Findings:</u>

<u>Fabulous Creature:</u>   <u>Report to Nathair:</u>
Argopelter   N/A

<u>Realm:</u> Human Realm

<u>Human Country it is Associated with:</u>
New England, USA. But can be found in
the forests of Georgia as well.

<u>Notes:</u>

A small monkey-like creature that lives in
dense forest areas and enjoys chucking
twigs and rocks at unsuspecting
intruders.

Fabulous Creature Findings:

Fabulous Creature:	Report to Nathair:
Lilithu	Must find an Advisor for further research
Realm: Underworld	

Human Idea it is Associated with:

Hell

Notes:

Personal demons of the biblical Lilith. Considered high level, everything they touch loses its life essence and turns into nothingness. Avoid at all costs.

<u>Fabulous Creature Findings:</u>

<u>Fabulous Creature:</u>	<u>Report to Nathair:</u>
Lilith	Must find an Advisor for further research
<u>Realm:</u> Underworld	

<u>Human Idea it is Associated with:</u>

Hell

<u>Notes:</u>

The mother of dark creatures. She stays in the underworld, and is the only Elder to live in her own domain. She represents darkness and evil, but makes bets/pacts with souls to have a fair chance. She gives a power boost to those who are descendants of her creations. Serpents especially. Andre says the underworld is the key to Nathair's goal. I wonder how and why?

<u>Fabulous Creature Findings:</u>

<u>Fabulous Creature:</u>	<u>Report to Nathair:</u>
Phoenix	Search for Bennu

<u>Realm:</u> No home realm, but Thebes was noted in a few of Nathair's books.

<u>Human Country it is Associated with:</u>
The oldest text ever written about the phoenix is from ancient Greece, but the creature has been written about in folklore worldwide. Other names include: Tsem Rinpoche, Firebird, and Fènghuáng.

<u>Fabulous Creature Findings:</u>   pg. 2

<u>Notes:</u>

A giant mythical bird that rises from the ashes. It gets its powers from the sun. Only one exists per lifetime and is known to do things that will only benefit them. They remember their past lives, and they may temporarily bind themselves to one being for fun or to gain something. Like serpents, they are rumored to be very manipulative and untrustworthy. We haven't met yet, but we have to find a way to attract him, in this reincarnation, his name is Bennu.

Fabulous Creature Findings:

Fabulous Creature:	Report to Nathair:
Lemuri	Must find an Advisor for further research
Realm: Underworld	

Human Idea it is Associated with:

Hell

Notes:

Evil spirits that terrify and can trick and transform living beings into Lemuri if they lose their lives in the underworld. Is known to whisper your deepest darkest thoughts to manipulate you. There is a hierarchy. The strongest lemuri can turn into Lilithu. Avoid at all costs.

·THIRTEEN·

Have you ever felt like everyone knows your secret, even though it is impossible to find out? It's not like people can stare into my eyes and instantly read my every thought. Still, when I hop out of Nathair's Mustang the next day at school, everyone in the parking lot stares at us like they know all about our plans and what we are. Well, what *they* are. I don't exist in this school without the company of Nathair. No one would even spare a glance at me if the mysterious bad boy didn't hold my backpack. With a couple of my books in tow, he shuts the car door with his hip. I think it's funny how he is the opposite of every girl in school, but they all can appreciate his innate beauty. Even Jasmine acknowledges his looks, but I'm sure she only says that to tease me. She's still convinced I'm going out with him.

Wait. Am I going out with him? My eyes drift to his hands, walking comfortably with my things. A pang of nervousness rings through my core. He's never dismissed any ideas of going out with me. Last night, we watched a movie together, eating popcorn and falling asleep on the comfy floor. He woke up before me and carried me to my room. That's boyfriend-ish, isn't it?

"Are we going to HQ today?" I ask, trying to take all of my things from him. He waves me off, slinging my bag over his shoulder. The spring wind blows my dress, my heavy, black lace tights keeping my outfit modest for school. I don't care that much in the first place. The green Grecian-style dress probably will get dress-coded anyway because it doesn't touch my knee. If I were caught, they'd write me up for this dress and my tights.

"Yeah, but you don't have to stay long. You look nice today, by the way." He tucks my books under his arm. I smile back. His warm eyes melt away the paranoia I had about everyone staring at me. Maybe they aren't worried about me and think I look nice today. I peer up at Snake Boy for a few moments, feeling warm and calm inside. At times, it feels like utter chaos with him, and then randomly, it feels blissful.

"Are Alister and Maebh going to show up?" I say, licking my lips slightly. I forgot to put on some lip balm before I left the manor. He shrugs, offering me a headphone. The bass of the song vibrates in my ear. Hard rock, what an emo way to start the day—I love it. I take it, feeling the depressing music soothe me. "Hey, are we going to talk about, you know, Bennu?"

Nathair shakes his head, frowning. "I thought we dismissed the treacherous journey idea and will try to find an easier route instead."

"What if there is no other way, Nathair? I can't live like this. If I'm going to be lying to everyone, why can't I fully have a taste of what you see? I study all these creatures and their abilities, but I never touch them, except for a few. I read about all these different worlds but can never see them. I want in, all the way." The different realms are just like my storybooks but real. I have the key to seeing all the true wonders of the world. Of course, I want to take it.

"There are some realms I wouldn't mind taking you to, but none have anything to do with my goal. We'll still have Alister, so maybe we can go after I change."

"Why can't we just do it for fun?" I tilt my head up at him, and his frown melts.

He shuts his eyes and turns away from me, blushing. "Stop trying to be cute. I'm not falling for it. We have our whole lives to have fun."

I tap his shoulder, and he looks back at me, smirking. I challenge him, "I thought you wanted nothing to do with me after six months."

"You're one of us now, Thomas. If you want to stick around." He enters the school, leaving me to think about it. That's an invitation.

"Hey, wait for me. You have my stuff!" I remind him, rushing into the building.

"Aw, how cute, the lovebirds are running to class," a sickeningly sweet voice coos. Nathair and I turn to look at the one and only Aethelfield.

"What do you want now?" Nathair grinds his teeth together, trying not to show his fangs.

"You know what I want." Seductive as ever, Aethel licks her lips like a hungry lioness. Her eyes, a haunting yellow, contrast with her caramel skin. Her mouth stretches into a long, thin grin. Her fangs poke out, flashing little hints of pearly whites.

Nathair hisses and wedges himself in between us. "Well, forget it, Aethel, and stop wasting our time."

"Did I hear you right? Did you say 'our time'? As in, you and her?" She glares at me as an awkward silence fills the air. The bell rings—time to go to class. I just stare at Aethel's angry features. Then, as fast as she changes her nail color, her face spreads a different mood: smug. I'm worried about what she's thinking. "Of course," she finally says and walks to her first class—*our* first class. I gulp, looking at Nathair one last time.

"Will you be okay?" he asks, watching her like a hawk as she struts to the classroom. I nod, collecting all my things from him. She can't hurt me with everyone around.

"Well, she's not strong enough to seduce the whole class and the teacher, right?" I ask, trying to bite back a tremble.

"Pfft, let her try. I think she can do like five, max. I'm next door. I'll keep my ears out." He says in a comforting tone, but my paranoid mind wonders how many *he* can control at once. I shake it off once I look at his sweet, goofy smile. I smile back and leave him to join my class.

Loud whispers run through the school more than usual. If you didn't look at the calendar, this is a clear sign that it is finally April. At Darlson High School, two things happen in April: Firecracker and prom. Firecracker is this huge talent show organized by our senior class. Even though the school itself doesn't fund it, everyone knows about it. Only popular upperclassmen are invited, and this year as a junior, they'd let me in if I can get a hold of one of the invites. Of course, since I'm a freak and invisible, I'm not likely to go, let alone perform.

I sit in my sixth-period Spanish II class. We are studying a more advanced food unit than last year. Tamara Jackson, the resident popular girl, watches me all period, which is unnerving. The bell rings. I pack up my pencils and books, feeling terrible for not taking notes, but everything is still easy to understand. Plus, Tamara keeps gawking at me all class. It is distracting me! If it is too bad, I can always cheat and drink that potion I use for magical research. I get up, only to be greeted by the popular chick who was visually stalking me all period.

"Can I help you?" I dislike setting crazy girls off, so I usually avoid snide tones. But today, I feel like playing one of those snarky girls in movies and showing people I don't have time for their crap.

Tamara smacks her unauthorized gum. Fidgeting, she mutters, "Ray, here's an invitation to the Firecracker." She drops it on my desk.

My face twists up in confusion. "What?"

"Please just don't try anything funny like your freak friends would, Ray."

"It's Raine, but why did you—" Tamara, not one to have a conversation with me, walks off, not bothering to let me finish my sentence. She side-eyes Nathair in the doorway, handing him one as well. I gasp at the low rattling in my ear. Oh no, not this again. I snatch up my things.

I walk over to him, blurting out, "What did you do?"

"Giving you what you want." He snickers, helping me with my bag.

"Oh, really, how is that? Do you know how painful that was?" I wave the invitation in his face. He tries to hold in a chuckle. I shove the envelope in my bag, bursting his personal space bubble. "It's not funny! I had to talk to her to get this. That's torture." I zip up my bag.

Leaning in, ready to whisper, he says, "Not going to lie, she fought me. That's why she couldn't deliver the invitation a little more politely."

"Nathair, you can't—" I grit my teeth.

"What? Make up your mind. Do you want to be antisocial or have some magical journey? Don't you want to make it to the city in the clouds?" He blocks the side of his face from possibly far away peers who might listen in.

I stare at him dumbfounded. "Are you serious?"

"This is what my father would want me to do. I thought about him in one of my classes, and contrary to popular belief, I don't like to piss you off."

"Since when do you listen to me anyway?" I ask, nodding my head toward Tamera, who is taking Tylenol from her brain invasion.

Nathair gives a dismissive wave in her direction. "She'll be okay." I start walking to my next class, and he follows behind. "And to be honest, I can't think of any other way to have a transformation without a spellcaster anyway. Most of those things we were looking up were *spells*. How would we use them if none of us cast spells? So hopefully the adviser can help us find someone," he ponders loud enough for only me to hear.

"That makes sense, but what does it do with the Firecracker?" I ask, blocking the way to my seventh-period door.

"Hey, get out of the way!" A classmate tries to move me, rudely squeezing in between us.

Nathair steps in front of him and throws him a nasty look. His eyes get dark and intense. That terrifying rattle goes off. "The password is *excuse me*," he says firmly.

The boy starts sweating and throws his hands up. "My bad, excuse me." His voice trembles. Nathair gently guides us to the side, holding that cold stare on the boy. Very unnecessary, since Snake Boy is intimidating enough to scare the guy into apologizing on a regular day. I watch the poor boy head to my seat, where he writes a note and leaves candy on my desk. Hmm, so I have a mind-controlling personal bodyguard now? Guess that's one of the perks of being a lackey.

"The candy is overkill," I mumble.

Nathair's hand touches mine, but we aren't exactly holding hands. Just an acknowledgment that the other person's hand is there. I feel even worse when the signature lightning jolts through our touch. Just from our hands touching, I find myself overreacting to this imaginary electricity. "Next time he'll remember his manners," he scolds, proceeding with our previous conversation before that interruption. "Anyway, I'm causing trouble. You being there and performing would cause social chaos," he proceeds, but I am stuck on one word: performing.

"Woah, we have one jam session, and now you think you can toss me in front of a few hundred kids! No, absolutely not!" I shake my head, already feeling sick to my stomach. "I hate them, and they hate me!" People stare at us, so I lower my voice,

"I'm not doing it. I'll set off a stink bomb and cause a mini-riot, but I am not performing."

"I know they don't deserve it, nor do I, but maybe this is a part of your journey too. The part where you stop caring what others think," he says earnestly, trying to convince me that I'd be fine.

"Don't you dare say this will help me in the long run because it will not!"

"Um, Miss Thomas, if you're done out here, it'd be nice if you came inside," Mr. Glen, my teacher, interrupts, "or do you want detention so you can continue to talk to your boyfriend?"

I'm not done biting his head off. "I'll take the detention," I grumble, walking off. My apprehension peaks as I hear rattling once again in the distance. He's insane. The cheap red, black, and white speckled linoleum is in my sights. Mixed with my anger and anxiety, the floor merges with the cold gray lockers.

Nathair's hastened footsteps trail behind me. "Mr. Glen was kidding about the detention by the way," he informs. I ignore him and keep walking. I can't feel bad for him. I am too busy trying to calm the storm in my mind. He lightly taps my arm, trying to get me to look his way. "It'll help with your stage fright."

I cross my arms, pulling away from him. He tugs at my arm for a moment before we stop moving altogether. I stand like a statue, face settling into a scowl, and look down at the ground.

"First of all, you have to stop using your powers to control people!" I say with my back to him.

"I only agreed not to use it on you." He sounds genuinely clueless. He knows it's wrong but still does it? Seething at the thought—we're going to break this bad habit of his.

From time to time, I worry if he allows me to feel my true feelings. However, as the rage boils in my body, ready to overflow, I'm sure he lets me feel everything.

"Don't use it on anyone! Only for emergencies." I urge, exasperated from protecting others from his *abilities*. I put my face in my hands, giving a small scream. My head pops back up, and I go back to his atrocious stage fright comment. "Also, in case you haven't noticed, I'm socially awkward. I can't dance, sing, or act sexy in any way, something you're looking for to make your plan work." I whip around to lay into him more.

Nathair's eyes look gentle, like a puppy's. He tries to hold my hand, but I snatch it away from his. Tucking them under my forearms. "I wouldn't make you if I didn't think you could do it," he says.

"That's the thing. Why do you have to make me? Why don't you pick another girl to make your servant?" I gasp and clamp my mouth shut with my hand. That was stupid and mean to say.

He hangs his head low, handing me my bag back. "Is that all you think of when you look at me? That you work for some evil monster or something?" My silence is deafening. He scoffs, meeting my eyes again. "I tried to make up for it. I tried to show you that you're my friend—not some slave. But I guess it was all in vain."

I reach out to him, but he takes a step back. "I'm sorry, that was uncalled for. It's just I'm getting overwhelmed. The information we got from Andronicus, you using your powers, my friends being weird. It is a lot to handle at once." He shakes his head, taking another step back.

"Don't forget you asked for this, and I was just defending you. When I see you get picked on, I don't like it. I thought this was the most civil way to handle it. I'm sorry for being such a *monster*." He spits out the last word and storms past me.

I refuse to do any rehearsing until he talks to me. This situation is so dumb. It's not like we are together. Why do I have to talk to him like we are? Sitting on the empty stage in the auditorium, Nathair works to attach chords to his computer. He looks at me from his peripheral vision but ignores me.

I click my teeth at him. "What am I going to do with you? You have really low self-esteem." Walking closer to him, I plop next to him.

I slide closer to him, but he scoots away. "Yeah, but I don't go around telling everyone like you do." He scoffs.

"True, but have you thought about why I'm like this? You're asking me to entertain the same people who broke me."

"Stand up for yourself. People are only this mean to you because you take it from them. 'You're ugly, can't sing, and can't dance.' These aren't facts, Raine. You just think they are. Different isn't bad. It's beautiful. It's what I like about you—"

I interrupt him, cynically laughing it off, "This isn't *High School Musical.*"

"So what if you aren't the next big diva? They are not even real themselves. The media makes them big. There are plenty of untalented and popular musicians." He looks me in my eyes again.

I blink away some tears, trying to swallow everything he's said. I start fidgeting with my fingers, hyperaware of my surroundings. I gulp as the nervousness piles up in my throat. "But what is this all for? Who is it for?" I choke out.

"Yourself and the team." I look down, disappointed, hoping for him to say, *For me.* Confused, he bends his head to examine me. I move my face away from his. "Hiding something over there, Thomas?"

"You have no idea." I finally look at him again, something I love to do. Even when he makes me mad, I still *enjoy* looking at him. Is that creepy of me?

"You know the whole school is saying we're going out, right?" he asks out of the blue.

"I figured, but it doesn't matter, does it? They're losing things to talk about, so they make up stuff. Do you want it to be true?" I ask, testing his ability to lie or not. Who knows with him?

He sits there, thinking for a second. "What? Me? No, I was just asking if you knew. Besides, being a giant snake kinda makes it hard to date." He shrugs, but it isn't as smooth as Nathair is famous for. Using my unique lie detector test, I lean my forehead against his. He chuckles, relinquishing some of his feelings. For a guy who can feel and control emotions, he sure hates using *his.*

"Didn't I warn you to stay away?" A voice echoes nearby. We whip our heads around in the direction of the phantom sound.

"You know, at first, it feels exhilarating. Like a tingle, then it turns into a shock. If done long enough, it starts to burn. The next thing you know, your body goes into shock. You pass out, and the venom starts working through your bloodstream. It slowly and painfully kills you. This is why monsters should stay with monsters," the voice hisses in the darkness. Our eyes strain to find the intruder. Under the shadow, a long thin tail creeps onto the dimly lit tiled floor.

"What do you want, Aethelfield?" Nathair asks. His tone contrasts with my terrified mind.

She reveals her terrifying yellow eyes with slits so sharp they can cut with a single glance. "I want to rip your little toy's neck out." Her fangs and pointed tongue slowly form in the shadows, and she cocks her head. Aethel's nails sharpen, out for blood. "I want to do you a favor and save you the trouble of hiding the body. Your method of killing her is an act of infatuation. Mine should have been done once your true nature was revealed." The room spins, and now I am in Alister's arms. When did he get here?

As if he read my mind, he answers. "I saw her slither in here and knew she was up to something."

I gawk at the true monster lunging for me. Nathair intercepts her, throwing her against a wall. He hisses back at her, the green eyes I witnessed at the club returning. "Go home, Aethel. If you're worried about power, then marry the king."

"You are more powerful than the king!" she hisses. "All of Thebes is waiting on you to accept that. Your mother is waiting, and so are your sisters!"

"You don't care about Thebes! You only care about yourself and your power! You can't get that through your venom!" he hisses back at her. His energy gets thicker, and his body tenses up.

"I won't give up on you until you stop breathing or you are sitting on a throne next to me," she points in my direction, "with her dead!"

"Run along, Aethel," Maebh says, pointing in her direction. Maebh wasn't with us before, was she? My brain is fried, and I can't tell who is there. For all I know, Richard could be fighting too!

"What am I supposed to be afraid of? Light magic isn't intimidating, sweet pea." Aethel laughs. Angry, in swift and graceful movements, Maebh's hands glow. A tiny crystal falls from the ceiling, clinking on the ground. Aethel grasps her mouth with both hands. Failing to hold in her squeals of excitement, she bursts into a boisterous cackle. Shoulders heaving, she bends over in pain from her laughter. Another crystal hits her head, halting her giggles. She wipes away a tear and looks up at the ceiling. Another crystal falls, then another, then another. They start to fall down like a gentle drizzle. Starting off small, a few crystals cut Aethel's face. Shock spreads across her face as blood runs down her cheek. The crystals grow longer and sharper, trickling down from the ceiling like a dangerous but gorgeous rain.

"You should be when your head is on the line, sweet pea," Maebh says mockingly. Even Nathair backs up, hiding behind the fairy. We all cower behind her, where it's safe.

Aethel's eyes widen, covering her head with her bag. The crystals scrape and cut her hands. She backs away, but the crystals continue to rain on her. A large stone drops, piercing her right foot! Crimson red flows out of her foot. Falling on her back, she tries to scurry backward, screaming in pain. She finally finds her feet and faces Maebh in fear. "This is malicious magic. How are you still a healer?"

"Aos sí are neutral, and since I'm using light magic for hurtful things, it cancels out. Now shoo before you get your head cut off, *snake.*"

Aethel hisses like the cornered animal she is, binding her legs into a long yellow snake tail. She sits upright and balances herself. With a deep wound still leaking at the bottom, she hisses one last time and slithers away. Maebh stops the crystals from falling.

She turns to me, walking over to check on me. "Are you all right?" I nod, picking up one of the crystals and inspecting them. It dissolves at my touch, breaking into thousands of fragments that float into nothingness. The other crystals follow, disappearing right before my eyes.

Alister brushes me off, glitter residue still on my shoulder. "Oh, Little Bear, I'm sorry you had to see that!"

"Me too." We all direct our attention to Nathair. He bites his lip, exhaling. "She didn't fully go to our second form, but I'm sorry you had to witness it."

"It's not your fault. Aethel's just crazy." I try to brush it off, but it doesn't make him feel better. He continues to sulk, looking down in shame. I pat his hand. What is he thinking? Is he still worried about if I think he's a monster?

He finally looks up but avoids my eyes. Instead, he looks at Alister and Maebh, holding back a grimace. They give him a supportive glance. "Raine," he says softly.

"Yes?" I perk up at his smooth voice calling my name.

"I will never hurt you," Nathair blurts out, looking at everyone except for me.

"I didn't think you were going to hurt me." I give a weak laugh. His stern gaze silences me.

He squeezes my hand back. "I know. It's a promise to myself."

FOURTEEN

"How can you use magic like that when you're not a spellcaster?" I asked Maebh the next day. Though I am still recovering from Aethel's attack, the rules of magic plague my mind. It's simple at a base level, but a web of intricacy hides underneath.

My Aos sí friend sits back in the kitchen chair, pondering. She snaps, finally coming up with an answer, and leans over the table to get close to me. It's like a secret between best friends, though it's nothing special to anyone from the world of Fabulous Creatures. She's so close to me that I can't help but pour all my attention into her following words. "Aos sí are born with specific powers that they know automatically after birth. Most of us can heal, but each gets a different elemental power. So, mine come from the Earth. So I can only use Earth elemental spells. However, a true spellcaster can use many different types of magic with no limits. And they can be light magic or dark magic," Maebh explains.

"Oh, so that's why I only see you use crystals. So what about light creatures? They can change and grow dark?"

"Yes, remember, Fabulous Creatures and humans are more alike than you think. You have bad people, and you have good people. Same with us. But we're all a little different. Unlike Nathair and Alister, Aos sí can choose what we want to be. Nathair is a dark creature, so he has to fight his *unsightly* characteristics. Alister is a light creature, so he has to try not to get corrupted." She closes her eyes, resting her chin on her hand. Her eyes flick open. "Which is why they are a strange pair," she says, sounding extremely dry. She murmurs mostly to herself, probably realizing that she is stuck with Nathair forever.

I wonder if my confusion comes from the fact that Fabulous Creatures are complex or if my brain is still fried. "I'm sorry, but I didn't follow."

She stretches high in the air and stands up. She fetches fresh ingredients out of the fridge and starts rinsing them. "It is confusing, I admit. It's not something you can learn in one day. You'll get the hang of it eventually. Ugh, just wait until we explain laws and treaties. The Elder Court alone is complicated enough," she says, cutting up some celery. One of the things I love about the manor is that everyone cooks there. At my house, we practically have take-out every night.

"What are my girls doing?" Alister busts into the kitchen, startling us. "Clearly something bad because you're both jumpy." We both give him an angry look. That jokester. He starts massaging his girlfriend's neck. She lightens up at the kind gesture and relaxes under his touch. Alister releases his tail, and it wiggles around for a moment. Then it gently rubs his lover's leg. Gross, is this what Snake Boy and I look like to people? Minus the tail action.

"We're having a magical girl talk, and I'm cooking." Maebh smiles, making the world a little brighter—her specialty.

"Sounds like I'm not eating dinner," Nathair says, following right behind Alister. He stops, sighing. His eyes are fixed on Alister's tail. "We're in the kitchen. Put that thing away!"

Alister laughs. "Are you mad because mine is bigger?"

"I'll have you know that I have a *grand* tail, thank you. Just because I don't have a butt doesn't mean you can make fun of it," Nathair says, getting defensive. Why are arguments like this so commonplace to me now?

Maebh sucks her teeth, making sure her back is turned to Nathair. "Oh, shut up. I didn't poison it. Remember, eating is a pleasure, not a right. I can starve you."

He pulls up a chair, swinging it toward him to straddle. "Fine. I can just make my own food or go hunting."

"What does it look like when you eat a cow anyway? Do you cook him or swallow him?" I ponder, remembering his original preference for diet.

"I would prefer not to answer that," he says dryly.

"Watch Animal Planet." Maebh cackles at me, wiping a tear from her eyes. Not sure if it is that funny of a question or if it is from the onions she is chopping up.

"More reasons why I hate you." Nathair glowers at Maebh. She returns his scowl by sticking her tongue out. He looks at me. "It's cleaner than the snakes here, thank you."

"Oh, your food just slides down. No chewing required?" I answer.

"Wow, out of all the awkward questions you could ask me." His voice trails as he scratches the back of his neck.

"No, 'how big are you?' is an awkward question." I laugh.

"Oh, I'll happily tell you my pe—"

"Don't finish that sentence." I cover his mouth before he says whatever perverted idea flies out. I hold my hand there for a moment. He tries to talk through my hand a few times and then gives up. Only when I feel safe do I lower it.

He shrugs. "Well, you asked."

"You know I meant in your snake form." I shake my head—thoughts interrupted by my phone ringing. Uh oh, lately, my mom has been complaining about how she never sees me anymore, but I've had good reason. Too bad she doesn't know that. I answer with a flat and annoyed tone, "Hello."

"Nice to know I still have a daughter. Where are you now, Raine?" Mom nags. I make a gunshot gesture with my hand. The Fabulous Creatures know that it means I'm in trouble.

"Maebh's," I lie.

My mom's exasperated voice huffs and puffs on the phone. Why do moms always have to be so dramatic? Why can't she enjoy me not sitting in her house and using her electricity? "You're always at Maebh's or out with your friends. This has been your third consecutive week that you've spent the night at someone's house! I miss you. Come home!"

"Now?" I whine. I was looking forward to Maebh's soup. They constantly spoil me with homemade food. I'm not ready to trade that in for frozen White Castle burgers.

The attitude radiates off her voice as if it is so hard to be away from me. "Yes, now. Since when have you become such a busy person anyway? Besides, you think I forgave you for burning a hole into my Persian rug? You're lucky I didn't ground you for eight weeks for that." Though I didn't like it when he used it, I silently thanked Nathair for 'convincing' my mom not to ground me and agreeing to get a new, less ugly rug instead. Though I told him to only use it for emergencies, at that moment, my life was at stake. You don't mess with a mother's expensive rug unless you have a death wish.

"Okay, Mom, I'll get a ride," I say, conceding.

"Good." She hangs up without saying goodbye. Yeah, that is the behavior of a mom that misses her child.

"My mother wants to pay attention to me now." I shove my phone in my pocket.

Maebh twists her face in confusion. "She chooses now after all those nights of you doing this? Haven't they been focused on your sister and her grades?"

"That and they think she has emotional problems because of our father. Richard thinks her acts of rebellion come from the trauma of losing a father figure. Like how people thought girls who love *Twilight* have daddy issues." I shrug.

"You serious?" Nathair spits out, slapping his knee in amusement.

"Yeah, I saw it on the TV when I went to my dermatologist. Old people dominate there." I get up, cleaning up my things. "Alister, can you hand me my camera?"

Alister complies, retrieving my digital camera. The sun sets, making the kitchen dim. The blue light of my camera's screen glows. Huh, strange. I could've sworn I turned it off earlier. Great, I'll have to charge it now. Alister flips through some of the pictures. Judging by the shapes, it must've been from the field trip to Emory University's art museum. I frown, remembering Aethel playing 'Keep Away' with my camera. But at least she didn't destroy it like she did with my book.

"These pictures are cool, Little Bear." He freezes at the image of the ancient Costa Rican crocodile seat. Light covers his body, and his eyes droop. His skin goes pale as he hands the camera to me. "Here."

"Alister, are you all right?" Maebh checks his forehead. She winces, removing her hand and shaking it. A red welt forms on her skin. "You're so hot!"

"Oh, I'm just tired." He checks his temperature with the back of his hand. He nods his head and puts it down. "I might have a small fever."

"Tell that to my third-degree burns!" Maebh runs her hand under cool water.

Nathair looks up at his friend. "You should rest then," Nathair adds, concern in his voice. He sits up straight. Eyes focused on Dragon Boy. Alister waves them off, acting casual, but I can see his shoulders slump the longer he stands up.

"Maybe a nap might help. I'll see you later, Raine." Alister turns and walks away.

"Bye," I say. The three of us lock eyes, telepathically telling each other to worry. Our silent three-way conversation says everything and nothing at the same time. Something is wrong. We need to investigate this to see if it gets worse. Alister stumbles back in for a moment to grab his phone. We all jump, pretending to be preoccupied with setting the table, and Maebh stirs her soup. The dragon drifts away without a word.

Nathair looks back and forth at the kitchen entrance. He opens his mouth to speak first, "I'll take you home."

"Thanks, Nathair." I get up and grab my things. We walk past Alister's room; his door is closed, but a handprint is burned into the doorframe. I whistle. That is one hell of a fever.

Later that evening, Jasmine waits for me at the front door of our house. I practically roll out of the car, hoping the 'rents don't see us. "Hm, still dating that boy, I see," Jasmine deduces, watching him pull away from our driveway.

"Yeah, you could say that." I shift my legs, not meeting her eyes.

"Richard is pissed at you. He said you're neglecting your family," Jasmine warns.

"Richard is a control freak. He's angry at himself because he can't manipulate me." I waltz in, shutting the door behind me. I look up at my darling sister. "How's your mental health?"

"Same as yours," she says.

I giggle, putting down my things. "Sounds like many years of therapy, then."

She changes the subject, "Yeah, how's your boyfriend?" I look at her, squinting my eyes. That is very suspicious. Her vibes are off, agitated, almost. "Lately, I've just been hearing some weird things about—"

"Um, it's complicated." My eyes dart around the room, trying to come up with an explanation. But I am at a loss for words.

"What is so complicated about you coming home, Raine?" Richard comes out of nowhere. Irritation is eminent.

I can feel myself shutting down. I mentally start withdrawing, not feeling up for a fight. With a straight face, I say, "I've been busy with schoolwork."

"Well, you can work at home," he nags.

I grit my teeth. "What did I do to be treated like a kid?"

"Are you talking back to me?" King Richard crosses his arms.

"Yes, because I understand if I was going around doing drugs and crime, but I'm literally at someone's house, working!" I say, not in the mood.

Richard storms over to me, towering over me. "Do not talk to me like I'm an idiot, young lady. I have authority over you!" His eyes cast down on me, trying and failing to look intimidating.

I fume, releasing my anger. "You are not my father, and I only tolerate you because my mother loves you, and no matter what you do, it's always going to be that way. Stop acting like the dad I never had. I don't want one. Just do your job and make her happy. Where I go is her business, not yours."

Richard jumps back, mouth agape. "Raine Alyce Thomas, you must have forgotten who you're talking to!"

Ready to make more snide comments, the thought of Alister flashes in my mind. If I piss off Richard more, I'll never be able to see if he is okay. Alister is like a brother to me, and letting my anger take over would make me a bad sister. I look up at Richard, having an epiphany. He is the ruler of this household as long as my mom loves him. Nothing I can say or do to change that. My mother doesn't want to be alone anymore. So I have to put up or shut up. She's letting him terrify us because she's scared to lose love again. I look at the tyrant and wave the white flag.

"No, sir, sorry," I reply, walking to my cold room.

The room lacks the personality and love my room at the manor has. It's been so long since I've been in this actual space. I forgot how *Richard* it is. The pastel yellow walls and the flower canopy bed look tacky and juvenile. It's Richard's vision of what a girl's room should look like. The lovely wood desk and drawers contain clothes that Richard picked. Sad how I feel more like myself with non-humans than with my own family.

There is a small polite knock at the door. "Come in," I answer.

"Hey, baby girl," my mother's soft voice greets me. A pang sets off in my chest. My dad used to call me that too. "I am just coming in to say hi. I don't see you that often anymore. You've been a busy bee."

My mother's under-eye dark circles are lighter today. And her tired smile is perkier, even showing a hint of her dimples. Her trip with Richard must have been nice.

It's a wonder how she would feel knowing that the happier she gets, the more miserable her daughters become.

Still, I smile through my discomfort. This house used to be my haven, but now it's a prison. "Mom, would you still love me if I wasn't perfect?" I ask.

"Perfect?" My mom makes a surprised sound, caught off guard. "I know we've been bumping heads lately, but that's just growing pains. Even adults get them. But it doesn't impact how much I love you."

I want to believe her, but her actions tell me otherwise. "What if I wanted different things than you? Would you be hurt?"

My mom sits next to me, rubbing my shoulder. Her red nails had a small chip, a flaw she normally never allowed. "You girls have hurt my feelings plenty of times, and I'm sure I've hurt yours. We're human. We make mistakes. As long as we can come back together, that's all that matters." The honesty of her words doesn't sink in. Maybe I'm more hurt than I let on. She emotionally abandoned me for a man. How can I believe her when we'll be strangers again as soon as the door opens?

"All Richard does is pick at my mistakes," I let it slip. Closing my eyes and biting my lips.

"Baby, I know it's been hard on you, losing your dad. But all he wants is to take care of our family. Try to get along with him, please. He's devoted to us." *To us, or you?* I try to sympathize with her. She wants a man who won't leave her again. A man who will promise her forever and mean it. My mom continues to rub my back, but unlike a child, it doesn't soothe me. It's the kind of comfort she gives when you scrape a knee or your favorite toy breaks. The one where she acknowledges your pain but can never truly feel it. She can feel sorry for you, but your issues are trivial to her in the long run.

I curl up in my chair. "I'll try."

She's too far gone, tied to her puppeteer.

Mom seems happy with my answer and kisses my temple, hugging me. I don't move but still accept her attempt at affection. She leaves the room after that, shutting the door.

The strings of our conversation tear down like the leftover spiderweb in the corner of my room.

I look around, already bored out of my mind, and walk to my old bookshelf. It is the only thing left of my dad and the only thing I am willing to keep. My chest feels heavy, and thoughts of him cloud my mind momentarily. No matter what I wanted, no matter what I asked, he always let me be myself. I didn't have to be the perfect daughter in front of him. I miss him. I forgot when my family was whole. Now my sister and I constantly battle for dominance when we need to be held and told everything is okay. To see my dad's face one more time would be a treasure.

I scan my books. In a dark mood, I decide to study one of the books from the library on Lilithu. I try to dive into my research.

Lost soul, why did you wander into a place like this? Were you a wicked person in your life? Did a dark creature lead you to purgatory? Or maybe our very own Queen of Hell sent you a personal invitation? Whatever your business is, repent for your mistakes and try to climb to the gates of Heaven.

You can still save yourself.

Make a bet with our lovely Queen. If you win, she will free you. However, exercise caution, for she is a tricky devil, ready to trip you up at every corner. This is where her nightmarish children come in.

Ready to do her bidding, the Lilithu will tempt you and drive you mad. Should they touch you, your soul will decay and rot in seconds. And you'll be lost in the circle of Hell that their master picks. Be wary. They can hold forms of people you love and visit you in the mortal realm. They are always watching, and once you are down here, they will enjoy the thrill of the hunt. You are their unfortunate prey.

Evil souls from above can join in too. The Lemuri were old pals of Lilith who journeyed to live with her in the afterlife. If you are in a half-alive state, they will try to get you to join them. Should you listen to their instructions to end your life, you will be lost in limbo and forced to become one.

Save yourself.

Save yourself.

For the first time in my entire life, it's terrifying to read. Unnerved, I slam the book shut. Perhaps that's why Nathair seemed so scared. A journey that will lead to Hell? From what the book says, it seems like a delicate process to get out safely. Will the adviser know? He's a dark creature, so maybe he will have a clue on how not to run into those horrifying monsters down below.

My eyes steer toward my bag. I borrowed a few other types with lighter topics, but instead, I take out my top-secret notebook. I usually leave it at Nathair's house, but since he even snoops, I keep it next to me twenty-four hours a day, seven days a week. Tapping my pen lightly on the paper, I think of what I want to write. Business or pleasure? Words pour through my fingers, spilling all over the paper. It's only safe in my care. Anything else is either dangerous information about the Fabulous Creatures or dangerously embarrassing to my psyche. There's no in-between.

> She can't see my pain.
> She doesn't want to.
> Because if she did, she'd break under the pressure.
> My back is stronger, so I'll carry this burden.

For the next three days, I am held captive in this house, only going to school and back. Alister is getting worse as well. According to Maebh, he won't even eat anymore. All he does is sleep. After an uneventful three days, I give up on trying to be good, something the old me would never do, and go to see Alister. Leaving my phone behind, I sneak out. Can't have another GPS incident.

I walk into the eerie bedroom. It resembles a cave, with clothes and books strewn all over the ground. A crystal bathtub lies in the middle of the room. Crafted by his lover, he lies in an ice bath. Eyes closed, he sleeps in the tub in his swimsuit. The ice melts in minutes, so I lug a heavy bag of ice and pour it in for him. He moans, shifting in the tub. His usually perfectly curled hair is tangled and dead looking, and his skin is pale. The most striking thing is his eyes, which are sunken in and deep purple.

Why is he so sick? My eyes widen as the realization strikes! I add another bag of ice for good measure and walk out.

"Guys, I have a theory of why Alister's sick!" I belt once I close the bedroom door.

"What?" Both Maebh and Nathair jump.

"Remember that snake necklace and how it reacted with Nathair?" I ask.

"I made it," Maebh says, her dryness radiating.

"I remember my death experience with this crazy bit—"

"Anyway, Alister saw a picture of a shamanic seat in the shape of a crocodile," I continue, not in the mood for a fight. "Is it a coincidence that right afterward, he gets sick? Maybe his body reacts badly like Nathair to that necklace!"

Maebh taps her finger on her chin, thinking out loud, "But it was just a picture. How did that hurt him?"

"Well, they say pictures take a piece of your soul. Its power over him may be so strong that he passed a piece of his soul when he saw the picture!" I theorize.

Nathair rests his head on his forehead. Looking off into the distance. He blinks, turning back to us. "Well, if that's the case, we need a shaman's help to heal him since a shaman's artifact cursed him," Nathair adds.

"Oh, that's a good idea!" I stop for a second and think about it more. "Wait, how would we do that?"

"Maybe if we get an item that a shaman is connected to, we can conjure them," Maebh volunteers.

"Oh, if that's the case, it has to be something with a jaguar!" I deduce. "I've seen many movies where someone tries to turn into a powerful jaguar deity. Plus, at that museum, they talked about it being an honor for a shaman to turn into a jaguar."

"Well, what's something there that you'd think would have the most connection to a shaman?" Nathair shuffles rampantly through some books.

"Um, this thing called the Jaguar Vessel. It looks like a vase with arms bent over its legs. It seems to be a museum favorite because they have it as the cover picture on their pamphlets." I place a hand over his, making him pause.

"Anything special about it?"

"Yeah, if you shake it, the ceramic balls inside should roar. That and the position of the jaguar matches the way shamans rest." I retrieve the pamphlet from my purse.

Nathair holds it up in the air. "So this is what we're gonna steal? Kind of ugly, don't you think?"

I gasp at him. "What do you mean steal?"

"Well, how are we supposed to summon a shaman if we have nothing to summon with?" he says frankly.

"Maebh, can you heal curses? Maybe my theory could be wrong!"

Maebh goes to open her mouth, but Nathair interrupts her. "She can only heal wounds, not curses. Anyway, it's for Alister. He'd do it a thousand times for one of us!"

"But do you have to use the word steal?" I'm not used to the idea of committing federal crimes!

"There's no way to sugarcoat it, sweetie," Maebh joins in, transferring her belongings from a smaller purse to a larger one. Imagine lip gloss and a rare artifact shuffling around in her crossbody. I cringe at the thought.

"We're borrowing it. We don't want to keep it!" I concede.

"Yes, superwoman, now get in the car. I don't know how long Alister is gonna last," I whine but listen to Nathair's command and drag myself to his car. This is all for Dragon Boy.

It takes us about forty minutes, but we step out of the car in wonder. The campus of Emory University looks straight out of a movie. The tall, white marble buildings contrast against the enormous dark trees with students resting under them. Many college students play Frisbee on the perfect green grass. I admire the campus. Emory University is one of the top choices for law or medical majors. After all, it is one of the most prestigious schools in Georgia.

A big, Grecian-style marble building reading Michael C. Carlos Museum appears after our five-minute walk around campus. My nerves come crashing down. "Stop looking like you're about to commit a felony," Nathair scoffs. Alister's illness has him on edge more than the thought of stealing a rare artifact.

"I am committing a felony, very sensitive to the fact that I'm a criminal." I swallow, walking into the entrance. On the left, a small bookstore greets us, filling the small hallway to the admission desk with the scent of new books—a smell I love.

"It's for Alister, the guy who saved your life and built a room for you in our house," Nathair says through gritted teeth.

"I know what Alister has done for me!" I fire back. I'm not just going to write Alister off like that.

"Just be ready to cut through the glass evenly so no one hears us." We both turn to our worried Maebh. Her eyes lack their usual sparkle. As bad as we all feel, we all know what must be done, and unfortunately, Maebh has a significant part. She nods in our direction, silently letting us know she is okay. Returning the gesture, we all walk in unison to the admissions desk.

"Hello." This nice old woman smiles at us. We return the favor.

"Hi, three students, please." I hand her nine dollars. She gives us our tickets, our devious plans unbeknownst to her. This takes 'do not touch' to a different level.

"Would you like some headphones for more information? It's only two more dollars," she offers.

"No, thank you, we like to read the information," Maebh chimes in, dazzling the poor woman with her perfect smile. Maebh's smile can trick anyone into thinking she's an angel put on this planet, though her true personality is the opposite.

"Very well." The woman shrugs. I give her a small wave before walking into the museum entrance on the right. The Jaguar Vessel is in the exhibit to the left. But we can look around at other exhibits before going to the one we need.

The first showcase we enjoy is Greek and Roman art. Highlighting a sea of busts and headless figures—Caesar, Brutus, Aphrodite/Venus, and many others decorate the walls mixed with their painting counterparts. What I find most interesting is the coffin. It has little boys riding a wolf on it. A flashback of last year's world history pops into my head. The two boys must be Romulus and Remus, founders of Rome. Legend says a wolf raised them.

Nathair appears next to me as I get a closer look at the tomb. Our hands touch, but he doesn't grab my hand. A classic move of his, which makes me wonder if it's his version of being shy. Still, he seems more relaxed knowing where to find the vessel. "Wanna know something cool?" he whispers.

"Yeah, sure."

Eyes wide and nerdy, he relays what he learned. This passionate look is what I give him at times. He looks at the art but relays his findings. "I looked into what we talked about at the fair. And I think it's confirmed. I'm technically Irish. I tracked my ancestry to a small realm whose portal is in Ireland." I snicker to myself, recalling Maebh might also be Irish. He would be so annoyed to know that.

"Nice to know what to put on demographics, huh?"

"Hey, guys, the coast is clear. I cleared out all the cameras, so I need Nathair to work his seduction magic and keep people out," Maebh whispers. We both nod, walking around for a few more minutes.

When we finally reach our destination, Maebh puts up a transparent crystal wall. Supposedly, it's made so we can see people, but they can't see us. With that advantage, Nathair can use his seduction abilities to steer them away from the exhibit we need.

Unfortunately, I have the challenging job of placing a crystal in the jaguar's place if an alarm goes off because of no pressure. If I don't do it fast enough, the alarm might go off, and then it'll be jail time.

So here I am, nerves pricking me like small needles. What if I had never followed Nathair to that stupid club that night? Knowing my past self, I would read a book and get into trouble mentally. No fake adventure in my mind can compete with my reality now.

"Okay, get ready, Raine, this is it," Maebh warns. I position myself. Slowly and nimbly, she scratches the diamond-hard crystal against the glass. Each second she takes feels like an eternity. My heartbeat grows faster and out of control. As if she had taken years, a wave of relief washes over me when she puts the glass circle on the ground. Her leather-gloved fingers flawlessly drift to the Jaguar Vessel. I prepare myself as she carefully removes the artifact. Quickly and clumsily, I slam the crystal into the missing artwork's place.

"Graceful," Nathair teases.

"Graceful," I mock, scrunching my face up as much as possible and sticking my tongue out, which he returns.

"Okay, if Alister were here, he'd say stop undressing each other with your eyes and help me!" Maebh demands as she puts the growling item on the ground. We rush over to her, observing it. It is pretty amazing to touch, even with leather gloves on. You can see the mini jaguars engraved in their fur. The clay color makes its bright red lips stand out. Not to mention the growl sounds like a real giant jungle cat!

"What do you need us to do, Maebh?" I ask.

"Hold my hand. I need your energy." I comply, but Nathair is too stubborn. Even though they both love Alister, Nathair still doesn't trust Maebh, but I don't blame him. The necklace incident was pretty traumatizing, and it wasn't me who almost died. Maebh cuts a glance at him. "He's losing his life as we speak, Nathair. Are you returning to your old ways of putting yourself first?"

"I could ask you the same question," he argues.

"Look, if I'm lying in a bed wasting away, you can screw around and not cooperate, but this is Alister, the guy who risked his life for you," Maebh throws back.

"I think we all realize Alister has saved our lives somehow, so stop guilt-tripping the other person, and let's get this over with!" I say, exasperated. Satisfied, Nathair finally grabs her hand. Maebh chants. My mouth drops in wonder as big, butterfly-like wings form on her back. Maebh glows, and her ears grow pointy. Her skin is now a burnt sienna. Her eyes turn into a brilliant hazel.

"Across the stars, realms, cosmos, and skies, I pray to the creator of the universe to hear my cry. When light creature, dark creature, and innocence combine, we summon a holy man from the divine. Though we are too imperfect to see perfection, please help us summon a shaman for resurrection. I love and hold dear, who love and hold dear to me, so please send a messenger to hear our testimony."

A flash of light ejects from the ancient jar, and wind forms around us! Surges of light energy flow through the tips of my hair to my toes, and I feel every part of it. A thick, black tribal tattoo wraps around my forearm, in the shape of a bird with its wings extended to my wrist. What is happening to me?

I look over at Nathair and Maebh, who are just as confused. Lighting flicks on my fingertips and flows through my body. Gingerly, I point, and a giant bolt dashes out of my hand!

The lightning sculpts a figure. Soon, a beautiful brunette stares at us. The winds grow more assertive, but where we stand is calm—the eye of the storm. Lightning moves through this strange spiritual plane.

"Where are we?" I manage to blurt out.

"Hello, my name is Illeona. You're in my domain," the stranger greets. Like Maebh, she possesses a smile of perfection. Her long dark hair is pulled into an impossibly long braid that touches the ground, and her tan skin and long face compliment her slim frame. Her almond eyes are sharp but kind.

"Illeona, I want to cut to the chase, my love is sick, and we know only you can heal his illness," Maebh pleads.

She takes hold of Maebh's hands. "With all of your collective memories of Alister's crusades, I should have enough power to save him from the Dragon Capsule."

"The Dragon Capsule?" I repeat.

"Yes, to reduce exposure to Fabulous Creatures, shamans would often capture dragons in these capsules and sit on them to hold them in. Of course, since not many humans can figure out the other realms, we holy people would tell them the capsules were religious seats dedicated to the crocodile," Illeona answers. This explains why it looks like a dragon.

"So, wait, can you heal him?" Nathair steps up to her, looking nervous.

"Yes, I have released that piece of his soul from the vessel. And I've increased your Aos sí's powers too. If you stick around, I can give you more information about your journey." We all look at her with hope, fully synced. "Go to the realm of Remone, and you shall find your spellcaster, but have caution.

This spellcaster isn't what you'd expect. They are very dangerous," Illeona warns. Her body fades, disappearing in waves, taking the lightning realm with her.

"Hey, wait!" Nathair pleads. "Please tell me more!" She doesn't heed his call and leaves us in the exhibit. Everything is untouched as if we had just walked into the display. I look down at my arm. The tattoo on my arm writhes around. As Nathair continues his plea, it gets weaker. I watch it fade, just like Nathair's hope.

Fabulous Creature Findings:

Fabulous Creature:	Report to Nathair:
Shaman	Confirmed we need
Realm: Human Realm	a spellcaster

Human Country it is Associated with:

More widely known in North and South America, but there is written evidence of Shaman in Europe, Asia, Africa, and Polynesian countries.

Notes:

People deeply connected with the spiritual plane, they are given the gift of sight and the ability to heal others with rituals and medicine.

· FIFTEEN ·

Violent scratches stretch across the innocent blue walls. Clothes are strewn all over the floor, ripped and broken. He hides in his room, flipping through any book he could find. Unlike his usual joking, sarcastic self, this Nathair is moody and irate. His face is full of remorse and regret. It's hard to look at.

Sick of seeing him stuck in this rut, I gingerly pick up some of his books. Covering his face in shame, he lays his head on the cold, wooden desk. "Please leave. I don't want you to see me like this."

I disregard him, still picking up his things. "We'll figure this out, don't worry. The unknown is super scary, but we'll be together. Alister and Maebh will be there too."

"Why aren't you scared of me?" His glossy green eyes are still beautiful, even with all the pain inside them. I kneel next to him, getting on his level, and continue to clean up. Clearing a space is all you need sometimes to clear your mind.

"Why should I be? We all have our bad days. I trash my room when I am mad too. Besides, there are scarier people out in the world than a frustrated band geek." The salvaged books make satisfying thumps, as the stack grows bigger and bigger on his desk. My hard work is paying off as the dullness in his eyes starts to clear. His eyes soften once they land on me.

"You shouldn't compare me to a human. I could snap at any moment. My room was the unlucky one this time, but it could be you next," he warns, hiding his face again.

"Oh, stop being so broody. That is so 2010's," I jest, poking him. He looks back at me once more. "Sulking boys are out of style, don't you know?" The small corners of his mouth quirk as our fingers intertwine.

"I'll hurt you if you keep calling me broody." He lightly chuckles.

"I know you won't hurt me unless I quit Firecracker," I joke, making him lighten up. It's time to stop moping. After we healed Alister, the house turned so cold when Nathair decided to hide away from his problems.

"You do realize it's tomorrow, right?" he reminds me, going with my change of subject. He sits up straight to look at me.

I throw my head back, already feeling overwhelmed. "Yes, and so much crap has happened since we decided to do it. I don't even know what song I'm doing. I need some magic to save me. ASAP!"

He chuckles, resting his head in his hand. "None of us have powers that can help you with that."

"Well, someone needs to get one, or else the only chaos will be my mental stability after being embarrassed for all eternity."

"You'll do fine," he insists, but I'm not assured.

"It isn't fair how you're hot, Alister is funny, and Maebh looks like a supermodel. I shouldn't compare myself to Fabulous Creatures, but what do I have?" With a slight grin, he looks at me with dopey eyes. "Why are you looking at me like that?" I ask. He continues his flurry of puppy-dog glances. It's so intense that I can vividly imagine myself popping a heart-bubble over his head.

Nathair pulls up a stool for me to sit on. He starts playing with a pen, glancing at me occasionally. "You're smart, brave, and kind."

"And I'm pretty?" I ask, not really caring about fishing for compliments. He's opening up again, and I'm milking this for all it's worth.

He chuckles, looking down for a second. "Very pretty."

"Thank you," I say, faking some confidence and flipping my hair. He sadly smiles at me and leans in close to my face. Our lips aren't touching, but I can feel that tingly warmth spreading through my chest. Phantom kisses dance on my lips as the sweet memories of us this close roll in. Even with those different scenarios, they all end the same: the lightning burning my core deliciously and painfully. Just centimeters apart, he confuses me when he moves away from me. He looks up at an intruder.

Maebh swings the door open, and their eyes meet, but she doesn't say anything to Nathair. "Raine, Richard is here to get you! Better hurry before he realizes that two guys own this house!" Maebh ushers me out.

"Raine," Nathair calls.

I turn around to look at him, stopping Maebh from dragging me out. "Yeah?"

"Thank you for always trying to understand me." He looks down, feeling shy.

I smile again. "It's like being afraid of a puppy because they could bite you. What's the point when they show no interest?" Determined, I make a mad dash to Nathair and give him a peck on the cheek before running away. He jolts up as if static shocks him, and then settles back in his chair red-faced. He puts his hand on his cheek, but before he can say anything to me, I'm gone.

When I finally reach Richard, Nathair is in the window, waving. I return the favor and get in the car.

"Who are you waving at?" Richard demands. "Is that a boy?"

I fake gasp. "Nadine would feel bad if you had said that in front of her!"

"Well, she shouldn't be dressed like a teenage boy!"

"That's just her style," I say, laughing.

"Wait, who is Nadine?"

"Maebh's sister," I lie. After that, we drive in awkward silence.

Most dads would ask about their kids' day or offer to get something in the drive-through. My real father let me be a radio DJ and then would poke fun at each angsty lyric. The mischievous wrinkle in his eyes as he turned up my music stuck in my memory. Or when my face was puffed up in anger, he'd pinch my cheeks and sing the song off-tune. Richard and I didn't have that kind of relationship. He never jokes, only criticizes.

Richard gulps, his large Adam's apple bobbing up. My face feels tight, and my scowl is apparent in the passenger side window. I fix my face since Richard hasn't offended me yet. He clears his throat, turning down his classical music. "So, your mother and I were talking." *This is never good.* I slide down in my seat, crossing my arms. Richard avoids eye contact with me, hyper-focusing on the road. "We think it might be nice if you ladies pick what we do for our annual summer trip."

"I'm sorry, I'll be busy for summer vacation. I am enrolling in a summer college program," I lie. Lie after lie piles up on me. That's all I know how to do these days. Thank God I'm not Pinocchio, or else my nose would be still in the driveway at the manor.

Honestly, I have no idea how Nathair plans to take me to the other realms over summer break, but it looks like some *influence* might be needed. My stomach rolls with guilt. No one deserves to be manipulated. Hopefully, we can come up with a better solution.

"Oh really? That's impressive." *I don't need your approval.* Staring straight ahead, he continues, "I'm sure it won't take up all your vacation. We can pick a date when you are free. Where would you like to go?"

He taps his steering wheel and fidgets with the loose piece of faux leather peeling off. How could a narcissistic, controlling man care about my opinion? I uncross my arms and sit up. "I like the beach."

"Oh really? I was just looking at hotels in Tybee Island. It has so many great seafood restaurants too. Your mother says you love salmon. How about I treat you to a nice fresh blackened salmon? I know a great place." Richard's voice softens, and his posture relaxes a bit.

I look over at him, for once a genuine smile is plastered on his face. He's trying. I guess I should too. "Yeah, that sounds nice."

We still need to agree on a song to perform tonight at school. So distracted by the events thrown at us—like Alister's illness—we can't rehearse or even pick a theme. It's easy picking songs I love, but it's hard picking something that everyone in my school will like. Since I'm not really into mainstream music, my choices aren't going to cut it. I give up and collapse into one of the seats in the school auditorium. The loud, empty bench vibrates from the impact. Alister is better at this type of stuff. He isn't popular but gets around with the ladies because of his big, curly hair. Too bad Nathair sent him off to set up for the Firecracker. "You seem to forget that I'm the opposite of sexy!" I yell at him after he turns down another song for the twenty-third time.

Nathair scrolls through the playlist on my phone. "You know a sexy song, but you just don't want to say it out loud."

"Why would I try to pretend like I'm some seductress when I haven't had a boyfriend in years?" I say. I swear he loves hearing himself argue with people. It is the only explanation for why he always fights with me.

"Because the social chaos comes from a nerdy girl like yourself, busting out of your shell and giving guys hard—"

"Keep it clean, please," I interrupt, holding my hand up in weakened defeat. Immediately after, it flops back down to my side. Slumping in my seat, I stare at Snake Boy in desperation.

"The point is that you need to think of a song you know you can perform and what people can like. I know they're morons. I understand most of the songs you like will hurt their brains, but you got to think of something, or else we might not get our adviser without desperate measures."

"How desperate are these measures?" Of course, if there is another way, I'll take it.

"Well, we can cause a riot, make a bomb threat, murder. It's your choice," he threatens, making me whine.

"This is not fair!"

He throws his hands up in the air. "Sorry, but I'm only doing this because you wanted this."

"Bull, you know help is needed, so you embarrass me."

"It's not embarrassing if you have talent. I keep telling you—" I intercept his oncoming speech with angry emo music. I blast Disturb's "Indestructible" and walk away from him, frowning. "Hey, remember who introduced you to this song!" He talks loud enough to hear over the tune. Lucky for him, I can't finish storming off because I run into Kasha and the kids from the Prom Committee.

"Hey," I say awkwardly.

"Hey, haven't seen you around in forever. I thought you were dead." She smiles.

"Yeah, a lot has happened." I awkwardly laugh, gingerly putting my hand in my hair.

"Well, I hope you can make it to prom, my parents forced me on the committee, and it would be nice if every one of us is there. Get your boyfriend to buy a ticket, more money for the school." She nods in Nathair's direction.

"He's not my boyfriend," I say harshly in his direction.

"Friend then, as I said, more money will equal a senior trip next year, and I definitely would love to go to New York or somewhere else."

"Yeah, that sounds wonderful," I agree.

"Nice music, by the way, very FML, and I love it!" she says, walking to the radio. Oh, Kasha had always been obsessed with emo music. "Are you going to the Firecracker tonight?"

"Um, no, not my type of thing. So many people to push through." I walk over to her, eyeing Nathair, hoping he'll catch on to my lie.

"Oh, are you going? I remember you performing at that club." She turns to Nathair.

Nathair sheepishly rests his hand behind his neck. "Nah, I'm sure those kids aren't into my type of music. How about you, Miss Prom Committee?"

She pouts. "I got grounded for my seventy-two in AP Mathematics, can't."

"But you have an A in that class," I say, feeling a bit relieved that Richard isn't that obsessed with my grades.

"Yeah, but I got a seventy-two on my test. My parents were pissed."

"But you still have an A," I repeat, incredulous.

"I know," she whines. Nathair gives me a confused look. He isn't well acquainted with her, or else he'd know that her parents are strict. Kasha and I were soul sisters in that way: overbearing parents. While mine focused on behavior and appearance, hers focused on academics and careers. I suppose that's why we originally bonded, because of our shared trauma of never being good enough.

"Kasha, we got to go through with this meeting," Miranda, an upperclassman, calls. "You know, minus Criss Angel and the Oreo." She looks us up and down, full of judgment. Kasha opens her mouth to speak.

"We should go anyway," I stop Kasha before she can reply to Miranda's rude comment.

"Oh, okay. Let's try to hang out sometime." She pauses to look at Nathair, awkwardly smiling at him. "All of us."

"Of course," I say, ushering Nathair to the door.

"Wait, Alister—" I shove Nathair out before he can finish his sentence.

"We can call Alister and tell him not to come to the auditorium," I whisper.

"Whatever," he says, leading me to his car.

The concoction of fabric Maebh calls an outfit is a visual overload. This isn't an outfit for the weak, but it is something a leader in a high school movie would wear. Bright and bold, screaming for attention. My knees buckle at the thought of people looking at me in this. Everyone will think I have lost my ever-loving mind. The black crop top complimented the red and black wavy pants. And my combat boots make it edgy but still comfortable. Maebh hands me the mirror to inspect her handy work. My jaw drops at the stranger in the mirror. She has slayed my makeup! Inspired by the monochromatic makeup trend online, I admire my bright red eyelashes, eyeshadow, and lip combo. I look like a red devil but in the best way. "Makeup is done. Now, all we're missing is the hair." Maebh pulls out a brush, spray bottle, and some hair gel.

"Hair? What are you gonna do to it?" I ask. My heart is beating a mile a minute, so fast that I can barely stand.

"Just make it more fantasy-like." Her smile spreads across her face, loving every minute of my makeover.

"Make it fantasy—" I jump when Maebh plunges her hands into my puffball. Her hands spread to every piece like a comb, and it grows longer and thicker! She pulls out my hair tie and brushes my hair into a high ponytail. Swooping my edges into cute swirls, she sets my edges with gel and a scarf.

"As beautiful as you are when nothing is done to you, today's a special occasion!" I look at the whole look in the mirror of my second bedroom. The girl in front of me is gorgeous. She's charming and brave. I touch the mirror only to have her mimic me. I wonder if she feels the same way that I do.

"I can't do this." I shake my head, and the girl in the mirror copies me. I turn around to face everyone.

I hear a soft knock at the door. The boys poke their heads in, fully breaking in once they see I'm dressed. Nathair gasps, stumbling into a chair. Eyes are wide in amazement. "Holy crap! You look amazing." His voice is full of excitement. But then he coughs, calming himself. "I mean, you look good."

Alister joins in, "You look like you are going to drag me to hell, but I'm kinda into it." Maebh playfully hits him.

"Of course, you can do this," Maebh says. She's the only one who is paying attention to my concerns.

"I really can't." I start hyperventilating. Nathair hops up, leading me to a chair.

"Why not, Little Bear?" Alister asks.

"Because I don't do stuff like this. I'm gonna fail, and I'll be the school's laughing stock." My world starts to spiral. Every horrible scenario of what could go wrong flashes before my eyes.

"All you can do is your best." Maebh pauses as if she just had a revelation. "You just need to have—*confidence*," she says, turning to Nathair.

Catching onto her drift, he begins to refuse, "No, I am not using my powers on Raine!"

Maebh charges at him, shaking his shoulders. "It's only to give her some confidence! You know she has the talent, just not the courage to deliver it!"

"No, I'll do it on the audience to love her even if she cries in a corner, but I will not do it on her!" He stands his ground, crossing his arms.

"Raine needs to overcome this, and you're going to deny her that?" Nathair looks remorseful. Maebh's guilt trip is working. "I thought so."

"Okay, just a little bit. Raine, come over here," I comply and face him. His face spells out how much he doesn't want to do this. Grimacing, his eyes flicker. I stare in wonder, hypnotized by the swirls of green. The rattling starts to ring in my ears. Can I do this? I'm horrible, useless, awkward, and—so pretty! My shoulders lift, and the pain in my chest fades away. I look in the mirror. That beautiful stranger is me. I fluff up the long spiral curls in the back of my head and give a bright smile to Nathair. He draws in a quick, sharp breath, looking away from me with a flushed face. I feel beautiful, thanks to him, and all my nervous feelings turned to excitement. It's time to get on stage!

"How are you feeling?" Maebh places a hand on my shoulder.

"I feel like one of you guys," I say, messing with my perfect hair. The mirror is now so hard to leave. I squeal, feeling giddy.

"I've created a monster because of your girlfriend," Nathair says to Alister.

I walk over to him and sit on his lap. "You think I'm a monster?" I throw an arm around his neck.

He shuffles around, words getting caught in his throat and stuttering over his words. "Call me when she's done." He slides me onto the chair and hops up. Wiping his clammy hands.

"Be careful what you wish for, Nathair. You said you wanted social chaos and got it, along with an extremely red face," Maebh snickers. She jingles the keys, holding them up mischievously. "Let's get that phoenix."

I saunter into the backstage area, touching up my lipstick. The rowdy crowd is clapping and singing along to some background music Tamara threw on. The posh girl stops in her tracks to give me a once-over. She checks her performer's list. "Raine Thomas?" Tamara Jackson calls, questioning if she read it right. I saunter up to her, my shoulders leading the way. Caught off guard by my stride over to her, she sucks her teeth at me. "I thought I told you not to do any funny business, Ray."

"I thought you were smart enough to read that my name is Raine, not 'Ray,' Tammy." A senior calls my name to go on stage. So, I take one last glance at Tamara and leave her in her tense silence. Adrenaline flows through my body, and my body feels light like a feather. I walk up the steps. Heavy white lights shine down on me. It is hard to see the crowd. I can only see a silhouette of black figures. Everyone stops cheering, sounding confused. I take a deep breath and put power into my core. I put the mic to my lips and start singing.

> *"Caught off guard by what I want to do.*
> *What I—*
> *I want to do—"*

I sway to the music, expecting people to hate it, but to my surprise, they start bobbing to the music. The song's beat picks up the tempo, and I move to the rhythm.

> *"Stop making assumptions and issues.*
> *People, just let me lose my mind!*
> *It's my life, and I can choose.*

Going round and round, all of these circles.
Bend me, and I'll break.
This is all I can take.
Just let me shine.
Let me see my greatness.
Let me rise.
I was born complicated.
I can think on my own.
I am not your perfect toy.
Let me discover the world.
Let me be my own girl.
Just let me shine."

The audience goes crazy! Beaming, I wipe the sweat off my forehead. I put the microphone to my mouth to sing my last line.

"Don't dim my light."

My senses come back when Nathair lifts his seduction off me. Instead of feeling accomplished, I can barely even remember what happened out there. The high crashes. The crowd cheers, chanting my name. I awkwardly walk off stage. My body locks up on me with each step. Couldn't he at least wait until I was off the stage? I bolt to the dressing room, tripping and shoving everything in my path out of the way. My hands tremble as I peel off my performance clothes. Exhaling, I manage to get changed without fainting—finally getting my shirt over my shaking body. No one made an escape plan for me?

I tiptoe out of the dressing room, whipping my head in all directions to find any of the Fabulous Creatures. "So she wasn't exaggerating. You have changed." I jerk my head at the sound of a familiar voice. Jay looks at me in disappointment.

"Hey," I say, trying to hug him like I used to. He moves away from me.

"So, is it his sick fantasy to have you lie to your friends all the time and perform on stage with this pretentious persona? Did he make you do this?"

"Jay, it was a dare," I say.

"*Did he*?" He raises his voice, putting so much force in it that I jump slightly.

"No, I already told you it was a dare," I say. My voice is small and weak.

"Who are you? You're not the sweet girl I met! You can't even look any one of us in the eye! Sofia is terrified for you, Raine, and I thought she was jealous of him. This isn't jealousy. This is you trading us for a guy! He doesn't even call you his girlfriend, but you act like he's worth more than us!" His voice breaks.

"It's not like that!" The raw emotion flows through me. "I can't tell you why, and all I can say is that it'll get better. I will change, though. People do it all the time."

"Are you doing it for the better, though?" It strikes a nerve when he says that to me. If only he knew the truth.

I can't look at him anymore. I'm not the same girl my friends fell in love with. She is just a sad person, a people pleaser. "Are you going to tell them?"

"I don't have to. They will find out about this. You're probably all over people's feed right now."

"Why can't I have you both? Why can't you guys accept that I'm my own person? I don't have to follow what Sofia says all the time!" I interrupt my friend, tears welling up.

"I can't even deal with you anymore. He's brainwashed you! Sofia just wants to keep you safe from a toxic relationship. That's it," Jay says, face twisted in frustration.

I ball up my fist, trying to hold in my fury. "Well, that's pretty toxic when you feel you have ownership over me and think you have the right to tell me who to have in my life!" I spit out.

Jay reels his head back, nostrils flared. "Well, once this gets out, I don't know if they'll be our friends, maybe mine, but not yours. Since we're so toxic, maybe it's a good thing." Jay storms out, taking all that's left of my former life.

The silent tears fall when Nathair drives me home. Swallowing nervously, he turns up the radio. I lay my head on the window, wiping away my tears. He touches my hand at a red light.

Jay claims I don't care about them, but if I didn't, would I be crying? It is hard to be close to everyone when you must keep this dark secret. Throughout history, humans have proved that they can't handle the knowledge of Fabulous Creatures, and those who did know were sworn to secrecy. As much as I want to be upfront, it's impossible to tell them. How would they react knowing I work for a highly poisonous giant snake? It might seem cool to fantasy lovers, but they haven't dealt with it in real life. I've already had a serpent try to kill me. Twice. What if others come after my friends? I couldn't let that happen because with knowledge also comes danger. Even Aethel doesn't want exposure. Ignorance is bliss.

It feels like an eternity to reach my parents' house. I swing open my bedroom door, bewildered that Jasmine is waiting for me. Calm and still, like an animal ready to strike, my sister gives me a glare I have never seen. It freezes me over. Moving slowly at first, Jasmine chucks one of my shirts out of my drawer! Unleashing her full fury, she starts pounding me with my clothes. "What are you doing?" I cry, seizing her arm. She shoves me off, continuing her rampage.

"I'm looking for my sister! My sweet sister is honest and would never lie to me."

"Maebh bought that stuff for me! What's wrong with you!" I exclaim. Unlike most siblings, we've never tried to kill each other, so this is out of the ordinary.

"What is wrong with you?" she screams, hitting me with one of my new shirts. "I thought I was the cool sister. One that you can go to for anything!"

"What do you mean? You are," I say, defending myself from the blows she flings my way.

She stops, staring deep into my eyes. "Dad disappearing destroyed us. Do you remember you wouldn't talk for three whole months?"

"What does that have to do with you destroying my things!" I shove her.

Jasmine stumbles, catching her fall and holding her furious gaze. "I had to be the strong big sister, hold in my feelings for you. And the least you can do is not sneak around behind my back. I thought it was us versus them. But now most days I feel alone, being tormented by *him*," she cries, breaking down. She hunches over, crying into one of my shirts. I look at my big sister with misty eyes.

"I didn't ask you to do that for me!" I say.

"No, but that's what sisters do. They help each other, be honest with each other."

"Why? You get to go out and party and drink. You can do whatever you please, but as soon as I do the same, it's a problem? Pretty hypocritical, *Big Sis*!" I yell back, now angry and hurt myself.

"All that stuff is to get Richard off of your back! He's had it out for you since day one, I just wanted him to be angry at me instead of you. It's ruined now that you performed at the Firecracker tonight and essentially talked shit about us in your little song." She continues to beat me with clothes I bought without Richard's supervision. "I sacrificed myself for *you*." She freely cries with each whack. "You're only the good girl because I made myself the bad one."

"You are demented! I don't owe you anything!" I fight back. All the anger and terrible memories flow into me. How dare she say she made me a good girl? I was a good girl because I wanted to be, not because my sister is the family screw-up.

"I never asked you to protect me. I never promised to walk behind you for the rest of my life. Deal with it." I punch her arm, using all my strength to toss her off.

"Fine." She stands up and fixes herself. "Since you don't need me to take care of you anymore. I won't bother anymore! I don't take care of liars."

"God, why does everyone think they are looking out for me? You guys have your own selfish agenda. Do you think I don't hear the rumors about you too? You're not innocent either!" I spit back acid. Jasmine pauses and walks out of my destroyed room, slamming my door. I lie there on the floor in dismay. I can't believe I just said that to her.

It takes me an hour to clean my room back up. Replaying "Fixed at Zero" over and over, depressing music is the only thing that keeps me moving. Deflated, I lie on my bed. How could I do something so amazing and many people get angry at me for changing? I cheated when Nathair used his powers on me, so in a way, they were getting mad over nothing. I've lost my friends *and* family. A light tap comes at my window. "Nathair?" I call, getting up to open it.

A burst of heat hits me! My feet lift off the ground, flinging me to the wall like a ragdoll. My back and head crack against a wall. I recoil, pain pulsating through my head and back. Slumping over, my head slides down my vanity. Wood scraping the side of my face. Iron-scented red liquid runs down my forehead. The world spins, and black spots creep into the corner of my eyes. Lead-filled eyelids drag down. I try to keep them open, searching for the source.

"Are you Bennu?" I croak out, pulling myself up enough to look at my assailant. A tan, blurry shape of a dark-haired man with fire-orange eyes appears.

"You know who I am, Raine. I'm your adviser, after all." He darkly chuckles. My eyes give up on me, and all I can see is black.

·SIXTEEN·

Dear Dad,

I don't understand why you left us. I remember when I was a little girl, you used to tell us that your family was the best thing that ever happened to you. Why can't we still be the lights of your life?

-Raine

The haze clears and blood rushes to the back of my head. I take a sharp breath at the searing pain. Though it is healed, the area still felt tender. The bed creaks under my weight. I lay down, looking at the sky in the window overhead. No idea how I got here, but at least I'm safe in the manor.

Wild, scary noises erupt from downstairs—yelling, glass breaking, and roars. I jump out of my bed and rush downstairs.

My head strums a wave of pain, but I focus on my feet, hitting each step. My hand grips the handrail, bracing myself for any accidents. The wood rubs my tacky palms raw once I get to the bottom of the step. Raw and red from the friction, I release my grip and turn quickly into the library.

Rage-filled, ready to kill, the boys pin Bennu to an empty wall. Neighboring bookshelves are tipped over, and poor books are spread across haphazardly. Nathair's sharp fangs are out, and his blue scales poke through. He hisses at the intruder, his forearm pinning his neck tightly against the wall. Alister's eyes are red diamonds, and his sharp claws look ready to dig into the mysterious man. The dragon's nose leaks smoke, and his chest glows a deadly orange, looking like lit coals are trapped inside.

The man, I presume is Bennu, looks bored. He stares back at the angry Fabulous Creatures, not a stitch of fear in sight. Not even a sweat drops from his brow, no trembling, nothing. He is perfectly still, in his full human form. He glances over at me, smirking. "You can call me *Ben*. I am so happy you are awake. We can talk about our contract now." As Bennu, I mean *Ben*, acknowledges my presence, Alister and Nathair let go of him like the fire he controls. With guilty looks, they switch back to their human forms as well. He struts over to me, looking at the boys. "Clearly, we need a contract to protect all parties from killing each other."

Nathair wedges his body in between us, looking down at me. "Are you okay? Alister could smell your wound miles away!" The stark height difference between these men and me is ridiculous. The two opposing men tower over me, one trying to protect me while the other is an enigma.

I didn't get the chance to get a good look at him when he was in my room. Tall with a slender face, sharp and pointy. His eyes are a burnt sienna in the light but look brown in certain angles. Ben's thick brows are close to his deep-set eyes. Everything about him is dark, like his full, lush dark hair. His most prominent feature is his nose. Like a heron, the bridge is straight, not curved, and long. It fits his full lips, which are hidden slightly under his five-clock shadow that is dangerously close to growing into a full beard and mustache.

"Yeah, I'm okay," I lie, my head throbbing. "What about a contract?" The guys pause, except for Ben. The firebird's eyes glow a haunting orange, and a Grinch-like smirk spreads across his face. He steps toward me, eyes glowing like a fire is about to spill out.

"It's just a written agreement saying no matter what happens during this journey, I am not responsible for the outcomes," Ben says smoothly. *Hm, very debonair of him.* Dressed in a blazer with a low-cut shirt, dress pants, and expensive shoes, this man could dazzle any woman into giving him the world. But I can see that he has similar 'quirks' to serpents. Beautiful, intoxicating, but deadly. Just one encounter with him let me know he doesn't have human desires like Nathair and Alister. He is unnatural and heartless.

How can I handle this Creature?

I shuffle from behind Nathair. "Okay, give me the paper." My hand shakes, but I say it firmly. I have to look strong, or he will run all over us.

"What? Raine, he just hurt you!" Nathair says as he blocks me from Ben.

"I'm okay, aren't I? Look, we've summoned him for a reason." I push him aside, walking over to Ben.

"Raine, this is in an ancient language. You have no idea what he could've written." Alister says, glaring at Ben.

"It's a contract, right?" I confirm, keeping my voice level.

Ben looks at me in surprise with a little mix of approval. "Yes, it is, my lady. So we can change it any way you'd like." He's making it too easy, which worries me.

"Write down that you won't betray us for the winning team if the situation arrives. Also, if you hurt any of us, we can do the same thing to you," I demand. "In English, so we can all read it."

Ben's sinister beam makes my stomach crawl, but he bows to me. "Your wish is my command," he says, pulling out an ancient-looking scroll and noting my request. He holds it out to me, showing me proof. The letters wiggle on the paper, sealing the ink with a golden hue.

The contract reads:

1. *The contractor must not harm the contractee and will ensure they arrive at their destination safely.*

2. *Magic can only be used to benefit both parties.*

3. *The contractor will provide a wish to <u>ONE</u> contractee and will only serve them. Other's requests will be considered if the main contractee wishes for it.*

4. *The contractor has a right to withhold information if*

deemed necessary.

5. *In exchange for the contractor's knowledge and escort service, the contractee will provide a favor to the contractor. The contractor will decide based on the extent of their service.*

6. *The contractee can break the contract at anytime, but only if the contractor agrees.*

"We all need to put our blood on this scroll for it to work," Ben explains.

I'm the first to step up, rolling up my sleeves. Ben hands me a needle. Raising it up to my finger, I hesitate. Alister grabs the hand that's holding the needle.

"Don't do it, Raine. He's already broken the first rule in the contract," Alister says. He lowers my hand and takes the needle from me. "Think about it. If he is here to help us, why does he even need a contract?"

"It has so many holes in it, and he holds all the power in it," Maebh seconds.

"Aren't you guys tired of playing it safe?" I ask, surveying everyone's serious faces, frozen in uncertainty. Why am I the only one willing to sacrifice? For once, I feel alone in this house. Divided from my magical friends. My fragility comes to mind. While they all have survival adaptations to protect them from obstacles, I have nothing. I'm just a mortal, so I can't hold any power in this room.

"I'm sorry, Raine, but I'm not signing it," Nathair puts his arms on each side of my arms and turns me to face him. He puts distance between Ben and me. "It's not safe."

"You don't trust my judgment?" I ask, losing the base in my voice now. My strong façade falls into dust. Giving up my friends and family for this was so hard. Yet, I can't have a say? Nathair's mouth opens to speak, but then it falls back down. His silence is all the answer I need.

"Take me home then," I snap, walking to the front door. Nathair gives Ben one more glance and gets his keys. Keeping my mouth shut, I walk to the car. Could anything go right?

The next day, the same school of fakes and hypocrites that cheered for me are all glaring daggers at me. How could you love me at the Firecracker but hate me now? That isn't the worst—sleazy jerks found their new prey in the hallway. Guess who the new lunch special is? So many harsh words are either thrown at me or whispered behind my back. Why is everyone so focused on me? Out of the corner of my eye, Aethel smiles to herself, watching something on her phone. I walk up to her, crossing my arms. Aethel keeps watching her phone and laughing.

"You know, I've underestimated the power of social media," she says. I swallow a lump in my throat.

"What are you talking about now?" I ask, spite dripping in my voice.

"I just learned this myself." She straightens up in her chair, leaning closer to me—as if the snake has the ability to be friendly. "Apparently, you can lace a TikTok with seduction. It's much less work than going around the school and seducing everyone, but I get the same results!" She holds her phone up to my face. My eyes widen at the recording of my performance plays. A small rattle goes off in the background, almost undetectable. It wasn't Nathair's, who was slower and lower in vibration. This one is more delicate in sound and higher pitched. The video title labels me as a quiet mouse who's a secret narcissist. I snatch the phone out of her hands and go to the comments.

My stomach drops as I read the massive amount of hate comments, calling me a fake, a liar, and a slut. Any horrible, misogynistic word you can think of is written down. All for everyone to see and agree with. Is this why everyone is so weird today? "You didn't," I whisper to her.

She beams, so proud of her achievements. "I hope the fifteen minutes were fun."

"Why are you doing this to me, Aethel?"

"You mess with my dreams. I mess with yours." Aethel's eyes glow a terrifying yellow.

"He was never yours to begin with," I say sternly.

"You're sheltered. You never have to worry about where your next meal is coming from or about your failing health. Have you ever lost loved ones to violence and destruction?" She hisses in my ear. "You can get anything you want. Some of us have to work to improve our quality of living. And the only thing I wanted, you took. I could never see a girl like you win. So, I'm going to make your life so miserable that you'll feel like you are in the ninth circle of Hell. Then you'll only feel a fraction of the pain that my people suffer." She reaches out to touch me, and I draw back, not wanting to give her a chance to hurt me again. I throw her phone down and leave for my seat.

All of my classmates whisper about me. Snickering at my expense and commenting on my appearance. Okay, so there's a magical spell that makes everyone hate me. How fun. But I can survive this. They've done worse things to me. The teacher calls me up. Trudging up there, I pass out the test results from last week's exam. "Don't look at my grade!" Tamara snaps, snatching her chemistry test from me.

"That's not even your test. It was the next one." The old me would've let her figure it out on her own and retain her dignity, but now I'm the one with no pride, so I might as well make her feel dumb too. Oh, I'm so bitter. After throwing the other paper back at me, she snatches another paper that isn't hers. It's my test, a one hundred. I crack up and hand her the forty-five she earned.

"You think you're so smart?"

"Yes," I reply curtly, exasperated with all the crap flung in my direction. In a slow, sarcastic tone, I continue, "I'm tired of you picking on me because you're not happy with yourself. I've lived with this for eight years, and I'm done. So, keep your attitude to yourself if you don't want to hear anything from me." I continue to pass out papers, letting Tamara feel insignificant for once. Energy stirs up inside me from all the anger I'm harboring.

The bell sounds once I'm done passing out papers. Frustrated, I hurry and collect my things. I hate to be the last one out of class. With awkward goodbyes to teachers or last-minute tasks, hanging around too long is uncomfortable. I strut to the front of the class, ready to head out the door. Travis bulldozes me over, and my items drop to the floor.

"Excuse you!" Usually, I'd get over it, but when Travis looks back at me and doesn't bother apologizing for knocking someone over, it's hard not to lose it and flick him off. As I gather everything, my pencil rolls away. I stretch out to drag it closer to me. The pencil starts to vibrate under my fingertips. The shaking under my feet grows wild and violent. Is it an earthquake? I slide under a desk, covering my head with a book.

The lights in the room just randomly explode with an electrical surge. One by one, rows of lights shatter and sprinkle glass shards everywhere. The whole row that I stood under crackles over my head! A deadly silence fills the air. I peek my head out to see if it stops. A lightning bolt strikes my eyes! I gasp, expecting pain, but lose my vision instead. Everything turns white.

Wings. All I can see are big, white, and undoubtedly beautiful wings. I reach out to touch them. The silhouette of a woman dances, fire pooling under her. I look at her in wonder as she draws fire with her majestic staff, creating strange creatures. Some are fearsome, and some are beautiful, but none look like they want to hurt her. A glorious white dragon stands out the most. With a long body like a serpent and brownish-red eyes, it is the most graceful thing I've ever seen. He has long whiskers like a Chinese dragon and no arms. The dragon floats, moving in ribbons. He stares at me, his beauty holding me in place. The woman stops dancing to look in my direction, the darkness blocking her face. A sliver of her warm smile cuts through the night. "He likes you."

"Raine, are you all right?" Coach Ramsey runs over to me to check on me.

"Yes, I'm okay, sir." I peek back at the ceiling in wonder. Nothing feels real right now.

"We both had a little scare today, huh?" Coach laughs with relief. "I need to call someone. Something must have short-circuited." I nod and let him walk me to drama class so that I don't get detention.

Today's drama class is calm and jovial. Everyone is practicing their singing. So talented and beautiful, the drama kids are fun to admire. It was a pure accident that I was placed in a class of gifted students. I've learned about playwrights, improved my memory, and even sing, but not enough to consider myself good enough to be in this class. Advanced Theater is the only class I can feel semi-comfortable in. However, I often keep to myself, never fully being part of the community. Nowadays, it is normal to feel alienated. A familiar sense of dread builds in me as my teacher calls out names for our auditions. Crap, I forgot all about it!

Of course, I haven't prepared anything. I can't even sing a song without Nathair's help. I force myself to sing the first thing that comes to mind and head to my playlist on my phone. One of my more alternative songs comes up. It's about a young woman trapped in a tower. Her only escape is the window. She leaves out of the window only to die in the freezing rain. It's a beautiful but sad song that matches my current mood.

The song pours out. My chest is heavy, but my body feels prickly jolts of energy. I tremble a bit but carry on. *Don't miss a note. Please don't miss a note.* I feel the tightening in my throat, but I try to hide it.

Just when I get off the stage, I notice a visitor. One of the guys from another class plops next to Diane Whittingham, our theater superstar. "Pfft, I came over here for the short skirt!" He snickers next to her. Silent, I sit back down and pull out a book. There is no use trying to fight. Feeling bad, I find it hard to pay attention to the story. Maybe it's the loud music of other's auditions. Perhaps it is the roar of laughter made in my direction. Whatever it is, Kasha's favorite phrase comes to mind because of it—FML.

Lunchtime isn't any better. Sofia has that horrible TikTok of me on repeat when I sit in my usual seat. She holds her hand together, looking down at the video in disappointment. "You are such a liar," is all she can say to me. I survey all my other quiet friends' faces. They don't smile, crack a joke, or anything.

"Sofia—"

"Don't talk unless you want to tell the truth for once. Ever since you met this guy, it has been non-stop lies. So, I'm going to let it run its course, and when you get some sense, call me." All I can do is stare desperately at her, begging her to understand.

"Oh man, the seats are already taken." My eyes follow the new kid, Giles. I didn't know my friends had accepted him into the clique. Then again, do I know anything anymore?

"Raine was just leaving to meet with her boyfriend." Sofia's eyes dart off in the distance, urging me to move with her eyes.

"So that's it?" I ask, still in *my* seat.

"Yeah, I think so," she says coldly. Speechless, I rise out of my seat. "I hope he's worth it," she adds. I walk away, not dignifying it with a comment. Where are my feet taking me? Who knows, but my soul is breaking in two at the thought of my life falling apart.

I swing the door of room three twenty-six and drop to my knees, leaning on a desk. I kick the door closed for privacy. The slams echo through the new mini library that Snake Boy built. A sloppy sign labeled "ancient mythology club" is drying on the desk. Little cut-outs of minotaurs and mermaids were left on the desk with string sitting next to it. Holding it together became almost impossible because these cut-outs were the closest I'll ever get to the real thing.

I cried. Big salty tears roll down my face, clogging my nose and dripping into my mouth.

"Raine?" Warm arms wrap around me from behind. Blue-stained fingers ball up, avoiding my shirt, and scissors fall on the desk in front of me. Even though I am pissed at him, I still relax in his body, desperate for comfort. I hit the ultimate low if I have to cry in *Nathair's* arms. Not to mention, I'm not a pretty crier like those girls in the movies. He crouches down to my level and turns my chair to face him. Without a word, he embraces me, tucking my head on his shoulder.

"Can you promise me something?" I ask.

"Sure, what is it?"

"Promise not to be a jerk and throw this back in my face."

He snickers. "I promise. By the way, how am I doing with comforting? Since you're so emotional, I'm trying to learn how to do it," he says playfully.

"*Me?*" I say high-pitched, shooting my head back up to look at the deluded Snake Boy.

"Well, me too, but I don't have to deal with P.M.S."

"You're turning into an asshole, Snake Boy."

"It's what I'm best at." Nathair wipes my tears away with the sleeve of his white hoodie. I sniffle, trying not to leave snot all over him and destroy the only white clothing he owns, but it's too late. Blue splatters decorate the edges of it. Nathair cleans his hands quickly with wet tissues. Once his hands are clean enough, he swipes away more tears with his thumb. Dabbing my eyes with a clean wipe after.

I melt under his touch, new tears forming. "I hate you, Nathair."

He smiles, showing off his bright white teeth. "I hate you too, Raine." If eyes are the window to the soul, then all I can see is his golden heart, ready for the rust to be polished off.

Even in the library, my problems seem to follow me. Thoughts of my friends and family disowning me plague my mind. I shake it off, turning a page in the hundreds of spell books Nathair has. With no spellcaster friends on our side, these are useless. I raise the book to slam it down but then freeze as my empathy returns. I put it away, placing the book gently on the shelf, and another book pops up.

I walk to it slowly as if it is going to jump out and bite me. The spine is a dirty concrete color, with clouds embossed on it. The book cracks as I put it on display.

Puffs of smoke come from the cover, and a feather pops out. What on Earth could this be? I turn the page, and angels fly out. I shut the book and stick it back on the shelf. A strange tune creeps into my head. Placing my palm on my forehead, the familiar song burns in my mind:

"Feathers, feathers falling through the sky
Feathers, feathers, like tears in the night
Heavens, heavens, wipe your teary eyes."

"You okay, Thomas?" Nathair asks.

I jump and drop the book. It tumbles down, bouncing between me and the bookshelf. It hits my foot, and pain follows after. I bend down in agony. Nathair hopelessly stares at me, picking up the book. I look up and wipe *my* teary eye. "You scared me!"

Nathair covers his smile with his forearm, royally failing to hold in his laugh. "I'm sorry."

He's not sorry in the slightest. I rub my foot before standing up straight. "What is it?" I summon another book, letting it fly to me. *Thank you, Maebh, for enchanting the library.*

Many great things have happened since another girl joined the house—the magic Dewey decimal system included. Small crystal pieces listen to our thoughts and search for the book. Once found, they surround the book and carry it to the person requesting it. She tried to make it completely invisible, but in certain lights, I could see them shift around in the air.

Playing with a few books that fly around like birds, I set them down and give Nathair an inquisitive look. His aura is darker now, his features sharpen, and he balls his fist.

Nathair's eyes slant. "He's here."

I put the new book in the nearby nook and saunter out. "Let's get this over with." The door opens itself like a pure gentleman. I pat the frame, silently thanking it. Nathair trails behind me.

We walk down the hallway, which always feels like it stretches the more stressed I feel. Nathair threads his fingers with mine, and I smile at him, letting him lead me the rest of the way.

In the middle of our cozy living room, Ben sits on the couch with his legs crossed. He rests his head on the top of his wrist. "How are you feeling?" He greets me.

"Fine," I lie. So casual and comfortable, Ben whips out the mysterious paper.

"Now, to discuss the contract." He holds it in front of us.

Maebh steps up to him. "We appreciate you coming from your original location to see us, but—"

Alister, usually so friendly, cuts off Maebh, "We're going to find a way to do this without you."

"Are you sure?" he asks, the flames in his eyes spread, seeping out of the sockets. We all stare into his eyes like moths to a flame. My mind starts to feel fuzzy, and I hear a loud ringing. My eyes unfocus and then refocus.

"Yes," Nathair says, sounding so unsure.

"Without an adviser, completing this journey would be almost impossible," Ben reasons, still holding the scroll out to us. We all look at each other, confused. We all agreed that we would find a different way. I feel stupid for even considering getting rid of Ben. "I can strengthen your bonds, which will be needed greatly in the future."

"Maybe he's right, guys," our stubborn bull, Nathair, agrees. Ben licks his lips, his pearly white teeth grinning at him. A reflection of Nathair's dazed expression shines in Ben's deep bottomless eyes.

"He can't hurt us without hurting himself, so I guess so," Alister seconds Nathair's notion. Dragon Boy's eyes fight to stay open. We walk over to the scroll, listless. Ben pulls out a small needle and pricks us on the finger. My blood hits the paper. The sounds of rippling water echo in my ears. Strong winds flow around us, rising with each person donating a drop of blood. Alister adds his portion, and flames engulf us. Ben laughs.

The wave of confusion lifts from me, and I can think on my own again. Regret rings through my body, but it's too late.

"What do we do now?" Maebh's eyes are empty, spaced out. She blinks, regaining some of her consciousness.

Ben rolls up the contract, putting it in his coat pocket. "Glad you are seeing my side now. Lucky for you, Andronicus gave me a key to open the portal to Remone, the coastal realm. This is a great place to start because I know of a dark spell-caster. They'll need a little taming, though." He puts a hand on Nathair's shoulder. Nathair shirks him off, still slow and lethargic.

Nathair rubs his eyes, life coming back to them. "I guess it is official. We will enter the portal of Remone during the summer." He doesn't say anything out of the ordinary, but his hands tremble behind his back. I can imagine how he feels.

Tonight, we've made a mistake.

Tonight, we made a deal with the devil.

·SEVENTEEN·

This is supposed to be one of the most precious memories of my life. As a teenage girl, one of our crowning glories is going to that magical prom night. This is our hallmark moment in movies, books, and TV shows. Our chance to dress in decadent dresses and feel like the royalty we see in the media.

And then there is me: hollow and bitter.

The glittering dresses line up in rows like fields of corn. The giant discount warehouse houses many colors and designs that fit every teen's taste. If this wasn't following such a traumatic event, it would be a core memory. I've read about this moment millions of times, and here I am, finally living in it.

There's a tap on my shoulder. "Can I help you, miss?" I jump out of my train of thought to fake a smile at one of my classmates, Gideon. He looks at me with his striking gray and blue eyes full of innocence. He has a rack of dresses that threaten to fall off their hangers with straps and skirts jumbling together. His lanyard dangles from his neck, tangling with one of the dresses. "Hey, why are you sitting here all alone?" he asks, putting some dresses back on their original rack. The dress pulls on his lanyard, and he jerks forward, looking for the culprit.

I smile at him and gently unhook it for him. Freeing him from the cute, sparkly trap. "Didn't you hear? I'm public enemy number one."

"They're just mad because of how great you looked on stage." He waves it off.

I have seen Gideon around the school before. He is in Jasmine's science class and holds study groups from time to time. A star football player with all his accolades decorating the halls of Darlson High. It's easy to see Gideon, but *talking* to him is another thing.

"Well, thank you." I play with my fingers, avoiding eye contact.

Gideon looks around and starts whispering, "Hey, if you get a dress today, I'll give you a family discount just because you're having a bad week." Oh, he is working. He has to help me. That's why he's talking to me. Of course, no boy would willingly talk to the social pariah without motives.

The will to look for a dress gets sucked out of me each second I stand here. "That's sweet of you, but I'm second-guessing about going to prom anyway." I blow a wayward curl out of my face.

"Why?" he asks, sorting through more dresses.

"Complications." I look away, blinking away a stray tear. Using my index finger, I wipe it away quickly before he can see.

"Oh, is it guy trouble? Need me to beat up someone?" he asks out of the blue, brandishing his fist for my non-existent boyfriend. My mind drifts to Nathair. I've been dropping hints about prom to him all week, hoping he'd have an open mind, but he doesn't care much about the event. He's been ignoring everyone to look for more information on ways to find a spellcaster. The only time I've seen him all week is when I walk to the library and force him to talk to me.

"No." I awkwardly laugh. It is hard having feelings for a guy when he practically runs away at the thought of taking you to prom.

"Are you going to prom with what's his name?" Gideon gags. "Green eyes."

"Nathair? Absolutely not," I scoff, sounding sort of pathetic.

Gideon drops one of the gowns. Bewildered, he picks it up and looks at me. "What, really? I thought you guys were dating." He chuckles. He puts his hand on his chest, fixing his shirt collar. He stands up straight, trying to tower over me. He looks down at me, his expression growing darker and more sensual. Puffing up his chest, he crosses his arms. "Doesn't he know another guy will ask if he takes too long?"

Yeah, right. I can't believe Gideon. He is too nice. No one would be that crazy after the stunt I pulled. But still, I lean on a wall, trying to stay calm. "Hm, I guess it never occurred to him."

"So, how about it, Raine?" I lightly bite my lip. I want to say no if Nathair changes his mind, but what if he never comes around? "I promise to be a gentleman." Gideon dramatically bows to me.

I giggle. "You know what? I like how you presented your proposal. I'll go with you." Gideon gives me an award-winning smile. My heart flutters a bit. This is the most excitement I have gotten this week.

"Well, since you're my date, I'll give you top-secret information on some of these dresses," he says, leaning closer. "There are some dresses that the owner likes to save. Rare dresses for people like Aethel, you know, good advertisers. Plus, my 20% off will take a bit off. Interested?"

"I'm no Aethel." I'm not a giant snake monster with a taste for breaking limbs and designer shoes. How can she afford all that stuff anyway? Alister would probably make fun of me for asking. Obviously, with *magic*. I draw my attention back to Gideon.

"You're the nicest girl in school, so I'm offering it to you." Do I really want this? I am already in the doghouse for changing so suddenly, so a fancy dress for popular girls won't help.

Screw it. Who cares? "I guess it doesn't hurt seeing it." Gideon leads me to this secret room in the back of the store. It is dark, and the only lights are on princess dresses. Most of them are very sexy looking, having short hems and considerable dips in the chest area, but one stands out to me. The sweetheart bodice is encased in silver sequins with a corset back and turquoise tulle ball gown gliding down to the ground. The ball gown's skirt is petite, and it looks like someone took a razor and cut all the princess out of it. It is dark looking but beautiful.

"Nice choice. Looks like it'll fit you like a glove," Gideon says, knowing which one I am drooling over. He strips the dress off the mannequin and walks me back to the dressing rooms. "Here you go, Cinderella. I prefer not to see it on you, so I'll be surprised." I have no problem with not showing it to him. I don't need a second opinion to confirm this is the perfect dress. Like a bride, this dress is 'the one.'

We run to the cash register. Gideon taps away at the computer, working his magic. I beam at him, making small hops in place. Handing him my mom's card, I get ready to show everyone my pick. Jasmine waltzes up with her dress and ignores me. "Jasmine, look, I found a dress!" I point to it as Gideon wraps it up in its protective cover. My sister ignores me, having no interest in seeing it. My confidence drops for a second, feeling a pit in my stomach. But Gideon comes to my rescue. His encouraging smile brightens my spirits. He hands me his phone number and rings up Jasmine. She animatedly talks with Serena about their dates.

We hop into Jasmine's car shortly after, and my phone rings. It's Nathair. "Hello," I answer, curious about what he wants.

"Hey, I need you to come over today and help me with these books." His voice sounds exhausted and low. How long has he been going at this?

I whip out my notebook and check which books I have already read for the week. I am behind. I have three more to check over, but Nathair stopped counting how many I read a while ago. I adjust the phone to my shoulder. "How about you take a break? You sound like you are ready to join the afterlife."

"Raine, he used a form of seduction on us," he stresses for the tenth time. "If he feels the need to control us and trick us, then he can't be trusted. You know, my father warned me of phoenixes. He told me the story of my grandfather. He didn't talk about him much, but he told me a story of how a phoenix helped his friend get dragged to the Underworld. I'm scared that will be one of us." Not that his feelings aren't valid, but it is too late to worry about it now. We've already signed the contract. Sure, we were all upset and kept Ben at a distance, but Nathair doesn't seem to understand what Maebh, Alister, and I seem to get. It's done. Now, all we can do is be careful.

The car gets quiet as the girls try to listen to my call. I clear my throat, watching my words. "Yeah, I hate that poem about the firebird too, but we're stuck with it."

"Oh, you're not alone right now?" he finally asks.

"Yeah, we just finished *prom dress* shopping," I say, hoping he'd come to his senses.

No such luck. Instead, Snake Boy dodges the advance. "Do you want me to come to save you? I'm in the car and know where you're at." I look down at my tracker bracelet. I sometimes forget it is even there.

I think for a second. My family would be more upset with me if I leave. I am so conflicted, but honestly, I'd chew off a limb to get out of the car. Jasmine has made it clear that she isn't talking to me until I break things off with Nathair—even though we are not dating. "Yes, please," I say a minute later.

"All right," he says, showing up next to us at a red light a few minutes later. I get out of the car.

"Raine, are you insane? I'm driving! Where do you think you're going? Our parents will kill me if you run off!" Her face contorts in rage. That is the first thing Jasmine has said to me all week. She whips her body around to look at me in the back seat.

"Places," I say, slamming the car door of the van. Moments like this make me happy to leave my old life. Why do I always have to be the one to compromise?

"You better get back in here or—" She rolls down her window to yell, but I hold up my hand.

"Or what? I'm dead to you, remember?" I hop into the car with my dress, and the green light turns on. "No one is going to miss me anyway." The car pulls off, separating from my sister's car in seconds.

We drive in silence for a few minutes. Nathair bites the dead skin off his lips and taps the steering wheel. I watch him as he fidgets with the radio, adjusts his mirror, and other small annoying things. I put my hand on his, stopping him from changing the radio station incessantly.

"What's wrong?" I ask, though to be honest, I don't have the emotional intelligence to deal with whatever he has going on.

"Raine, I know you're going through a hard time right now," he laments. "Do you need help," his voice trails off, looking at the endless trees passing by in a green swipe, "to fix it?" He finally spits out. "Only if you want, that is."

Too high-strung and irritated to let what he's implying sink in, I can't help but snap. "NO!"

"But I can make everyone friendly to you again."

I shake my head and slap my face, dragging my hand down my face like a cartoon character. "Nathair, you're learning to be human. You can't solve all your problems with your powers."

He clears his throat, "I understand, but it's not hard for me to undo what Aethel did. They can see the performance for how it's supposed to be!" He looks at my evil side-eye. "Just let me help you this one time."

"No!" I say sternly. "Mind controlling—manipulating—" I draw my breath in and correct myself, "*convincing* people is not good. You can't control how people feel or think."

"How come they can do it to you? It's not fair." His eyes glow, and that familiar rattle starts. "At least let me make your sister happi—"

I smack his arm, knocking the color out of his eyes. Outrage pulsates through me as I grit my teeth. Nathair pulls over and looks at me pathetically. "Don't ever use that power on my sister, or I'll never forgive you! Remember how violated you felt when Ben did it to you?"

The color leaves Nathair's face, but he stays calm and still as if I was Medusa. "It didn't feel good," he mumbles.

My eyes pop out of my head, and I continue my onslaught. "So why would you do that to others? Give people a chance to come around or give up. But whatever it is, never take that choice from them!" The seat belt chokes me in the midst of me talking with my voice and hands.

"It's in my nature, Raine." His guilty-laced voice drops as my name slips out of his mouth.

"Then ask me first, don't condemn others for being manipulative, and then do the same!" My voice cracks, "I'll help you be a good person. I'm on your side, but if you're constantly abusing your powers, how can I know you're going to let me feel my own feelings?"

He stays silent for a second, his Adam's apple quivering. "Okay, I'll try to keep my seduction magic to a minimum."

"How do I know you're telling the truth?"

"I don't want you angry at me anymore, but you still look pissed." He says, his big hands clasping over the entirety of his face.

I have to remember that he is coming from a good place. So I cool down, laying my head on the passenger side window. I'm so tired, stressed, and unable to handle another one of his incidents. Next time, I won't be so forgiving. "You have to swear to me. Please, only use it for emergencies." I hold out my pinky. He stares at it incredulously. "Promise," I say sternly and so out of breath from my fury.

He gulps but hooks his pinky with mine. "I promise," he says.

"Stamp it," I demand. We press our thumbs together and seal the pack. "It'll be really bad if you break it. It can ruin our friendship." I warn. He nods, finally understanding the gravity of his actions.

I think about that book that Aethel destroyed a while ago with her heels. I never found out the true way to stop a serpent from using their powers, but turns out I didn't need it after all. The true way to stop a serpent from controlling you is with a pinky promise.

Nathair puts the car in drive, staying stiff and cold for the rest of the ride.

Maebh throws every shoe in her closet out in the living room to see which style would look good with my dress. "You look so pretty!" She gushes, messing with my thick hair. For the past week, I've been confining it in buns to hide it from the people at school. It is nice to have this nice, healthy, thick, coily hair, but with no tracks, wig, or extensions, my newfound hair growth has to be a secret.

"Are you guys done yet? I'm tired of being blindfolded." Alister refuses to see my dress until prom, as if he is a proud dad or something.

"No, they're not." Nathair flips through a book, seemingly recovered from our fight earlier. He hasn't looked up from his books the whole time I have been here. To be invisible to even Snake Boy hurts a bit, but I let my darling fairy friend keep dressing me up. "Love Like Woe" plays on Maebh's phone, and Nathair wrinkles his nose. "Ew, I can't believe you like that Justin Bieber wannabe."

"I love this song," I defend.

"Forget about him. What about a date? I know this loser didn't ask you," Maebh sneers at Nathair.

"Gideon asked me to go with him. He's a senior in my sister's class," I say dreamily. He looks great on paper and is someone everyone would approve of. Even Sofia would come around to Gideon. The thought of having a crush on Gideon makes my stomach flip.

Maybe if this date goes well, I can learn to like him.

"Let me see a picture," Maebh says, pulling out his phone. We search for his name on Instagram. She nods in approval. "Good choice. He's really cute!"

Nathair lowers his book and finally looks at me. "Rumors are floating around that there is a Fabulous Creature hunter around here." He says, changing the subject.

"They're urban legends. FC hunters don't exist. Most Humans aren't strong or dumb enough to take on a Fabulous Creature," Maebh dismisses.

"I'm open to anything since an Aos sí is doing my hair. How'd you find out?" I ask Snake Boy as Maebh fidgets with my hair.

"I talked to some pygmies the other day, and they told me to visit one of their cousins to hear the news that might affect us. He lives here, so I went to see him, and he told me how he was worried about the FC hunter catching him. He is the only one of his kind to live in Georgia. I also went to see some of the Brownies that live here. They worried they would be after them too." Nathair informs.

Maebh turns me around to adjust my dress. I glance at Nathair through my peripheral. "Well, be careful. I'd imagine that you and Alister would be on his to-kill list. After all, you're highly venomous, and Alister is a possible Elder."

"I hate pygmies. They look like mini rejects from *Where the Wild Things Are*," Maebh interrupts, clearly trying to stop FC Hunter's talk.

The terror ringtone goes off again, but I silence it. I am already doomed, anyway. It can't get any worse. It goes off again until I shut off my phone. Before the phone powers off, the last thing I see is a message from Step-Terror.

*Raine, if you keep up this terrible attitude, you will be—*The phone screen goes black. "Hm," I say, slamming my phone on the table.

"Am I interrupting something?" We all snap our heads to Ben. Nathair clenches his jaw, and Alister growls, losing the eye mask. "Is this how you treat your adviser? I was handpicked to serve you, you know."

"Handpicked from hell?" Nathair hisses, his eyes turning into slits.

"Like you can talk serpent, you're on the same scale as me. The difference between you and me is that I have lived more lives than you. So, I'm more useful. I have helped someone transform before you, and I know it is possible with the right tools." Ben's eyes spark, fire floating out in small embers.

"Who was it?" I ask, earning glares from my friends.

"I'll tell you when the time comes." Ben smiles at me.

"How convenient," Nathair scoffs.

Ben waves off his animosity. "Anyway, don't mind me. I'm not here to talk business. I got Raine a gift, an apology for our first encounter."

"She doesn't want anything from you." Maebh looks him up and down and scowls. Going back to her alterations.

"What is it?" I ask quietly, getting exasperated looks from the three of them.

"Why don't you see?" Ben waves his hands and a blue flame forms on the ground. The fire dances around for a moment. A blue Pomeranian puppy with cute white wings materializes, putting out the fire. "This is a Japanese Yokai called a Ha-Inu. Once he gets older, he will be an excellent guardian."

"Are you stupid?" Nathair shuts his book. "She doesn't need a guardian. If she needs protection, she has us." Nathair stands up. I walk over to the sleeping thing and stroke his little body with my finger. His fur is so soft.

"I like him," I say.

"He can also transform into a regular Pomeranian for walks outside. Did I do good, your majesty?" Ben bows.

"Don't call me that," I mumble, picking up the dog. He is a ball of fur in the palm of my hand. Suddenly, in a flash, he switches to a calm brown color with hints of black and gray.

"How do we know that's not a leyak you disguised as a puppy?" Maebh rushes over to me and takes the dog from me. I look at her quizzically.

"What is a leyak? You guys have mentioned them a few times," I ask.

"Leyaks are terrifying spellcasters that shapeshift and eat the entrails of humans. It's a perfect gift for Ben to give you." Maebh hands the dog back to Ben.

"Well, if you don't believe me, you could always kill the poor thing by stabbing it through his mouth," Ben proposes. Maebh glares at him but backs down. "I thought so." He smirks evilly and walks away, tossing the dog at me. I scramble but catch the terrified pooch. The little puppy whines in my hands and shivers. I don't understand how an already dead dog could grow or, for that matter, be tangible, but I put the poor thing on the warm couch.

I spend the night despite Jasmine's threatening texts about my "boyfriend." Still, instead of worrying about it, I just want to sleep where I am most comfortable. Greer—the new name of the puppy given to me—sleeps beside me with a towel under him. Greer's blue fur shows in the moonlight on his sleeping form. The cute little boy has been asleep since I got him. I want to follow him into a deep sleep. It takes me a while, but I dig my face deeper into my pillow until all I can see is darkness.

No longer in my bed, I drift to a different world. It is raining hard, and lightning strikes, thunder follows it. Wherever this was, it was not in the human realm. Nothing around me looked familiar.

A thousand needles tickle under my skin, and lightning jets off my arms. My fingers twitch, needing a release. Pointing my jittery hand to the sky, a giant lightning bolt jolts out of me, crashing into a strange tower! The tumultuous, crooked tower nearby calls to me, echoing my name faintly. I walk inside, a cooing sound greets me. On a different floor, a spell is cast in a foreign language. I follow it up the stairs and walk to a room on my left. Inside, a tiny transparent being hovers over Ben. "Go lure the hunter to us!" he commands. The being flies off at the speed of light. Like a ferocious villain, his head snaps in my direction and snickers.

"My Liege, you must not be so nosey." His body turns black, and wings rip out of his back, the blood splattering everywhere! I stare into his haunted orange eyes as he turns into a giant bird, slowly cracking disgustingly with every bone in his body to the desired shape. The black phoenix roars at me, and I back up. Ben flings himself at me and impales my stomach with one of

his claws! I cry as the fire burns my insides, crawling up my torso and neck. The sizzling pain silences my screams. Falling to the ground, my head grows light, and I writhe on the floor, hearing his evil laugh echo in my ear.

My sweat muddies all my senses as I sit up in bed. I touch my face. Asphyxiated, I gobble air into my lungs like I haven't in a thousand years. Isn't that a bad omen to see your death in dreams? Whatever it is, I still step out of bed and touch everything on my body. Impulsively, I pick up Greer and walk into Nathair's room.

When I open the door, the serene blue comforts me. I don't waste any time and pathetically crawl into bed with him. Greer is placed in a safe spot where no one would roll over on him. One sleepy eye pops open to survey me. I wait for him to say a mean comment and kick me out, but all he does is close his eyes again to sleep. He throws his arm over me and pulls me closer. My mind is put at ease as I listen to the rhythmic beat in his chest. I lightly smile to myself, snuggling up to him. The soft skin on his neck brushes up against my face. Right now, I am where I want to be. I finally float off into sleep. Dreaming of darkness never felt so sweet.

The next day seems uneventful. I pass through my classes with good participation and peacefully eat lunch alone in room three twenty-six, our headquarters. Honestly, I have yet to find out where the others are today. I haven't seen anyone since last night. The strange thing is that I woke up in my own bed this morning. Nathair thought out how I would get to school. He called a car for me, letting me sleep a bit before heading there.

It isn't until the afternoon bell rings that the day turns strange. I innocently walk to my bus when I am stopped by tiny men hiding in the bushes. They are about the size of a hand and wear thick clothes made of leather and wool with small workers' shoes. Judging by their brown skin, I think they are brownies! "Hey, miss, come over here to Hamish, will ya?" I tiptoe over to Hamish and his tiny crew of six. "Nathair sent us to come to drive you home."

"Drive me home?" It would take about four to see where they are driving!

"Don't worry, sweet. There are more of us in the car. This is Ian, Cameron, Glenn, Brody, Clyde, and Tyree." He introduces the girl last, especially beaming. I shyly smile and wave.

"Well, don't just stand there. Follow us!" Hamish laughs with a strong Scottish accent. I shrug and carefully walk with them, ensuring no one else can see them. It would be hard to explain why tiny brown people the size of my hand are running around the school. They lead me to a lovely, recently-restored '96 Cadillac. As promised, twenty more brownies excitedly wait for me. They bombard me with questions on how they can help with my homework, care for my puppy, do chores, and do many other things I should do alone. When legends say brownies are helpful, they forget to mention how they need to do something to pass the time, which includes chores. The ones that aren't talking up a storm are driving. As I expected, they stand up on each other, and Hamish steers at the top.

He would yell brake or gas to four brownies stationed down where feet usually are placed. Surprisingly, they are pretty good drivers.

"So, guys, why'd Nathair want you to come to pick me up?" I ask nonchalantly. This is just a regular Tuesday to me now.

"He's out trying to find that hunter. We're scared for our lives in Dahlonega." As if on command, they all—except Hamish—shiver in unison.

"That's sweet of him to help you guys out."

"Yeah, after we told him we could help around your house, he said he'd track this guy down," Basil says proudly. That's Nathair for you. Even when being selfless, he finds a way to be selfish. "We're here, sweet," Hamish announces as I look at the manor with a gleam in my eye. My eyes focus on a strange note on the door. I gasp as I get closer to read it:

<u>Fabulous Creature Findings:</u>

<u>Fabulous Creature:</u>	<u>Report to Nathair:</u>
Pygmies	N/A

<u>Realm:</u> Human Realm

<u>Human Country it is Associated with:</u>

They originated from Russia and Ethiopia.

<u>Notes:</u>

Small dwarf-like creatures that build houses underground and weld axes. Aristotle and Pliny wrote about them. Since they are so small and keep out of sight, in fear of humans, Elders have allowed them to live in peace with humans. There seems to be one in Georgia that needs Nathair's help.

Fabulous Creature Findings:

Fabulous Creature:	Report to Nathair:
Brownies	N/A

Realm: Human Realm

Human Country it is Associated with:
More widely known in Europe around Ireland and Scotland.

Notes:
Helpful little brown men from Scotland and said to help families when they are sleeping with chores. Like pygmies, Elders have allowed them to live in peace with humans. They will stay in the manor until further notice.

Fabulous Creature Findings:

<u>Fabulous Creature:</u>   <u>Report to Nathair:</u>

Ha Inu   N/A

<u>Realm:</u> The spirit Plane

<u>Human Country it is Associated with:</u>
A type of Yokai from Japan.

<u>Notes:</u>

A yokai that is a blue dog with wings. In Japanese folklore, it is said to guard the home of its master after its mysterious death.

Fabulous Creature Findings:

<u>Fabulous Creature:</u>   <u>Report to Nathair:</u>

Fabulous Creature   Yes, if spotted

Hunters aka FC Hunters

<u>Realm:</u> Human Realm

<u>Human Country it is Associated with:</u>

More popular in Europe, but there seem to
be divisions in each country.

<u>Notes:</u>

A small group of humans actively hunting
and searching for Fabulous Creatures. Like
Elders, they believe in balance, but they
think no Fabulous Creature belongs in the
human realm because they have supernatural
advantages. They are a glimpse of what
humans might do if everyone discovers that
magic exists. There is one hunting my
friends. I need to find out who it is.

·EIGHTEEN·

On a lovely sunny Saturday, a torrent of emotions stirs inside. Nathair has put his barrier back up. If he gets within a five-foot radius of me, he always leaves to make himself busy.

"Raine," Maebh calls in a cheerful sing-song voice. She practically floats into the room, eyes bright with a slight golden hue. Speckles of her dust still on her face, she holds up my newly altered dress with a triumphant smile.

"Yes, Mae?" This is her third time telling me that this is the last alteration. It's official, though fairies are very stylish creatures, they are also perfectionists! She happily scurries over to me with my poor, chopped-up dress.

"Today is the day! Try this on, and I swear this is my last time improving it." I cock an eyebrow since my good friend has been delusional all day. "Oh, and I made your shoes!" she adds. I gingerly take both items and go to change. "Where do you think you're going?"

I glance at her, befuddled. "To my room?"

"Why? Just strip here!" Maebh starts by pulling off my jacket.

"But what if Nathair or Alister walks in?"

"Pfft, Nathair is too obsessed with Ben right now to care, and Alister better not look at you *or* I'll kill him!" Maebh says, shouting the last part. The whole house shivers. Not even the wind wants to speak. Her terrifying reasoning is good enough for me. So, I proceed to try on the dress.

Before I can get the dress over my hips, everybody's favorite Snake Boy busts in. "An A Bao A Qu is running amuck in downtown Atlanta!"

I swiftly pull the dress up to cover myself. The glow leaves Maebh's eyes as her gaze follows his frantic packing. "Let me guess, Ben is up to this?" Maebh replies dryly as she zips up my dress.

"Well, who else would want to?" Nathair calls back, throwing potions and small traps in his bag hastily. My phone goes off again. Disgruntled, we all moan and groan. Nathair snatches my phone away, answering it. With a glint of frustration, fangs poke out of his mouth. "You will give her some space and deal with this at a later time, old man!" My phone makes a soft click. Nathair's human face returns, handing me my phone. "I'm sorry, I'm just so tired of hearing that stupid ringtone."

I snort. "Me too!" Normally I would be angry for him using his powers, but the 'rents are a lot to handle by myself. I need the backup.

Maebh joins in, "Me three."

Nathair looks me up and down. "And Raine, get dressed in your room. We're not nudists." Before I can reply, he speeds off out of the door.

"So that's it? 'Get dressed in your room?' So he's really ignoring the fact it's prom day?" I ask Maebh, gesturing to the door.

She shrugs at me. "No worries, Gideon will appreciate you." Maebh pats my back and places my shoes in front of me. She has done an excellent job with everything. One side of the dress is short and flows delicately to the floor on the other side of me. Then the heels are just plain pumps encrusted in genuine crystals. A full-on diva shoe.

"It's pretty, Maebh, but only Cinderella deserves this."

"If you're not Cinderella, then who are you?" Maebh combs her fingers through my hair, adding volume.

"I don't know. The ugly stepsister? I can't get Nathair to admit he likes me or go to prom. So ridiculous! Isn't Cinderella supposed to be this beautiful, nice girl that gets a happy ending? Almost everyone I know hates me," I vent.

"You're right. You can't be a Cinderella. I see you as a stronger character." Maebh pauses for a moment to think. "Like Mulan!"

"Okay, now you just want to hear your voice, Mae," I scoff.

"No, listen, we're making an adventure to see if we're more than just rejects. Mulan formed her own fate, and that's what you and the rest of us are doing. You may not feel like it yet, but you'll realize you're strong like her one day." Maebh smiles as she braids the front part of my hair.

"All I'm feeling is the rejected part."

"It'll come," Maebh assures.

My mother and Richard proudly crowd around Jasmine and her date, taking hundreds of pictures. I haven't gotten the same treatment. 'The van incident'—when I ditched my sister to ride with Nathair—made my mother lose all hope for me. Any progress we made about our feelings is gone. Lost. Deleted from her memory.

Overthinking once again, I make myself sick. The smell of bleach and cleaner fills my nose, contributing to my not-so-sunny disposition. Richard must've gone on a cleaning rampage.

"Congratulations, Jasmine, such a beautiful young lady." Richard smiles, patting her shoulder. I silently agree. Jasmine's dress is a striking red dress that flows beautifully down her legs. Form-fitting at the top, with boning in the bust area and gathering into a pretty halter tied in the back. However, Jasmine has long hair with curls cascading down her back to give some modesty. For once, her makeup is simple but has a commanding lip color that only makes her plump lips look even more attractive.

My sister is beautiful, but I wish she could say the same. I want to feel pretty, just like any other girl. And like any little sister, I want to look up to my big sister. She's the oldest and the wisest. What she says matters to me. I hope she can understand that. Maebh does, and she isn't my blood sibling.

"Raine," my mother calls. I snap my head a little too eagerly in her direction.

"Yes?" I ask as sweetly as I can sound.

"Bring me that other camera. This one is going dead. I need more pictures of your sister." My head drops. Even my mother hates me. I can't seem to win. With that familiar choking feeling, I walk to my mom to give her the camera. She looks me right in the eyes and pauses like she wants to say something but turns away from me. She doesn't ask me if I want any pictures before Gideon shows up. I look down at the ground as she returns to taking photographs of Jasmine. I pathetically sit down again. Maybe next year, for Senior Prom, my mom will take photos of me. Maybe next year, Richard will say I'm beautiful too. Perhaps, I am just being selfish. This is Jasmine's last year of high school, and I have all next year.

Whatever the reason, I get up, walk to "my" room, and dial Nathair's number. I dab my eyes with a tissue, trying not to ruin my makeup. The dial tone rings continuously. The voicemail answers a minute later.

This is Nathair.

Please leave a message.

Unless you're Thomas and Alister, just text me, dweebs—

Well, I'm flattered.

I chuck my phone onto the bed. He must've made this voice message before our disagreement. *Fight?* I have no idea what to call it since I cannot find the source without him opening his mouth and communicating. His favorite word.

I want to talk to you, call me back. I text him. My eyes squint as the read report changes to *read.* I nod my head, anger bubbling up to a low simmer. Cool. He's ignoring me. I could've found the A Bao A Qu, and he wouldn't have known.

Desperate, I plop down on my desk and write to the only person who will listen:

Dear Dad,

I'm going crazy! It feels like everyone hates me. Even this guy I like is acting like I have a disease! Dad, I don't understand why people can't just accept that I can't tell them the truth. Instead, they label me as a liar when I'm working for a serpent in reality! It's getting so hard that I want to shout at the top of my lungs, `MAGICAL CREATURES EXIST, AND I NEED TO HELP ONE OF THEM!' Especially Jasmine and Sofia. You should feel honored, Dad. You're the first human I've told.

–Raine

A strange breeze blows past me, knocking over my cup of pens. I jump up, trying to catch them before they fall off the table. My eyes land on one of my pink pens. I turn my head, curious. It says, '*I love you*.' Grabbing all my things, I set them back in their proper place. The doorbell rings. I glance over at my letter. Some hand sanitizer fell on it, rendering it un-readable. The door rings again. I hide the remains of my stupid letter and walk down the stairs.

Walking down, it looks like it is straight out of a movie. The girl walks downstairs, and the guy stupidly gawks at her and says an unintelligible one-word description of his feelings. It is so cliché but cute. All my insecurities about myself disappear. I don't mind being that girl walking down the stairs for once.

"Wow." Gideon smiles.

I innocently smile back. Sure, it is nice to be admired for once, but I still have this weird desire to have Nathair staring at me in a suit. "We should go," I suggest since my mother and Richard take no interest in taking pictures of me. It's official: I'm the new family screw-up.

"I hope you don't mind that I got a limo." *He's perfect.* This can't be happening. Perfect, a word I once hated, is the only description I can give the guy.

"No, I don't mind." I lightly laugh as I hook arms with him. In pleasant silence, we walk to the limo. My corsage sits in the leather seat and greets me—Baby's breath. It is a pretty shade of blue, making the pathetic rose I bought Gideon look unanimated. Awkwardly but sweetly, he ties it to my wrist, and his cute smile plastered on the whole time. It isn't until I pin his rose that I feel optimistic about going with Gideon. I feel like a teenager again, awkward and so imperfectly perfect. No one calls me a liar or expects me to do impossible things like find shamans or mages. Gideon represents the things I miss about my old lifestyle. The only thing missing is my friends.

I am thankful we don't run out of things to discuss at our Pre-Prom dinner. Gideon is the perfect guy. I can fall for him more if I hang around him. That would fix everything wrong in my life, wouldn't it?

"I'm a total alt-rock fanboy. I'm surprised I don't have a bunch of posters on my wall or something," Gideon says, snapping my attention back to him.

"Really? You're gonna have to send me some of your favorites." I pull out my phone and scroll through my playlist. "What else do you like?"

He grabs my hand, admires it, and takes the opportunity to give me a quick massage. "Like the nails, Raine," he explains. My eyes shoot wide open and I start to sweat under my armpits but let him continue. I smile through my shyness, taking in slower deeper breaths to cool down. He pauses, finally letting my hand go, and taps his temple. "Oh, I can rap."

"No, you can't!" I twirl my hair with my glittery nails, compliments of Maebh's salon.

"I swear!" Gideon crosses his fingers.

"Okay, freestyle then!" I laugh, gesturing for him to go on. He fake-clears his throat and makes some dramatic gestures of his own. I lightly hit him, and he starts his rap. He pulls this lame rap about a prince searching for his Cinderella. Though it is simply worded, he does have poetic flow and great use of figurative language. Is that lame of me for liking that it has figurative language? After he finishes, I make fun of his G-rated rap.

Everything is fine until a small leather-bound book slips from Gideon's bag. On it is a rough red carving that resembles a six attached to a cross. With one hand, I pull it out and show it to him. "What's this?" I ask, nervous.

"Oh, that," Gideon says calmly. "My mom is obsessed with occult stuff. She got me into it too. There is a crazy urban legend that a magical world parallels ours. This is a different language from a realm called Carmena. It means 'hunter.' It's not real, just a fun hobby of ours. These are just dumb little fairy tales," he assures.

I nod, taking a closer look at it. "Oh, so Mothman is real. He is just from the parallel world?" I say. But this is no laughing matter. His mom is carrying some strange artifacts. How would she get these without the help of a Fabulous Creature? I hold up the book, still looking skeptical. "Your mom lets you take this stuff with you?"

"Not really. I kind of borrowed it from her." He shyly scratches the back of his head. "You don't think I'm some cult freak now, do you?"

"Oh no." I lightly laugh, going through my purse to see if I brought a potion to translate this book. After the note left at the manor a few days ago, I must be careful of everyone.

"Raine, you okay? You know it's fine if you're a little freaked out. It is a third-date kind of topic." I just innocently smile as I look harder for that darn potion.

"One second, I'm a little sick. I need to take my medicine." I brightly smile, looking at him. I find one in my purse and take it in one gulp. "I'm an occult nerd myself. When I turn eighteen, I want a tattoo on my shoulder. How about you? Tattoos are really hot." I stumble out, failing again at this flirting game. Nathair taught me a thing or two, and one of the things he mentioned was hunters and how they always have a tattoo of their insignia on their right shoulder. One that looks awfully familiar to this book.

"Trying to check for something, Raine?"

"Well," I glide my hand toward him. Please don't let whatever sliver of feminine wiles I have fail me, "let's pretend it's our third date."

"All right," he says on cue. I laugh. Winking at me, Gideon shows me his right shoulder. It holds a tattoo, all right, but not anything fabulous or mythical. It is just a cross—which looks attractive on his arm. I can't help but feel relieved, but that still makes his mother a suspect. "Is my shoulder to your liking?" he asks.

"Yes, it's a nice shoulder." Relief washes over me, ready to flirt. He is no Nathair, but he is perfect.

They do an excellent job picking out this expensive hotel in Atlantic Station. All the kids chose 'A Night at the Emmys.' So they've put up anything red and shaped like a star. Gold stars hang from the ceiling, and it lacks effort, honestly. They've only depended on the beauty of the hotel. The music varies. Thanks to Kasha, we have a good range of songs that most could agree on. Sure, they play some rap, but I got a little pop and a rock song. I have been dancing with Gideon about as much as I can. With the stress of Nathair, having to tend to his dilemma of the missing Fabulous Creature, and Gideon disappearing randomly—the date hasn't been as lovely as the dinner.

Snake Boy has been pacing around prom all night. He got a tip that a Fabulous Creature needs help in the area. The pounding rain is so loud that you can hear it between song breaks, and the blinding lightning is a dead giveaway that the A Bao A Qu is running amuck. "Any news?" my tormentor, Nathair, asks me for the third time. My eyes twitch.

"I think his mom may be the hunter," I say, annoyed. I haven't seen the A Bao A Qu all night, and Nathair constantly has me walking around searching for it.

"If his mom is one, then he is too. Mama didn't raise a regular human. Sorry, your perfect guy ditched you again. Maybe he's stabbing the A Bao A Qu as we speak," Nathair says as he hands me a cup of punch. I down it, crushing my cup. Darn, no one spiked it.

"Listen, you're acting like it's my fault this thing is out! By the way, Gideon isn't a hunter because I checked his shoulder like you told me to."

"Raine, it's okay if you're madly in love with a baby mermaid killer, but you must have some standards. He's just going to shank a leprechaun at your wedding." He cruelly laughs, taking a sip of his drink.

"At least Gideon isn't scared to admit what he wants and doesn't lie about it," I say, tipping his drink so it falls on his black t-shirt and jeans. "By the way, this is a formal event. Put a tie on," I whisper in his ear, hitting him on the side of his stomach, and I'm not gentle either. I walk away to enjoy a few moments before he follows me.

"Raine!" Gideon calls in the distance. This is the fifth time Gideon has disappeared from my sight. I start to wonder if it is the fact that Nathair keeps interrupting our time together with questions on the A Bao A Qu or if he has a "good reason."

"You're great when you're here, Gideon, but I should go home. I have no business here, honestly." I sadly smile.

"I feel bad, but I don't want to leave it like this. The dinner went so well."

"It could always be worse," I joke.

"I want to make it up to you, take you somewhere nice whenever." Gideon's eyes dart to Nathair. He pulls me away and puts distance between Nathair and me. He clears his throat. "I can't let a pretty girl get away and not know I like you."

"But we've only talked for a week?" My face feels flushed.

"But we've known each other for three years, and quite frankly, you can do much better," he whispers, nodding in Nathair's direction.

"I'll call you if I find the time then, and whatever our make-up prom is, it better be good." I playfully poke him, and that's when he leans in to kiss me. My nerves shoot up as I feel Nathair's eye burn into me. Turning my head, he misses my lips and gets my cheek. *Smooth one, Raine. So smooth.* I mentally slap myself, calling myself a series of expletives. I can't believe I did that. My body freezes, and I look over at Nathair.

Snake Boy hides behind the drink table, pretending to get a refill, but the ladle misses and pours back into the communal bowl. We lock eyes for a moment, and he whips around, taking a sip from his empty cup.

I look back at my date. My confidence is annihilated. "That's okay. Just be careful, please. I can't help but think you're getting mixed up with the wrong type." He gives me a small, crooked smile, and I finally frown. I've smiled all night at him, had fun hanging out with him, and he is almost perfect, but I can only think about the idiot over by the drink table, who looks back with an hors d'oeuvre in his mouth.

"I'm sorry, but bye, Gideon." I finally run off, too mortified to keep up this charade.

It's time to find that damn A Bao A Qu.

The huge conference doors close behind me with a loud thump. I rest against it, letting the wood cool down my body. My eyes close as I re-center myself. A familiar cooing sound reaches me. My heels click on the gorgeous marble tiles ahead of me, only to be silenced when my shoes hit the bright red carpet. My dangling earrings jingle in my ears, making it hard to make out the strange noise. My body pulls me to a hallway on my left that is remote from the rest of the hotel. I walk down, fully alert to my surroundings. In front of me lies a doorway that looks like where the hotel staff goes to take out the trash. Not again. This is how I met Alister. I groan and crack open the heavy twin doors.

A silvery being bobs in the air. The A Bao A Qu has a silver light with many tentacles dangling down its body. It coos once again and flies away. "Hey, wait! I'm not trying to hurt you!" I call and run after it.

The A Bao A Qu leads me to the back alleyway in the rain. I hesitate. The black girl within me doesn't want her hair or dress to get wet. It coos again, forcing me out into the rain.

"All right, I'm a drowned cat because of you, so you're going to come over here peacefully and let Nathair take you home!" I nag the creature. The A Bao A Qu trills and zooms over to me once I mention home. It wants to get to its perfect form. The A Bao A Qu has to follow a pure person up the stairs in the Tower of Victory. It sure can't do that if it's running around town! "Aww, good boy," I praise, patting it. Its skin feels like the surface of a peach.

The door slams, and I jerk in its direction, still having a hand on the A Bao A Qu. Nathair runs out, looking worried. "Raine, you okay?" He jogs to me.

"Yes, why wouldn't I be?"

"The A Bao A Qu scared the caterers, and they knocked over a heater! They just now put the fire out."

"That can't be true. I just caught him." I gesture to my little friend. The little creature trills in agreeance with me.

"He's been here? Then wh—" A giant sword slices through the air, parting us! We jump away, opposite sides of the sword.

"Get away from her, *serpent*!" a familiar voice demands. My neck creaks in the direction of the attack. Gideon, now jacket-less and with rolled-up sleeves, holds the giant sword. His big, red tattoo is fully visible. The cross is now gone, replaced by the mark of a hunter. My eyes widen in horror. "You better not have hurt her!" Gideon calls, his voice ricocheting through the alley.

Nathair chuckles, his eyes turn to green slits, and his fangs sharpen. He steps toward Gideon. "You stab fairies for a living, and you have the nerve to assume *I'm* hurting her." He pushes his hair out of his face. "Look, just let her go inside, and I'll deal with you alone." The air around Nathair stiffens, and his scales start to flare, crawling up from under his shirt. Nathair cracks his neck, fiercely staring at Gideon.

Gideon gulps, backing up and pointing his weapon at Nathair. "It is worse than I thought. It's a high-level one. Raine, get behind me. I'll protect you!" Gideon insists, seizing my arm. I pull away, fighting to get from behind me.

Nathair rattles, and the humanity in his eyes drains the longer he stares at his prey. "Let her go, and you can have me," he hisses, stepping closer to him, "Or are you scared?" He mocks as his rattling continues. My arms quivered in fear, or so I thought. I look down at the hand that Gideon held captive and realize that I'm not the scared one. Nathiar's cold eyes look hungry, ready to tear into him.

"Your seduction doesn't work well on me, you know," Gideon presses his sword into Nathair's chest, not breaking skin yet. "Raine, stay behind me."

"No!" I yank my arm from him and dash behind Nathair, ripping him away from the sword. Nathair snaps out of his bloodlust, and his snake features vanish at my grasp. "Look at me. You don't want to do this. Neither of you." My eyes sting from the raindrops as my head shifts back and forth between the two boys.

"He threatened us first. I am just doing everyone a favor!" Nathair's chest heaves under my hands, but I keep him in place.

"Raine, I am here to save you. I know this monster has been tormenting you for months." I turn only my head to look back at Gideon. His eyes.

They have slits in them.

"What are you?" I say, keeping one hand on Snake Boy's chest. I turn to face Gideon once more. Gideon's duo-toned eyes flicker at me. His skin is a pale gray, and his blue veins are more prominent. I squint to see his fangs. "You're a Fabulous Creature." It wasn't a question.

"Listen, I am not the enemy. I'm just a—"

Nathair cuts him off, "He's a Dhampir, half human and half-wraith. Those eyes are a clear giveaway. Careful, he can use seduction too," Nathair warns.

"Half human is better than a full serpent. I can assure you of that." Gideon scowls, charging at us. He shoves me out of the way and swings his sword at Nathair. Snake Boy dodges it with the blade only a centimeter away from his face! The serpent doesn't even flinch.

"Stop it!" I exclaim and run back in front of Nathair. I push Snake Boy directly behind me. Giving Gideon a dirty look. "It was you who was hunting the brownies and the pygmies. You're scaring everyone! Leave them alone."

"I'm sorry, Raine, but this is my job." He smiles sadly at us. "I can't let creatures like him run around and hurt people."

"You're the only one here hurting people! All the creatures here just want to live peacefully." He is supposed to be perfect. How could he be so cruel?

"I can't believe you are defending him. I am the good guy. My organization restores order and balance to the world. He's brainwashed you into thinking otherwise." Gideon says with full conviction. I keep Nathair behind me, holding him back from going for Gideon's neck. No need to prove the hunter right. Gideon exhales, putting his sword down. "I'm disappointed, serpent, getting your girlfriend to save you?" Gideon says.

Nathair's voice shakes in amusement. "Hm? Is that so? From my point of view, she's protecting you."

"Please don't think I am done with you. I will get back up. Only because I know an angry dragon will be at my heels once I take you down," Gideon threatens. He looks back at me in disappointment. "Raine, it looks like we'll have to postpone our date."

My face falls, unamused. "Yeah, let's take a rain check."

He holds his arms up, putting away his sword. Gideon glances at me once more and then leaves into the darkness.

Nathair reaches for the white glowing creature hidden behind the storm drain above us. He holds the white ball in his palm, trying to rub my shoulder with his other hand.

"No." I shake my head, shrugging him off. "You're just as bad right now."

His face softens, and his soft human features come back. "Why?"

"I hate you too!" I yell, walking away from him with the A Bao A Qu. "You ignored me all day, and then you try to get into a fight with my date. And if I let you, I feel like you'd have no problem killing him." I hunch over, rubbing my destroyed makeup off my eyes.

"I was definitely going to kill him," he jokes.

"That's not funny. None of this is a joke!" I yell, spiraling into madness. I hear that dreaded rattling. "Stop reading my emotions! Anyone from a ten-mile radius can see I am PISSED OFF!"

My whole night is ruined. My family ignored me, I had dinner with—and liked—a murderer, I look like a drowned rat, and I had the guy I wanted to be my date try to kill someone! All because I decided to be an idiot. I saw the book and chose to believe his fake tattoo.

"Hey, you guys found it!" Maebh prances out of the backdoor, Alister behind her. Their smiles fall once they see my stone-cold face.

"You guys take this back to its home," Nathair orders before anyone can ask questions. Not knowing how to handle the situation, they awkwardly hold onto the A Bao A Qu. The thing squirms in Maebh's arms. "I'll take care of her, don't worry," Nathair says. Maebh and Alister look at each other, hesitant, but agree. Assuming Alister will fly there, I don't say anything. I can't say bye even if I want to. The closed feeling in my throat stops me. The rain doesn't help, either. It's making everything feel worse. "Raine," Nathair says. He kneels to my level.

"What?" I cough. My nose is two clogged straws.

"Come on, let's get you out of the rain." He points to an awning. "I'm sorry about everything. I was trying and *failing* to stay under your radar. After you got upset with me for using my seduction powers too much, I just tried to give you some space. When I heard the guy was taking you to prom—" He sighs, turning his body away from me for a moment, and then looks back. "I admit I got jealous." His hands start to rub my wrists and back gently. He helps me stand up. I tumble in my heels, but he steadies me. "But just because he was dumb and a coward doesn't mean he deserved to get swallowed alive—"

"You're hurting me!" I yell in his ear, still heaving.

"Where?" He jumps, checking for any injuries.

"Not physically, stupid!" I huff. "Emotionally. It's always extremes with you. Anytime something gets hard, you force it to go your way, or you go cold and ice me out."

"You're right. How about I let some of my pride go away?" He grabs my hands, holding them to his chest. I look up at him, and his sincerity pours out from his eyes. In the rain, they sparkle like gems. "Raine, will you have this last dance with me?"

I look at him like he is nuts. "There's no music."

"Sure there is," Nathair replies, pulling out his headphones. I laugh a little. Placing a bud in my ear, I am surprised at his song choice. It's "Love Like Woe," the song he insulted earlier on Maebh's playlist. I sniffle a little and hesitantly take his hand.

We dance under an awning in the rain to the tune of Nathair's off-beat singing. I lean back my head, grinning ear to ear, and take a deep breath. The anger and sadness from the day leave with my exhale. Warm, fat raindrops run down my face. The sky is crying tears of joy.

Fabulous Creature Findings:

<u>Fabulous Creature:</u>	<u>Report to Nathair:</u>
A Bao A Qu	No- crisis solved

<u>Realm:</u> The Spirit Plane

<u>Human Country it is Associated with:</u>

India

<u>Notes:</u>

A spiritual being who follows people up
the stairs in the Tower of Victory. It gains
more power and grows little arms as the
person ascends the stairs. Only people
with complete purity can help the A Bao A
Qu reach its perfect form, but when they
descend the stairs, the poor thing loses
its shape and falls back to the first step,
weak and defeated. A Bao A Qu will reach
Nirvana if it succeeds.

<u>Fabulous Creature Findings:</u>

<u>Fabulous Creature:</u>	<u>Report to Nathair:</u>
Dhampir	If Problems persist

<u>Realm:</u> Carmena and the Human Realm

<u>Human Country it is Associated with:</u>
European Countries have legends of Wraith and Dhampir.

<u>Notes:</u>
Half-wraith and half-human. Wraith are gray-skinned, blood-sucking monsters. Wraith use their seduction powers to trick humans into mating with them. A dead giveaway is their heterochromatic eyes! Dhampirs are natural hunters and have a habit of hunting wraith because they believe they can achieve a complete form if they consume their flesh. This may be why Gideon is an FC Hunter. But does his organization know?

·NINETEEN·

The month of May always goes the slowest. Our last month in school before summer vacation consists of reviews and busy seniors ready to graduate. It's always a bittersweet time, full of reminiscence and fear. Depending on your age, you must say goodbye to friends for two months or forever. Even if you manage to keep in touch, you're both different. Adulthood is scary, and May makes many seniors see that.

At my old lunch table, my friends are laughing and smiling. I fumble with my things, feeling lonely and nostalgic looking at them. I remember our post-final exam sleepovers. The air always had the sweet smell of pizza from the local shop that Cassie's mom would order for us. And how could I forget sneaking my friends into our neighborhood pool? All these summer treats were just fleeting memories now.

My eyes dart around, looking for a table to set my stuff on. I glance at the O.C. kids' table and deny myself. I can't go over there.

The lunch bell rings, and as the gang gathers their things, I gather the courage to go over there and greet them. "Hey, guys," I say. Everyone's eyes avert in every direction except for mine. They rustle through their stuff and quickly sling their backpacks over their shoulders. Speed walking away, they lean into one another and whisper. Sofia laughs out loud, tossing me a wayward glance before disappearing to her next class. "See you later," I mumble, sitting lonely at their table.

"Raine." I look up at Gideon. He gulps, sitting down next to me. I slam my bag between us on the table. Prom flashbacks run through my head as I shove my books into my backpack. I need to get out of here. "Will you hear me out?" Gideon asks.

"No," I say.

"Just give me five minutes!" he says as he runs in my direction to block me.

"I'm sure you didn't give anyone else the same courtesy when you killed them," I whisper, biting back my anger.

"I haven't killed anyone. I'm still in training. I just joined last year." Huh, no wonder he seemed so shaky when facing Nathair. Gideon stumbles over his words, "Raine, I didn't come over here to talk about that. I wanted to tell you about Nathair. You think this guy isn't so bad, but his uncle is a big deal. I don't know what he's told you, but—" I make eye contact with him.

"I already know, Gideon."

"But don't you know how a serpent's venom measures its strength? He's a pure-blooded royal. He could take down hundreds of people if he wanted! You're in grave danger." His eyes turn dark.

"How do you know, huh?" I say sarcastically.

"Don't you think it is weird that he isolates you from your friends and family? That he pretends that you are friends, but in reality, he has all the control over you? That is what dark creatures do, Raine. They manipulate their victims. That is a serpent's real power," Gideon whispers, getting closer and closer to me. His eyes flicker, and the wind rushes past us, despite no windows. Everyone walks past us, unaware of the situation.

"He's right. You can use seduction. That's why people are ignoring us. You're no better than he is." I step away, putting my bag between us. "Besides, you don't even know the whole story."

"Well, tell me the whole story so I can help you! Raine, I have no emotional attachments to these creatures. Most are dark creatures that hurt people. Just like him. He's a predator. It's in his instincts!"

"This is coming from a half-wraith, a bloodthirsty, violent, animalistic vampire," I argue.

"My human half makes me neutral like you, and I hate wraiths. Look, please don't be upset. I am only here to help you. I am a friend! I'm sorry I didn't help sooner. I had to report him, which is a lot of paperwork for an underling like me."

"Report? What do you mean?" I ball his shirt up with my fists.

"Yeah, I have to. You seem so sure he is harmless, so I'll warn you. He better get out of town before H.Q. gets here. You saw him that night. He's very powerful and violent." I do remember the look in his eyes. He looked like he was having fun toying with Gideon. If I wasn't there, I worry about what would have happened to Gideon that night. That was a different Nathair than I was used to. Perhaps that's the side of him he was protecting me from.

"He's not normally like that, and you were terrorizing all the Fabulous Creatures in the area," I dismiss, finding it hard to shake that cruel side of Nathair.

"I'm sorry, but the professionals are coming. I can't have him go into his full form," he gulps, trying to grab my hand, but I snatch it away from him. "Please, just let Aethel take him back to his home."

"Wait. You condemn Nathair, but you talked to Aethel? You should be trying to hunt her too." Bewildered by the audacity, I shove him.

"She's just worried about you too. She doesn't want to cause trouble. All she wants is to take him back to Thebes." He adds fake concern to his voice.

"Defending my mortal enemy, huh? Wow, you are not helping your case," I say, slowly clapping. "When did she tell you this?"

"Right before I asked you out," he admits.

It's all coming together. I thought it was so random that one of the most popular boys in school asked me out to prom. Aethel doesn't just want a fight. She wants chaos.

"Gideon, if Nathair is the monster under my bed, you are the one in the closet. I hope you get all that's coming to you for disturbing these poor creatures. Call off your hunters. I will make sure he won't be a problem anymore." And with that, I leave him alone in the lunchroom.

When I return to the manor, I try calling all my friends, but only Cassie picks up the phone.

"So, why were you acting so weird around us?" Cassie asks, making me inhale.

"I can't tell you why."

"Raine, are you in trouble? You know we can help if—"

"No," I interrupt. "It's just not my story to tell, Cassie."

"If you're involved, it's your story too. Look, I'm on Sofia's side. Talk to me when you get your priorities straight," Cassie says in an exasperated tone.

"Cassie, please," I beg, my throat tightening again. "I miss you guys. You're the only one who answered my call."

"Raine, you picked a guy over us. It hurt. That's what everyone was trying to tell you. I can't give you any more chances if you can't give yourself one." Cassie hangs up before I can respond.

My phone falls onto my neon sheets. I stare at it, hopelessly praying she'll call me back. This is my life. I'm not some heroine in a fantasy novel. I'm just plain old Raine Thomas.

"Raine," Maebh calls from the kitchen, probably cooking. I walk over to her location. A tight dress sits on the table, looking at me. "I made you a dress, so try it on."

I look at her, amazed. Don't I already have a closet full of handmade or store-bought beautiful creations? "Maebh, you're always doing stuff for me," I say while changing. You'd think I learned from the last time.

"You're like a sister to me. Isn't that what you're supposed to do?"

"Well, if that's the case, I'm a horrible sister to you, Jasmine, and Sofia," I snort. Maebh notices my slightly sad tone.

"One day, they'll understand, Raine, but until then, kick Nathair in the stomach." Her optimism chirps at me.

"Where is Snake Boy anyway? I need to talk to him."

"The smirky punk is in his room," Maebh says dryly.

"Is smirky even a word?"

"I don't know. I just use it."

"Nice." I giggle and leave Maebh to finish her meal.

As promised, everyone's favorite guy is lying on his bed in a daydream-like state. I creep in, making sure not to be seen, and jump on his bed! Nathair is so out of it that he is surprised by my presence. I laugh as I pin him down playfully in my new, short dress. "What, are you a tiger now? Are you going to eat me?" he jokes.

I childishly shake my head. "Nah, I just ate." I get serious for a moment, sliding off of him. "I talked to Gideon today."

"I know," he smirks. I blink at him, confusion spreading across my face like wildfire. "For people who hunt Fabulous Creatures, they sure are clueless on who's *actually* human."

"Nathair, what do you mean by that?"

"I found his mom at that art gallery. Turns out it would be a huge scandal if they found out she's his wraith side. Not his dad." Snake Boy winks and rests his hands behind his head. A small patch of skin rises up at the bottom of his shirt. Focus, Raine!

"You blackmailed her?" I direct my eyes back up to his mischievous face. He can be an evil genius when he wants to be! Though I'm a little proud that he handled it civilly. The look he gave me when he snapped back into his human form crosses my mind. It was one of shame—apologetic. That's the side I'm used to. This is his true self. Clever and ready to compromise. I smile down at him, looking sweetly back up at me. He's not a threat.

"Hey, Thomas, we should go out tomorrow," he says, changing the subject.

"You mean on a date?" I jest, crossing my arms, now next to him. That's not normal for Nathair to ask me to go places.

He takes a moment to decide for himself. Seconds later, he nods and smiles at me. Call me sappy, but I can't help but melt slightly at his smile, something he rarely does. "Yeah, it's a date," he says low, happy but unsure. It is very human of him to look this vulnerable.

I purse my lips, lightly tapping them. "I guess I'll go on a date with you."

"I knew you would," he says, sitting up. I playfully push him over. Tucking his arm behind my neck, we lay together in harmonious silence.

It's weird when your significant other sees you getting ready for a date with them. He sees me pick out my dress. He sees me doing my hair. He sees everything a girl does to get ready for a date and doesn't seem to care much about it, either!

"Okay, so wear the Converse during the day, but when it gets dark, put on the heels." Maebh, my fashion fairy, is the perfect person to consult. "Do you know what type of lipstick you need to wear?"

I shake my head, ashamed of my ignorance. "I have no clue."

"Wear clear Mentha ultra shine lip balm during the day and a sexy red at night." She instructs as if I am a helpless toddler.

"The mint one is the mentha?"

"Raine, it is your favorite one, and you don't know its name?" Maebh nags.

"I just buy the same color every time," I whine.

"Raine should just keep wearing the Converse and the clear gloss ladies. I promise I won't pay any attention or care." I turn my head at the beautiful Nathair and his asshole-ish comment. Sadly, you can't help who you like.

"Will you go away? I'm not ready yet!" I shoo him off.

"I'm glad I'm not a girl. All I have to do is shower and throw some clothes on," he teases.

Maebh doesn't look amused. "I can't wait until he screws it up. Your honeymoon phase is making me sick."

"What makes you think he's gonna mess it up?" I ask.

"It's Nathair. Enough said." I crinkle my nose at her and continue my makeup consultation with her.

For our date, Nathair decides to have us travel around for a metropolitan adventure. I don't mind that he doesn't have some storybook plan. Honestly, I just want him to call it a date. Funny how guys think girls are complicated, but all we want is something sweet and simple.

It is a sunny day with a light breeze—a rare occasion in Georgia because of its extreme heat and cold. We travel across downtown Atlanta, visiting museums and parks. He even buys me a book at this fancy Barnes & Noble!

"You ready for the trip this summer?" I ask at our final destination, a micro food hall on Ponce. The beautiful foundation in an old, renovated Sears store shines through the industrial pipes and aesthetic decorations. Stacked with small shops selling food from all over, the food hall is an excellent place to be adventurous. Holding big communal tables and small, intimate ones. We squeeze together into a booth, the moody lights shining on us.

"No," he says low, picking at his pork bao buns.

"Why? By the end of summer, you'll be human for your senior year. For most kids, a big change for senior year is a haircut, and you get a new identity. You'll be Nathair Vanos, not *Nathrech of the Realm Thebes*," I belt out my most resounding voice, extending my arm dramatically. He shakes his head in amusement too.

"How do you know my real name?" he asks, chuckling.

"Alister and Aethel let it slip a few times. What is the real story on that, by the way?" I pull apart a steamed bun, devouring it in seconds.

"Well, that is my birthname, but I changed it. All I did was directly translate the name from my language to English and use the phonemic spelling. It's like Maebh's name. The spelling and pronunciation are different," he explains.

"Well, I want to be closer to you. Aethel, Alister, and Maebh all knew you before the name change. I feel left out. Which one should I use?" I ask, a little sad.

He looks down at his lap, then back up at me. "When I hear Nathrech, all I feel is pain and sadness. That's why Alister and Maebh switched. But when I hear Nathair, I feel hope. Especially when you say it." He licks his lips, drawing closer to mine. He flinches, reeling his head back. "But enough about that."

"Oh, I got an idea," I say, tapping my fist into my palm. I'm sure everyone around could see the lightbulb going off. "Let's rapid-fire questions at each other." I nudge Snake Boy smiling from ear to ear.

As if it is impossible for him to agree to something without giving me a hard time, he does his famous eye roll. Special for me, he drew it out for dramatic effect. "Why does everything have to be a game with you?"

I bat my eyes at him and bump a shoulder against his. "There's nothing you're curious about me?" I say with a disgusting high-pitched voice.

He shakes his head and crosses his arms. Maybe once he is human, I can write a manual on how to deal with Nathair.

First, I'll list all his mannerisms and then their translation. Following his own formula, he says, "You're an open book, Thomas." I flutter my eyes again and cause him to grumble. "Fine. How many boyfriends have you had in the past?"

"Three." My voice is nonchalant, but Nathair blinks and makes a face. A slight smile creeps up on my face. Not going to lie, seeing him squirm at the thought of other guys finding me attractive satisfies me. I'm sure he had a certain view of me, pure and innocent, but it's fun to have him sweat a little.

Stretching out every muscle in his face, he settles into his response. "Not going to lie, I'm surprised by that answer."

I debate if I just want to have him running around feeling jealous, but it's not a nice thing to do, so instead, I pat his shoulder, snickering. "Two were online boyfriends, but I was so in love with them. During my Twi-hard phase, we met on a vampire forum. I was caught in a love triangle and living for it! We broke up cause my dad found out I was talking to strangers online, so he deleted my profile. As for the third one, I only dated him because I thought he might be a werewolf."

His face falls, unamused. "So you've always been this desperate?" I burst into full laughter, lacing my fingers with his. Serves him right for being nosy. Girls don't have to conform to some purity standard. I never viewed myself as pure or innocent. It was just hard to find a connection with a person. He finally lightens up and laughs with me. The plush skin that forms under his eyes when he grins catches my attention. I pinch it and cause his cheeks to flush. He laughs it off, taking my hand off his face and holding it. Well, I've never found a connection like this one.

"It's my turn to ask the question! What's your biggest re-gret?" The sunset pours through the large stained-glass windows in the food hall. Nathair's body is backlit, the sun making him look as angelic as his healing character. It hurts me to keep looking his way, but how could I ignore the beauty unfolding? I can see everything, his mind—the real him.

"If it's my biggest, why would I want to bring it up?" Nathair rolls his eyes at me, still holding back a laugh.

"I want to know everything about you," I say with a voice so gentle. Unable to stop myself, I touch his face with my other hand. He brushes me off again, holding both of my hands for ransom.

His dark loose curls fall forward and frame his face. He releases me and tucks one side behind his ears. I push back the other side. He swats me away, holding me captive again. "Fine, your singing," he teases.

"For real!" I hit his shoulder. He rubs his arm, placing his fingers under his chin like a cartoon character pondering his next scheme.

His eyes widen, looking past me in the background. I turn around to see a little boy about eight years old playing with his friend in a nearby shop. I look back at him. He presses his lips tight as if he wants to seal what he will say. His lips grow purple as he chews on them, and his fingers turn yellow from gripping my hands. He looks down at my hands and lets go of them. "I don't want you to look at me differently."

It hurts seeing the anxiety radiating off his body. I lean in, tilting my head at him, full of empathy. "I won't, I promise!" Throwing a scout's honor at him.

He swallows, seemingly accepting my answer. "Serpents test their strength on each other. When we're about eight, we must turn into our snake forms and spar." He pauses, staring at the corner of the table next to me. His eyes follow my hand, which slides across the surface of it as I adjust myself for the story.

"That sounds dangerous," I say, crossing my legs.

His eyes freeze in place, glued onto the corner of the table. "Very, but most of us were weak because we lived in the Cursed Lands. Most serpents can only make you pass out. Only the rich serpents at the capital are truly poisonous." He continues, blinking his eyes more than usual. His chest hitches, taking in air.

"Who made you guys do this?"

"We have a cruel Duke who follows the king's teachings religiously. So, the area he owns is where I live. I remember it was a rule that only children had to do it since they are more venomous than older people. The longer you live there, the sicker you are," he continues, his voice losing power with each word. Nathair's voice is rarely quiet or meek. He always carries his tone with the fierceness of a lion, but at this moment, he sounded so small, like a mouse. His voice trembling with the memory haunting each vibration. He pauses again.

My heart shatters. I am scared to ask, but I prompt him anyway. "So, what happened when you had to take your test?"

Unrelenting, he stares at the corner of the table, refusing to blink now. "You know, I had a friend before Alister. His name was Sergey. I called him Ser." Redness creeps up in his eyes, but he still is focused on the table. Before I can ask what he is staring at, I realize what he's trying not to look at: me.

I gulp as I continue to listen to this horrific story. His name *was* Sergey. I couldn't help but cling to that detail. "Nathair, what happened to Ser?"

Out of nowhere, he slams his hands down on the table. He vaults out of the seat. "Let's go home." His volume is back, but the tiny shaking mouse is still in his voice.

I stay rooted in my seat, hooking his arm. "Hey, hey, hey! It's okay!" He stops, letting me turn his body to him with a slight tug of resistance. Even in his arm, I can feel his intense pulse. "Stay with me, don't shut me out." I gently guide him back to his seat, waiting for the confused gazes of onlookers to go away.

Nathair starts to whisper so no one can overhear our conversation. "The royals control almost everything about us, but the one thing they let the parents do is to pick which partner we test against. My mother picked Ser." He hunches over a little with his fingers digging into his torso, pulling at his shirt.

"Tell me what happened." I try to get him to look me in the eyes, but he avoids me again.

He looks up at the ceiling, his emerald eyes cold and bottomless. I give him a moment. His head is upturned as he continues his story, "Most of us have a natural antivenom against each other, so we're just sick for a few days after. I didn't know I could—" His lip trembles. "I'm sorry, Raine, I can't say it out loud." He finally looks down, a tear falling on the seat.

I embrace him, letting him hide away from the world in the crook of my neck. My hair shields him, guarding his secret against any outsiders. Maybe this was the wrong place to ask such a personal question.

I close my eyes and let him sit in mental solitude. I pat his back, letting all his anxiety, anger, and sadness pour into me. Maybe most people wouldn't know what to do with information like that. Would they be scared? All I can feel is gratitude. I am thankful that he feels comfortable enough to tell me such a traumatic thing, and I can eat his pain and relieve him. He carried this burden for so long, the idea that everyone he cared about will eventually leave him. He probably thought that everything I told him was a beautiful lie.

He won't feel like that as long as I am alive. Even if I die, I will crawl out of Hell itself to get back to him. He's never going to be alone again. I promise this to myself.

My mother crosses my mind. I don't want to be like her, full of codependency and regret. Instead of sewing him to my heart, I will give him the needle and thread to stitch himself together. Then I'll cheer him on when he embroiders new memories onto the patches.

Pulling away, I place a comforting hand on his shoulder and give him a sweet smile. "That's okay, I understand. Thank you for telling me about it." He cleans himself up with the sleeve of his shirt. I dab his face with a tissue from my tray. "Let's go back to the car," I suggest. He agrees. We clean up our trays and head out. We walk in silence to the car.

Once we reach the garage, I am the first to break the silence. "I know it hurts, but can you tell me your favorite memory with him?"

He nods, still hoarse, but he answers anyway. "Ser, my sister, Maeta, and I were inseparable. I remember we were racing in our snake forms and getting big. We didn't pay attention, and

I accidentally knocked into the Duke's house. I burst into his kitchen. Since I was in there, I ate all his food."

"Jesus, all of it?" I ask, hyping up my cheerful voice to turn his mood around. We finally hop into the car, slamming the door behind us. Our tired bodies settle into the seats.

He has a wistful smile for a split second and is back to looking me in the eyes. I look expectantly at him to finish the story. "I had a big mouth and an empty stomach. He tried to take me to trial and banish me for it, but Ser lied and said an angry dragon came and must've done it. What saved us both was that everyone in town resented how well off the Duke was to even have that much food. So Ser quoted the dragon saying, 'That is enough bread for the fat guy.' Everyone laughed and voted me innocent after that."

"Do you miss him?" I think of my own lost one for a moment. I damn sure miss him. He's a pain that pops up in a flash and then goes away. Like a splinter, my father pricks my heart and exits when he feels like it. I can stew on my loss for weeks or for minutes. I can feel him checking on me now, possibly worried about why his daughter is so sad. I wonder if Ser is watching Nathair.

I'm okay, Daddy.

Just like that, the pressure goes away.

I bring my attention back to Nathair.

He pushes through the pain. "Every day, but I was going to take that day to my grave," he says. I'm happy he got that off his chest. "Thank you for lending an ear."

"Oh me?" I say, placing my hand on my chest and looking around. I bounce forward, beaming. "I'll be here all week! Or anytime you need me. You said you feel alone. Sometimes I do too. Even when I got along with my friends, I felt so alone because everyone was satisfied with their lives, but I wasn't. You're the only one who gets it. I want more in life, and you, Maebh, and Alister are the only ones who make me feel comfortable exploring it. So the least I can do is to remind you that I'm here for you."

"I've been a jerk to you this whole time," he argues.

I wave him off, calm and collected. "I dish it back. That's what friends are for. Or whatever we are."

"Yeah, whatever."

"Still hate me?" I say, sticking out my tongue.

"I think I only slightly dislike you now," he jokes back.

I flip my hair, biting back a smug look. The warmth and giddiness build up in the pit of my stomach. "Hold my hand, you freak." Offering my hand for sacrifice, he gently caresses it before holding it and sends butterflies shooting through me.

He rubs his thumbs over my skin. "Don't you ever wish for a nice, normal guy who can hang around your old friends? A guy you can take to your parents?"

"No, I don't need to. I don't like normal." I dismiss.

"I'm jealous of him," he mutters.

"Who?"

"Boyfriend number four. Whoever he is." He smirks at me. At times, his smile is a cool summer day, caressing me with a gentle wind.

Magnets draw me closer to him. I run my tongue over my bottom lip, biting it. If I don't do that, I won't be able to control myself any longer. A wave of desire washes over me.

My face grows hot, and memories of our kiss come flooding back. Lightning bolts ricochet around in my stomach. "Then be him." My feelings pour out. I bite my lips, trying to suck back in the words, but it is too late. My lips demand us to be closer.

"Raine, you know the answer to this—" He lightly gasps as I take his lips to mine. Gentle at first, we grow hungry for more and deepen our kiss.

His fingers creep up my torso and send an icy shiver in its place. White dots spin and dance under my eyelashes. Nathair nibbles at my bottom lip. My eyes fight me, fully closing—accepting the sweet elixir pouring from his kiss. A blissful blur, time passes before I fall into a satisfying slumber.

Raine...

Raine...

Raine...

Raine!

"Raine!" I jolt awake at Maebh's frantic voice. Air rushes into my lungs. "Oh God, baby, are you okay?"

"Yeah, why wouldn't I be? When did I get back to the manor?" I ask with my voice hoarse.

"Raine, you almost died!" The unfamiliar sentence echoes in my head.

Then it hits me. "Where's Nathair?"

"You two got a little carried away, and you reacted to his—"

"Venom," I finish the sentence for her.

"Yeah, thank goodness I was here to heal you, or else you would've—"

"Yeah, I got it, died." I jump out of my bed, only to fall to the ground. Maebh calls after me. I get up and run out, my footing out of control. My dog, Greer, follows me, whining.

"Raine, don't go in there!" Maebh cautions as I enter the room.

Alister pins Nathair against the wall, looking ready to mangle him. "How could you be so irresponsible? You have to learn when enough is—" Alister stops mid-sentence to look at me. He drops Nathair. "Mae, I thought she was sleeping."

Maebh, who finally reaches us, tries pulling me away. "She ran off because she was worried."

"I'm sorry you had to see that. I just flipped when he told me," Alister says, attempting to make up an explanation.

I push Maebh away. "It's my fault. I should've told him I was feeling sick."

"You know I would never actually hurt any of you, right?" Alister asks low.

"We're all entitled to a violent moment," I say calmly, even though I know it would hurt his feelings. As promised, he flinches and walks out of the room. I finally look over at my broken snake, disheveled and lost, and I feel sorry for him. Weakly, I crawl over to him.

"What are we doing?" His voice breaks into a thousand pieces.

"It was just an accident," I say, touching his hand.

Nathair shakes his head, sliding his hand away. "How many accidents are we going to have?"

"It won't happen again. You'll be human soon enough."

Avoiding my gaze like the plague, we break as Nathair stares at the ground. "And what if I'm not? I'm tired of being stuck in limbo with you. You don't feel the same?"

"But I'm happy when I'm with you." My mouth is heavy and dry with sawdust.

"You can't be happy if you're dead." He quickly leaves me on the floor. Heartbroken, I lie where his body used to be, all alone again.

After last night's trauma, I went home to my family's house and rode the bus to school in the morning. With magic in sight, it's easy to worry. Typically, I would at least see Nathair twice by lunch.

"Raine." I look up to see Sofia and the O.C. kids staring at me.

"Yes?" I ask, feeling that horrible sense of ending.

"We need to talk to you," Sofia says.

"Okay." I get up and walk with them to our old table.

"I don't like seeing you like this," Sofia confesses.

"Like what?"

"I told her about our conversation," Cassie adds.

Sofia puts her hand on my shoulder. "We miss you, but you're not healthy. Nathair has messed you up, just like I thought. He's screwing with your head. You don't even know right from wrong anymore because of him," Sofia continues.

"Sofia, it's not like that."

She solemnly shakes her head. "Yes, it is, and I'm afraid you'll have to choose *now*."

"What do you mean?" I ask, dreading the anxiety building in my gut. I feel like it will burst out of me, and I want nothing more than to hold it in.

"It's him, or it's us." The words sound like a death threat, and I am speechless. I drown in my ominous feeling of the end. "So, who is it?"

"She chooses you," Nathair says behind me. I twist my head his way. Anxiety suffocates me. What about our adventure? What about us? What about his promise to take me to the city in the clouds? He snatches my tracker bracelet off me. The click of it is a gunshot to my ears. He emotionlessly grazes my side with his hand and leans into my ear, "I'm so sorry," he whispers, breathy and raw. I hear the dreaded rattling sound trail behind.

Pain sears through my chest, so intense that I must hold my lungs in place. My eyes are full of pressure with tears that never come. The hyperventilating slows down. "No! Why are you—" A calm wave washes over me. My body feels like it's floating. White dots float around as I watch Nathair slink away, unnoticed by everyone around him. With each step he takes, our memories together follow him, and my head gets lighter and lighter. Finally turning back to my friends, I say without hesitation, "I choose you guys, of course."

·TWENTY·

The sound of breakfast sizzles in the pan. Only the best for my graduating sister, Jasmine. My mom hums as she cooks this rare meal. I sit at the table, posture straight and perfect. My hair is slicked back into a pristine bun. With a smile plastered, I turn to my mother. Pose me like a doll and tell me what to do. This is my real life. Not some fantasy world. I don't know what I was thinking. I have everything I need and love here.

"Do you want some pancakes?" My mother asks me, now that I am back in her good graces—Richard's good graces.

"Yes, please." Happy to have her little girl back, my mom fills my plate. After all, I have finals today. I need a big breakfast to give me the energy to excel.

"Careful. Too many starches will make you gain weight, and your boyfriend won't want you anymore whenever he decides to show up," Jasmine mutters, stabbing a pancake. My eye twitches, I haven't thought much about him, and it is for the best. After I explained to everyone that I wasn't with Nathair anymore and they wouldn't have to worry about him, everyone pretends that he never existed. I don't mind, though, because each memory is a series of dust specks floating around in the air. I can see them but never catch the finer details. It's all a blur, but it's okay. Memories are replaceable.

Sometimes I see him in my dreams and wake up in tears each morning, but I have no idea why. A rattle shakes in my ear, and I lightly press my ears. My head aches a bit, but I just take another sip of water. "Mom, I think I have tinnitus. Can we go to the doctor to get it checked out? It's been bothering me for a week."

My mom settles down with her plate, kissing Richard after she sits down. Her eyes grow wide with confusion. "You need to stop listening to your headphones at a loud volume, dear. Try that first, and if it keeps bothering you, we'll check." Richard rubs my mother's hand and smiles at her. They are so in love. Maybe I'll find something like that one day.

Pain cuts into my head, and I bend in agony.

His striking green eyes are glowing in the dim light. The corners of my eyes grow peppery, black spots creeping up to the center of my vision. Shivering at his touch as it tempts me and calls me closer to him. We are only a centimeter apart. His eyes are the size of saucers, with deep emerald flecks—

Never go into the mountains or the desert, for she is not the only one to live. These dark Fabulous Creatures will be waiting for you. If you are so unlucky to meet one, then to avoid its call, all you need to do is—

Remember—

The pain dissipates, and I sit back straight in my perfect posture. Jasmine squints her eyes, mouth agape. "Are you good?"

I turn to my sister and place my hand on hers. "Yes, I'm okay. Thank you for asking."

My family look concerned but continue to eat their breakfast. My mom clears her throat. "Also, Raine, I was cleaning up your room and found this weird notebook with snakes and doodles. What is it? It talks about giant snakes, dragons, and other wacky creatures."

I cut up a piece of dry pancake. Taking a bite, I gently place my fork down and take my notebook from my mother. "It's for my college portfolio! I am applying for a writing scholarship," I say.

My mom's eyes droop down, rubbing my arm. "Why are there letters to your father in there?"

"Do you want to talk about it?" Richard pries.

I shake my head, smiling. "I'm fine. I don't need to."

If you are so unlucky to meet one, then to avoid its call, all you need to do is—

Remember you are—

I feel another sting in the back of my mind. Excusing myself, I stand up from the table and bump into the dishes. "Oops, clumsy me!" I laugh it off.

Jasmine laughs dryly. "Yeah, that's a normal reaction."

Slapping my dear sister's shoulder, I chuckle at her joke and walk to my room. "Jasmine, you're so funny!"

I walk into my room full of clean bookshelves. Once packed with silly books, I only keep small knickknacks that my mom had bought. But at least I donated most of my books to charity. Let those stupid thoughts go to someone else who needs them to tolerate their lives. I don't need absurd fairy tales to wake up in the morning like I used to. I can get by just fine. Right?

I tried throwing out all the clothes Maebh bought and made for me, but for some reason couldn't bring myself to do it. I close the armoire and see a red thread tied to my finger with a little bow at the end. Huh, that's weird. A loose thread must've gotten on me. I open the closet back up to find the culprit, but none of my clothes are red. I shut my wardrobe with a thud. The phantom thread now gone. I look around, only to see a loose black string on the ground. Shrugging, I pick it up and toss it in the trash. A low hum turns into a whisper in my head, and my heart aches.

If you are so unlucky to meet one, then to avoid its call, all you need to do is—

Remember you are in—

"Raine, time for school," my mom calls from the kitchen.

"Okay." My head feels hollow, but I stretch and prepare for a beautiful day.

It is the last day of school, and one more test separates us from our summer. Everyone is ecstatic, but I find myself dreading the thought. The O.C. kids ramble about their summer plans, but I tune them out. "I'm going to an anime con in California for the summer. What are you doing, Raine?" Cassie asks.

"Probably nothing," I say. The rattling in my head echoes in my ears, but I ignore it. I can't worry anyone because who would want to burden others with your discomfort?

Sofia slings her arm around my neck, tapping my head with hers. "Aw, nonsense, we're going boyfriend shopping. That way, I'll be the one to choose her next boyfriend."

Performing for them, I laugh on cue. "Yeah, sure. I'm sure we'll have many great years together, and I'll thank you." My chest hurts again as my friends laugh at my joke. If I keep my smile, nobody will notice that I rub the spot where my tracker bracelet used to be. Flashbacks of our kisses and time together flash through my mind. My throat closes up some. His green eyes haunt me.

"Raine," Cassie snaps me back into the present.

Perform. "Yeah?" I tilt my head, forcing a seconds-late smile.

Jay taps my shoulder. "You okay? Kind of spaced just there." The memories start flooding my mind. I can still smell his fresh scent. I can still feel his warm body hugging me. I can still hear his voice. It's hard to stay in the present when your mind is slowly unraveling. The mask of losing someone special to me cracks. I don't feel well, but I still play it cool, casually waving off my friends. "Pfft, yeah, just thinking about stuff, you know."

"What kind of stuff?" Kasha walks up with her usual microwave lunch.

"It better not be about that guy." Sofia stabs her chicken nuggets with a fork. Maybe she imagines Nathair's face in her meal. I don't want any more drama, so I lie. "I didn't end things well with some people, and I regret it." My mind goes to Gideon. Did I want him? Or did I like him because he was easy? I'll never know. "I'm going to use the bathroom," I say, leaving them at the table.

Sofia runs after me. "You know, it's okay if you're sad. He did mess with you for a while, and you like to see the good in people." She places a hand on my shoulder, sending a violent shockwave through me.

He rubs his thumbs over my skin. "Don't you ever wish for a nice, normal guy who can hang around your old friends? A guy you can take to your parents?"

"No, I don't need to. I don't like normal," I dismiss.

"I'm jealous of him," he mutters to himself.

"Who?"

"Boyfriend number four—"

He clears his throat. "I understand, but it's not hard for me to undo what Aethel did. They can see the performance for how it's supposed to be!" He looks at my evil side-eye. "Just let me help you this one time."

"No!" I say sternly. "Mind controlling—manipulating—" I draw my breath in and correct myself, "convincing people is not good. You can't control how people feel or think—"

"I'm so sorry," he whispers, breathy and raw. I hear the dreaded rattling sound trail behind—

*If you are so unlucky to meet one, then to avoid its call, all you need to do is remember you are in control. **Take back your power.***

"I'm not sad. I'm angry!" I snap, whipping around to face her. How. Dare. He. I'm going to murder him. Everything goes red to me as the betrayal settles in. Seething, I cross my arms and look at my clueless best friend.

Sofia swallows and looks at me teary-eyed. "Any guy that steals my best friend is bad to me, Raine," she admits.

I turn to look at her, tired of things unspoken. "You don't understand."

"Raine, he doesn't belong with us. He's different."

Something in me breaks. I walk slowly to her. "You're no better than he is. You dumped me and left me in the dust as soon as I started talking to him." I prod her chest.

She glances at my finger, calmly pinching it and putting it to the side. "You're really about to stick up for a guy that left you in pieces? Do you not comprehend that I'm here? That we're here? Raine, he left, and we're dealing with the broken pieces! I know you miss him because you've been walking around like a mindless zombie! I'm not some heartless person who doesn't care, but if I don't rip that rose-colored band-aid off your arm, no one will! He doesn't care about you, Raine. When will you realize that I do?" Sofia yells.

"Ignoring me for weeks isn't helping or supporting me, Sofia!" I yell back.

"That's because I don't reason with stupid, and that's what that guy made you! Cutting you off was best for you so you could see the truth."

How could she understand? It was like a play. We had a connection, a natural, magical connection. Our line was pulled to its limits, but I know it was there! The anger implodes inside me as every blood vessel in my face goes with it. "I am so sick of people doing things that are 'for the best.' I am not a toy for any of you to play with! I am a person with thoughts and feelings. I don't care if they are wrong. They are mine to feel!" I shout, slapping my chest and getting into Sofia's face. She needs to understand. He needs to understand. The raw emotions go downhill, and I glare at her. "Why are we still friends if I'm such an idiot?" I ask, my voice laced with its own venom.

"Because I love you, and that's what people do when they love someone! They let them make their mistakes and help sweep up the pieces and glue them back together!" Something dawns on me once she says this. I turn away from her and look at her over my shoulder.

"You're right," I say, running off. I have to go to him. If he wants to run away from his feelings, fine. But I will shout mine from the top of my lungs, and he will hear them. If my feelings are such a burden to him, I'll pounce like a lioness and tear into him. He will know the pain he caused me and feel my wrath.

I don't get far once I am out of Sofia's sight because Aethel stands in my way, looking very pissed. Here she stands, the antagonist in my story, a story that feels like it has already ended. "Where is he?" Her forked tongue slithers out of her mouth.

I step up to her, getting close to her face. Scales shine under the light. "Gone."

Her eyes shift to diamonds. Two-tone scales cover her body. "What do you mean gone?"

"He went to become human," I say. She lunges at me, pounding me into a wall. Her hand has a firm grip on my neck.

"If I bite you. It will take a day to kill you," she snarls.

"Then do it. He's not here to protect me now, is he?" I spit. I know she wouldn't, though she is crazy enough. Her threat doesn't scare me.

"Don't you want to live? Why are you tempting me as an insignificant human?" she asked dangerously.

I only laugh, my craziness setting in. "You're just a scared, puny snake. You wouldn't dare."

"Don't mess with me!" She shakes me, slamming my back onto the wall. Her snake tongue flickers near my face.

"It's not a joke. If you want to kill me, just do it now. I dare you." I chuckle at her. "I wonder how people will take it once they find out a serpent killed a human?" She glares at me, releasing me.

"Mark my words, human, I will find him. He will marry me, or he will die." With that, she walks off, her five-inch heels clicking furiously with each step.

With my anger subsiding, the ecstasy of summer doesn't feel the same this year. Everything is bitter, nothing sweet. I sat on my bed, my head nestled between my blanket and my hands. Everything is falling apart. How could he do this to me? *No, I don't have time to mope. I need to think this through.* I wipe away the stray tears. I know him. He'll turn me away or act cold and distant. Maybe even throw me out of the house, so I need to be as calm as possible.

The door clicks open, and my big sister pokes her head in sheepishly. "I know I am one of the last people you want to talk to, but you do know it hurts me too when you are sad," Jasmine says softly as she enters.

"So what?" I muffle my voice with the blanket.

"I don't get it, Raine. What is this big secret that you can't tell anyone? Is that boy worth all this trouble?"

I sit up more to look at my sister, allowing her to crawl next to me. "It's not my secret to tell. I was helping him. I started falling for him along the way, and now everything is ruined."

"What did you guys do?"

"Just kissed, went out, and *read books together*." I snort at that last part.

"Wow, so you really like him?" Jasmine asks, which strikes a big nerve. Can falling into 'like' with someone hurt just as much as love? And how do you know when it tips dangerously to the other side? I want him. I *miss* him.

Tears fall from my face like a sink faucet. I nod since facing my truth makes it impossible to talk. "I do," I confess.

"I'm sorry for saying all those things that night. I just got into a fight with the 'rentals, and it utterly sucked. I took it out on you. You didn't deserve it." Jasmine tucks one of my pillows under her arms, getting more comfortable. "I hear your boyfriend left. Is it true?"

"He left because he's afraid of me." I wipe a falling tear.

"What do you mean?"

"He's messed up in his past with people because of his upbringing. He was so terrified of hurting me that he did it anyway." I wipe my tears away, looking down, ashamed.

"Well, tell him he hurt you." Jasmine rolls over on her stomach to look at me better. "You seem like you know where he is."

"It's complicated," I say, playing with my pillow. "He left me for a reason, so I need a plan."

Jasmine hops up and puts her hands on her hips. "A plan? He's a dumb boy, and you're a Thomas! We're beautiful and fierce women! We don't fret over dumb boys. End it on your terms, not his. You know how to get to him, don't you?" she declares like a princess. To be honest, my sister is a bratty royal with good intentions.

"No, but I can think of something." I only have one person or creature that I can go to. "Jasmine, you're right. I need to finish what he started," I say, retrieving my phone to order a car.

"Aren't I always right?" she says, getting up and heading to the door.

"Jasmine," I call. She turns to me. "You're the best sister in the world."

She tosses me some money. "For the car," she answers before I can ask, leaving me alone. I smile warmly and type in the manor's address.

The gentle wind blows my hair in the opposite direction of the long uphill walk. It warns me not to go up there. I trek up the driveway and look around at the dim state of the manor. The green grass turns yellow and brown, crunching under my feet. The trees no longer shine, each leaf matte and dull, falling with each wind swipe. Even the garden's rainbow fruits and vegetables lack hue and look like someone sucked their juice out with a straw. How could this happen? How could it ever lose its magic? I shiver under the breeze, which picks up and grows angry with me for proceeding. Is my welcome overstayed? Seeing the remnants of the glittering lights of Alister's potion-making and the smell of Maebh's latest cooking experiment, I know it is no longer there. Riding in Snake Boy's car up this same hill and mocking him on his latest gripe. It is all just a distant memory now.

Were all the relationships I made genuine or conditional? Growing up to make them happy was a way to survive. Keep them happy, and I will be satisfied, right? I gave myself empty promises, filling my head with hope time and time again. All for my surface-level happiness to erode away with the wind. It's never what I wanted.

How ironic is it that the snake tempted me from the Garden of Eden? I had everything, and yet I still looked elsewhere for fulfillment. I only belonged to my books, following their perfect story. But when it's my turn, it ends like this?

Take back your power.

Chirp. Chirp. I crane my neck to see a small orange bird perched on the branch above me, with feathers so bright that they burn the blue sky. He tilts his head at me.

"What should I do?" I ask as if the little bird would know. But my heart, once filled with sorrow, is bursting with strength. Maybe magic is not only for those born with it but also for those who keep it alive. I went from being the dull girl with boring dreams in a boring house with a boring life to just being myself. That's right. I am Raine, and I write my own story. With no peep or sound from the bird, he comes to me and lands on my shoulder. His small beady black eyes are as dark as space, but it tells me all I need to know.

This isn't the end. I won't let it be.

· Acknowledgements ·

Wow, I can't believe this is thirteen years in the making! I originally wrote the first draft at sixteen when the idea randomly came to me while listening to Lady Gaga's "Monster." The original story was sixty thousand words of terror and cringe, but underneath the incredibly rough draft was an idea I adore even to this day. To be honest, I have the biggest impostor syndrome known to man, so it took so long to see the light of day because of my insecurities. This story was locked away for twelve years because I didn't believe in myself or my writing. When my father passed away, I felt like my life was falling apart. But one day, he came to me and told me to write again. I got a second wind and have been writing and editing ever since. Life is too short to hold back on your potential.

So, first of all, thank you to anyone giving this book a chance because I never could even guess that it would make it to your hands. No matter how you felt about the story, thank you for supporting it. I am so grateful that you chose this story.

Thank you to my mother, who has been my cheerleader since day one and has listened to my countless spiraling rants about my writing process. She recognized that I had this passion, and when I was mentally lost in the world during my adult years, she always reminded me that I had that love of writing inside me. Thank you to my sister Shayla for always sticking by me when so many people walked out of my life and showing me that I am loved. Thank you to Tanisha for teaching me how to be strong and persevere. Thank you to Carinda for showing me how to bounce back from tragedy and rise from it. And to the rest of my family and friends, thank you for cherishing me and valuing me as a person. Without you, this book would've been forgotten on a dusty flash drive.

Thank you to all the freelance editors and beta readers involved with the project. Without you guys, I couldn't have experimented and expanded on the world and the character's relationships. You all gave such valuable feedback that made me create a book I am proud to show the world!

As I grow more in my craft, I hope we can continue this journey together. You all are amazing people.

Raine's Rainy Day:

ACROSS THE SKY
EMILIE AUTUMN

BAD ROMANCE
LADY GAGA

MONSTER
LADY GAGA

FIXED AT ZERO
VERSA EMERGE

ONE AND ONLY
TIMBALAND FT. FALL OUT BOY

NOT A FRIEND
SORN

WONDERLAND
ALEXA

TOO LOUD
ICON FOR HIRE

PAIN
THREE DAYS GRACE

Follow for updates on the sequel and Bonus Content:

@Venenumous_Books

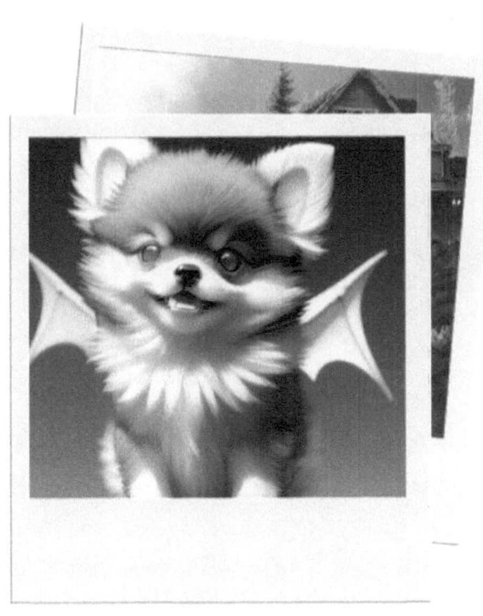